They could never have imagined that the world would be so vast.

Back then, it had only been as wide as the arena, and they had loathed its very existence.

Is it WRONG to try to PICK UP GIRLS IN A DUNGEON? ON THE SIDE

Sword Oratoria

CONTENTS

LOKI:
Goddess of the greatest familia, *Loki Familia*.
LEENE ARSHE:
A human supporter, healer, and member of *Loki Familia*.
ALICIA FORESTLIGHT:
An older elf in *Loki Familia* with a gentle disposition.
LEFIYA VIRIDIS:
An elven magic user who deeply admires Aiz.
TIONA HYRUTE:
An Amazon and first-tier adventurer. Tione's younger twin sister.
ANAKITY AUTUMN:
A catgirl and member of *Loki Familia*. Everyone calls her "Aki."
TIONE HYRUTE:
The elder of the two Amazonian sisters and a member of *Loki Familia*.
RIVERIA LJOS ALF:
The vice-captain of *Loki Familia*. Elf. The strongest magic user in all of Orario.
AIZ WALLENSTEIN:
A Level 6 adventurer and Orario's strongest swordswoman. Afraid of swimming…?
© Kiyotaka Haimura

"You'll be facinggggggggg me."
All of a sudden, Aiz found herself veiled in an enormous shadow from behind.
© Kiyotaka Haimura
BACHE KALIF:
An Amazon who leads Kali Familia with her older sister, Argana.
"Rjada ru jheeda... die Hyrute."
"I couldn't help but miss you, my beloved daughters..."
KALI:
The warmongering patron deity of Kali Familia.
"You've changed, Tione!"
ARGANA KALIF:
An Amazon and leader of Kali Familia. Bache's older sister.

VOLUME 6

FUJINO OMORI

ILLUSTRATION BY
KIYOTAKA HAIMURA

CHARACTER DESIGN BY
SUZUHITO YASUDA

NEW YORK

IS IT WRONG TO TRY TO PICK UP GIRLS IN A DUNGEON?
ON THE SIDE: SWORD ORATORIA, Volume 6
FUJINO OMORI

Translation by Liv Sommerlot
Cover art by Kiyotaka Haimura

Yen On
1290 Avenue of the Americas
New York, NY 10104

Visit us at yenpress.com
facebook.com/yenpress
twitter.com/yenpress
yenpress.tumblr.com
instagram.com/yenpress

First Yen On Edition: June 2018

Yen On is an imprint of Yen Press, LLC.
The Yen On name and logo are trademarks of Yen Press, LLC.

Library of Congress Cataloging-in-Publication Data
Names: Ōmori, Fujino, author. | Haimura, Kiyotaka, 1973– illustrator. | Yasuda, Suzuhito, designer.
Title: Is it wrong to try to pick up girls in a dungeon? on the side: sword oratoria / story by Fujino Omori ; illustration by Kiyotaka Haimura ; original design by Suzuhito Yasuda.
Other titles: Danjon ni deai wo motomeru no wa machigatteirudarouka gaiden sword oratoria. English.
Description: New York, NY : Yen On, 2016– | Series: Is it wrong to try to pick up girls in a dungeon? on the side: sword oratoria
Identifiers: LCCN 2016023729 | ISBN 9780316315333 (v. 1 : pbk.) | ISBN 9780316318167 (v. 2 : pbk.) | ISBN 9780316318181 (v. 3 : pbk.) | ISBN 9780316318228 (v. 4 : pbk.) | ISBN 9780316442503 (v. 5 : pbk.) | ISBN 9780316442527 (v. 6 : pbk.)
Subjects: CYAC: Fantasy.
Classification: LCC PZ7.1.O54 Isg 2016 | DDC [Fic]—dc23
LC record available at https://lccn.loc.gov/2016023729

ISBNs: 978-0-316-44252-7 (paperback)
978-0-316-44253-4 (ebook)

1 3 5 7 9 10 8 6 4 2

LSC-C

Printed in the United States of America

VOLUME 6

FUJINO OMORI

ILLUSTRATION BY KIYOTAKA HAIMURA

CHARACTER DESIGN BY SUZUHITO YASUDA

PROLOGUE

A Mid-Spring Night's Dream

Гэта казка іншага сям'і.

Начны сон вышыні вясновага

Her vision trembled.

A sound buzzed in her ears.

The moment she realized what had caused the shock and constant tremors in her body, the first thing she felt was nausea.

A murderous roar echoed around her as the sound of hundreds of thousands of feet shook the earth.

The world of stone and rock quivered along with that distant bellow. The blue sky and the light of the sun seemed so far, far away through the iron latticework of her small window. All she could smell in the cold, dank room that served as her prison was the stench of mold and rust.

Abandoned in a corner of the room sat her two cutlasses, blades clinking as she waited for her turn.

The scene changed.

Suddenly, her field of view shrank—she was wearing a mask. Before her stood an odious gate, light filtering through its bars. The moment she passed through it, leaving the darkness behind, she found herself enveloped in a thunderous cacophony of screams and shouts. All around her, spectators howled as she stepped into the arena.

She saw her enemies come charging from the opposite gate, and she rose to face them, weapon gripped tightly as she sprinted forward.

Each opponent was different from the last as they came one after another. First, a pack of white wolves, saliva dribbling from their mouths in great heavy globules; then, a cudgel-wielding gladiator; and after that, a chained dragon—finally, there was a girl just like her. Weapons collided, but in the end, it was she who was left standing.

As her fallen opponent lay at her feet, around her the arena erupted as the sun blazed overhead.

"*—Se wehga! Se wehga! Se wehga!*"

Shouts in a language that wasn't Koine poured down on her.

The praises of her fellow female warriors engulfed her as the twilit sky trembled and shook.

Face turned up toward the heavens, she lost herself in that never-ending sea of red.

The scene changed. It always did.

She saw the blurred smile of a goddess.

Then a female warrior was looking down at her, beating her into the ground over and over. Laughter rang loudly in her ears.

Excitement mixed with rage in an endless frenzy.

Within those emotions was a mumbled scream and splattered blood.

On the gleaming surface of the weapon, she could see her own eyes blurring.

Still it repeated, over and over, as the world faded around her.

That was when she glanced down, only to see her own hands, stained the deepest red—

Then Tione woke up.

"...Great," Tione murmured as she stared up at the ceiling of her room in Twilight Manor.

It was dark inside, and the world outside her window was still dim. Glancing in the direction of her clock, she saw that the short hand had only just passed four.

"Haven't even gotten any decent rest since the expedition..."

She frowned, a crease rising to her brow as she continued to stare listlessly at the ceiling, eyes heavy.

All of a sudden—*boof!*

A pillow arced toward her.

She quickly snatched the cushion out of the air.

Sitting up without so much as a noise, Tione turned to where her sister currently slept soundly, spread-eagled on her own bed with the blanket kicked off. This was Tiona.

That innocent face, that unconscious pillow toss—Tione felt anger bubbling up inside her. She chucked the pillow back at her snoozing sister. But even in her sleep, the younger Amazon was able to deflect the shot with ease.

Tione clicked her tongue in annoyance as her projectile simply tumbled across the bedding.

"...She hasn't changed at all," she muttered, half in jealousy and half in irritation, as she glanced over at her sister's serene face. "Guess I'll take a shower or something..."

With a long sigh, she slid out of bed.

Then, grabbing a change of clothes and dressed in nothing but her undergarments, she made her way out of the room.

"Tioneeee...mmghh..."

Mere minutes later.

Tiona rolled over in bed, her sister's name on her lips as the very same dream invaded her own thoughts.

CHAPTER 1

Quest Results & Next Quest

Гэта казка іншага сям'і.

Quest Вынік & Наступны Quest

Loki Familia's expedition party had returned to Twilight Manor.

They'd collapsed into their beds and slept soundly their first night back, and their lips curled into smiles as they awoke to the light of the surface. They were home—free from the chill dark and far from the unceasing howls of monsters.

A certain elven maiden squinted her azure eyes as she peered through her window at the sun. Outside in the courtyard, a golden-haired, golden-eyed swordswoman had awoken for her early morning training regimen, already hours into her routine as she lost herself in the fragrant breeze and clear blue sky.

The late risers trickled out of their rooms one by one, eager to sate their appetites with the bread, hot soup, fried eggs, and meats they'd been deprived of for so long. The warm sunlight, the good weather, the fresh foods—all the pleasures of the surface they'd previously taken for granted soothed their weary bodies.

Before long, the manor was as lively as ever.

"All righty, then! I know we've got plenty of things to deal with… but how's about we start off with yer Status updates, yeah?"

Loki announced her intentions amid all the renewed hustle and bustle.

And so, while the familia members who'd stayed behind were busy with organizing the resources, equipment, and spoils of war from the expedition—a task they'd been busy with since the night prior—the party members formed a long, snaking line leading to Loki's chambers on the top floor of the manor's central tower. Given how easy it had been for their Statuses to develop during the expedition, nearly everyone had to pay the goddess a visit, which meant there was no way to get through the whole throng on the same night they returned. Even Aiz had spent the evening merely resting, waiting until the next day to take her turn.

Updating the Statuses of more than thirty adventurers was no easy task, but Loki hopped to excitedly, as prompt and efficient as ever.

It was during this time that—

"Level Six!! I caught up to Aiz!!"

"Heh-HEH!"

Tiona's and Bete's exclamations echoed throughout the tower.

Both of them had leveled up. The high-grade excelia they'd obtained after their decisive battle in the Frontier had been enough to bump them from Level 5 to Level 6. Just as the phrase implied, leveling up involved pushing their Status past its current limit to reach even greater heights in terms of skills and abilities.

Tiona clutched in her hands the updated parchment she'd received from Loki, grinning as she jumped and skipped about. Even Bete cracked a smile for once, not caring who was watching as he let out a howl.

"Guess there's no point in even asking you, hmm, Tione?"

"Heh. Well, you know. Anyway, what about you guys? Aki? Narfi?"

Tione asked the question while she tried her best to keep her own excitement in check after leveling up just like her sister.

"We still have a ways to go, it seems..." The catgirl and human responded with strained laughs, their shoulders slumped. It would seem *Loki Familia*'s alternates were stuck at Level 4, if Raul's drooping head was any indication.

"Hey, Aiz! Look, look! Level Six!"

"Mmn...congratulations, Tiona."

"Eh-heh-heh...I told ya I wasn't gonna lose to you! Better watch out or I'll blow right past ya!"

Tiona dashed forward to greet the swordswoman, still brimming with excitement as the group made its way down the tower steps and out into the courtyard. Aiz responded with a faint smile, spurring on the Amazon's cheer.

Tiona launched herself onto Aiz's back with a practically audible *sproing!* "What about you, Aiz, huh? You didn't level up *again*, did you?!"

"Don't be silly..."

That's impossible. Aiz finished the thought privately as she glanced down at the parchment in her hands.

Aiz Wallenstein

LEVEL 6

Strength: I30->84 Endurance: I39->89 Dexterity: I58->98
Agility: I57->93 Magic: I45->H101 Hunter: G Abnormal
Resistance: G Swordsman: H Spirit Healing: I

Her abilities had increased more than 230 points in total after she'd first embarked on the expedition—ever since the night of the black raid she'd weathered with Bell and Hestia, actually. From that point, she'd taken part in the attack on The Dragon's Urn, then the life-and-death battle with the corrupted spirit, and even dueling with the Warlord, Ottar. Taking all these into account, it was no surprise that her gains were substantial, even if she was already Level 6.

The numbers made Aiz happy—relieved, almost. They were her reward for breaking her previous limits and reaching new heights. At Tiona's urging ("Show me! Show me!"), she relinquished the parchment with her new Status. When the Amazon gave an "Ohhhh!" in approval, it brought smiles to both their faces.

Meanwhile, back upstairs where Lefiya was just now getting her own Status updated—

"Congrats, Lefiya! You should be able t'level up!"

Loki cried out triumphantly from behind the elf, whose clothes were undone to reveal the smooth curve of her back.

"...What?"

Lefiya froze, halfway through retrieving her clothes.

The crimson hieroglyphics on her back, which were not unlike an epitaph, pulsed with light at regular intervals.

It took her all of ten seconds before she was practically stumbling back toward the grinning goddess.

"L-l-l-level up? D-did you say...*level up*? M-me?!"

"That I did, little missy. To Level Four!"

"I...I did it!!"

Lefiya shouted, unable to contain herself. Even though she was still only half-dressed and covering herself with her discarded shirt, she wanted to jump for joy.

She'd certainly looked death in the face rather often recently, yet she had lived to tell the tale.

In fact, she'd been fully prepared to meet her end more times than she could count. As a Level 3, she'd already descended to the Dungeon's depths—a place where even first-tier adventurers like Aiz and the others couldn't be sure of victory—and returned in one piece. If the high-grade excelia Tiona and the others had earned was enough for them to level up, then it made sense that the quality of Lefiya's excelia was worthy of a "feat."

Desperate to catch up to Aiz and the others, she'd put her own life on the line to complete her adventure.

"Quite a few of you kids came back with all kinds'a new magic and skills...Seems like this expedition was well worth it."

Loki was talking to herself, but Lefiya wasn't listening, her face still flushed and her head dizzy.

She was beyond happy. Her heart was filled with the feeling that she'd truly grown stronger and that she might actually have a chance to catch up to Aiz and the others.

And that rabbit—yes, that *rabbit.*

—I did it! Did you see that, hmm? How's that for size?

Pictured clearly in her mind was the boy she'd dubbed her rival for many reasons. She puffed her chest out with pride—on the inside.

Her rival had taken down a minotaur all by himself when he was only Level 1, earning him a chance to level up. Even though she had faltered when the boy's accelerated growth led him to pull off his own feat, Lefiya was sure now that she hadn't lost yet.

For the time being, at least, she was in the lead.

Still, I mustn't let this go to my head. His level may be lower than mine at the moment, but he's reckless to a fault and wields strange magic to boot. That's why I have to take advantage of every bit of strength I have—with even greater effort than he uses—and widen the gap between us as much as possible...!

Lefiya began to settle down, practically tingling with energy. Loki could almost see the blazing flames emanating from behind the elf, but her expression soon turned confused.

"Hmm...y'know, Lefiya? This is just a tiny suggestion, but...could ya be patient for a little while longer? About leveling up, I mean."

"Wh-whaaat?"

Lefiya came to a sudden halt again, a puzzled question escaping her lips. Her goddess's "suggestion" had completely snuffed out the fiery sense of victory within her.

As she turned around, asking why with her eyes, Loki handed over the parchment with her updated Status.

Lefiya Viridis

LEVEL 3

Strength: I84->86 Endurance: H121->184 Dexterity: G207->210
Agility: G252->271 Magic: B723->797 Mage: H Abnormal
Resistance: I

No new skills, though her abilities had improved quite handily since before the expedition, in particular her endurance and magic.

Holding her clothes in one hand and the parchment in another, her gaze rose from the page.

"You get a good look? Then let me take you through it step-by-step, okay? Lefiya...what level was yer magic at when you went up to Level Three?"

"It was...S..."

"Right? Soooo...you can see why this time you don't have quite enough, yeah? At least that's what I was thinkin'. Don't want you losin' out to Riveria, huh? Gotta make you a ridiculous magic powerhouse."

"R-ridiculous magic powerhouse..." A bead of sweat worked its way down Lefiya's temple as the words hit home.

She knew what Loki was saying. That she still had room to grow as a Level 3.

Her Status had not exceeded the limits of her current "container" the way Aiz's had when she leveled up.

"Now, if you were anyone else, I'd level you up as soon as I was able to. After all, the ability points of a higher level aren't even comparable to the level below it."

"Yes, this is...true..."

"I can't stop you from focusin' on numbers, numbers, numbers all the time, either. Maxin' out an ability takes a lot of time and effort, and it'd be much easier to just up and at 'em to the next level. *But...*" Loki set herself down on the bed then continued. "Those eensy-weensy little numbers you'd be giving up on could prove fatal in a familia like mine."

If two adventurers of the same level were to go head-to-head, how those figures matched up could mean the difference between victory and defeat. In other words, it was an ability gap. Acquiring more points at an earlier level could confer a distinct advantage, since it would be reflected in a person's current level as "extra" power.

Of course, numbers weren't the only determining factor when it came to victory and defeat. An adventurer's expertise—their techniques, tactical finesse, magic, and skills—all played an important role, as well.

Still, it was a great advantage to have.

And it went without saying that the higher one's level, the more excelia required to raise one's numbers.

"Lucky for you, you've got Finn and the others who can help you get the experience you need. One more expedition like this and you'll shoot right up, don'tcha think?"

"Ah...ha-ha...ha-ha-ha..."

The fact that other familias *did* prioritize leveling up was the problem.

In a departure from how *Loki Familia* operated with its legion of powerful elites, adventurers in less influential familias had to risk their lives in the Dungeon for any hope of leveling up. This made the level-ups themselves, along with the increase in fighting power they brought, absolutely essential. They didn't exist in an environment where they could easily collect high-caliber excelia whenever and wherever they pleased.

Lefiya could only force a laugh as Loki shot her a somewhat sadistic smile.

"I know, I know…you may be thinkin' life's a little bit cruel right now, but…Lefiya, think about it. Your level-ups have been comin' faster ever since you converted to my familia, yeah?"

"They have, yes…"

Lefiya's first level-up had taken her three years to achieve. She'd been a mere eleven years old, still in the middle of her studies in the Education District.

After one more year in school, she'd joined *Loki Familia*, and after only another year's time, she'd reached Level 3. Now, two years after that moment, she'd received the golden ticket that would accelerate her to Level 4.

Putting aside a certain white rabbit's insane growth, Lefiya's progress was nothing to scoff at, either. It was steady and sure, thanks to the strength of Finn, Aiz, and the others.

"I know it's a lot of pressure hearin' it again and again, but Finn, the other top spots, and I all want ya to follow in Riveria's footsteps. Super Lefiya's great, but *Hyper* Lefiya's what we *really* want, no matter how much time 'n' energy it takes," Loki continued with a grin as Lefiya looked on quietly. "Remember what your last Level Two Status looked like? We want something like that again, yeah? Leavin' yer magic at a B would be such a waste…so let's get it up to a high A."

"…"

"O'course, I'll admit this isn't really my decision to make. You should do whatever you feel is right. If you wanna level up right now, I won't stop you. So…whaddaya think?"

Lefiya was silent for a moment.

Thinking.

Finally, she nodded.

"I understand. I'll continue at this level for a while longer."

There *was* pressure, just like Loki had said.

All these expectations from those around her made her timid to the point of shame.

But now she would rise to meet those expectations.

Being Riveria's successor—that's what she needed to be thinking about if she hoped to compete against her boy rival. If she hoped to lend her strength to Aiz and the others. And it was the expedition, and its intense battles, that had allowed her to do so.

Something in Lefiya had changed on that expedition, and even she had realized it.

"Thanks a million, Lefiya. Finn and the others already filled me in on everything that happened down there, and it'll probably be a bit before we organize another. I know it might not feel great, but try and hold out till then, okay?"

"I will."

As Loki smiled, Lefiya turned her head over her shoulder to look at the Status on her back, currently stuck in its arrested state of development. The glowing hieroglyphs affirmed that a level-up was possible at any time as long as her patron deity allowed it.

Once Loki had redone the lock and the light of her Status had faded, Lefiya redonned her garments and left the room behind her.

"Well, I'll be. Still no Level Seven for ye?"

The mad rush of Status updates had just about ended when Gareth made his comment, arms folded as his fellow elites took their turns.

"Seems it wasn't quite enough. Perhaps I should go to Ottar, hmm? Ask him for his secrets."

Finn turned toward the dwarf from his spot outside Loki's chambers, a wry grin on his face.

"Then there yet remain only two Level Sevens, the strongest in the world…" Riveria finished for them.

It would seem all three *Loki Familia* elites, updated Status parchments in hand, had to spend a bit more time as Level 6s. As they glanced out the window, down to the courtyard where their friends either celebrated or lamented various Status updates, the trio felt the undeniable sting of impatience as well.

"You guys are natural-born leaders. Fact is, I don't think there's anyone alive who could lead the three of you. Which is kinda the problem, yeah? I know it's tough, but y'all still have a ways to go before you can match the big mom 'n' pop, Zeus and Hera."

Loki curled an arm behind her head as she explained.

For all the excelia it netted them, the three upper-class adventurers might as well have been floundering around in the Dungeon's upper levels. The value of any experience points received from the floors they'd already cleared wasn't very good. For Finn, Aiz, and the other first-tiers, this created a sort of wall, prohibiting any real growth.

Even the experience they'd earned from their fight against the expedition's final boss, the spirit, had had to be divided up among the entire party—which was exactly what Loki was alluding to now.

"Aaanyway, that's an issue for another time. I'm behind schedule! Y'all take care of tradin' in the spoils, all right?"

"Of course. We've dropped well into the red thanks to this expedition. There's the cost of the magic swords and Durandal weapons before we even left, plus all that poison-vermis antivenin we were forced to buy…"

"And the drop items, too, aye. We had to give 'em to *Hephaistos Familia* in exchange for their services…"

"Hnnnnngh, stop, stop, stop, please! Yer givin' me a splittin' headache!"

"Will we be holding a party tonight, then?"

"'Course we will! Gotta celebrate your homecomin', after all!!"

The conversation continued as the *Loki Familia* elites discussed the day's schedule with their patron deity.

Almost as they were done wrapping things up, though, Finn seemed to remember something. "Ah, right. There was something I forgot to tell you…about the incident with the minotaur down in the upper levels. Considering we were forced to face off against Ottar, it would seem the goddess Freya may have played a part in the attack."

"…Hrmm?"

"I'm sure we'd be able to uncover evidence if we investigate. Though we avoided any casualties, Aiz in particular had to cross swords with him…so at the very least, we should report it to the Guild, yes?" Finn posed.

"Ah, right…It came up at Denatus, too. Whole thing got pretty much left up in the air, though…so diggin' any further probably won't do much good. Let's just ignore it!"

"Are you sure?"

But Loki merely flapped her hand in nonchalant disregard. The unusually forgiving demeanor of their goddess was enough to draw questioning glances from all three elites.

Loki, however, simply ignored their looks.

"Anyways, I got somewhere to be! Meetin' adjourned!"

She offhandedly dismissed them as she made to leave the room. On the inside, however, she was sweating up a storm.

Actually, Loki had a secret agreement she'd made with the goddess Freya.

Moreover, it hinged entirely on Loki's own Achilles' heel.

She wasn't allowed to interfere in any of Freya's doings. Naturally, she couldn't talk about those things with her followers, either. It certainly felt like her dignity as a goddess (nonexistent though it might seem) had taken a hit.

As their patron deity scrambled out of the room, the remaining three adventurers could only stare at her back in disbelief.

"Somethin' happen between the two of them, ye reckon…?"

"More drunken dealings? Really now…"

"Hmm, or perhaps something more like a debt."

Followers could not lie to their god.

Similarly, Finn and the others were not about to be taken in by their goddess, either.

Their time together had been far, far too long for that.

Their Status updates completed, the members of *Loki Familia* made their way into the city to finish off their remaining expedition obligations—namely, the exchanging of loot for money.

Heaving bags on top of more bags, they set off from the manor en masse before dispersing into every corner of the city.

"Finn Deimne of *Loki Familia*. As relayed previously, my familia has returned from its expedition, and I'm here to trade in magic stones."

"You got it! Misha Frot at your service! Welcome back! We've been waiting for you!"

"We encountered many unreported monsters down in the Dungeon's depths. Though this will only apply to a small selection of familias, I'd like you to issue a warning for all floors below fifty. I've included further details in my report, along with a list of all our members who've leveled up."

"Understood, sir! Now, let's see…Whaaaaaa—?! Three Level Sixes?!?"

Some spread word about the fruits of their adventure, along with the new intel they'd gathered, before carting their haul of magic stones to the exchange room.

"I, uh…erm…Mr. President? You don't, uh…think you could buy them for a bit…more…do you?"

"What do you mean, Raul? This is already a generous amount! Or are you saying you're dissatisfied with my offer?"

"N-no, of course not, just…Well, this expedition left us…pretty deep in the red. So money would be greatly appreciated…"

"Oh, come on, Raul! Put some oomph into it! Pleeeeease, Mr. President! We're desperate!"

Geez, Aki! What are you—some kind of devil in disguise?!

"Yes, we're begging you, Mr. President, sir! You'll be our go-to shop from now on! Think of all that business! Right, Leene?"

"E-exactly, Narfi! It's just like the captain—like *Braver's* always told us! That you have such a big heart! You're truly a man worthy of respect!!...Or, you know, something like that."

"Though I have to ask—you didn't change your cologne, did you? That elegant scent, it's almost...spellbinding. And I'm an elf. I should know! In fact...I must say, you practically look awe-inspiring today, Mr. President."

"Is that so? Heh...heh-heh-heh...Well, I suppose I could raise my offer a bit. You *are* such valued customers, after all."

""""""Thank you, sir!!""""""

"...Yeesh! W-women are so scary."

Some threw themselves into heated episodes of haggling with the merchant familias, bringing out their drop items, ores, and other Dungeon finds.

"You here, Tsubaki?"

"Ohhhh!! Been waitin' for ya, Gareth! Get yer butt in here!"

"No need t'rush, lass...Now then, the drop items from the depths, just like we agreed."

"*Aha!* This is it, this is it! Dragon fangs...dragon scales!! *Bwa-ha-ha!!* The goods I can make with these babies...!! C'mon, don't get cheap on me. I know you got more in there!"

"If we already promised these...then why does partin' with 'em cut so deep?"

Some relinquished contractual payment to those who'd lent their aid during the expedition.

"Oh-ho? Bete Loga? On bag duty? A rare sight indeed!"

"Aw, can it! There weren't enough people, so Gramps asked me. Make sure this gets to that smith woman, will ya?"

"And what's this?"

"Money. For fixin' up my Frosvirt. It's not the whole amount, but…I'll get her the rest soon."

"Heh…you really haven't changed, have you?"

Some repaid their debts via a certain goddess of the forge.

"Oh, Riveria! You're back! And in one piece to boot."

"All thanks to you, Lenoa. Though I need to apologize first, since I've gone and broken it again."

"Whaaaaaaaaaaat?! A-are you *cursed* or something?!"

Others still took in their staves for repair, given that the magic stones adorning them had cracked.

"Amiiiid! Long time no see!"

"Shhhhh! Inside voices in the store, please!"

"Ha-ha-ha. Nice seeing you, Amid."

"Hello again…Amid."

"Welcome back, my friends. Miss Tiona, Miss Tione, Miss Lefiya, and…Miss Aiz."

Lastly, a certain set of girls made their way to a certain clinic, where a certain friend awaited.

It was the clinic of *Dian Cecht Familia*, complete with emblem of herb and light, a facility they'd not visited in some time. Today, as always, its rooms were filled with upper-class adventurers. From within the hustle and bustle, the human girl Amid greeted Aiz and the others with a smile.

"Congratulations on the completion of your expedition. I had heard you ran into an Irregular and were forced to stay for some time on the eighteenth floor…Nothing *too* serious, I hope?"

"It was a formidable battleground to be sure…but thanks to your potions and elixirs, we were able to pull through by the skin of our teeth. Well, there was the antivenin, too, of course."

"Your magic potion helped me a lot as well! I cannot thank you enough!"

After Tione spoke, Lefiya added her own thoughts.

"It brings me nothing but joy to hear that my medicines were able to assist you."

The warmhearted healer answered with another smile, her long silver hair fluttering. Her delicate, doll-like features softened at the news that Aiz and the others had escaped unharmed.

Then, all of a sudden.

Her eyes turned toward Tione, almost as though she'd just noticed something.

"Miss Tione…is something wrong?"

"…You can tell?"

"I am a healer, after all."

What with the countless sick and injured patients Amid had treated in the past, it was all too easy for her keen eyes to notice the change in the girl's pallor. The fact that the rest of her friends had not noticed anything yet was further proof of Amid's skills as a healer.

Tione brought a finger up to scratch lightly at her cheek. "It's not really, you know, a big thing…I had a bad dream is all. You don't have anything that might help me sleep better, do you?"

"I see. Perhaps I can recommend some Argelica Root, as it promotes restful sleep."

"Thanks…Uh, would you mind keeping this from Aiz and the others? Especially that idiot?"

Tione spoke in a low voice while the girl behind the long counter responded with a kind smile.

"Whaaatcha guys doin', huh?" The aforementioned idiot came bounding over when she noticed the two's conversation.

"Merely discussing the details for an exchange of drop items," Amid answered dutifully before moving on to a new topic. "I assume all of you are quite busy again today, yes?"

"Yup, yup! After this, I'm headin' over to *Goibniu Familia* so I can get my Urga fixed up. You're comin', too, aren't ya, Tione?"

"Yeah. I ran out of spares for my Zolas…and I could definitely use some more Filuka throwing knives."

"Will you be going as well, Miss Aiz?"

"Yes, I need them to take a look at my Desperate…"

The first order of business was turning in magic stones and drop items, but the second would be repair (or replacement) of their weapons and armor. For as many times as they'd done it now, it still always felt like a mountain of things needed doing after they returned from an expedition. Even as Amid gathered materials and replenished the supply of items from across the counter, Aiz and the others were already focused on the great many other tasks they still had yet to do.

"Now that you mention it, didn't Loki leave the manor with us, too? I wonder what she could be up to," Tione mused, almost to herself.

"She said she had an errand to run, I believe…"

"Probably gettin' the goods for the big bash tonight, yeah?"

Lefiya offered her own thoughts on the matter, as did the younger Amazon with an accompanying belly laugh. The conversation made Aiz think back to earlier that morning, when she'd seen Loki exit the manor before disappearing almost immediately.

It almost seemed like…something was wrong? she thought with a curious cock of her head, her gaze traveling nonchalantly toward the ceiling.

"Oh? All alone, are you?"

"Aizuu and the others are all busy settlin' matters now that the expedition is over."

The man who had been waiting for Loki inside the room had a regal demeanor about him, almost like the prince of some well-to-do nation. His elven servant accompanied him.

They were in a certain high-class establishment somewhere in the Shopping District. This bar and its soundproof room had become the "usual spot" for their secret talks.

Loki pulled out a chair from the round table before thumping herself down across from Dionysus.

"Where's our mutual friend?"

"Not back yet, it seems. Rumor has it he was seen heading for the Dungeon…but he's sent some of his followers in his stead." Dionysus directed his gaze toward the wall where a young chienthrope girl stood. She responded with a nod and a stiff smile. Next to her, a sizable war tiger let out a sigh.

"He went to the Dungeon all right. Pushed himself on Finn and my guys on the eighteenth floor, too. Y'think he's okay? He didn't up and die down there, did he?"

"Well, seein' as our blessing's still alive and well, I know *I'm* not worrying…And even then, he's always seemed like the type you can't quite kill. Before I know it, he'll be back, laughin' all the way. Asfi's with him, after all."

The chienthrope, Lulune, spoke up from her spot by the wall, her voice trembling from hesitation and nervousness. Forced to join them in this meeting, she could only let out a string of strained chuckles as she expressed her (albeit questionable) faith in her patron deity.

Those in the room were already fully aware of Hermes and company's unannounced sojourn upon *Loki Familia*'s base camp down on the eighteenth floor. What they didn't know was why, despite the rest of the party returning to the surface the day prior, he and the others had chosen to stay behind.

"Now that you're here, why don't we move to the subject at hand?"

But Loki and the others had gathered for one thing and one thing only—to formulate a plan of attack to deal with the organization threatening their city. Namely, the remnants of the Evils, along with the vibrantly colored monsters and their strange "creature" friends that dwelled underground. It was to fight back against this city destroyer "Enyo," the mysterious puppet master controlling the strings, that Loki, Dionysus, and Hermes had formed this alliance of theirs in the first place. They had plenty of reasons to sniff them out, too, from a thirst for revenge to debts in need of repayment.

And now that the core of *Loki Familia*'s strength had returned from their expedition, the alliance was ready to launch a full-scale attack.

"Well, whether we agree or not, our next course of action's already been pretty much decided, yeah? We've gotta find *it*…the second entrance to the Dungeon."

Their enemies' movements left them with only one explanation: Another entrance to the Dungeon besides the one found within Babel Tower.

There was no doubt that there was a secret passage somewhere—a tunnel that would allow someone to transport monsters to the surface away from the prying eyes of the Guild and its adventurers.

"You are, of course, correct. But before we get to that…surely you were able to make some progress in your own investigation after your followers' expedition, yes? They *did* descend to the Dungeon's depths, which is where those delightfully colored monsters are known to spawn," Dionysus pointed out.

Every eye in the room went to Loki.

The goddess remained quiet for a moment, narrow eyes widening ever so slightly as she surveyed the reactions of those around her, before she spoke.

"Seems like there was some sorta fallen spirit. Strong enough to give even my Finn and his crew a run for their money. And from what we can gather, our enemy apparently wants to summon this thing…to the surface."

The "her" all the creatures kept referring to was none other than the corrupted spirit.

A messenger of the gods, devoured time and time again by the monsters of the depths but who continued to live, constantly changing its form. The crystal-orb fetuses were at the core of everything. They were products of "her," just like the creatures, and they used the viola flowers as arms to collect magic stones in order to evolve into demi-spirits.

All with the main goal of eventually being summoned to the world above.

A gargantuan demi-spirit unleashed beneath the open sky, completely decimating the city of Orario—the Dungeon's "lid."

—*"I will destroy Orario."*

That was what Olivas Act had proclaimed down in the pantry on the twenty-fourth floor. His words ran through the minds of Hermes's and Dionysus's followers who happened to be present for the current conversation. Lulune's face paled, and something caught in her throat as the young war tiger's eyes widened in surprise. Filvis glanced toward her patron deity, too, as she attempted to suppress her own feelings.

Dionysus brought his hand to his face with a quiet sigh as he digested the hypothetical scenario. He was silent for a moment, then raised his head, glass-like eyes distorting.

"Then we need to find it posthaste…not only the second entrance but this crystal orb as well," he said slowly, the weighty timbre of his voice filling the ears of those in the room. The glow from the magic-stone lanterns reflected off the deep-purple wine atop the table, creating a bewitching display of light.

The other deities' followers didn't make a sound. Loki let her chair creak back and forth in a show of bad form as she began to respond.

"…Yeah, but…why do me 'n' my guys have to take all the responsibility, huh? You're givin' us the hard stuff."

"Ha-ha-ha, no worries. Have no fear, for I will lend my aid as well. But there is such a thing as 'the right man in the right place,' no?"

Dionysus replied with a laugh, forgetting his soberingly serious expression when he saw Loki's eyes that seemed to say, *Don't bullshit me*, and he met her half-lidded glare with a flash of sparkling pearly whites.

The thinly veiled battle between the will of two deities was enough to send a pang through Lulune's stomach as she thought, *Awww I wanna go hooome* and tears welled in her eyes. Once again, the war tiger next to her sighed, present only because Lulune herself had tearfully begged him to accompany her.

Filvis, on the other hand, stood beside her god with her eyes closed, silently watching over the proceedings.

"...Well, whatever. Too far in to back out now, as the sayin' goes. Where d'ya think we should start searchin', huh? I mean, I know we'll prolly end up havin' to search everything with a fine-tooth comb, but there's gotta be someplace that's especially suspicious for us to start—"

"—I, erm...About that...Lord Hermes actually, uh, asked us to tell you all something after he came back from his trip...just in case he wasn't able to make it to this meeting..."

Lulune suddenly butted in with a nervous raise of her hand.

Loki's brows furrowed.

Not this again...

But even as the annoyed thought crossed Loki's mind, Dionysus let out a laugh.

"I already know what you're going to say, and don't worry, Loki. I don't believe this should be of any concern for you. In fact, you might find yourself pleasantly surprised."

"?"

At Loki's dubious look, Dionysus's face hardened.

"There is, however, something you should be worried about. Loki, I'd like you to leave the search to us. In the meantime, I'd appreciate it if you would take care of another task."

That night.

Around the time dusk began to blanket the sky, a strange commotion was working its way into every nook and cranny of the city.

News of *Loki Familia*'s post-expedition feat—Bete's, Tiona's, and Tione's ascent to Level 6—was making the rounds. In their love of frivolity, the gods of Orario hadn't even waited for the official Guild proclamation, disseminating the news across the entire city at blinding speed.

"I heard *Loki Familia*'s on par with *Freya Familia* and the Warlord now."

"I heard they *surpassed* them."

"Well, I heard they're now the leading familia in all of Orario."

The heated debate could be heard in every corner of every bar—arguments over which of Orario's two leading familias was the strongest. Bards filled the streets with their songs—lyrics touting the feat of those brave first-tier adventurers. The gods naturally made merry with mirthful cries and loud laughter. The news also drew envious reactions from adventurers who could only dream and aspire to such greatness. Exuberant demi-human children ran about the streets in tattered capes and helmets fashioned from pots, pretending to be adventurers.

Loki Familia was the hot topic in Orario, the first ones to make it to the Dungeon's fifty-ninth floor since the deities Zeus and Hera had so long ago. Once more, the blessed light of stars shone down on the city from above, the coveted seats of hero-hood beckoning the next generation of adventurers.

Gods, adventurers, and citizens alike celebrated the familia's mighty deeds.

"Shall we toast, then? To another successful expedition—cheers!!"

Meanwhile, the familia in question was in the midst of its own celebration at a certain bar where their alcohol-loving patron deity had led them.

The Benevolent Mistress, to be specific—a little place down on West Main Street.

Its walls were filled to the brim with noisy patrons as a mighty *clang* of steins echoed through the air. Aiz raised her glass as well, though more like a skittish animal than anything else, quietly bringing the citrusy juice to her lips.

"Control yourself, Bete! You're not getting drunk on my watch!" Riveria directed a warning look toward the werewolf.

"Hey, I'm always in control!" he shot back in annoyance.

"Lefiya! Mind if I have that meat you got over there?"

"O-of course, Miss Tiona! But...that's your fifth piece already..."

"The food's not showing any signs of stopping, so why worry? Ah, could I get a refill of this?"

Tiona was indulging even more than usual. Tione was helping

herself freely to the food and drink as well while Lefiya simply shuddered.

"Heavens, Finn. We've not accounted for this kind of festivity in our budget."

"Surely a party won't break the bank, hmm? And if worse comes to worst, we can always appropriate a bit from Loki's secret savings."

As Gareth mused with a wary eye at all the revelry while nursing his large drink, Finn merely laughed.

"*Hey!* I heard that!...And I don't give a damn! Hey, everyone! Everything's on me tonight, so go wild!" Loki announced, face already a brilliant red.

"Yahooo!!" The celebratory cries from Raul and the other familia members practically shook the roof.

Obeying their goddess's wishes, they continued to order more—frothy ales and the house's specialty fruit wines—and drain every cask. The table was lined with colorful vegetables, cheesy quiches, baked fish, and thick steaks. Tiona's tongue was restless as the waiters brought them out one after another. The waiters themselves, the cat people in particular, could only let out harried mewls as their eyes darted this way and that.

Loki Familia's wild celebration was even attracting the attention of other patrons. Customers seated at neighboring tables showed curious astonishment as they watched the group.

Sensing the attention (and feeling very much like a beautiful flower drawing the interest of the surrounding bees), even the normally impassive Aiz found herself enjoying the party.

"Miss Aiz, would you like me to get you some food?"

"It's fine, really...Thank you, Lefiya."

"...Is...something wrong? You look as though you've got something on your mind."

"?"

"You were staring off into space...B-but I apologize if my assumption is incorrect!"

Aiz found herself taken aback by Lefiya's observation.

Her mind really had drifted somewhere else.

A cluster of voices rose up above the others from farther within the room.

"Syr! Lyu's back!" "Lyu?!" "What are you girls yapping about? Get back to work!!"

As the owner and her waitresses shouted back and forth, Aiz's thoughts, however, were focused on the information she'd received about Bell and his party only a short while ago.

Earlier, sometime between the start of the celebration and around the time she finished exchanging materials then dropping off her weapon for repair, Aiz had made the rounds, informing the few acquaintances she had outside the familia of her safe return from the expedition. Just as she'd been about to thank Lulune for the portable rations the girl had given her, she'd been updated on Hermes's and the others' return. Bell and his party had been with them.

She still didn't know why he'd chosen to remain behind on the eighteenth floor and not join the rearguard on their return to the surface, but hearing that he'd made it back was enough to bring her relief. Unfortunately, however, it seemed that something had happened on their return trek, as he'd looked considerably worse for the wear upon appearing from Babel's entrance.

Maybe I'll...check up on him tomorrow...Ah, but I don't even know where his familia's home is...

Her brows furrowed in concern. Tiona's and everyone's raucous voices buzzed in her ear as the strange lack of any concrete information on *Hestia Familia*'s whereabouts weighed upon her mind.

"Oh, right! Tomorrow we're gonna make a trip outside the city!" Loki suddenly declared, red-faced and ever so slightly unhinged.

"Oh? What's all this out of the blue?"

Riveria, ever the voice of the whole familia, raised the question as she regarded their goddess suspiciously. Around her, the rest of the familia sported weak smirks and looks of exasperation.

Loki, however, just smiled complacently as she looked out across her followers.

"The expedition's over, yeah? So I thought we could have ourselves a little vacation! You know, some R&R!"

"Huh? A trip? That sounds fun!" Tiona piped up, only for Bete to immediately shoot her down.

"You're not seriously believing her, are you? Idiot..."

"What'd you call me?!"

The Amazon snapped back angrily, but it was just as the werewolf had said—Loki's explanation was hard for any of them to swallow. While this wouldn't be the first time their patron deity had made a similarly offhand proclamation, whenever she did, it usually signified something was about to happen.

This time, too, everyone was already bracing themselves for whatever it was the trickster goddess was planning. Finn, on the other hand, simply smiled, as if already aware of her true motives.

"Where in blazes are we goin'?" Gareth finally popped the question.

"Well...I'm not gonna go into too much detail here, but..." Loki prefaced with an upward quirk of her lips. "Let's just say it's right outside the city. Port Meren, to be exact."

CHAPTER

2

PORT MEREN

Гэта казка іншага сям'і.

Порт вуліца нямераных

Meren was a port city to the southwest of Orario.

With only about three kirlo between the two, it was no more than a hop, skip, and a jump from one city to the other. It served as Orario's portal to the sea due to its proximity to the banks of Lolog Lake, a large brackish body of water that led to the ocean.

Day after day, countless ships from countries all over the world made port in the city's harbor, dropping off their hefty loads of cargo. The majority of the goods would be further transported into Orario as imports. In fact, just about everything that eventually made its way to Orario's marketplaces was first gathered together in Meren. The sea route's ability to transport large quantities of goods was one of its key advantages, and Orario, too, was no stranger to using it for its own exports. The city had long made use of the port as its go-between for exchanging its world-renowned magic-stone goods for foreign imports.

Needless to say, Port Meren was an important point in Orario's oceanic ventures.

"Wa-*hah*! I haven't been here in forever!"

Just as Loki had informed them the night prior, Aiz and the others of *Loki Familia* had made their way to the port city. Tiona cried out boisterously from the middle of the great sloping street connecting the port with the bay. Though Aiz didn't react as drastically, she also found herself rather in awe when looking past the crowds of people at the vast lake and countless ships moored there.

"Seriously. How many years has it been?"

A smile appeared on Tione's face as she checked out the port.

"I don't think I've been here since before I even started heading into the Dungeon!" Tiona responded with a happy laugh.

Much like how many goods made their way through the port city, quite a few people bound for Orario did as well. Those already on the continent could make their way to the Labyrinth City by traveling along its northern and eastern roads, but travelers from the Far East or various island and ocean nations first needed to pass through Meren. Tiona and Tione had made that very trip many years ago.

Only Aiz and a few others found themselves entranced by the surrounding scenery. Most of the group reacted similarly to Tiona and Tione—with a sort of nostalgic excitement.

"Check out this huge dodobass! I know they sell 'em in the city, too, but I've never seen one this big!" Tiona's eager shouts continued as she spotted a gargantuan fish on display in one of the nearby shops. This one boasted a length of well over one meder.

"It seems fish undergo the same development as monsters..."

True to Lefiya's words, the fish's enormous warped scales certainly did make it look more like a monster than a fish. Most likely, it had evolved as such to ensure it didn't become prey to those same monsters. Dodobass weren't the only sea creatures available, either—shrimp, crab, and a whole assortment of other seafood could be seen for sale in shops, most so fresh they were still alive (something unseen outside of port cities).

The road lined with stone buildings was bustling with activity as foreigners, merchants, and fishermen milled about. Off to the side of the road were carpets laid out with rare fineries and tents lined with fish, snails, and other fresh seafood, all of them filled with the haggling voices of prospective buyers. This small snapshot of Meren—the bazaar-like atmosphere, the tanned skin of the fishermen and merchants, and the salty aroma wafting in on the breeze—was enough to make it clear that this was truly a seaside city.

"You came through here when you got to Orario, too, right, Lefiya?"

"I did, yes. Back when I was a student, my friends and I would come to this port often."

"Really? Then you know any good restaurants? You gotta take us to one!"

Tiona latched onto the young elf's back as she responded.

Despite Lefiya's surprise at the sudden attack, she, too, felt a giddy excitement building inside her, as did the rest of the group. Bright smiles appeared on all their faces as they made their way down the road, eyes flitting back and forth around the environs and its endless distractions.

Aiz brought a hand to her chest.

I don't remember this lake...nor this city...

Her own memories of ceaseless fighting with monsters were rusted with the blood of her many victims, so she couldn't be sure whether she'd visited this city before or not. The Dungeon was everything she knew, leaving nothing behind but a vague feeling that she'd once been outside Orario.

...But this smell...I feel like I know it...

Somewhere in the back of her mind, the lake's unique smell tickled her memories.

The humid breeze brushing past her was something she could never have felt when she was surrounded by the great walls of Orario. It had a gentle aroma, saltier than fresh water but not as strong as the sea, and it wrapped her in a warm embrace.

Her eyes narrowed instinctively as the wind played with the golden strands of her hair.

"Is something wrong, Aiz? You're rather quiet over there, though you seem happy," Riveria prodded her, the only one who'd noticed the Sword Princess's spellbound expression.

"...Have you ever been to this city before, Riveria?"

"I have, yes." The high elf nodded. "Once before I arrived in Orario and a few times after, as well. Though some believe the smell of this lake is trying on a forest elf's nose...I'm actually quite fond of it. When I first laid eyes on this scenery, it seemed so different from the confining village in which I was raised—it was exhilarating." A soft smile graced her lips as she looked out across the lake, toward the horizon and the glimmer of the far-off sea.

Hearing this, Aiz couldn't help but think of everything she'd heard about Riveria's past—how she'd left her elven home in hopes of broadening her world and discovering the unknown, similar to how Finn had hopes of restoring the pride of the prum race.

The first time she'd met Finn and the others was when she'd

strong-armed her way into *Loki Familia* with such force, Loki herself had described it as "making a deal with the devil," apparently leading to countless days of contention. Her journey to Orario had been far more than the "simple trip" she'd originally described it as.

All of this, however, would mean that Riveria, too, had experienced a great many wonders as she made her way to the city. Her longing to discover the unknown, her curious heart—everything about her had the makings of an adventurer, and today she was every bit a citizen of the great dungeon city of Orario. Having said that, even she herself had remarked at one point that she'd like to see it all again—to traverse the world a second time.

The sudden memory of this stole Aiz's thoughts, her mind questioning what she would do if Riveria were to leave.

As improbable as it seemed, she found herself imagining what such a future would be like…and the resulting pang of heartache, like a child unwilling to leave her mother, brought an embarrassed flush to her cheeks.

"What're y'all hangin' about for, huh? C'mon! The sea is…I mean, the *lake* is callin' us!" Loki shouted joyfully from her spot at the front of the group. This was in spite of the fact that she herself was contributing the most to this "hanging about."

"Sometimes I really wonder about her…" Tione muttered wearily.

But continue behind her they did, and as Aiz watched her patron deity humming and strolling along in front of her, her thoughts drifted back to the night prior and the events that had led them here.

"We've gotta find that second entrance to the Dungeon, and the first place we're gonna look is Port Meren," Loki had announced from within Twilight Manor's large dining hall once everyone had returned from the party.

"Meren's that little port city just outside of town, isn't it? How come we're not searchin' inside the city itself, huh?" Tiona questioned from her spot next to Aiz at one of the hall's many tables.

Most of the other familia members, however, ignored her question, instead reacting as if they understood perfectly.

"Tiona, do you know how marine life-forms first emerged on the surface?" Finn turned toward the girl.

"Erm, well…from beneath…Babel?"

"And how are they going to do that? Grow legs and walk? You idiot!"

Tione immediately balked when her sister answered with a curious finger to her chin.

Riveria was much more amiable in her explanation.

"We've always been told that the hole directly beneath Babel was the only entrance to the Dungeon…but that's not, in fact, correct. There exists another tunnel outside Orario—one that connects to the waterfront and through which the aquatic monsters of the deep can reach the surface."

"And that's…Meren," Aiz finished the thought for her.

"There's a hole that leads to the Dungeon's lower levels right below our noses—in Lolog Lake. It's how the water beasties make their way to the surface. Seems no one even knew it existed ere the gods' descent," Gareth added.

"Really? Whoa! I never knew!" Tiona exclaimed somewhat obtusely, garnering another look of disbelief from her sister.

"About fifteen years ago, the familias of Zeus and Hera worked together with *Poseidon Familia* to close up the hole at the bottom of the lake, making it impossible for any more monsters to use it as a path to the surface…or, at least, that's what everyone thought," Finn began as his green eyes turned toward Loki.

The recent activities of Levis and the Evils, however, strongly hinted that the hole may have been reopened. While it wasn't a sure bet…the mere possibility that the violas and other vibrantly colored monsters were being transported via the hole at the bottom of the lake was one they couldn't ignore.

"While investigating wouldn't do any harm, I personally feel it's a bit unwarranted…" Riveria added her thoughts on the matter, closing one of her eyes.

"Same. I've got two words—im-possible! You all saw those things on the twenty-fourth floor, right?" Bete piped up in agreement.

Next to him, Aiz and Lefiya exchanged glances, both of their thoughts traveling to the situation back in the twenty-fourth floor's pantry.

It was there that they'd seen all those violas trapped in cages by the Evils' remnants. While it certainly wouldn't be impossible for associates of the Evils to transport them all the way down to the lower levels and release them into the water…it was still a bit far-fetched.

"I get what you're tryin' to say—I do! But accordin' to Dionysus, some new, never-before-seen species of monster was just sighted off the coast of Meren…some kinda nasty snake thingie. Real ugly green color, too."

The color drained from every face in the room at the news.

A "nasty snake thingie" and an "ugly green color"…That could mean only one thing—carnivorous violas.

As the group shared worried glances, Finn opened his mouth.

"In light of this news, I believe we've no choice but to investigate. If anything, we should be able to uncover some sort of clue."

His proposition was met with unanimous support.

Thus, it was decided that *Loki Familia* would travel to Port Meren.

"But don't we need permission from the Guild to go outside the city? The procedure is actually, uh, pretty annoying. Not sure we'd be able to finish things up in time to leave tomorrow."

Tione was resting her chin somewhat dejectedly in her hands as she pointed this out.

Orario's biggest fear or, in this case, the Guild's biggest fear, was losing their first-tier adventurers. Aside from a few special cases, they weren't allowed to leave the city whenever they pleased, and the process to obtain permission was nothing short of exasperating. Not only that, it could take as many as a few days for the paperwork to get finalized.

"Never fear! I already got permission!" Loki quickly asserted.

"…You're kidding."

"No, I'm serious! Delivered the form to ol' Ouranos himself! Well, it's mostly 'cause I made a big scene at the service counter. But I wrote specifically in hieroglyphics 'We're investigatin' the violas. Don't get in our way!' so it's all good."

The goddess laughed triumphantly as Tione's chin slid off her hands in disbelief.

At any rate, for whatever reason, whether barring them permission would raise suspicion or he actually wanted to use *Loki Familia* to solve this whole problem with the violas, the Guild leader had acquiesced to their request to leave the city.

As Loki proudly waved around the scroll with the Guild's seal on it, even Finn found the corners of his lips curling upward.

"She must've obtained it earlier today after she left the mansion with us..."

"B-but still! Don't you think this is all happening a little too quickly?"

Tiona offered her thoughts, and Lefiya was quick to respond.

"...You don't trust her?" Aiz spoke up as well.

"It's a little suspicious..." Tione finished. All four at the table felt a very real sense of foreboding sweep over them.

Everyone in the familia was more than used to their patron deity's bizarre nature, but even as their caution rose, Loki never lost her wide smile.

"So! Will you and the other guys hold down the fort while we're gone, Finn?"

"What?!"

"Aiz and the other gals plus little ol' me want a few nights to ourselves. Wouldn't want any men around to bother us, ya know."

She continued rather teasingly, completely ignoring cries of injustice coming from Bete and the other men.

"What the hell?! You better have a damn good explanation for this!" Bete roared.

"What?" Loki shrugged him off. "We can't just leave the manor unattended, can we? Who knows what could happen! But we already decided to go to Meren, sooooooo. Plus, I reassured the Guild that I'd leave at least half the familia behind."

"That's not what I'm askin', you cow! Why do only the girls get to go, huh?!"

"Oh, right. Finn. I also want you to keep an eye on Dionysus and the others, okay? Always givin' me the grunt work—would be nice if I had something to hold over him. Also, I don't trust Hermes at all, sneakin' around all the time."

"LISTEN TO ME, WOMAAAAAAAAAAAAAAAAAAAAAAN!!" Bete was practically fuming at this point. Raul and the others braced themselves while Finn could only sigh alongside his fellow elites as the familia's women watched everything unfold in weary silence.

Aiz, Tiona, Tione, and Lefiya exchanged glances among themselves. It would seem their lady-only investigation in Port Meren was about to begin.

"We really were the only ones who got to come…Ughh, I wish the captain was here…" Tione grumbled to herself, surrounded by the hustle and bustle of Meren's streets.

"Ah-ha-ha…" Lefiya forced a somewhat awkward laugh. True enough, the only ones allowed to join the investigation at the port had been *Loki Familia*'s women.

The womanizing goddess had invited her pride and joy—gorgeous elves, an elegant catgirl, an adorable human—making for a sight that attracted the notice of the surrounding crowd. Aiz and Riveria in particular garnered quite a lot of male attention with their beauty that rivaled even goddesses.

"Now then! We should be reaching the harbor right about now…"

Loki continued along aimlessly, still refusing to tell them exactly where they were going. The large pack on her back—a pack that she refused to allow anyone else to carry—was stuffed to the brim with an apparently "secret" item.

Under the dubious gazes of her followers, she finally cut through the crowd and made her way toward the harbor proper.

"Ah! It truly is a sight to behold!" Lefiya gasped in awe upon seeing the grand port up close. Its docks were bustling with sailors, their heads wrapped in towels for a truly "seaman" look, and all around them ships had laid anchor along the marina.

They bobbed and lilted in the pure breeze below a blue sky—

sailboats of all shapes and sizes, more than they could count. And in the middle towered the merchant ships, so tall you had to crane your neck just to see them in their entirety. Every one of them found their gazes stolen by these seaworthy masterpieces, Aiz included.

"You've fallen in love with the ships, huh, Aiz?"

"Yes, they're…amazing."

Tiona asked her question with a laugh, arms behind her head. Aiz surveyed the breathtaking view, watching in fascination as one of the mighty vessels pulled out of the harbor.

The arc-shaped port city wrapped around the banks of the brackish lake was so alive with activity, it nearly put Orario to shame. Brawny seamen lugged crates and barrels down from their ships where horse-drawn carriages carted everything away to locations unknown. Passenger ships unloaded their cargo of people—everything from finely dressed elves to traveling animal people making their way down the wooden bridge connecting the ship's deck with the dock below.

Beyond the dock itself, the wide expanse of Lolog Lake was a sight to behold. Big enough that its opposite bank remained hidden along the hazy horizon, it could easily have been mistaken for the sea itself, spread out beneath a swath of fluffy white clouds. As the radiant sun reflected off its surface, it glittered the same brilliant blue as Lefiya's eyes.

Amid the scent of the water drifting in on the breeze, the seagulls cawing in the distance, and the cries of the sailors going about their business, even closing one's eyes couldn't diminish the feeling of standing on the threshold between land and sea. It was a different experience from the unknown discoveries they made deep within the Dungeon. As Aiz felt her mind and body grow calm, she found herself at a loss for words.

"Over here, y'all!"

Aiz and the others followed the sound of their patron deity's voice toward the southern wharf.

Loki herself wove her way through the mountains of casks and cargo until she seemed to find what she was looking for—and raised her voice to meet the figure in her sights.

"Hey, Njörðr!"

"Hmm? Well, I'll be. If it isn't Loki!"

The god who turned around was a finely built specimen. His brown hair was pulled back in a ponytail that dangled from the back of his head, and the smile he gave the group exuded a sort of calming warmth despite the virile gallantry of his features. He was about the same height as Bete, and his upper half was bare, revealing a muscular chest and arms. His physique was one not often seen in the streets of Orario. For Aiz and the others, their first impression of him said that this fellow carrying a fishing net slung over his shoulder was unmistakably a man of the sea.

"Feels like just yesterday we last saw each other. How many years has it been? Or should I say, how many decades?"

"Well, considerin' our scale of time, a few years feels like a blink of an eye. You forget to catch up and suddenly it's been half a century. I really did mean to visit more often! On my honor!"

"You lie the same, too."

Njörðr laughed as sweat glistened on his pearly white skin. The strange fact that no part of him was tanned proved he was a deity. His shorts stopped at the knees to reveal two shapely legs that looked as though the sea itself had washed them clean.

As he put down his fishing net and walked over to Loki with an amiable smile, the long-standing relationship the two shared was clear.

"Seems you're doing fine, too, Riveria. Word of your fame reaches even beyond the walls of the city." The carefree god shifted his attention to the nearby high elf.

"There's no need for flattery, Njörðr. It does nothing but swell one's pride."

Riveria responded with a small smile.

"Lady Riveria, are you and this god acquaintances?" Lefiya asked somewhat timidly.

"He did much for me before I came to live in Orario. He's a friend

© Kiyotaka Haimura

of Loki's from the heavens. Surely you have heard of *Njörðr Familia* and their famed sea products, yourself?"

"Oh, yeah!"

"Now that you mention it..."

Tiona and Tione piped up as even Aiz's face mellowed in realization.

Besides its important role in trade, the port of Meren was also famous for its fishing industry, with a fourth of its area devoted to the craft. The ones in charge of the business were none other than *Njörðr Familia.*

The familia itself was made up of a system of fisheries, prevalent mostly in cities along the coast. This included, of course, Lolog Lake but also the ocean it flowed into. The large catches Njörðr's followers brought in from the water were sold not only in Meren's shops but also in Orario, bringing a fresh taste of the sea to the city. Both *Njörðr Familia* and *Demeter Familia*, the latter with its rich agricultural industry, had long histories of supplying food to the Labyrinth City.

"What brings you here, then? You even brought the whole family along, though I see that Finn and Gareth are missing. Quite the bag you've got, too..." Njörðr shot Loki's bulging backpack a dubious look as the fishermen around them continued their work.

Loki just grinned. "I'm actually on a bit of a treasure hunt. But I decided to have some fun while I'm at it. To that end, I was hopin' I might ask ya a question or two."

"And what might those questions be?"

"You're pretty familiar with this area, yeah? I mean, obviously..."

The two deities continued their huddled chat, faces close. Aiz and the others standing nearby could catch only a few phrases here and there—*"A 'hidden gem' kinda place," "Somewhere nobody else knows about, yeah," "A real paradise, if you know what I mean...!"*

Njörðr threw a suspicious glance at Loki's bag and her pack of followers, apparently inferring what the goddess was up to before leaning in to whisper in her ear.

Loki responded with a series of nods, the smile on her face growing with every word.

"Amazing! Thanks, Njörðr! I'll tell ya all about it later, yeah?"

"You're sure I can't join you—?"

"No can do!" Loki promptly turned down the other god before spinning around to call out to her followers. "Got everything I needed to know! Let's skedaddle!"

As the excitement in their patron deity's voice neared its climax, so did the sense of foreboding everyone was feeling.

Following Njörðr's recommendation, the group headed even farther south, putting distance between themselves and the city proper. They stopped when they reached a small alcove, hidden from sight in the shadows of the surrounding trees and rocks.

"Oh, wow! The sand is so white!"

"It's a beautiful beach. And here I'd always thought the port was nothing but rocks and cliffs..."

"It's gorgeous..."

Tiona, Tione, and Aiz couldn't hide their wonder at the view of the sandy white hills spreading before their eyes.

It was a fairly sizable inlet just off the side of the lake's banks, completely surrounded by towering trees and giant boulders. Cliffs scraped the sky to either side while the beach itself was devoid of life—a true "hidden gem" if they'd ever seen one.

The sound of gentle waves lapping at the sand drew them in like moths to a flame. None of them could keep the smiles off their faces as they took in the sight of the sculpted coastline.

"All righty then! I brought y'all a change of clothes!!"

The squawking voice of their goddess put a stop to their appreciation of the beauty.

She'd struck a strange pose, as if she'd been waiting for just this moment, and was now riffling through her pack and exposing its contents.

—Long, long ago, when the gods had first descended from the heavens, they'd brought with them culture and inventions to impart upon the peoples of the world below. Among those inventions was a set of things commonly referred to as the Three Sacred Treasures.

Despite "three" being included in their name, their numbers actually varied depending on the race or cultural sphere in question. They included everything from special ears one could wear to make one look like an animal person, elastic spats popular even among adventurers, bloomers, stockings, sailor uniforms...the list went on, oftentimes instigating debates over which of the inventions should actually be considered "sacred treasures" (and occasionally even resulting in bloodshed). Even to this day, the heated debate between those who sought the truth—people whose eyes had been opened after the desecration of a god—refused to die down.

There did, however, exist one treasure that not a single soul in all the world would deny.

And that was the bikini.

"So this is the real reason we came to Meren..."

Aki lamented, red-faced, as she used both her hands to cover her chest and belly, where the skin was bare thanks to the ridiculously skimpy bits of cloth her patron deity had forced her into.

The slender tail poking out from her rear lilted back and forth as she and her fellow familia members came out from behind some nearby rocks after all of them had changed into similar attire. They were now hiding themselves behind their hands. Aside from their chests and hip areas, every bit of the blushing maidens' skin was exposed to the brilliant sun overhead.

"Even after all those baths we took down on the eighteenth floor..."

"...Somehow this is still more embarrassing!"

Lefiya and Leene awkwardly swayed back and forth.

The majority of them had been forced into two-piece suits, and the size of the bottom halves only added to their shame. Lefiya's still-developing breasts formed a graceful valley that peeked out of her suit's top, the lower half (complete with short miniskirt) snug against the smooth curves of her bottom.

"You carried that big bag of bikinis all the way here…?"

Alicia raised the question. She wore a one-piece suit that made her turn a brilliant shade of red that spread all the way to the tips of her long, pointed ears. Nearby, her patron deity was eyeing the elf's fully developed body with a sense of satisfaction.

"Whoa! Wooow! This is amazing! Bodies glistening in the sun! Is this paradise?!"

The womanizing goddess's excitement was reaching its peak. Though Loki had denied her true motives for investigating the lake, it was clear as day to her followers what was most important in her mind. Fist raised toward the sky in triumph, her bloodshot eyes examined every detail of the embarrassed and incredibly uncomfortable girls and their bodies.

"Hey! Where's Riveria? Where's my darling, adorable little Riveria, huh?!"

"She's frozen behind that rock, still holding her suit…"

"Whaaaaat? C'mon, I need to see the goods! Hurry up or I'll put that thing on for ya!"

"—You will do no such thing!!" "Stop right there!" "You'll not defile Lady Riveria!!" The elves in the group were to their feet immediately, racing toward Loki as she dashed to the rock where Riveria was paralyzed. With Alicia in the lead, the elves sent the goddess facedown into the sand.

"Guwwagh!!" Loki yelped, though her cry of surprise quickly devolved into a bout of lascivious laughter at the sensation of naked skin pressing against her from all sides.

Meanwhile, just as Lefiya had described, Riveria remained as still as a statue behind the rocky outcrop, risqué outfit clutched between her hands.

…Th-they're not lying…It really is embarrassing… Aiz thought, eyes traveling down the length of her bikini-clad body as she blushed.

It was a white two-piece, similar to the others aside from the long pareu-style skirt dangling from her bottom half.

She'd put up a fight, too, when Loki had first coerced her into wearing her standard battle attire, but even that didn't hold a candle to the shameful bits of cloth she'd been forced into now—even if no one besides her familia was present.

Rubbing her naked arms uncomfortably, she mentally thanked no one in particular for the fact that the men hadn't been allowed to join.

"M-M-M-M-Miss Aiz in a bikini...?!"

"Wooow!" "I knew she'd look good in that!" "Nice!" "I'm jealous!"

There were many compliments once Aiz emerged a few moments after the others. And not only from Lefiya, either—her smooth skin, slender frame, and shapely breasts left the group agape in awe.

It was also enough to make Little Aiz inside her, dressed in a tiny swimsuit, dizzy from the attention. As her cheeks grew redder, she found her eyes dropping toward the ground, unable to meet the gazes of her normally indifferent peers.

"You and your sister don't feel the least bit embarrassed...do you?" Aki threw a glance in the direction of the two Amazonian sisters.

"Why would we? It's not like it's a big deal."

"These aren't even that different from what we usually wear!"

They responded nonchalantly. True to Tiona's words, the blue bikinis they sported now showed no more skin than their normal battle gear. The feather-like cloth was so thin that it was practically see through, yet they felt no shame in baring copper-colored legs or ample chests.

Before long, Loki called out to them, having forsaken her quest to see Riveria suited up.

"All right, everybody! It's time to put aside our work for a while and have some fun!! Instead of swimming in the ocean, swim in the lake! Some dearly needed relaxation for my battle-weary maidens!! Complete with wardrobe malfunctions, of course!!"

"As if!!"

The cry from the group of red-faced girls was unanimous.

No matter the reason behind it, the group of adventurers had certainly earned themselves some time in the sun, and they were going to take advantage of it.

"Mmm, salty! But I thought this wasn't the ocean!" Tiona immediately took a running jump into the water. Shaking her head like a wet dog, she brought a hand up to wipe her bangs out of her eyes, clearly enjoying herself.

"M-Miss Tiona! How can you just jump in like that?"

"Easy peasy! Come on in, Lefiya!"

"I, well, here I goooooo!" Taken in by the innocent girl's antics, the elf's lips curled into a smile as she made her way across the white sand and into the water.

Though summer was a ways off and the water still had that mid-spring chill, the Dungeon-hardened adventurers rushed in en masse. They played in the waves and splashed one another, their laughing voices quickly filling the deserted inlet.

Jostling breasts, wriggling hips, hands reaching to fix bits of cloth that had gotten themselves wedged in a little too far—Loki, too, was having the time of her life as she watched the girls enjoying themselves in the lake waters.

"Beautiful. Just beautiful. I may not have the ocean, but I still got me a gaggle of bikini-clad girls to ogle...hee-hee-hee, the perfect combination!" She sighed.

"She really is a perverted old man..." Tione grumbled, not surprised in the least as she saw the drool bubbling out from between the goddess's lips. She turned her eyes skyward. "I wonder if the southern kingdoms feel like this..." she murmured, her voice swallowed up by the never-ending sky.

It was almost as if the dazzling sun overhead was shining just for them and their private beach.

"..."

Meanwhile, Aiz had found herself a small corner of the beach and was currently idling about without much to do. Somehow, she looked less and less like the aloof Sword Princess and more like a small child hesitant to approach the white waves breaking on the sand.

"Miss Aiz! Would you like to join us?" Lefiya called out exuberantly once she noticed her seclusion.

"...Um..." Aiz's gaze turned in the opposite direction of the sea-drenched elf.

Just past the beach, she could see the heads of the others in their group floating in the water. Even farther out, Tiona could be seen gliding cheerily back and forth among the waves.

It looked deep. Very deep.

"...I'm, uh...I'm fine...really..."

"?"

Lefiya cocked her head to the side in confusion at Aiz's more hesitant than usual demeanor.

"Whassup, Aizuu? Don't tell me you still can't swim?" Loki approached the beached girl.

"Urk!" The goddess's assumption was right on the money.

"..."

"You...can't swim, Miss Aiz?!"

—This isn't good!

Aiz's behavior grew even more suspicious. The nervous flitting of her golden eyes gave away her secret.

Lefiya's cry of surprise was enough to draw the attention of Tiona and Tione, who both made their way over, babbling excitedly. ("What is it? What is it?") Their brows furrowed doubtfully upon first hearing Lefiya's explanation but then softened in acute realization.

"You know, now that you mention it..."

"Even down in the Dungeon, she never got too close to the water..."

"And anytime it looked like she was about to fall into any, she'd just use her wind magic to kick herself off the surface..."

As Tiona and the others discussed the situation among themselves, Aiz gave a tiny gulp. Clasping her hands, she awkwardly rubbed her slender fingers against one another.

"...When I try to swim, I only...sink..." she finally uttered, red-faced and quiet as a mouse.

"Whaaaaaaaaat? Really?!"

"You can't be serious!"

"B-but you've never had a problem bathing in the Dungeon's pools! Like down on the eighteenth floor, you seemed just fine..."

Tiona shouted with surprise, and Tione and Lefiya echoed her sentiment.

The reactions only increased Aiz's discomfort. "I'm...fine if I can touch the floor...I just can't...put my head under the water..." Her eyes fell to the ground as she felt shame well up inside her.

Lefiya couldn't contain her shock. To think that the girl she'd adored for so long could have such a monumental weakness!

The Sword Princess, Aiz Wallenstein.

Sixteen years old...and a human anchor.

This was a result of her delving again and again into the Dungeon, focused on nothing but honing her combat skills.

"Heavens above! To think that ya still can't swim. I woulda thought for sure you'd be able to by now after goin' to the Dungeon's beach floor so many times...Huh? Wait a second! This means—if I can get her in the water, *I win!* She'll have no way to resist my advances when she's struggling just to stay afloat! *Prepare yourself, Aiz!*" The boorish grin that accompanied Loki's words was positively obscene. She promptly launched herself at the water-fearing girl—

"—gngh?!"

"Yeeeow!!"

—only for Aiz to respond in kind, her eyes glinting with sudden vehemence.

The full-force slap she inflicted upon her patron deity sent the goddess tumbling across the sand with an addled "*Gwwuoooof?!*"

Meanwhile, Tiona hurried over to Aiz's side and grabbed her hands.

"How 'bout we teach you, then, Aiz?"

"Er, well..."

"Yeah! It'll be a great opportunity for you to practice! It'll only get worse if you keep putting it off, right?" Tione added with a smile.

"I—I will help as well, Miss Aiz!" Lefiya assured her enthusiastically.

"...Mmmmm..."

The pressure building, Aiz ultimately had no choice but to nod in agreement. And thus, though the heart of the girl in question was whirling in turmoil like a typhoon, the first-ever swimming lessons for the human anchor began.

"Why don't we start by seeing just how bad you really are, hmm?"

"Could you walk just a little ways into the water for us, Aiz?"

"O-okay..." Voice trembling slightly, Aiz unwrapped the pareu from around her waist. Knowing that she had no choice but to accept her fate at this point, she set her jaw and tied her long golden hair up into a ponytail. With a sidelong glance at the other girls farther off who were now eyeing the situation curiously, she ever so slowly, ever so warily inched her way into the water until it reached the vicinity of her hips.

"If you just lie on your back, you'll float. Give it a try, yeah?"

"..."

"Ohhh! She did it! She did it!"

"I knew you could, Miss Aiz!"

"There you go. See? It's easy! Now let's try putting your head in the water and using your arms and legs to move—"

"——*glug, glug, glug, glug...?!*"

There was an almost inhuman noise as Aiz sank to the bottom of the lake.

"N-no way!!"

"That was so fast! She just disappeared!"

"T-Tiona, aren't you going to save her?!" Tione asked fearfully as Lefiya and Tiona simply watched in shock.

That was enough to elicit the attention of the other familia members, causing everyone to rush into the lake with panicked screams.

"Miss Aiz!!"

"It ain't gonna work. The trauma from Riveria's special training's rooted too deep..."

"What did Riveria do to her?!"

Loki explained, having recovered but still boasting a leaf-shaped red mark on her cheek, and Tione responded with a shout forceful enough to send flecks of spit from her mouth.

The high elf in question, however, remained petrified behind her rock, still motionless with her hands on her suit.

"Talk to us, Aiz!" "Miss Aiz, are you all right?!"

"...I'm sorry..." Aiz mumbled as Tiona and Lefiya dragged her safely to shore. Her eyes spun, and her shoulders heaved with each breath.

Many of the other lower-level familia members had never seen their Sword Princess like this before, and the shocking scene was enough to elicit gulps of anxiety from the entire group.

They kept trying, having her attempt a few more back floats once she'd recovered, but nothing seemed to work. Every time she tried moving her feet, she sank straight to the bottom.

"This is even worse than I thought..." Tione bemoaned.

"But that's exactly why she needs to practice!" Tiona this time.

"More than being afraid of the water...it's almost like when the time comes for her to swim, she tenses up and completely loses it..."

"A reflex, then? Riveria really must have done a number on her..."

As the two Amazons lamented the situation, faces grim, Lefiya sympathetically rubbed Aiz's back.

As for Aiz, her legs had given out beneath her, and she was currently supporting herself with both hands in the sand; she could only watch as Little Aiz inside her gurgled from deep below the water's surface.

The other familia members who'd been watching the spectacle unfold began to gather around her.

"Hmm...how 'bout you practice with me, then, huh, Aiz? You can hold my hand!" Tiona suggested, reaching out to her.

"Um...okay..." If her friend was willing to do so much for her, then Aiz couldn't just back down. Resolving herself, she took Tiona's hand, and the two of them made their way back toward the water.

Tiona walked backward across the bottom of the lake, both hands clenched tightly in Aiz's as she helped support the other girl in the water.

Slowly, slowly, with tiny little kicks like those of a small animal, Aiz began moving herself forward, determined to keep her head above water and remain afloat.

"No need to be so tense, Aiz. Yeah, yeah, there you go. That's how you do it."

"R-really?"

"Okay, I'm gonna let ya go now!"

"?!"

"One, two—"

"I'm not ready, I'm not ready, I'm not ready!"

"—three! Here you go!!"

"————————ghn?!"

The moment Tiona released her, Aiz began to writhe like a panicked rabbit. With a horrendous gurgling noise, she began to sink beneath the water.

Desperate now, she reached toward Tiona, somehow managing to clasp both arms tightly around the Amazon's body. Pressed against her friend's bosom, she simply trembled in fear, not unlike a frightened child.

So cute. Tiona couldn't help but think this while she smiled.

"Sooooo cute."

"Isn't she adorable?"

"Absolutely precious."

"Oh, Aizuu. You're adorable even like that. So different from usual, you know?'

The sight prompted comments aplenty from the peanut gallery back on the beach (Loki included). The only one who wasn't looking at Aiz was Lefiya. Her azure eyes were currently locked on Tiona as a jealous moan rumbled within the depths of her throat.

The beach party didn't last long after that (and Aiz's swimming problems remained unresolved). Having played to their hearts'

content, it was time to move on to the real focus of the trip—their investigation.

"If we're supposed to examine the hole in the bottom of the lake… doesn't that, erm, mean we need to venture down there?" Lefiya seemed somewhat fretful as she threw a glance in Aiz's direction.

The Sword Princess flinched at the non-combat-related implication.

Then Aki turned to Loki. "Of course. You know where the hole is, don't you, Loki?"

"Sure do! I did my homework! It's in a ravine just a smidgen farther south. Tiona? Tione? I'm leaving it to you girls!"

"Got it!"

"This'll be over in a snap!" The twins responded with identical winks.

While Lefiya and the others had been fully prepared to help (as inexperienced as they were with water combat), Loki had entrusted Tiona and Tione with the task of investigating the spot.

As the two stepped forward, Aiz's head shot up with a snap.

"Those swimsuits…are they made from Undine cloth?"

What with all her drowning and bouts of shame, Aiz hadn't had a chance to look at the two's outfits until now.

The cloth was a deep shade of blue while the fabric itself was endowed with the divine protection of the spirits.

"'Course it is! Prepped 'em for the girls myself. Not about to send 'em on an underwater quest without it," Loki broke in proudly.

The cloth, woven with the spirits' magic and bestowed with specialized attributes, could outperform even the armor of the most advanced smiths. Undine cloth, in particular, boasted improved resistance when it came to water-element attacks and could even fend off intense heat waves, making it an integral asset to any adventurer's wardrobe.

That being said, the only way to truly invoke its power was to wear it underwater.

Even the strongest adventurers' movements were still heavily sluggish when trying to navigate underwater; however, by equipping

Undine cloth, one could zoom back and forth with ease beneath the waves, greatly expanding one's range of mobility. It boosted not only water resistance but movement and speed underwater, as well.

While it was pricey, it was an essential piece of equipment if one hoped to engage in any sort of underwater monster culling.

"But to desecrate the cloth of the spirits by turning it into a pair of bikinis…" Lefiya and the others warily eyed their patron deity, who ignored the condemning looks and simply continued talking.

"What's more, my two lovely Amazons have the Dive ability. Fact is, they can already swim like the fishes! So equipping them with Undine cloth is like throwin' wings on a tiger…or should I say, givin' a halberd to an Amazon!"

"And just what is that supposed to mean?!" Tione shot the aphorism-spewing goddess a look of indignation.

The two Amazonian sisters had learned the Dive ability upon their recent level-up—an ability that carried with it the same basic effects as those provided by Undine cloth. The difference, then, was made up by an increase in attack power, making their underwater combat abilities that much stronger.

It was said that this ability was absolutely essential to all those in *Poseidon Familia*, what with their many endeavors in the wide-open sea.

"I thought that Dive was a fairly rare ability…?" Lefiya questioned.

"Though I've heard it's much easier for members of more seaworthy familias to learn…" Aki pointed out.

"But then how did those two learn it…?" "Yeah, how is it possible…?"

As the dubious voices of their peers rose up around them, Tiona and Tione met them head-on.

"Before coming to Orario, we often accepted requests from fishing villages of the island nations to hunt monsters in the sea. It was how we obtained money for food."

"Yeah, yeah! Sea monsters can be super hard to take down! But we spent so much time doing it that somehow we got really good at fighting underwater!"

The fact that neither of them liked to lose only spurred their abilities further, as they'd often compete against each other as to who could bag the most kills.

As Lefiya and the other familia members listened to all this with somewhat forced laughs, Loki began rummaging around in her giant bag before pulling something out and handing it to the two girls.

"Here ya go. Weapons! In case ya run into any of those nasty flower critters. These should give it to 'em!"

"And these are?"

"Corbel Edges! Had 'em custom-made by *Goibniu Familia* from under-coral and sea tiger fangs. Snatched 'em outta the manor's storage."

The two daggers were about the same length as Tione's Kukri knives and surprisingly light, too; the blades resembled water crystal in their translucent marine-blue color. After receiving two each, the girls gave the daggers a few practice slashes before taking off down the beach with a "Be back soon!"

Cutting straight across the sand, they dove deftly into the lake.

"…You know…It might be too late to ask this, but if Misses Tiona and Tione are the only ones necessary for the investigation, why did all of us have to change into swimwear, too…?" Lefiya mumbled as she watched the bikini-clad sisters disappear into the water.

Loki, however, feigned ignorance. "Go, go, go! You can do it!" she shouted, completely disregarding the mage's question.

The clear, brilliant blue of Lolog Lake was enough to rival even the waters of the south. Drainage from magic-stone production in Orario and Meren was purified via large distillation apparatuses, keeping the water in the lake so clear that people could see far beneath the surface. It was through this translucent blue world that Tiona and Tione swam now, making their way quickly away from the inlet where Aiz and the others had waved their good-byes and gripping their Corbel Edges in one hand.

"Bwuuaterssh's swwhooaw bbbreeeeaaaar!" Tiona exclaimed with a burst of bubbles.

Tione just rolled her eyes in the other girl's direction. *How the hell am I supposed to know what you're saying?*

There was a peaceful tranquility down in this watery realm that was quite different from anything that could be found on land. Schools of green, blue, and gray fish swam past them as they continued farther and farther through the brine. Down below, seaweed poked up from among the scattered rocks and crags, undulating gently in the current.

Soon, clumps of driftwood and scattered remnants of a past shipwreck came into view. Swarms of dodobass scuttling from view, the two girls looked down silently on the vestiges of the once great ship, its hull eaten away by erosion and decay.

"!"

A strange light suddenly caught Tiona's eye.

Something shone from deep within the shadows of the ship.

The moment they realized it was the glowing red eye of a giant monstrous fish, with the body easily equal in size to the two sisters', the creature emerged abruptly from the darkness.

It was a raider fish, and likely the reason the ship had capsized in the first place.

Its red eyes darting back and forth, it zipped out with a swift jerk from a recess on the lake floor in hopes of catching this new prey.

"Whuuuuuuaaaahhhhh!!"

As the monster fish rocketed toward them, Tiona raised her right hand, the one not currently holding a weapon, in the air.

"!!"

"Guwah?!"

With a speed and intensity no less fierce than when on the surface, she brought her arm down on the fish with a watery *bash*.

Her iron-like fist shattered the creature's face into dust. The would-be predator's blood sprayed out in every direction as its body was sent careening toward the lake floor below, sending up a whirling cloud of silt.

We might not have done this for a while, but we certainly haven't gotten rusty!

Well, the suits probably help.

Tione shrugged in Tiona's direction, and the other girl rotated her arm to stretch.

The telepathic twins communicated with their gazes as they felt the power of the Undine cloth burgeoning their Dive ability.

How long you think you can hold your breath?

An hour or so easy.

And so they continued on, the information Loki had given them guiding their descent.

Deeper and deeper they dived, constantly surveying the area around them. They followed the sloping lake bottom as it curved downward, and the light of the sun from the water's surface overhead grew fainter and fainter the farther they swam.

A short while later, and after they'd already taken care of more than a few of the brackish water's denizens—

That must be it…

—they arrived.

The deepest part of Lolog Lake. In front of them, there was a lid so giant it was enough to take their breath away. It was a colossal circular seal, more than ten meders wide.

It appeared to be constructed of either seiros or varmath, and its white surface was so different from the surrounding rock, it looked like the entrance to some kind of sea temple. Though the lid seemed firmly closed atop the hole in the ground's sloping surface, it was easily sizable enough that dragons and other large vermin could have passed through it in the past. In fact, countless aquatic monsters had made their way to the surface via this very tunnel ages ago in the Ancient Times.

Tiona and Tione sank toward the lake floor, looking up at the imperious form of the gargantuan lid.

What's that thing…?

A monster fossil…? No, more like a drop item.

In the white stone of the lid was a jet-black figure.

It appeared to be some kind of giant skeleton—no, the leftover bones of something even larger. Its skull was sharp, like a dragon's, but its spine was long, almost like a snake's, and two mammoth fins protruded from its back like wings. The broken, cracked bones wound their way around the surface of the white stone like a coil, looking very much like the fossil of a creature long gone, just as Tione had said.

What was this thing? Knowing very little about this hole or the connecting tunnel, they found themselves momentarily at a loss until, finally, it came to them.

Leviathan…

The ancient beast who'd made its way to the surface long, long ago.

The monstrous sea calamity whose defeat was listed as one of the Three Great Quests of humanity, together with Behemoth and the One-Eyed Dragon, who had been brought down fifteen years ago by the party of adventurers led by Zeus and Hera.

I've heard that the scales of the Black Dragon can be used to ward off monsters…

Around a thousand years ago, the One-Eyed Dragon left Orario and scattered its black scales in every corner of the lower world. No monster in all the land would come close because of the ceaseless waves of power rolling off them, thanks to the King of the Beasts' presence still alive inside. It was undeniable after a few indisputable instances of this.

The scales of this Leviathan were the same.

The divine will of Ouranos had barred passage to the surface for the monsters of the Dungeon. Even if any were to make their way through, the moment they saw the black bones, they'd high-tail it back to the Dungeon. As trying to simply kill all of them would be impossible, this was the easiest way to ensure none got through.

Upon defeat of Leviathan, the familias of Zeus and Hera had

© Kiyotaka Haimura

brought back the beast's skeleton, using it here on the tunnel's lid to complete the seal.

The "Leviathan Seal," as the Guild officially called it.

As Tiona and Tione looked out upon this unbreachable gate of contrasting black and white, they found themselves losing track of time completely.

...We should check to make sure there aren't any gaps in the lid.

Turning their gazes away from the fossil's empty eye sockets, the twins returned to the task at hand.

Searching the entirety of the great hole, they looked for any signs that a monster had passed through—anything that could serve as a secret path. Each taking a different side, they searched every nook and cranny of the mighty lid, including the surrounding rock.

Their efforts, however, seemed to be in vain.

Not a single scratch! Tiona floated upside down as she waved her arms back and forth in the water.

Yeah, there's just no way a monster could have broken this seal, not that we didn't already know...Doesn't seem like anything even came close, and there aren't any gaps around it, either... Tione threw a sidelong glance at her sister with a sigh.

Even the many monsters they'd had to tackle just to get to this spot had all but disappeared. The lid, with all its monster-warding properties, was intact and in good health.

Monsters don't wanna get close, right? So maybe we should search a little farther out? Maybe they built another *hole a ways away or somethin', yeah?*

I'm not too keen on scouring every inch of this place without even knowing where to look...

As always, the two sisters found themselves at an impasse. Sending bubbles toward the surface, they took another look around at their environs.

——!

All of a sudden, Tione's eyes grew as sharp as a hawk's.

Far, far off in the distance, she caught sight of two long figures floating in the water.

Decidedly yellowish-green figures.

Tione!

That's them, all right! Violas!!

They were off without a second thought, zooming through the water.

The two monsters were swimming not more than ten meders or so from the lake's surface. And a great many ships were cutting through the water above. The two sisters swam as fast as they could to intercept the giant flowers.

!

Their heated pursuit sent intense ripples of water in the direction of the violas, who quickly became alerted to their presence.

Great buds opening with a *snap*, they revealed their ghastly fangs and jaws. Then, every one of their mighty tentacles came careening toward them.

"Bweyyh mreallwy *mwarh* ere!!" Tiona exclaimed unintelligibly as she glided out of the way of the incoming tendrils with grace and speed that could rival a mermaid's. She used the opportunity to brandish the Corbel Edge in her hand before neatly severing the tentacles.

?!

As the tentacles scattered in the water, Tione dove forward.

She was at the beast's stiff torso in a flash, marine-blue blade flashing as she neatly divided it in two, just as her sister had.

"Gnngh!"

——————hwwwuuaargh?!

The weapons, forged specifically for use in the water, cut through the normally impervious skin of the flowers with little resistance. And as the gracefully curving blue glint of the blade separated its head from its body, the flower itself quickly shriveled into nothing.

The remaining viola took one look before turning tail.

Crap! It's getting away!

After all these years out of the water, the twins' attacks didn't cut quite as deep.

Severely injured, the giant flower quickly made its way to the water's surface, almost as though seeking salvation in the light of the sun.

Tiona and Tione followed after it—until a new ship appeared from the direction of the ravine.

——*Shit!!*

In a fit of rage, the viola shot its tentacles toward the ship's hull.

"Loki!" Aiz shouted sharply.

She'd noticed it before anyone else, and her voice prompted the rest of her *Loki Familia* peers on the beach to look up at the situation forming in the middle of the lake.

"A boat?!"

"And there's something wrapped around it!"

The galleon that had just appeared on the lake was currently grappling with a set of yellowish-green tentacles from within the brackish waters. Just when it appeared that the severed tentacles would bring the ship down, the viola itself reared its ugly head. The giant flower opened its jaws, fully prepared to sink the vessel with it.

"Holy hell! Aiz! Everyone! Get out there!" Loki shouted.

Immediately, Lefiya and the other mages up and down the beach began casting their spells as Aiz and her fellow frontliners found their footing in the sand and raced toward the ship.

——*Gnnghh?!*

When all of a sudden.

A shadow jumped down from the galleon's deck, delivering a blow straight to the viola's head.

"What…?"

The beast's giant head went tumbling through the air before plummeting into the water.

Not long after, the tentacles that had been gripping the ship separated themselves from the hull as the rest of the flower's body sank back into the deep. Aiz and the others could do nothing but stare at the spectacle in shock.

"What just happened?!"

"Someone killed the viola?!"

Tiona and Tione, too, heads bursting out of the water a short distance away, were stunned into silence.

The giant flower, a creature that could give even first-tier adventurers a run for their money, had been slain.

As an excited clamor built up aboard the surrounding ships floating on the water, Tiona and her sister could only stare up in wonder at the giant vessel before them.

Then—*THUD!*

The dark shadow that had so readily ended the viola's life landed atop a nearby fishing boat, scimitar flashing.

"Rjada ru jheeda…die Hyrute."

Tiona reacted almost immediately to the non-Koine words—the words of her people. Spinning around with a jolt, she came face-to-face with the woman standing on the boat.

All eyes of the men on the boat were focused squarely on this newcomer and the copper skin laid bare by her revealing clothes. A silken neckerchief covered her mouth, hiding the lower half of her face.

She was watching Tiona silently, eyes staring out from beneath her sand-colored hair.

"Bache…"

First Tiona, then Tione went wide-eyed in wonder, unable to believe what they were seeing—when suddenly, a voice calling out from the galleon's deck landed the final blow of surprise.

"Now there's two faces I haven't seen in a long while."

"————————"

The sound of the not quite young, not quite old voice brought time to a screeching halt.

Their gazes moved upward to find an entire group of Amazonian soldiers staring down at them from the boat's deck—along with a certain young goddess.

Her skin was the same copper hue as her followers', bloodred hair billowing in the lake breeze. While her short stature may have given her the appearance of a child, the necklace of fake bones around her neck, the fanged mask over her face, and the two eyes glinting behind it projected nothing if not pure authority. Next to her stood an Amazon with hair the same color as the woman still behind them on the fishing boat.

As Aiz and the others watched the spectacle unfold from their spot on shore, Tione's eyes flashed with a sudden fury. She screamed up at the group of women smiling down at them from above.

"Kaliiiiiiiiiiii———!!"

CHAPTER

3

KINGDOM of the AMAZONS

Гэта казка іншага сям'і.

Краіна жанчыны салдатасалдата

The enormous galleon pulled slowly into port.

From its anchor shaped like two swords, to its warrior-esque statue adorning the ship's bow, to the towering mast protruding from the ship's hold like a mighty halberd, it was every bit the ship of a tribe of warrior women—and it garnered the attention to match it as the troupe alighted to the land below.

Even the brawny fishermen littering the dock were immediately abuzz with excitement and confusion as the Amazonian women disembarked, led by their young, masked goddess.

"Kali!!" Tione shouted, still clad in her blue swimsuit. With Tiona on her heels, she made a beeline toward the incoming ship that, by chance, had pulled halfway into the city port. The gathering crowd quickly moved aside at the menacing aura radiating off the two sisters.

By the time Aiz and the others arrived, back in their normal attire, the air choking the wharf was liable to explode at a moment's notice.

"What are you doing here?!"

"We haven't seen each other in years and that's the first thing you say to me?" the masked goddess, Kali, countered disenchantedly, indifferent to Tione's rage.

"Answer me!!"

"A little sightseeing is all. Problem, Tione?" Kali posed before sending one of her girls to meet the highly flustered city official headed their way. Given they already had the proper port-entry permit, it did seem they'd made prior preparations for the trip.

"That's bullshit…!!"

"No, it's undeniable truth. Wanted a change in routine is all. A little stimulation, you know?" Kali's lips curled upward coyly as the crease between Tione's brows deepened. Behind her, Tiona kept quiet, unable to conceal her look of dubiety.

Aiz, on the other hand, couldn't seem to keep her eyes off two different women in the group—the two sandy-haired Amazonian warriors next to the goddess, so alike there was no way they weren't sisters.

—They're strong.

The battle-hardened intuition of the Sword Princess told her as much. Both women before her could easily stand shoulder to shoulder with the best of their first-tier adventurers.

Level 5s maybe…? No, Level 6s?

A thought that, if true, was a little terrifying.

She was certain they belonged to a familia outside the city. And while Aiz herself didn't know much about the world outside Orario and the Dungeon, she did know that leveling up outside the Labyrinth City was a difficult task. When taking that into account, these two sisters and the first-tier aura they were giving off seemed even more remarkable.

Aiz couldn't help but wonder just what kind of training they'd undergone that would give them the ability to take out a viola with such ease.

And that one…she hasn't taken her eyes off Tione this entire time.

Her gaze flitted to the woman who'd killed the viola, her face expressionless beneath her semi-long hair. The vibe around her suggested she was even more taciturn than Aiz herself.

The woman next to her, hair tied up in a ponytail that descended all the way to her waist, was currently eyeing the confrontation between Kali and Tione with a little smile.

As though feeling the pair of eyes on her, she threw a glance in Aiz's direction.

Aiz's muscles instinctively tensed at the almost reptilian way those two eyes bored through her.

"Aaaanyway! It's been a long time…" the tiny goddess continued, looking up at Tione and making a rather lewd gesture toward her chest as her eyes traveled downward to stare pointedly at Tione's breasts. "…You've grown."

"And just where do you think you're looking…?!"

A husky murmur escaped Kali's lips as her eyes flicked toward Tiona.

"Meh…you haven't changed at all," she finished disinterestedly.

"What're you lookin' at, huh?!" Tiona barked back. As the girl began stomping her feet in indignation, Aiz stepped forward like always to hold her arms behind her back.

"I've heard of you guys before. *Loki Familia*, yes? Where's your goddess?"

"I'm right here." Loki stepped out from the crowd of people, walking past Tiona and her tantrum to face Kali head-on. The scarlet-haired goddess's gaze was surly, her lips curled upward in a grin that exuded impertinence. "I thought somethin' was goin' on… Heh. No biggie. As you can see, these two kiddos are mine now. You need somethin', runt number two?"

"Hmph. Our first time meeting and you're already being a disobliging asshole. Now, if you'll excuse me, I have business with these two."

"Oh-ho-ho! Pickin' a fight, are we? On our first date? Come at me, you vertically challenged piece of trash!!" One provocation leading to another, Loki erupted—a magnificent first impression if ever they'd seen one.

"P-please calm down!"

"You're making a scene!!"

Lefiya, Aki, and the others pleaded, moving forward to calm their raging goddess.

Kali, on the other hand, completely ignored the entire spectacle, turning, instead, toward where Tione was still glaring daggers in her direction.

"At any rate, we're going to be here for a while. If you folks are doing the same, perhaps we'll meet again."

"Don't make me laugh…"

"I'm sensing some animosity. Do you really hate me—and the rest of your tribe—so much?"

"I never wanted to see you again…ever!" Tione practically spit, both at Kali and at the rest of the Amazons behind her.

Kali's eyes narrowed behind her mask.

Then she turned on her heel, taking the rest of her troupe with her.

"I couldn't help but miss you, my beloved daughters," she finished before she and her familia left the wharf behind them.

"Daughters…?" Lefiya murmured curiously as she watched the departing group and Tione, who remained stock-still on the dock. Ever so hesitantly, she turned toward Loki, whose peers were still restraining her. "Do Misses Tione and Tiona…know that goddess?"

"…Hnnnngggghh…Guess there's no point hiding it…" Loki let out a disgruntled sigh, completely spent and breath ragged. Pulling away from her captors, she brought a hand to her head with a scratch. "That's their old familia. Their very first one, too, from before they joined ours."

Lefiya, Aiz, and the others sucked in their breath.

Tiona, however, simply gazed quietly at her sister's back before turning her eyes toward the infuriatingly sunny sky above.

"*Kali Familia* consists of the goddess of Telskyura and her followers."

Later that night.

They were in the room they'd reserved at a local inn—their home base for the length of their investigation—as Loki and Riveria explained the situation, everything about Tione and Tiona, and the deep connection they had with this *Kali Familia*.

"Telskyura…that's a peninsular country far to Orario's southeast, right?" Aki confirmed.

"It is," Riveria continued. "A solitary island surrounded on all sides by sea and cliffs…known for belonging to no one but Amazons. I'm sure many of you have heard of it."

"S'just like with Ares and Rakia. A nation-state familia or whatever you wanna call it. I mean, not that I think that tiny tramp's fit to rule or anything…" Loki added. "It's pointless! That brat and I'll never get along! The only one who grinds my gears more than that pip-squeak is that Jyaga Maru midget tramp…And what's with that creepy mask, huh? *Ugh!* Pisses me off!!"

Everyone withheld their comments as the goddess grumbled with increasing contempt before Riveria continued.

"It would seem the only men allowed on the island are slaves or those used for breeding."

"From the little we learned about it in school, it seems to be a very savage country. Or, at least, that's the impression I've always had…"

After Lefiya added her thoughts, Riveria explained further.

"You'd be correct. From what I've heard, a day there doesn't go by without battle cries and cheering crowds filling the air, everyone devoting themselves to relentless combat. It is a nation of blood and war…the Holy Land of the Amazons. It's one of the few world powers besides Orario, and they possess incredible capacity for war. And not only that, they're completely isolated compared to other countries. Information about what goes on inside their borders is extremely limited…"

It was here that Riveria stopped.

Eyes traveling back and forth between Aiz and the other women seated on the sofa, she continued.

"There are rumors that their two captains, the sisters Argana and Bache, have both reached Level Six."

There was a simultaneous gulp of dread from all those listening.

First-tier adventurers were rare enough already, even in Orario, but for them to be the same level as Riveria and the other elites was something else entirely. It was so easy to forget about the world outside the walls of the great Labyrinth City, and this piece of news was enough to leave them speechless.

"Riveria, how did they get that strong? Without the Dungeon… how were they able to level up?" Aiz asked, unable to wrap her thoughts around the perceived dilemma.

The group of Amazonian warriors they'd come face-to-face with earlier that day immediately sprang to her mind. It wasn't just the two sisters in question, either—all of them seemed strong enough to hold their own against a top-tier adventurer. How could they possibly have grown that strong without the boon of the Dungeon?

Riveria was silent for a moment. Then…

"Through the rites they perform every day in the arena…ruthless fights to the death, not only against the monsters they capture but even against their fellow warriors."

Once again, Aiz and the others found themselves at a loss for words.

"Yeah, some explorer wrote about it in his chronicle or whatnot. About how he snuck into Telskyura and barely made it out with his life…and the constant killing that took place day and night in those rites," Loki explained.

"You mean the *Curious Tales of Rastillo Furough*?" asked Riveria.

"That's the one! There's a copy in the manor's archives!" Loki replied with a fervent nod, reciting it for them now as though flipping through the pages then and there. "'I, too, shall emulate their hymns. An Amazon of the land is a true warrior'…I can still remember that line."

Silence settled over the room.

Whether they'd heard of Telskyura before, like Lefiya, or were just learning about it for the first time, like Aiz, they were all at a loss for words. But not because they'd learned the truth about the island of Amazons.

No, it was because they remembered that Tiona and Tione, too, had once been members of this *Kali Familia*, and the realization was enough to shake them to the core.

Lefiya was the first to speak, voice straining from her parched throat. "Then…Misses Tiona and Tione both…?"

"Born and raised in Telskyura. Least, that's what they told me upon joining. So I can assume they went through the whole rigmarole, too…"

It had been five years since the two sisters had converted to *Loki Familia*. Loki leaned on the back of the sofa, eyes traveling toward the ceiling as though she was reliving that very day in her mind.

"We've killed so many of our brethren, and you still want us to join you?"

That was what Tione had asked when Loki had approached them with her invitation.

Riveria closed her eye in silent reflection. She'd been there, too, together with Finn and the rest of the elites.

Lefiya and the others could barely contain their shock.

There was no way they could have known that the eternally innocent Tiona and the lovestruck Tione constantly attempting to court the captain could have had such horrific pasts. Even hearing it now, they could barely believe their ears.

While, certainly, none of them had ever asked about the two girls' history, neither Tiona nor Tione had ever shown signs that something darker resided within them.

I never knew…

Not even Aiz had known.

Back then, Aiz had been even less interested in matters aside from her training and had known only that they were getting some new members in the familia—nothing more. She didn't start interacting with them until Tiona had approached her: Aiz, the inarticulate, flustered girl and Tiona, the ever-smiling, audacious Amazon.

Aiz knew it was due to—or perhaps "thanks to" would be the more appropriate phrase—the two sisters that she'd grown into the person she was today ("mellowed out," as Tsubaki had put it). With not a shred of ulterior motive between them, they'd both played a big role in Aiz's life.

"…"

The conversation coming to a close, Aiz turned her gaze toward the open window.

She could see Tione outside, standing on the wide balcony with her back to them.

"C'moooon, Tione. Let's go back inside!"

With Tiona's incessant pestering in her ear, Tione continued to stare out at the city beyond the balcony's railing. The hotel they'd booked was a grand Southern-style inn right in the center of the city. And from the balcony on its fifth and highest floor, one could take in the entire port and its connecting bay in a single glance.

The lights from the anchored boats flickered like will-o'-the-wisps across the dark waters of the lake, and toward the east, the gleam of a lighthouse cut through the darkness.

"...Why did they come here?" Tione murmured through her fatigue, letting her eyes drop to the city below. It was a question aimed at a certain goddess and her followers, currently located somewhere within all that shadowy darkness.

"I know how you feel, but thinkin' 'bout it's not gonna do us any good. Maybe they really did just come to sightsee," Tiona posed, acting no different from usual despite her sister's melancholy. As she leaned over on the railing into Tione's line of sight, Tione looked at her long and hard.

"Why are you acting like this is no big deal?! Kali, she—None of them would have any reason to go somewhere if there wasn't fighting involved!"

"..."

"Do you even remember what they made us do? Do you?! If you do, then wipe that stupid grin off your face!!" Tione exploded.

The outburst was enough to spark Tiona's rage, as well. "What're we supposed to do, then, huh? Tell me what it is we can do! Just put our heads down and charge right in? Are you even listening to yourself?"

"That's not what I'm saying, you idiot! Stop putting words in my mouth!"

"Then stop putting words in mine!!"

"Yeah, well, I couldn't stand you acting all 'la-di-da, nothing's wrong'!"

"Oh, couldn't you?!"

Aiz and the others in the room were listening in on them now, shocked into silence at the scene taking place on the balcony.

Having had enough, Tione turned her back on her sister with an angry jerk. She marched past Aiz and the others already gathered at the window, past Loki with her arms folded behind her head, and past Riveria with her one eye closed to make her way out of the room.

No one knew what to do for a moment. After throwing a glance at Tiona, shocked and silent on the balcony, Aiz raced out the door after Tione.

"Miss Tiona...are you all right?" Lefiya asked as she and the other girls drew around her once Aiz had left.

"Mmn...I'm fine..." Tiona nodded.

"...We, um...heard that...that you and Miss Tione used to belong to the familia of that Lady Kali we met today..." Lefiya continued cautiously.

"It's true." Tiona's response came without hesitation. The elven mage—and the other girls around them—swallowed hard.

"Then...erm...well—"

"Sorry, I don't really know if I should be talking for both of us if Tione isn't here..." Tiona cut in before Lefiya could find the right words, her eyes dropping to the floor.

Silence wrapped itself around the room until, after turning her gaze skyward, Tiona spoke again.

"But..." she started, looking somewhere far off into the distance, "...I can say that we never wanted to see them again...ever."

"Tione."

There was a voice from behind her.

Tione turned away as Aiz ran to catch up with her, the bluish shadow of the corridor tinting the world around her.

"Isn't this a sight, you chasing me? Usually it's the other way around," Tione muttered sarcastically, averting Aiz's gaze.

"Because...because you and Tiona were...always the ones who helped me...whenever I caused trouble for everyone else..." Aiz spoke bit by bit, coming to a halt. Tione could tell she was trying to speak her mind, and the usually taciturn girl was selecting her words with the utmost of care.

But the warm support of her friend did nothing but irritate her now.

"Aiz, please. I want to be alone. I've…become something I didn't want to become."

"Tione…if there's anything at all I can do—"

—let me know.

Or, at least, that's what she would undoubtedly have said before Tione interrupted her.

"You have secrets, too, right? Things you don't wanna tell us?"

"!"

"So don't you think that's a little unfair? Saying nothing about yourself but expecting everyone else to bare everything to you?!" Tione snapped, thrusting Aiz's goodwill right back at her.

Aiz's gaze fell.

"I'm sorry…"

The near-whisper seemed to echo in the corridor.

But it was Tione who was truly sorry at what had just transpired. Quickly, as though running away from the other girl, she hurried on ahead.

"What's wrong with me…?" She cursed at herself, filled with self-loathing as she made her way not back to the common room but to an empty private room, yanking open the door and stepping inside. She let herself collapse onto the bed.

All of a sudden, she was overcome by an intense feeling of fatigue.

"Why…why did they have to be here…?" she moaned, hands clenched around the bedsheets.

As her eyelids grew as heavy as lead, her dreams called her to sleep.

Ever since she could open her eyes, Tione had been a part of that country.

The forsaken island of Telskyura.

A nation of female warriors, Amazons, whose ceaseless rituals of bloodshed had been continuing since their goddess had come into power. The first two things she could remember were a searing heat on her back and the sound of someone crying—she didn't know if it was herself or someone else.

Falna. Since the moment they were born, Tione and the other girls of Telskyura had been christened as children of their goddess.

It was said that the Amazons of Telskyura knew how to kill a goblin before they even knew how to speak. What with their latent abilities unlocked by the Falna, along with their first baptism—being placed in front of a goblin child and forced to fend for themselves—by the time they could take their first steps, they were every bit a warrior. In fact, for as long as Tione could remember, her hand had been gripping a sword.

She didn't know what the warmth of a mother's hand felt like.

She wouldn't know her parents if she saw them. She wouldn't be able to pick out their voices.

She had no semblance of family save one—the girl she'd recognized instantly as her other half the moment they saw each other. And she was sure it had been the same for Tiona, too.

"They told me you're the big sister and I'm the little sister!"

"Hmph."

The word *sisters* had been nothing more than a word to the young twins, but it would grow to become a powerful bond.

To be respected in Telskyura, one had to be a true warrior.

Strength was everything in this holy land of the Amazons. It was truth. Those with strength were lauded, given status and prestige. Contrastingly, the weak, who were defeated in combat and denied even the honor of a noble death, were forced to serve their country and superiors as part of the labor force. Bloodshed was a means of attaining true warriorhood, a staircase, a time-honored national custom. Telskyura was an embodiment of Amazonian instinct in every way.

Enter the goddess Kali, who was every bit as fond of combat as the Amazons.

Her blessing further developed the Amazons' abilities, making their battles all the more violent. The warriors revered this bringer of strength as their one and only god, and the perpetual fighting and bloodshed flourished.

Did Tione feel remorse for the endless days she'd been forced to fight? No.

Truthfully, she'd had no real problem with it.

Had she been unable to fight off the monsters coming at her, she'd have been killed. This was simply basic instinct. Above all, she was an Amazon—it was in her nature. Fighting gave her a natural high that got her blood pumping.

No, it wasn't the days and nights she spent in combat, experiencing all that power, that filled her with such enmity. In fact, that was all she'd known back then. Defeat the monsters in the arena, then return to her large stone room with naught but the necessities of life—her days had consisted of nothing but this back-and-forth path. Her entire world had consisted of the zealous cries of her brethren and the cold, cold stones of the battlefield.

It was when she'd first had to face off against her own sisters that her days of fighting had begun to lose their appeal.

By the time the monsters in the arena had turned into her fellow Amazons, it had already been too late for Tione. Her peers, similar in age and height, had fought harder than the monsters she was so used to, and though it had been difficult at first, soon, she was picking them off as quickly as the monsters that had come before.

"Ahhh..."

The first time she'd heard one of her sisters' dying cries, it had sounded so weak.

Though the same blood spilled from their veins as the monsters she'd slain, it seemed somehow even more vivid.

As she'd watched the life fade from the eyes of the girl beneath the mask she had to wear, Tione had felt her heart stir. It had been a strange feeling she couldn't quite describe. Upon returning to her room of stone, she'd found her sister, Tiona, normally uncontainable in her excitement, simply staring off into space with the blood of her brethren staining her skin. That night, Tione had washed herself again and again and again in the icy cold water.

The number of girls she'd had to fight only grew from that day forth.

She cut them down with her weapons, bludgeoned them with her fists, wrung their necks using the skills she'd acquired. She'd practically been born on the battlefield, and she knew nothing of right from wrong. And yet, the stirring in her heart refused to be assuaged. She couldn't understand why—why was this any different from the monsters she'd once slaughtered so easily? She could still feel the give of their skin beneath her fingers, the crunch of their bones against her fist. Even long after the battle was over, she could still hear their screams, those agonizing wails that escaped their lips mere moments before death.

The cheers from the women in the audience would go on and on and on when she won. They'd revered her, the devourer of the weak. *This is right*, their voices had said, as her goddess Kali sat on high, looking down at her with a smile on her face.

Maybe she'd just grown weary and learned to ignore the stirring in her heart, dulling it with apathy. Still, she began to yearn for the days when she'd had to fight nothing but monsters.

And yet, even in the darkest of times, light finds a way.

It had come in the form of another Amazon who was almost like a sister, generous and caring. Tione, Tiona, and the other girls, too, had all been quite fond of her. Every time Tione would return to their room after another battle, she'd been there to greet her with a warm smile. She'd been strong, too, the strongest of them all, always there waiting before anyone else.

Perhaps Tione even thought of her like a mother. Her hands had tended to her wounds, rough yet gentle. They'd all gathered around her, craving the warmth of another's touch as they'd slept side by side on the floor. That room, that cold stone room, more like a prison than anything else, was the only "home" Tione had ever known.

The rites had a law that prohibited combat between Amazons of the same room—a law that the girls had begun to discover the longer they fought.

This law had been a breath of relief to Tione. She wouldn't have to fight the girl who'd long taken care of her, nor the girls whose faces she knew so well, nor her own sister, Tiona. That place, the home she'd created, would never change.

That's what she'd believed.

And then her fifth birthday had arrived, and she'd been summoned to the arena, the same as any other day…

"…"

Tione opened her eyes.

It felt like she hadn't slept a wink thanks to the flashback that had served as her dream. It was the same way she'd felt upon waking for the last two days.

As she sat up and wiped the sweaty bangs from her eyes, she noticed someone else sleeping in the bed right next to hers.

Tiona.

Though Tione hadn't returned to their shared room, Tiona had still found her and spent the night here next to her.

Tione was silent as she watched her sister sleep.

She'd always been like this, wanting to be by Tione's side whenever something happened. She wouldn't say anything, simply gravitating toward her, as though seeking out her other half.

Just like she'd done back then.

Before they'd joined *Loki Familia*.

When it had been just the two of them.

Giving her sister one last look, she quietly slipped out of the room.

"…"

Tiona's eyelids flicked open the moment the door closed.

The next morning, Aiz and the others split up into groups before heading out into the city.

They needed to gather as much information as they could on the sudden appearance of the violas in the lake.

"A giant, man-eating flower? No idea. Weird stuff's always coming up out of the lake and ocean around here."

"If we're countin' hits to the hull, these ships are takin' constant beatings from monsters and whatnot. That's how we shipbuilders make a profit!"

"Haven't had many casualties wound here lately. Mewen's been pwetty peeshful."

"Whenever beasties crop up, we just leave 'em to *Njörðr Familia*. Those fishermen are a lot stronger than your average adventurer. If things really got out of control, well, we'd simply contact the Guild and they'd send us help from Orario."

Aiz, Lefiya, and the rest of the recon group went from person to person—a young human man managing an open-air shop, an elven ship captain (rare as they were), a tanned catgirl wandering around selling ice-cold juice, and a dwarven bar owner currently in his apprenticeship—asking for any info they could offer on violas or other monsters in the lake.

"It would seem no one knows anything about the violas."

"Yeah, yesterday's sighting must have been the first..."

Lefiya and Aiz looked out across the bustling crowd of the city's main street from their vantage point in front of a small alleyway. They and the rest of their group were taking a much-needed respite from the sun's rays.

"I guess that means..." Aiz continued with a murmur, "the lake and the sea are both safe..."

"It would seem that way...If those giant things really were appearing frequently, they'd be causing quite a lot of damage."

If the violas were tough enough to give even first-tier adventurers a run for their money, frequent spawnings would be a cause for panic. From what they'd heard from the laymen of the area, however, the lake and its surrounding sea had been perfectly calm as of late.

Which meant they'd reached something of an impasse.

"Certainly there's no way the violas are being killed before they're able to cause any damage...right? Then what could possibly be going on?"

As Lefiya racked her brain next to her, Aiz simply stared off into the busy street.

"The drainage channel seems...in order."

Aki and Leene were on their way back to Meren after checking out the river nearby that acted as Lolog Lake's drain receptacle. The Guild had long been banging their heads against the wall at the raider fish and other monsters that used the river as a way to gain access to Orario's sewer system, turning it into a cesspool for breeding. In fact, only a short while ago, Loki and Bete had even discovered a viola in the old sewers. Rather than using it as a way to travel from the lake to the city, it seemed more likely that the flower had been using the sewers as a way to return to the lake. Which was why Aki and the others were checking up on it now.

"The mythril grate seems firmly in place..."

"I'd heard they were going to fix it ever since those monsters did a number on it, but I didn't know it was finished already."

Drainage water gushed out in great, heavy deluges from behind the silver barricade at the hole to the main sewage pipe. They were a short ways to the northwest of Orario, having descended the gently sloping hill that led to the entrance of the city's sewers.

True to Leene's words, the drainage pipe, with its view of the city walls and their accompanying guard post, had been effectively sealed off thanks to the mythril grating covering its opening. Not only would it be able to hold back large monsters like the violas, it looked as though it would have no problem keeping out mid- and small-scale monsters like the raider fish, too. And it showed no signs of breakage.

The girls watched as the clean, purified water, free from its preprocessed stink, poured into the pool below.

"Then there's no way those flowers could have reached the lake from here…unless it made the trek quite some time ago." Aki followed this up with a grumble as she brought a hand to her slender chin in thought.

"Nasty-looking flower creatures, huh…? Come to think of it, we were pretty shocked by those things yesterday," Njörðr mused in response to Loki's question, a large sack hoisted up on his shoulder.

She was in Nóatún, *Njörðr Familia*'s home.

As Aiz and the rest of her followers went about on their investigative missions, Loki was off collecting information herself. Currently she was interrogating Njörðr, her old friend, in his home's storehouse connected to the lake-facing port.

"You're the main man around here, ain't ya? You haven't heard about any, you know, suspicious goings-on recently, have ya?"

"I'm afraid I'm only the 'main man' when it comes to matters of the fishing variety. I don't dip my fingers into any other pots and have no delusions of becoming the next Poseidon," he pointed out with a wry smile as he hefted his sack—"Alley-oop!"—into a corner of the storehouse. "I'm constantly up to my ears in fish. No room for talk of these 'suspicious goings-on' of yours."

"Oh, gimme a break!" Loki shot back from behind him, seated cross-legged on a nearby crate.

"You'll have to forgive me. I must admit I was quite surprised when I heard of your true intentions in coming to Meren…" he explained with a sigh as he rubbed the back of his neck.

Loki stared at his back in silence.

"Things have been peaceful here in Meren for many years now…at least, until what happened yesterday. Ask anyone around here and they'll tell you the same."

The violas' attack on *Kali Familia*'s boat the day prior had been the first thing to rile up the port in quite some time. Though Tiona and Tione might have been the ones who forced the giant flowers to the water's surface, the fact still remained that the violas had been there in the first place. To think they'd simply have stayed there on the lake floor, minding their own business and not attacking anyone was unreasonable...right? It seemed much more probable that some creature tamer had set them loose there—or, at least, that's what Loki thought.

"That reminds me, you still on bad terms with the Guild?"

"Hmm? Ah...same old, same old, yes. Even though we aren't adventurers, they still constantly try to bring us over to their side, and every time we refuse, they tax the hell out of our shipments of fish," Njörðr explained none too enthusiastically.

This same practice had been going on since, or perhaps even before, Loki and the others had first come to Orario through Meren's harbor.

"Not much we can do, unfortunately, given that Orario's not only right next door but our biggest business partner to boot. They say it's the general consensus from their side, but I know it's a lie—more like a petty revenge tactic. I could see through it from the very beginning. Makes me jealous of *Demeter Familia* and the preferential treatment they get despite their different affiliation."

"We've had troubles of our own, too."

The "Guild" Njörðr spoke of that was making life miserable for him here in the lower world wasn't the main Guild Headquarters in Orario.

There was another Guild here in Meren.

"Have you already gone to the Guild Branch Office?" Njörðr suddenly asked, returning to the business at hand.

"Yep," Loki responded. "Riveria's actually there right now."

The stone lobby of the Guild Branch Office was considerably smaller than that of the main headquarters in Orario.

While it was a decent-size building in and of itself, the giant pantheon that was the lobby of the headquarters, bustling with activity day and night, was simply too big to make a proper comparison. Most of the relatively few uniformed attendants who worked there did so not at the front counter but, instead, performing routine office work such as filing port entry permits and checklists of commercial goods.

It was just one of the sub-branches the main Guild in Orario had established outside the city. While the roles of each branch varied depending on their location, this building in Meren acted as the gateway to the sea, directing all matters relating to the port and managing the import and export of goods—magic-stone commodities, for instance—for the city.

This atmosphere, so different from that of the main headquarters, currently surrounded Riveria as she stood alone before the front desk.

"Giant man-eating flowers…? Hmm…can't say I know 'em!"

Riveria returned her attention to the man in front of her.

The attendant at the front desk was a long, oval-faced human man. Tall and skinny, he was almost what you could call lanky, and the features below his perfectly coiffed dark hair were expressing some impatience.

Rubart was his name.

The head of the branch and the one in charge.

"You're quite sure?"

"You think I'd lie? We haven't heard anything about this kind of new species, not even from the main headquarters in Orario," Rubart retorted, clearly annoyed at having to respond to the same question three times.

It was puzzling. Even if the upper echelons of the Guild (Ouranos, in other words) were limiting information on the new monster species, for information not to be shared even within the organization—especially considering how many people had already witnessed the violas during the Monsterphilia and the event on the eighteenth floor—it wouldn't make sense to try to cover things up.

Sure, there wasn't any pressing reason to involve the branches outside the city, but still…

"And yet this monster was spotted. Does this not call for an investigation and preventative measures on your part?"

"We can just leave it to *Njörðr Familia*. Even if we did try to look into it, that lot'd likely tell us to mind our own business—that the waterfront is their jurisdiction. It's the same every time," Rubart spat out, his words evidence enough as to the shaky relationship the two groups shared.

As obvious as it may have seemed, there was no reason for the Guild to hold sway over familias outside Orario. And the fact that they had no legal right to force *Njörðr Familia* to do much of anything surely made them an annoying lump they'd rather be rid of.

Riveria, however, knew the fishermen would be no match for the violas—their strength was simply too great. Unfortunately, her words were getting her nowhere.

"What's more important right now is that gaggle of Amazons that made port. We'd like you to do something about them." Rubart's brows arched in irritation.

What's "more important right now"...? Riveria couldn't believe what she was hearing. But even as she shot him a one-eyed look of disbelief, the branch manager continued.

"While they haven't caused too much trouble yet, we've already been getting complaints from our citizens. Terribly hard to approach, it seems. Words just don't get through to them! And apparently they've even been running off with merchandise without paying..."

"You are the ones who permitted them entry to the port, yes?"

"Well, yes...but...it's a little more complicated than that," Rubart continued somewhat ambiguously. "The city has an autonomous government that operates separately from the Guild."

"And the city granted the Amazons their port entry permit?"

"Yes," Rubart replied with a disgruntled nod. "Meren used to be nothing but a tiny fishing village constantly threatened by monsters. But after *Poseidon Familia* set up camp and Orario's prosperity helped it develop, it really flourished into the 'Gateway to the Dungeon City' it is today."

It was a well-known story—*Poseidon Familia* deciding to use Meren as its base—and it made sense considering how many aquatic monsters appeared offshore. They'd plugged up the hole in the bottom of the lake and, ever since, had been monitoring and maintaining the giant lid while upholding peace on the water's surface. Then, once the Leviathan Seal had been put in place fifteen years ago,

Poseidon and his followers had left the port city with the assurance that the seal could never be broken, off to quell the threat of sea creatures all over the world. *Njörðr Familia* stayed behind, supplying the city with their fish.

Though Riveria already knew much of what Rubart was telling her, she listened in all the same.

"The Guild invested in the city early, even going so far as to help it expand...but after all these generations, the head of Meren's still never given up its autonomous government."

Of course, what Rubart failed to mention was that any city would resist being commandeered if given the chance.

"You probably know this already, but Meren isn't just a company under the Guild's patronage. It's also an entry point for people and communities all over the world, so there's that to think about, too."

"Yet this gives you no trouble with Orario?"

The neutrality of the large-scale port was one of its key factors. After all, a controlling government would only lead to decline. Though Meren focused the majority of its efforts toward Orario, there were still many ships that used the port as a relay point on their journeys to other destinations. There were also the shipments of cargo destined for its surrounding cities and towns to consider. If the Guild started being fastidious about who could use the port, their clientele would simply move their business elsewhere.

Even from an outsider's perspective, preventing the Guild's unilateral reign over Meren was in everyone's favor.

"Well, a compromise was reached, and it was decided that the government would be split in two. To put things simply, all matters related to Orario, trade included, are to be handled by this branch office..."

"And everything else is taken care of by the city?"

"Exactly," Rubart confirmed, face still sour.

At the time, the decision was heavily influenced by the support of *Poseidon Familia*, which still acted independently despite cooperating with Orario, and *Njörðr Familia*, which was acting as a good neighbor.

All in all, it was just as complicated a situation as the branch manager described.

"True, we didn't actually raise any objections to *Kali Familia* being granted a permit, so I suppose we are partly responsible...but it was the city that fought tooth and nail to get them in here, thanks mostly to that bastard Murdock," Rubart finished with a curse, a disgusted look on his face.

At the end of all things, *Njörðr Familia* was loyal to the city of Meren.

While the relationship between them and the Guild wouldn't necessarily be called antagonistic, given the Guild branch's history of conflict with the city, they certainly weren't the best of friends. Riveria was already well aware of this, at least.

"At any rate...it feels like we've got some wild animal prowling around the city."

"..."

"Which is why the Guild, as your administrative body, is asking for your cooperation."

As Rubart laid down the law, Riveria could do nothing but sit in silence, one eye now almost perpetually closed.

"So please! We promise we've no ill intentions...If you'd be ever so kind as to hear us out!" Alicia pleaded, holding in her urge to cringe as she forced an ingratiating smile.

"Go away," was the curt reply from the elderly gentleman in question.

They were in Meren's west town, at a building that seemed to have been built to glower at the Guild Branch Office in the east—the Murdock estate, home to generation after generation of Meren's governors.

Alicia and Narfi were there to collect information but hadn't even made it inside; they were presently being barred entry at the door by a Mr. Borg Murdock, the current head of the family.

"I have nothing to say to you, Guild dogs."

Borg was an aging human man with a tuft of white hair protruding from his chin. With no sign of a sagging belly, instead he boasted a physique that could rival any of the fishermen's on the wharf. His eyes were sharp, and though he lacked hair on his head, by simply adding a cap to the picture, one could easily picture him as a ship captain from the old stories.

"Gods' honest truth, we're not here on Guild business. We're here about the giant flower creatures that appeared in the lake yesterday… as part of an investigation. If you have any relevant information you could give us, we would be ever so appreciative," Alicia pleaded.

"…"

Borg was silent.

Simply looking at the elf for a few moments in all her innocent sincerity, he finally opened his mouth.

"…Go away."

He said nothing else.

Then he turned around and disappeared inside the manor. Alicia and Narfi could do nothing but make their own exit back through the gate, at a loss as to what to do.

"I'll admit, I had higher expectations for that interaction, considering he's the governor and all…but apparently that was asking too much," Narfi mused, scratching at her cheek in dumbfounded astonishment.

Alicia sighed. "I've heard the city and Guild don't exactly see eye to eye on things…but to think it was this bad! Guess we're outta luck. No point in beating a dead horse."

Faced with a feud that had been around longer than either of them had been alive, the girls had no choice but to leave the mansion behind.

"…"

From one of the windows of the mansion, Borg watched them leave, eyes narrowed with acrimony.

The sun, having reached its peak, had already started its afternoon descent toward the western horizon. Aiz, Lefiya, and the rest of the reconnaissance groups were making their way back toward the pier.

They didn't have to go far past the commerce area with its trade ships, passenger ships, and fishermen's dhows to reach *Njörðr Familia*'s fishing pier. The merchants and travelers dressed in their foreign clothes gave way to fishermen and women, all bustling about in their work. This rare type of familia—neither adventurers nor merchants—was still novel enough to the group of girls that they couldn't help but scan their environs in wonder.

Most of the trawlers wore nothing over their broad chests or donned a set of short sleeves and long pants. Everyone was going about their own business, from the burly dwarf who passed by with an unbelievably large fish on his shoulder to the group of harpoon-wielding prums currently maneuvering their boat out to sea. Some were hard at work hauling great nets full of fresh and saltwater fish alike to shore—everything from giant dodobass to shiny red shrimp—while still others were grilling up their catches of fish and clams for an afternoon snack. The smell of salt and sound of popping oil were enough to draw in the eyes (and appetites) of Lefiya and the others as they walked along, none of them having taken their lunches yet.

And among all the crunching and the munching of seafolk ingesting their freshly caught fish, they caught sight of Tiona and Tione.

"M-Miss Tiona? What are you two...doing?" Lefiya asked, somewhat taken aback.

"Got hungry while asking these folks for info. They said we were free to have a bite, too, so long as we paid up, so...here we are!" Tiona responded, her mouth currently full of enough grilled fish to rival the surrounding workers'.

It would seem Tiona and Tione's luck collecting info had been about as good as Aiz and everyone else's. The others in their group, already having eaten their fill, were taking a load off nearby.

"...How is...Tione doing?" Aiz whispered discreetly as she threw a glance at the Amazon in question.

"Mmmn...still a little testy, but I think she'll be fine. We made sure to keep away from Kali and crew this morning, and I kept an eye on her to make sure she didn't get into any trouble."

The atmosphere around Tione had been tense since the night prior, and the others in her group, hume bunny Rakuta included, had found it hard to truly relax. Currently, Tione was masking her irritation with food, asking for seconds, thirds, and fourths—"More"—with stern glares daunting enough to elicit stammers of surprise from their brawny mealtime companions.

"Usually it's her keeping tabs on me..." Tiona laughed awkwardly. Even she could see the irony in the role reversal.

"What about you? Are you okay?" Aiz asked.

"Me? I'm fine! You know me—thinking's not my strong suit," the young Amazon responded with her usual smile, almost as though completely indifferent to the entire situation. Perhaps it was just Aiz's imagination, but something about the innocent smile was different than usual—strained. But she wasn't about to press any further.

"Geez...you girls can eat! Even for adventurers! I guess first-tiers really are in a class all their own," one of the particularly strapping men gushed as he watched the two sisters stuff their faces together with the other fishermen around the grill. He was a human man nearly two meders tall with a crop of black hair above his jet-black eyes. "What about that skinny little thing over there, huh? The Sword Princess? Can she eat like you two?"

"Nah, she never eats as much as us. Really likes her Jyaga Maru Kun, though."

"And you are...?" Aiz turned her eyes in the young man's direction.

"Me? I'm Rod. The captain 'round these parts," Rod boasted warmly.

Aiz was silent a moment as she formulated her words. "Mister Rod, then...do you and the others in your familia fish a lot?"

"That we do. S'bout all we're good at, really. We fish the lake, a'course, but even all the way out to the sea, too. I've probably spent more of my life on the waves than here on land."

Fishing was *Njörðr Familia*'s be-all and end-all. As burly as these men of the sea happened to be, neither they nor their patron deity had any delusions of grandeur or bones to pick with other familias.

In fact, they seemed more like an organization of fishermen than a true familia.

"Most men in this city grow up to be fishers. Guess it's thanks to Skip Njörðr."

"Are there any fishermen in the port who don't belong to *Njörðr Familia*?" Lefiya asked curiously.

"You probably could if you wanted, but no one does. The Skip's a great guy, and his blessing comes in real handy. Gives you more strength than the average trawler," Rod replied, glancing toward one of the storehouses where a slender young human was lugging around a giant net all by himself. No doubt, a Status was carved into his back, as well.

"If your goal is just to make a livin' with fishin', you'll do it a lot faster at the feet of the Skip. And even if it's sailin' on the high seas, you'll have a much easier time with his blessin', especially given how many monsters are lurkin' out there," the *Njörðr Familia* captain explained. In today's day and age, even fishermen needed the power of the Falna, if only to give them a better chance at defending themselves. Out on the ocean and surrounded by water, a man had no one to rely on but himself. "And besides, well...we all love Skip Njörðr! He's taken care of us since we were knee-high to a minnow...and he's been protectin' this city for centuries, all the way back to the time of our fathers, and even our fathers' fathers, may they rest in peace."

Njörðr had been in charge of the fishing in Meren for so long, no other familias had ever even tried to set up their own fishing gigs—which was one more reason why *Njörðr Familia*'s grip on the city's fishing industry was so strong. The love, respect, and trust Rod and the other fishermen had for their patron deity was all too evident in the intrepid captain's smile.

"Do you ever hunt monsters purposefully, Mister Rod?"

"Hmm? Ah...sometimes! Every once in a while we'll get a request from the folks here in among the orders of fish."

Then what the townsfolk had told them earlier had been correct.

The fishers here, what with the help of the Falna, would probably have no trouble taking care of the type of monsters that appeared on the surface—weakened from generations of breeding and never having stepped foot in the actual Dungeon. They were strong enough to take out their fair share of sea pirates, after all. Rod himself had already reached Level 2, what with his many years spent on the open ocean and the countless battles he'd seen. And from what Aiz could see, there were at least a few others in the group besides him whose strength could easily rival a low-level adventurer's.

So long as things didn't get too crazy, they'd be able to deal with any trouble themselves, meaning the times they were forced to send for help from Orario were few and far between.

"In all your experience on the lake and ocean, did you ever see...a large flower-type monster?"

"You mean that thing from yesterday? Didn't get to see it myself, as I just pulled into port this morning, but...you sure that thing wasn't an aqua serpent?" Rod asked, lacing his thick arms across each other.

Aiz and the others nodded.

The captain's brows furrowed. Out of all the fishermen, he was easily the most acquainted with Meren's waterfront. "I do have an idea. I've often seen it when I'm fishin' in the lake and ocean. A real long thing, like a snake, almost...swimmin' in the water below the ship..."

"...!"

"Even I thought it was an aqua serpent at first, but—" Rod started before cutting his words short and quickly raising his head. "This thing you're talkin' about's never attacked us. Not even once!"

He looked around at the rest of his men, who all nodded in agreement, both at never having been attacked and never having gotten a good look at the creature in question.

Befuddlement crossed the faces of the group of girls.

"...? Hey, what's that little bag hanging from your waist? I've noticed most of you fisher guys have one," Tiona suddenly said.

True enough, there was a similar bag—a little bigger than a typical adventurer's pouch—tied around the waist of every fisherman walking along the dock.

"Ho-ho! You've got good eyes, little missy." Rod laughed. Grabbing ahold of the bag, he held it aloft for the group to see, almost like a child showing off his favorite toy. "This here's magic dust! Sprinkle a little of this beauty on the water, and monsters won't come close!" he announced proudly.

"What?!" Tiona (and the rest of the girls) blurted back in surprise. Bewildered as to what could be inside, she took the bag from the captain's hand and worked the stubborn tie open.

"Hey, hey, careful now!"

"Huh—? Bwwwwwoooaaaagh, that stinks!" she cried out, reeling back and away from the pungent smell wafting out of the bag.

It was strong enough to elicit cries of disgust from Aiz, Lefiya, and the surrounding girls, all of them quickly bringing their hands to their noses.

"Why didn't you say something?! What is this stuff?!" Tears forming in her eyes, Tiona attempted to peer into the bag. The others followed suit, doing their best to hold out against the overwhelming odor.

"Is it raw? Seems like a bunch of different things all ground up into powder..."

"And that color! Gives me the heebie-jeebies!"

Reds, yellows, blacks—all variety of different colored powders appeared to be mixed together, which almost looked like the crumbled remains of something dead when paired with the rancid smell. Tiona's face curled in on itself like a dried prune as she surveyed the mysterious glittering dust.

"A dust that repels monsters...We don't have anything like this in Orario, as far as I know," Lefiya mused.

"You sure this doesn't actually attract monsters? You know, mix it with some blood and meat and toss it over the side of the boat like bait to keep things from attacking the boat itself?" Tiona posed as the rest of the group exchanged similar thoughts behind her.

True to Lefiya's words, this kind of convenient "monster repellant" certainly couldn't be found in any stores in Orario. Aiz, however, knew of another item with remarkably similar properties. It was something she'd heard about from Bell, after he'd fled to the eighteenth floor during his escape from certain death. A "stink bag" that an apothecary from an ally familia had whipped up by chance. The bag and its terrific monster-repelling odor was what had helped him and his party make it all the way to the safety point with their lives.

Perhaps this powder in front of them now was one and the same.

Still...could this smell really keep even marine-type beasts at bay?

"But...we heard this thing was invented in Orario," Rod mused as confusion crossed his and the other fishermen's faces. "Yeah, you know! By that...that...Herseus...Persimmeus...oh, whatever her name is..."

"Perseus?"

"That's it! She's the one who invented it!"

While it certainly did seem like something the rare item maker could whip up...Lefiya and the others remained skeptical. They simply couldn't understand why, if such an item truly existed, no one in Orario knew about it.

"Erm...from whom exactly did you receive this powder, Mister Rod?"

"From the big man, Papa Borg...head of the Murdock family. He bought it up in the city and gave it out to us free of charge. Not only to us fishermen but to all the boats that pass through Meren. It's been forever now. That old man does a lot for us," Rod explained. "Well... can't say it's perfect, as we do still get some raider fish attacks and such, but it's certainly helped us avoid a lotta excess damage to our ships. Ships 'round here never sail without it!"

Could that be why Kali Familia*'s ship got attacked yesterday...?* Aiz immediately thought.

Every ship that docked in Meren, and even the passenger ships and sailing boats that often passed through, had these bags...but *Kali Familia* wouldn't, given that this was their first time making port in the city. They wouldn't have known that the powder even existed.

"..."

Aiz took the bag of powder from Tiona, reaching her hand inside. She scooped up some of the colorful, sparkling dust with her fingers, letting it cascade down into her palm.

All the while, she watched, studying the tumbling, flowing particles.

"Speaking of...what's going on between you guys and those Amazons, huh?"

"...Why? Did something happen?"

"Ah, no, no, just...us'n everyone else in the city are rightly pretty terrified of 'em. You can tell how strong they are just by lookin'! And then they march right through the middle of the street like they own the place..."

Rod explained as he scratched the back of his head. By strange coincidence, the conversation turned toward *Kali Familia*, similar to what had happened to Riveria during her visit to the Guild.

"Yeah, they're scary!" "Savages, the whole lot of 'em!" the other fishermen were quick to add as Tiona grew quiet. The teary-eyed appeals from the burly men were enough to draw troubled looks from Aiz and the others.

"..."

Meanwhile, Tione was standing a short distance away from the group, focused in the direction of the city.

The conversation, however, didn't last much longer.

"—Rod! We've got trouble!" an out-of-breath animal-person trawler shouted as he came running out onto the dock. Before anyone could so much as ask what the matter was, he continued his hysterical rant. "Those Amazonian ladies are causing a huge ruckus on the main road. One of 'em's got ahold of Mark!"

All at once, the entire wharf plunged into panic.

As the color drained from Rod's and the other fishermen's faces, Aiz and her group found themselves thrown for a loop.

Amid the building clamor, however, Tiona was the only one who quickly scanned the area around them.

"Crap—!!" she hissed beneath her breath.

Mere moments later, Aiz, too, noticed the cause of her alarm.

"Miss Tiona, Miss Aiz, is…is something wrong?!" Lefiya inquired hesitantly.

"Tione's gone."

"She's flown the coop!"

Aiz and Tiona responded in unison.

Before Lefiya and the other girls could register their surprise, the two were off, sprinting away from the pier.

"Lefiya! Get Loki! She should be in the storehouse nearby!"

"We're going on ahead!"

The two first-tier adventurers called back as they raced as fast as their legs would take them. Even as the commotion built behind them, they kept their sights set straight on the city.

It was a gorgeous day.

Fluffy white clouds lingered lazily in the cerulean sky overlooking the city, and the gleam of the sun reflected a beautiful emerald green off the waters of the brackish lake below.

But despite the peaceful calm of the weather, the main street of Meren, normally filled with the hustle and bustle of passersby, was currently blanketed in a strange hush.

No one moved.

Or, more accurately, no one could move.

All eyes were glued to the middle of the street, where an Amazonian warrior was single-handedly holding one of the local fishermen aloft by his throat.

"Is there…problem?" she asked with a smile, her use of Koine maladroit at best.

Her long sandy hair was tied back in a ponytail that fell all the way down her back. The revealing clothing practically drawn on her copper skin was undeniably Amazonian, and around her waist she wore a belt not of fur but of scale—a drop item, perhaps, from some kind of dragon.

Despite her obvious beauty, between the glint in her eyes and the

upward curve of her lips, she gave off an aura, purposeful or not, that reeked of reptilian malice. Far from what anyone would describe as "bewitching," she looked more like a giant serpent anxious to gorge itself on its prey. Even her tongue seemed inhuman, impossibly long as it darted out to wet her lips.

The well-built young man currently in her clutches said nothing in response to her inquiry. A raspy, wheezing breath worked its way out of his mouth as his legs dangled uselessly in the air. The Amazon gripped his throat and held him aloft with one slender arm. Desperate for breath, he clawed at the fingers digging into his skin.

"P-please f-forgive…him…! Y-you were just so b-b-beautiful that he…couldn't stop staring and…and didn't watch where he was g-going, so p-please…!!" another fisherman nearby—his companion—pleaded.

The Amazon's head turned toward the tear-stricken man with an almost audible *creak*.

"In my country, bumping into a warrior…is a challenge to fight to the death."

The man's face paled instantly.

Her grip on the fisherman's neck tightened with a series of cracks, and the man's body spasmed in response.

As frightened screams began erupting from the crowd, the woman's companions, another group of Amazons, simply watched in amusement. Her sister, too, hair of the same sandy hue, merely stared out across the goings-on in apathy.

The man appeared to lose consciousness, his arms going limp, as his assailant narrowed her eyes in amusement.

Only then.

"Let him go."

An arm reached out, the same copper color, and grabbed her wrist.

It was Tione.

"…Tione?"

"I said let him go, Argana."

But the Amazon's—Argana's—smile never faltered, even at the bone-crushing grip on her arm. In fact, if anything, it deepened.

Finally, as Tione's murderous glare continued, she released her grip on the fisherman's neck with a shrug, almost as though having lost interest. The man's body fell to the ground with a thud, and she shook off Tione's hold on her arm.

"Where were you? We searched for you…you and Tiona."

"I see you can speak Koine now. So fighting's not the only thing in that monkey brain of yours." Tione snorted, glaring daggers at the woman in front of her as the fisherman's companion rushed forward to drag him out of the way.

Argana didn't so much as flinch, her eyes filled with amusement.

"Kali taught it to me. She teaches us many things. The pleasure of growing stronger…and how to understand those who are different from us," she added as her eyes passed over the crowd. "We wanted to know…what are our prey screaming? Are they angry? Are they begging for their lives?"

The naked sadism elicited a look of pure revulsion from Tione, who stuck her tongue out at her former comrade.

They were still the same as ever. Interested in nothing but power, bloodshed, combat.

Tione felt her blood begin to boil, face-to-face with the red thread of fate that connected the Amazons to their native country of Telskyura.

Her hand instinctively curled into a tight fist.

"Have you heard, Tione? How strong the outside world has gotten?"

"…"

"They have turned into snakes…just like us."

"—No one's the same as you, you evil witch!"

Something snapped inside Tione.

With an almost audible *crack*, all the years spent remedying her brash nature, her coarse tongue, came undone as her features lit up with rage.

Argana continued to smile that same crescent moon smile, head slowly twisting to the side.

"Then—shall we see just how strong you've become?"

For a single moment, no one so much as twitched along that wide road.

Then.

"Gnnngh!!"

The two women launched themselves at each other.

Argana's left arm blocked Tione's kick, and Tione's left arm blocked Argana's kick.

In less than an instant, the grand hand-to-hand duel had begun.

"Tione?!"

Tiona and Aiz arrived a second too late.

Screaming at the throng of onlookers to stay back, they made their way toward the center of the panicking crowd, where a barefoot battle of fist against fist was currently taking place. Long sandy hair tangled with jet-black as the two women exchanged punches and kicks that would leave an ordinary person crippled. The thick, dull sounds of the blocked blows thrummed in the ears of everyone present.

They seemed on par with each other. No, Tione was slightly—.

The skill with which they delivered their blows was nothing short of exemplary, and as Aiz watched them, she felt tiny prickles of apprehension stab at her heart.

When it came to weapons-free combat, Tione and Tiona were unquestionably the best in *Loki Familia*. Though Gareth might have been the strongest and Bete might have been the fastest, from a technical perspective, the Amazons' unique style of martial arts was easily the fiercest. Aiz herself knew that, without a sword, she'd be out on her ass in five seconds flat.

But that same Tione now was slowly, ever so slowly, being "out-fierced" by Argana.

Those long limbs, almost like snakes, pecked away at her in ever-quickening strikes. And Argana's ability to read her enemy's next move was uncanny. Before Tione even began her attacks, Argana was already preparing for a counterstrike. There was no question as to her Level-6 rank, and she seemed to have the advantage when it came to Status, too.

Argana's eyes flashed as Tione's face twisted in frustration. That same frustration was quickly painted over with pure, concentrated rage as her unwillingness to lose spurred on her attacks at an even greater speed.

Aiz and Tiona sailed over the crowd of pushing, shoving onlookers, just about to put a stop to the fight, when—

"!"

Someone else stepped forward from the crowd to block their way.

It was the other sandy-haired Amazon, the one who shared the same blood as the woman in the brawl.

"Move, Bache!!" Tiona screamed.

"...rhu muu," was the only reply from the stoic Amazon's neckerchief.

Aiz couldn't understand the words, but she could understand their meaning—that the woman had no intentions of letting them pass.

Tiona's eyebrows positively bristled, and she charged toward the woman's right side, fully prepared to push her way through, as Aiz zoomed forward at a similar breakneck speed on the woman's immediate left. The very breaths of the two first-tier adventurers were perfectly in sync as they prepped for the combo technique they'd cultivated in the Dungeon's depths—only for Bache to take on the two of them at the same time.

Catching Tiona's iron fist in one hand, she let loose a simultaneous kick in Aiz's direction.

"""?!"""

Despite being airborne, Tiona found herself instantly in the clutches of a circular throw, while Aiz, despite her speed, felt the Amazon's kick slice through strands of her golden hair.

But there was no time for gawking. Hands slamming the ground, the two of them prepared to right themselves for the next onslaught. Bache, however, was already two steps ahead. Spinning like a chess piece, she let loose a rapid-fire barrage of blows and kicks to their heads, torsos, and legs, coming at them from every direction and striking both Aiz and Tiona at the same time.

—She's fast!!

Aiz could barely believe her eyes at the sheer velocity of the attacks coming from the seemingly dispassionate warrior.

She knew right away that this wasn't an opponent she'd be able to defeat without her sword. Pulling her backup sword out of its scabbard—Desperate was still in maintenance—she looked up to see the rest of the Amazonian warriors joining the battle.

"...!"

They must have felt Bache was at a disadvantage now that the two first-tier adventurers were fully prepared for battle, and they charged forward with weapons flashing.

Bache kept her focus on Tiona as the group of Amazons targeted Aiz, who quickly found herself drawn into her own free-for-all as the bare-fisted duel between the two Amazons intensified next to her.

"Ah-ha-ha-ha-ha-ha-ha-ha-ha! You've changed, Tione! You've really changed!"

"Ggh—!"

Meanwhile, the battle between Argana and Tione continued, Argana's laugh eliciting even deeper rage from the younger Amazon.

But it wasn't just rage directed at her opponent. It was frustration at herself, too. The more damage she took, the more her combat power skyrocketed, and the more her fury bubbled, the more effective her Berserk skill became. And yet, despite the building power behind her each and every punch, Argana continued to fend them off with ease. Even the most powerful of attacks, enough to completely demolish an enemy, were useless if one couldn't land them.

Argana's techniques had the advantage when it came to polish, and she countered every one of Tione's strikes like a mirror—the very same steps, the very same moves.

Which was natural, really.

Considering that the style of martial arts Tione practiced had been beat into her again and again at the hands of this very Amazon.

"Gnngh!!"

One of the kicks connected directly with Tione's back, sending her sailing toward the side of the road in front of a nearby food stand.

Somehow, she'd been able to absorb the blow, and her arms tingled from the impact, but she shook it off, fully prepared to dash back into the fight when—she noticed it.

"Huh...?!"

A kid?!

Right behind her, a young human girl was crouched in fear.

What are you doing here?! she almost screamed, only to remember she was the one who'd lost her senses and recklessly begun fighting in the middle of a crowded street. No doubt, this girl simply hadn't been able to run away in time.

Tione found herself at a loss for words as she stared down into the girl's tear-stricken eyes, when all of a sudden, a shadow overtook them.

"——"

It was Argana. And her laugh was enough to make Tione's blood run cold as she held her fist aloft.

Tione would have just enough time to duck out of the way. But the girl wouldn't be so lucky. Considering the incoming strike was powerful enough to send an entire carriage flying just by grazing it, the small body would be crushed. Even the resulting shock waves would be enough to snap her tiny limbs.

Argana, however, showed no concern. She had no reason to be concerned.

The only person in her eyes was Tione.

"———ngh!!"

Tione yanked the girl out of the way, leaving herself wide open for Argana's incoming fist.

"Tione?!"

There was a thunderous crash as Tione's body was launched through the food stall, splintering it into pieces as she careened into the wall of the building behind it.

Tiona and Aiz forgot about their own battles, whirling around to see a giant cloud of dust billowing up from the nearby building.

"Gn—...ghnn...!" Tione grunted, spitting up blood. While she'd somehow been able to defend herself against the full force of the attack, the impact had still created a giant crack.

Argana, on the other hand, simply stood there blinking in silence, a strange look on her face.

"Did you really just…protect that girl?" She threw a glance at the girl in question, currently sprawled out on the ground and trembling in fear, before returning her eyes to Tione. "You really have changed, Tione…You've gotten stronger…and you've gotten weaker." A look of pure, unadulterated disappointment crossed her face. "You are… no longer a warrior."

Her body drooped, almost as though she had lost all will to fight.

There was the sound of weapons dropping from the direction of Aiz and Tiona, both of them still stopped where they stood, as Tione slowly staggered to her feet.

"The old you would never have protected garbage like that. I see now that you shouldn't have left…You should have continued your battles in Telskyura…with us."

"Are you…seriously saying that to me…?! Who would…who would ever want to stay in that place…?!" Tione hissed, glaring with deep-rooted resentment.

Argana's eyes narrowed as a small smile formed on her lips.

"You still regret…killing Seldas, don't you?"

In that instant, time seemed to stop.

"And yet, by killing her, you grew stronger, did you not?"

Tione's eyes went red.

"————NNNGGHH!!!"

An unintelligible roar erupted from the depths of her throat.

Forgetting herself, forgetting the pain, she let the madness take control and charged toward the other woman in an uncontrollable rage.

"—That's far enough!"

It came the moment before her fist hit its mark.

The sound of two short claps echoed throughout the street.

Though quiet, the voice that called out to them possessed a godlike sovereignty, and Tione's body gave an instinctive shudder. Her tightly curled fist loosened as she returned to herself. Argana turned in the direction of the voice.

It was Loki, together with the rest of *Loki Familia*'s adventurers, including one very out of breath Lefiya.

"If things get any more heated 'round here, people are gonna get hurt. Not cool." The goddess narrowed her eyes; she had only just arrived from the direction of the wharf but was already holding the battlefield in the palm of her hand. Rakuta, looking even more like a rabbit than usual, darted forward to grab the young girl, still sprawled out on the ground, and pull her out of harm's way.

Tiona and Aiz lowered their fists and sword respectively, eyes directed toward their goddess.

"Argana. Bache. You two, too."

The voice came from closer this time, from the opposite side of Loki and near where Tione and Argana had been fighting.

It was Kali, carting along a number of her followers.

"Apologies, Loki. Seems the outside world was a little too much for my girls." She shook her head with a sigh and a (seemingly forced) grumble as her eyes met Loki's. "Shall we share the blame? After all, your Sword Princess and her friends did a number on my girls, too."

"Oh, whatever. Just scat, will ya? And I don't wanna see you or any of your 'girls' again," Loki scoffed, brushing her hand at them as though swatting at a bug.

While Bache had come out of her battle with Tiona unscathed, the group of Amazons Aiz had been fighting hadn't fared so well and were in various states of injury. The girls in question were glaring daggers at Aiz and her sword while Aiz herself seemed none the worse for wear despite having been vastly outnumbered.

Kali simply smiled, then turned on her heel.

"Ta-ta, Tione."

"..."

Argana and Bache walked past them, Bache as silent as ever and Argana throwing them a sidelong glance as they made their way first past Aiz and Tiona and then, finally, Tione. The rest of the Amazons, too, fell in line obediently behind their goddess and made their exit.

"M-Miss Aiz! Miss Tiona! Are you two all right?!" Lefiya immediately started for the two girls.

"I'm fine…thank you," Aiz replied as she resheathed her sword, appreciative of the elf's efforts in fetching Loki.

Tiona rubbed at her arm. "Yeeeouch…she really did a good one on me!" she hissed, and, indeed, bruises were already beginning to pop up all across her copper skin.

As much as she bemoaned the pain, however, there was something more important on her mind, and she threw a glance toward her sister.

"Miss Tione…" Lefiya and Aiz, too, noticed the direction of her gaze.

The girl in question was standing in the middle of the deserted road, her back to them.

Her eyes followed the retreating group of Amazons until they'd disappeared in the distance.

"Seems this is more serious than I thought…" Loki murmured, and the words caught on the breeze and circled their way toward Tione.

Tione brought a hand to her still-aching chest, oblivious to the blood that stained her mouth, as the wind played with her long black hair.

"Ngh…"

Seldas.

The name stirred in her heart—a name she'd kept buried for so, so long and, with it, the memories that haunted her. It was a piece of her past she didn't want to remember.

She felt lost, confused, simply staring up at the sky overhead, as blue as the landscape of her memories.

The sky had been blue that day, too.

And it was stifling hot, baking the arena in the fiery heat of the sun overhead.

The ground of packed earth was already stained a brilliant red from the day's fresh blood.

"Se wehga! Se wehga! Se wehga!"

The deafening roar surrounded her. Cheers. Cheers for her, Tione, standing her ground in the middle of the arena. Praise and adoration rained down on her tiny frame from every corner of the stands.

"Se wehga" was a phrase unique to the Amazons of Telskyura.

Translated roughly, it meant "Thou art the true warrior."

She couldn't make out anything over the thunderous ovation, her sense of hearing all but useless as she made her way toward the opponent in front of her. Hands shaking, she pulled the mask off the prone body—from the Amazon she'd killed—as the girl's blood spilled out like a fountain onto the ground below.

She knew this face.

It was the face of the girl who'd tended to her wounds, who'd slept beside her so many nights, who'd breathed life back into her cold, dry heart.

The girl who'd been like a big sister to her, a mother to her, one of the most important figures in her life.

"Seldas..."

Though the name passed Tione's trembling lips, Seldas's eyes had already descended into darkness. Never again would they respond to her voice.

There had been a rule regarding who fought whom in the rites.

But Tione and the others had misunderstood that rule.

The reason they'd not yet had to fight any of the girls from their same room was simply that the right moment hadn't come. As they strengthened the vessels of their flesh, so, too, did they strengthen their bonds with their roommates. They created friends, family for them to love.

And then, they were made to kill those loved ones.

This was their way of unleashing their anger. Of forcing them to overcome their grief. Of drying the tears from their eyes.

This was how they created "true warriors," ones free from all manner of emotions and perfectly molded for combat.

Everything was part of this procedure for manufacturing warriors.

No...NO...

Something shattered. The world Tione had once known crumbled around her the moment she removed that mask.

For the very first time in her life, as she laid her hands upon the girl she'd loved, she knew how to differentiate right from wrong. She realized how twisted, how mistaken she'd been—cutting down her peers without so much as flinching, just as she'd killed the monsters before them.

On that day and in that place, the girl she'd so looked up to, the only mother she'd ever had, had taught her an important lesson—the agony of losing someone you loved.

She'd hurt her. No, her country, her goddess, these warrior-manufacturing traditions, her brethren had—

As tears of fury cascaded from her eyes, Tione turned toward the sky and roared.

"Se wehga! Se wehga! Se wehga!"

Thou art the true warrior. Thou art the true warrior. Thou art the true warrior.

The chant was deafening. Lauding the tiny girl in the arena, howling at the heavens. Christening her a warrior of old, having passed the test and now one step closer to the gods.

But to Tione, the words were nothing but a curse.

It was her fifth birthday. The day Tione had killed the one she loved…and advanced to Level 2.

Tione's eyes would never see clearly again.

The moon in the sky overhead cast its light across the mountains, forest, and lake.

Night's curtain had descended over Meren.

Off to the north, the great walls of Orario stood tall, visible from every corner of the small port city and its comparably undersized parapets. Not even the shadow of night masked the view. The glimmer of light from the city itself, hidden within its mighty walls, flooded out in harsh contrast to the surrounding darkness. Orario wasn't called "the hottest city in the world" for nothing—one would almost think night never fell the way the sleepless city's brilliant lights stained the sky. While the sight of the bustling city was old hat for the denizens of Meren, it was enough to stir the hearts and hopes of those for whom Orario was their journey's end.

And while the nightlife of Meren couldn't compare to that of its bigger sister, by no means was it going to go down without a fight.

Magic-stone lanterns hung from the port's columns and buildings, bathing its main road in warm orange light. A festival-like atmosphere buzzed about the marketplace and its open-air stands, the whole street brimming with endless throngs of passersby. Travelers joined the ranks of shipwrights and fishermen, all of them solicited by the sounds and smells of freshly cooked seafood as they wandered from one tent to the next.

Needless to say, the port was a busy place—a true melting pot of foreigners.

In the bars, too, demi-humans and even a few gods mingled, hitting it off with all manner of new conversation partners.

"How's Tione lookin', Riveria?"

It was in one such bar—a little establishment not far from *Loki Familia*'s hotel—that Loki bided her time now. When the high elf appeared, she called out from her place at a small two-person table surrounded by the din of the enthused clientele.

"Even with Tiona and Aiz at her side…she isn't faring well. She took quite the beating. Especially her heart," Riveria explained as she pulled out the chair across from the goddess and sat down. "It doesn't look good," she added, guiltily almost, as though blaming herself for not having been at the scene of the fight. Still busy collecting information, by the time she, Alicia, and the others had rushed over upon hearing the commotion, all that was left was a deserted street and the girls of *Loki Familia* watching over a motionless Tione.

Once they'd finished repairing the storefronts they'd destroyed after apologizing to a very flustered Rubart and company, it was already evening. Since then, most of them had returned to the inn, which was exactly where Riveria had been prior to this meeting, doing her best to heal and soothe a broken Tione.

As Riveria sighed, Loki took a swig from her mug of ale.

"I know we've gotta continue this investigation, but...it's startin' to look like we might need to get Tione and her sister back to the city sooner rather than later."

"Tiona should go quietly, but I doubt Tione will back down without a fight..."

"Hmm...You and I'll talk to her."

As concerned as they were for the two Amazonian sisters, however, they had a more important topic to discuss. The real reason they were meeting in this bar was to exchange the information they'd uncovered regarding their elusive violas.

And so, the goddess and vice captain of *Loki Familia* began their conference, away from the prying ears of the rest of their familia.

"All righty then, let's go over everything we know first. We know that Tiona and Tione found nothin' off-kilter on the lake bottom. The ol' seal was tight as ever. While they didn't probe every nook and cranny down there, I think it's safe to say the second Dungeon entrance we're lookin' for isn't in the lake..."

"Which would mean that however our flower fiends got there, they used a route on the surface."

"'Zactly. If I had to guess, they're in the sewers. And someone's cartin' them to the lake. We just need to look for somethin' fishy... boxes or cages or somethin'...and then we'll find the mastermind behind this whole thing."

Riveria nodded.

The remnants of the Evils, and perhaps their one possible connection to the creatures, could well be somewhere within this very port.

"You learn anything new from your huntin' today?"

"Mostly more of the same. Given how calm things have been on the waterfront lately, everyone's more concerned about pirates than they are about any sort of monster. No one had even caught a glimpse of a viola before yesterday's attack."

"What about the folks at the Guild?"

"I was only able to speak with the branch manager—a human man named Rubart. Admittedly, I...have my suspicions," the high elf conceded, one eye closing.

"Anything you can pinpoint?"

"There was just something unnatural about the whole conversation. The way he brought up the topic of *Kali Familia*, completely drawing my attention away from the violas..."

Loki wasn't one to second-guess Riveria's judgment.

While Finn may have been the brains and intuition of the group, Riveria was surely its all-seeing eye of perception. Her ability to discern others' hearts could prove victorious even against Aiz's defenses, much like a motherly sort of insight.

"What about Alicia and crew's trip to see the gov? They learn anything?"

"Unfortunately, they were thrown out on suspicions of Guild involvement. Nigh unapproachable, it seems. The conversation itself was entirely one-sided."

"Hmph...Involved with the Guild, sure, but we're still not from around here," Loki grumbled, bringing her mug to her lips.

Riveria was silent as the goddess picked at her food—a fish fillet with faintly greenish oil and sauce—before finally speaking up.

"And what of you? Were you able to acquire any new information? You went to see Njörðr, did you not?"

Loki grew even quieter.

Fork hand coming to a stop, she threw a quick glance up at the high elf.

"Hey...you don't think Njörðr could be dirty, do ya?"

Surprise flashed in Riveria's jade-colored eyes. "You really suspect Njörðr could have anything to do with this?"

"It was just a thought..."

"I find it difficult to believe, even absurd. While I may not have spent a great deal of time with him, the lengths he went to in order to help others like me when we first arrived on our journeys to Orario were extraordinary. He is, above all else, a man of character," the high elf asserted, not a trace of doubt in her voice.

Loki scratched at her head awkwardly.

Having known the other god since their time in the upper world, this was something she knew all too well, herself. And yet, there was something she just couldn't shake from their earlier exchange.

"Us gods have a hard time tellin' when another god is lyin'. S'not like with you kids. Still...Njörðr, he...was never very good at it. At least from my perspective," Loki explained, recalling the image of Njörðr with his back to her, avoiding eye contact.

It had been that moment that Loki knew.

"He's hidin' somethin' from me. I know it."

"...And that 'something' is related to the violas?"

"That I don't know...but he's certainly got a guilty conscience about something."

Riveria shook her head. "I don't believe it..."

As Loki sat there, her follower's eye narrowed at her in disbelief, a strange feeling washed over her—one she'd never before felt. There was a flower-shaped shadow looming over this peaceful port town. And while it didn't unsettle her, so to speak, it was still in sharp contradiction to everything Aiz and the others had uncovered today. That's what bothered her. The fact that she just couldn't figure it out.

Loki let her head fall.

"This whole thing might be bigger 'n all of us...or maybe more tangled would be the better way to put it."

There were a number of characters she couldn't bring herself to trust. Three, if she only included humans and gods.

Rubart at the Guild, Borg at the manor, and the patron deity of *Njörðr Familia* himself.

There was a good chance one of those three was the puppet master Loki was searching for.

"...What are we to do about *Kali Familia*?" Riveria finally asked, still mulling about Njörðr.

Loki grew quiet.

"Do you believe they've nothing to do with any of this?"

"As much as I worry 'bout Tione and her sister, they're not high on my radar. Whether or not they're completely innocent, though..." she trailed off, displeased with her vague answer. Finally, after another moment to think, she continued, trying to put her instinct into words. "...I can't help but feel like there's some sorta thread connecting 'em. It's tiny, one you can't see no matter how hard you squint...but a thread nonetheless," she mused, almost to herself, as her eyes widened ever so slightly.

Riveria brought a hand to her chin in thought.

The din of the pub around them wove itself through their silence. Craving alcohol to lubricate the gears of her thoughts, Loki sought out her mug only to find it devoid of ale. She stuck out her tongue in displeasure before waving the empty stein high. "I need a top-up over here, old man!"

"Guzzlin' them down tonight, I see, milady. Somethin' on your mind?" the owner of the bar, an old raccoon, asked as he traded out the empty mug on her table for a new one full of ale.

"Oh, this and that. Lots to think about when my cute little kids are involved, you know? Only choice is to drown my troubles!"

"If you have any Alb Water, I'll take that," Riveria spoke up when it came her turn to order, never one to touch the drink herself.

"Come to think, you notice anything weird goin' on lately, old man? Doesn't have to be big. Just somethin' you might have noticed in passin'," Loki said nonchalantly, downing half her ale in one gulp.

"Anything weird, huh...?" the raccoon murmured. "You know, just so rightly there was somethin'! Amazons! Been seein' 'em everywhere in the streets lately..."

"Amazons...?" Riveria inquired.

"The very same! From that one lady god's familia," he continued. "We might have our fair share of brothels on the backstreets, but these ain't no ladies of Meren! Don't recognize a one of 'em... Then again, could just be my mind playin' tricks on me. After all, this town's the gateway to Orario, so we get all sorts of folks comin' through here from one day to the next..." he mused, head cocked to the side as though suddenly unsure of himself.

Loki and Riveria could only look at each other in silence.

Velvet curtains lined every wall in the magic-stone-lit room.

The velvet rug, the vases, the sofa—everything was dyed a deep crimson. There was something almost licentious about it as every corner oozed a brothel-like aura. It contained not a single window; the entirety of the room was underground. Inside, its walls were filled with Amazons of *Kali Familia*, clothed in warriors' attire.

Argana, Bache, and others were lounging around the room, each one idling about on their own, as Kali lay sprawled out upon the couch, petite lips parting for a lethargic yawn.

"..."

Without warning, Bache, who was standing off by herself in silence, turned her eyes toward the entrance.

As if in response, the room's sole door opened.

"—You're all here. Perfect."

The newcomer was a copper-skinned goddess.

Her body was adorned in gold, from the circlet around her head to her earrings, necklace, bracelets, and anklets. As far as clothing was concerned, she wore nothing but a loincloth and a few strips of fabric for a top, all of it tied together by a belt at her waist. Everything about her seemed molded to incite the lust of male eyes, from her ample chest and supple limbs to her salaciously curved hips. She was stunningly gorgeous. So much so that clothes would only hinder her beauty.

The Amazons of Telskyura, having known nothing but combat their whole lives, were taken with her immediately.

Even if the "femme fatales" they'd heard of only through word of mouth did, indeed, exist, something told them they'd still pale in the face of the beauty before them now. It didn't matter that they were all women the same as she—the mouths of everyone in the room dropped in an entranced stupor, and their cheeks flushed a brilliant red. As Argana directed her eyes toward the newcomer in delighted curiosity, Bache furrowed her brows in an attempt to resist before turning her gaze away.

A fiendishly bewitching allure filled the room, strong enough to captivate men and women alike and liable to put even other gods in their place.

The goddess twirled a long kiseru pipe between her fingers as her eyes narrowed in provocation.

"Finally! We've been waiting for you!" Kali piped up with her usual smile of confidence as she rose from the sofa, the only one in the room unaffected by the newcomer's charm.

As the goddess entered the room, a trail of women followed her. They, too, were Amazons, similar to *Kali Familia*. Every one of them boasted a monstrous body, practically mistakable for a two-meder-plus monster, yet stunningly beautiful with long legs.

There wasn't one among them who was nothing short of a goddess herself, clad in combat garments that accentuated the cascading valleys between their breasts and the bare curves of their hips. And yet, even in spite of their beauty, it was clear from how they carried themselves, with not a single visible opening, that they were every bit living, breathing weapons of destruction.

Their beguiling patron deity took her seat on the sofa across from Kali.

Kali's followers, in turn, took their places behind Kali, while their visitors did the same opposite them.

With the table in the center of the room between them, the two goddess-led factions faced each other.

"This may be a little off base this late into the game, but I just wanna confirm—you're Ishtar, correct?"

"That I am," the goddess Ishtar confirmed with a smile.

Ishtar Familia.

A large familia known for its superior combat prowess even among the familias of Orario.

Reigning over the Pleasure Quarter in the southeast, its enormous sphere of influence was said to be the greatest in the city, and its warrior courtesans, known as the "Berbera," were easily strong enough to rival the most skilled first-tier adventurers.

Their patron deity was the goddess of beauty Ishtar.

A goddess whose enchanting guiles could ensnare the hearts of thousands—the very embodiment of beauty itself—and who kept the brothels of the city firmly under her thumb.

Kali, however, didn't hesitate a moment in the face of Ishtar's authority.

"You're a bit of an odd duck, you know that? Sending a request to a far-off country like ours."

"Which is why I explained my reasoning in great detail in the many letters we exchanged. I'm not afraid to use whatever means necessary."

In fact, it was at Ishtar's behest that Kali and the rest of her followers had journeyed to Meren in the first place—a certain request letter, signed by the goddess of beauty herself, had simply shown up on her doorstep one day.

"...I will bring down that woman—Freya," Ishtar asserted, a dark flame burning in her amethyst eyes.

There was no one Ishtar despised more than Orario's other twin head, and coincidentally the other "goddess of beauty," Freya. It was jealousy that spurred her hatred—she envied the other goddess's prestige, renown, and, most of all, the fact that she was considered the most beautiful goddess in all the world.

Ishtar refused to be known as simply the "Goddess of Jealousy," deity of an envy so powerful, the gods had warned them it would upend the fate of humans and plunge the lower world into chaos.

No, Ishtar had pledged herself to bringing her rival down.

Which was exactly why she'd requested the help of *Kali Familia* in realizing her scheme now.

"I had no idea what to expect when that first secret message of yours came," Kali remarked, thinking back to the first letter she'd received from Ishtar more than a year ago.

Freya Familia was easily the strongest in Orario, and Ishtar wasn't stupid enough to think she could take them on herself. Her only option if she had any hopes of proving victorious was to request help from one of the world's much smaller powers—*Kali Familia*, with its warriors that rivaled Orario's first-tier adventurers. And so she'd felt them out time and time again, not only with her letters but through the observations her messenger Amazons brought back from the island nation.

Though Kali hadn't believed the letters at first, after multiple envoys and tributes of Superior-grade armaments, she'd finally agreed to give Ishtar's request some thought.

"All things considered, it didn't take much to catch your interest."

"It's a great opportunity! To do battle with the famed *Freya Familia*…and really, you musta done your homework before comin' to us. You knew this'd be right up our alley."

The true reason *Kali Familia* had decided to heed Ishtar's request, even going so far as to leave their own country, was because of the chance it offered—to fight against the irrefutably powerful *Freya Familia*, the strongest in a city already known for its capable factions.

This was an offer Kali and her combat-craving Amazons simply couldn't refuse, and it was a serendipitous meeting of interests for the two goddesses.

Ishtar crossed her slender, tanned legs as she and the young goddess across the table exchanged smiles. Catching the sidelong glances of Kali's followers eyeing her every move, she brought the tip of her kiseru pipe to her lips.

"I'll only let you know my initial plan for now. Wouldn't want you and your girls to run wild or anything, now would we?"

"What, you don't trust us?" Kali scoffed.

"I'd watch my tongue if I were you, little Neanderthals."

Ishtar's warning was accompanied by a puff of purple smoke from between her lips.

Behind Kali, Argana and the other *Kali Familia* Amazons sported contentious smiles directed at Ishtar's followers. The enormous women behind Ishtar responded in kind. Though the alliance had been formed, the atmosphere in the room seemed liable to combust at a moment's notice.

"Samira," Ishtar called out, slicing through the tension.

An ashen-haired Amazon approached the short-legged table between the two goddesses, unfolding a scroll atop its surface.

It was a map of Orario.

"Our territory is here—the Pleasure Quarter in the southeast. *Freya Familia*'s home, on the other hand, is located here, right in the middle of the Shopping District. To put things in perspective, Meren is located to Orario's southwest," Ishtar explained, her thin finger pointing out each location on the map.

"Hmmm...interesting. Then the enemy's already nicely sandwiched between us," Kali mused with a nod, leaning forward across the table. "A pincer attack, then?"

"Precisely," Ishtar confirmed with a smile. "My familia will begin the attack, and while Freya and her followers have their full attention on us, you and your warriors will sneak in from behind."

Ishtar had chosen an ally outside the city itself not only to ensure her plan's secrecy but also to guarantee their attack would come as a complete surprise. Even the strongest familia in Orario wouldn't expect an attack from outside the city's walls. Even more so if the attackers boasted Level-6 combat power.

"And what're we supposed to do about those crazy-high walls, huh? I'm sure they've got guards, yeah?"

"There's a certain...company I've got wrapped around my finger—Albella. Simply come in by freight, and you should be able to pass by without an inspection. If you'd like, I can even open the gate for you myself the day prior," Ishtar explained, the corners of her mouth curling upward as her irresistible charm did its work. "Once you've finished preparing, we'll invade Freya's territory...And once the fighting begins, that will be your sign to attack," she finished. Her aura embodied callous ferocity despite her commanding allure.

Helping an outside force infiltrate the city was a serious crime, but Ishtar had no qualms about making enemies with the Guild. Such was the tenacity of one who'd spent too long ruminating on her own humiliation.

As Ishtar finished relaying her plan, Kali's eyes narrowed.

"Heh. The jealousy of a goddess truly is a terrifying thing. A shame, really, that one so beautiful could have fallen so far," she mused, chuckling at the irony. While her outward appearance and voice resembled a young girl's, the bite behind her words and the way she stared daggers made it plain that she was no child.

Ishtar made her rebuke while she smiled.

"Say what you will, but I will do anything to bring that woman's world crashing down around her." As the goddess's smile widened, her gorgeous features bordered on the demonic.

The sheer intensity exuding from her every pore had reached the point where it was overwhelming Kali's followers.

"At any rate, that's as much as I can tell you now. Even barbarians like you should be able to follow such simple instructions, yes?"

"Heh, charming as ever. But simple's good. After all, this is our first time meetin' face-to-face. Can't expect too much, now, can we?" Kali agreed, playing off her opponent's effrontery with congeniality. "What day we lookin' at?"

"Preparations are taking longer than planned; however, feel free to use this inn as you like until the day arrives."

"How generous."

"I know. You should feel honored."

Ishtar had taken care of everything since the Amazons' arrival, from their port-entry permit to their lodgings, while her followers made constant treks in secret between Orario and Meren. In fact, the "Amazons" mentioned in a certain bar in another corner of the city were the Amazons of *Ishtar Familia*.

"Still, even with the lavish fineries, we're still here just twiddlin' our thumbs...My girls wanna get out there and fight, don't you, Argana?" Kali leaned back against the sofa and glanced back to where Argana was currently standing behind her.

"We do," the Amazon replied, a snakelike smile gracing her lips. "That Warlord especially. Gotta see what he's really made of."

"That boaz is just one of many in Freya's entourage. Don't act out of turn," Ishtar hissed, purple smoke escaping her teeth.

"I know, I know! We'll wait like good little girls," Kali responded with a wave of her hands, looking more and more like a mischievous child. "Speakin' of, this your whole familia, Ishtar?"

"Are you really that imbecilic? My familia is equally as large as yours. I left most of them back in the city and brought only my top girls with me here. Why do you ask?" the goddess of beauty inquired with a tilt of her head.

"Just wondering if your girls here would be the only ones tackling the front end of the pincer attack, is all. Our friend the Warlord's a Level Seven. He alone would be enough to take down my Argana and Bache. Just don't want the whole thing to be over before it even starts," Kali remarked none too delicately as she glanced at Ishtar's entourage. She, too, had left the majority of her familia back in Telskyura. From her point of view, what with her party of mostly Level 5s and 6s, *Ishtar Familia* didn't exactly seem the best choice for a frontal attack.

While Ishtar's followers were quick to anger at the remark, Ishtar herself simply smiled.

"There's no need to worry. I have something special up my sleeve," she assured, throwing a glance at one of the women behind her.

The woman in question was the only one in the group of a different race.

Though her face was hidden by a pure-white veil of feathers covering her head, from the tail protruding from her hips, it was clear she was of animal-person descent. Her curves betrayed her femininity and, when coupled with her robes, gave off the impression of a priest or kazuki-adorned Shinto shrine maiden.

She didn't respond to her patron deity's knowing glance, remaining completely silent and apparently devoid of any sort of enthusiasm.

"...Hmm?" Kali eyed the girl curiously.

In return, she found a set of gorgeous green eyes staring back at her from behind her facial covering. Almost immediately, however, the long-legged woman next to her blocked her view, face stern as she hid the veiled girl behind her back.

"I'm basically serving you victory on a platter. Any leftovers are yours for the taking...Feel free to have a ball," Ishtar offered, and her followers behind her responded with bestial smiles.

Kali's followers couldn't help but grin in return at the alluring proposition.

"While I'm not sure how I feel about this trump card of yours...I guess it'll have to do. So long as I get the gist of it. For now, we're just supposed to sit tight, yeah?"

"Exactly."

"That bein' the case, I'd like it if we finished this whole business of my compensation, then."

Ishtar's dark hair fluttered, glimpses of purple visible amid the rich obsidian. "I'd be glad to pay you as much as you'd like. Simply name your price, and I'll—"

"Keep your money. I don't need it anymore. I want somethin' else."

"Oh?"

"And I want it before all this goes down, too," the miniature goddess asserted, the tiniest of trembles audible in her voice.

Ishtar scowled. Eyes sharpening like needles, she looked at the other goddess head-on. "...Go on."

"*Loki Familia*'s currently here in this port. Don't get me wrong—it's got nothin' to do with us. Just a coincidence, is all. Seems like they're here huntin' some kinda man-eating flower monster or whatsit."

"Man-eating flower...? Ah yes. Those." A disdainful smile crossed Ishtar's lips as she made the connection in her mind. "And? Don't tell me...?"

"You got it. I was hopin' to go up against 'em."

Ishtar's eyebrows rose in identical arcs. "You can't be serious. Going up against Freya and her followers is ludicrous enough. *Loki Familia* would be even more so. I can't have you bloodied and bruised before the fight with Freya even begins!" she snapped, voice cracking.

Kali raised her hands in supplication. "Sorry, sorry...I wasn't being clear. By 'them' I didn't mean the whole familia...but two certain sisters within the familia."

At the word *sisters*, Argana's lips broke into a smile behind the goddess.

"You see, Loki's gotten her hands on a few of my kids. Well, former kids, at least. I lost the two of 'em in a rather...unfortunate incident. Still tugs a bit at my heartstrings, you know?"

"...You speak of the two Amazonian twins?"

"One and the same! I'd very much like it if my Argana and Bache could go up against 'em."

Ishtar tossed a puzzled glance at the two Amazons in question.

The two were sisters, the same sand-colored hair falling over their shoulders. While one wasn't even trying to contain her mirth, the other remained stony and silent.

And yet, while their attitudes may have differed, both of them were imbued with the same carnal desire to fight.

"Two sisters who left...two sisters who stayed...Which ones turned out stronger, I wonder? Will the ones who come out on top break free of the vessel they're trapped in? Will they reach new heights—a new level?" Kali mused, half to herself, as her eyes stared off in the distance. "I want to see that battle. The carnage. I want to witness for myself which choice was correct...in a shower of blood."

With a quiet intensity, Kali's voice grew more and more heated as she spoke.

Her eyes glinted beneath her mask, her throat trembling in imminent ecstasy.

This time, it was the Amazons on Ishtar's side who shuddered, nerves on edge at their glimpse of the goddess of war, blood, and mayhem in all her glory. It was clear that the woman before them now sought not just combat but a brilliant fight to the death.

What gratified Kali the most, and what had been her sole purpose in descending to the lower world, had been nothing but war itself.

The fact that her true motivation focused solely on the taking of lives made her all the more detestable. But it was this simple purpose that had drawn Ishtar to her in the first place—somehow it made her seem more "manageable"...Still. Not even Ishtar could have calculated the true extent of the tiny goddess's bloodlust, and faced with it now, she could only glower in disgust.

There was a gasp from the veiled beast woman behind her—fear, perhaps?

"But in order to make that happen, I need you folks to keep the rest of their familia at bay. We learned well enough today that they've got a number of girls in their ranks who'll cause us trouble if we try again, their Sword Princess in particular. And I want this to be a fight between sisters only," the petite goddess demanded haughtily.

Ishtar, however, would have none of that, and she was just about to tell her as such when—

"—Hee-hee-hee. Let them have their funnnn, Lady Ishtar."

A certain giant of a woman who'd been silently watching the scene unfold from behind Ishtar finally opened her enormous mouth.

"Phryne..."

"It's finnnne, isn't it? A warm-up for the fight with Freya, if you will. Besidesssss, sooner or later even Orario will find out Kali and her followersssss are here in Meren. If they're convinced their purpose in coming was to fight *Loki Familia*, there's no chance of the Guild or Freya and her lot raising any suspicionsssss..." the Amazon explained.

While her limbs were strangely short, her bust size was substantial, and atop her large body and even larger head was a patch of short bobbed hair, the profile almost reminiscent of a toad's. Her voice, too, hoarse and guttural, sounded as though it had been ripped straight from a frog, the husky croaking eliciting looks of disgust from both Kali's and Ishtar's entourages.

It was none other than Phryne Jamil, *Ishtar Familia*'s captain.

At Level 5, she was the strongest in the familia.

"I'll take care of that Sword Princesssssss for them."

Despite the good argument the toad woman had given, Ishtar still suspected she had ulterior motives, and, indeed, she didn't miss the deep-rooted enmity burning in those giant ogling eyes the moment Phryne mentioned the Sword Princess.

She sighed, long and low, but finally recovered her earlier smile.

"All right, then. Phryne does make a good point. And I can't say I'm all too fond of Loki and her merry men, either," she finally agreed, her distaste for *Freya Familia*'s rivals all too obvious. "Having said that, if we find we've bitten off more than we can chew, I'm pulling my girls out, and you'll have to handle the rest yourselves."

"I'd assumed as much." Kali nodded coolly. The inklings of a smile were finally beginning to show on the cherubic goddess's face. "There's nothing that excites me like the spray of blood, and nothing lights a fire in my gut like the cries of agony when some poor soul crosses over the line between life and death. There exists no greater thrill in all the world! And a treat my more frivolous brothers and sisters will never get to taste—real war, with real lives at stake. That…that is the true thrill of the lower world…and exactly what I seek."

"…"

"The only truth my children know is that of fighting and bloodshed."

From Ishtar's point of view, as someone whose entire being revolved around love and sex, love was the true, unchanging universal truth, but since they would never see eye to eye on such things, she kept her mouth shut.

"—War is the future," Kali continued caustically, her bloodred eyes narrowing within the empty sockets of her mask. "And I'm gonna be the first in line to see it."

CHAPTER 4

SISTER & SISTER, DUSK & DAWN, SHADOW & LIGHT

Гэта казка іншага сям'і.

Старэйшая сястра і малодшая сястра ноччу і раніцай цемра і святла

Tiona remembered it all too well.

The look in her sister's eyes. The moment she began to lose her way.

The day Tione reached Level 2, Tiona had leveled up, as well. It was by the same method—killing one of the girls in their shared chambers.

However, Tiona's mind hadn't been nearly as developed as her older sister's, and even when she realized she'd killed one of her beloved roommates, she'd barely felt a thing.

Oh, poo. I killed someone again.

She liked to fight. Kali and the other Amazons had always congratulated her when she'd won. And yet, every time she was forced to kill one of her sisters, she got a funny feeling in her heart. Tiona had been too young to know how to put it into words, and so it had just built and built and built.

So long as she focused only on the excitement stirring in her blood, things would be fine. She could still be like the other Amazons. That's what she'd believed. That's what she'd understood innately. But the funny feeling in her heart brought all of that to a halt. As a young girl who acted on instinct rather than reason, the more her blood churned in excitement, the more she was troubled deep within her heart. The line between the two emotions was paper-thin at best.

When she returned to her stone room on the day of her fifth birthday, Tione had already been there. Alone in the corner, her weapon and mask tossed to the floor and her face buried in her knees.

"Who did you fight?"

"...Seldas."

Tione didn't even look up upon her approach, voice no more than a whisper.

Seldas.

Tiona, too, had thought warmly of her. Besides her sister, Seldas had been easily the most generous and kind of anyone she'd ever known. But the rites didn't end until someone was dead. And both Tione and Seldas had had no choice but to fight to the death.

The funny feeling in Tiona's heart grew even stronger.

"...Good."

She replied. And the word had been genuine.

Tiona might not have been able to truly feel the connection in their blood, but that didn't keep her from understanding that Tione was someone special to her. She was relieved that Seldas had died and Tione had lived.

I'm glad you're alive. I'm glad you weren't killed. That had been what Tiona had meant with her word.

But all she'd been met with was a fist.

It was heavy with unadulterated ferocity.

While the two sisters may have argued often, none of their fights had ever been this extreme; Tione was aiming to kill as she shattered Tiona's jaw.

Pain flared across Tiona's face. She saw red and, with an enraged howl, prepared to leap upon her sister...

...only to come to a stop at the sight in front of her.

Tione was crying.

Her body was shaking, her features contorted in a strange mix of rage and despair as giant tears rushed from her eyes.

Tiona's fist loosened, her arm falling limply to her side.

And then she'd simply stood there, in silence, watching her sister weep.

Tione grew even wilder after that.

She'd never been the most eloquent of girls, but now her words had begun to border on the obscene. She became aggressive toward everyone and everything. Even her sister wasn't an exception to her abuse. With every day that passed, her eyes grew more stagnant, more clouded, indicative of the turmoil in her heart.

Tione wasn't the only one, either. Everyone in their room had felt it now that their numbers had dropped by more than half. Now that they fully understood the truth behind the rites, not a one of them spoke. Some feared forming any more of an emotional connection with their peers, while others worried about being killed themselves. There were also those who reached a sort of understanding, surrendering to their own instinct and awakening as the "warriors" their country so craved.

Their days of fighting sped by.

Those who survived the rites rose up in rank and were eventually selected, one by one, by their more senior Amazons. It was an acknowledgment of their own strength and abilities, and a binding relationship as teacher and student.

Tiona was chosen by Bache. And Tione was chosen by Argana.

The two sandy-haired sisters were ten years older than the five-year-old girls. As they were also twins, it could only be assumed they'd thought pairing up the two sets of siblings would lead to some sort of benefit. Argana was the older of the two, and both had already made quite the name for themselves. At the time, they were ranked high among the few candidates in the running for the familia's next captains.

The training was grueling. Not a day went by where the young girls didn't see blood in their vomit, and there were even times they left with broken bones. Merely surviving from one day to the next meant desperately stealing every move, every technique they could from the two Amazons deemed their instructors.

"*...On your feet.*"

As Bache looked down at her, icy and unfeeling, on the cold stone ground, Tiona felt fear for the first time in her life. It wasn't until later, once they'd both escaped, that she'd learned Tione's training under Argana had been even more arduous.

Between the rites and their training, the time they spent in their room inevitably grew less and less. As did their roommates. In fact, by the time they realized it, they were the only two left in their little stone room.

But they weren't allowed time to despair. The constant training wore down their bodies and minds, their emotions all but dulled, and their only happiness came from their victories in battle. Tiona found herself lost, drifting aimlessly through her day-to-day routine—the same routine Telskyura had used already to mold most of its warriors, stripped of everything but their will to fight.

It was an entire year before she reached her turning point.

She'd been crawling about the empty arena like a cat, having stolen a moment's peace before her training was to begin, when she'd found a balled-up scrap of paper that had been carelessly tossed away down one of the empty aisles—a piece of a story.

The epic.

"..."

Tiona opened her eyes.

The faint lapping of the lake's waters and the cries of nearby seagulls pulled her out of her dream as reality came into focus.

Sentimental scenes of her past still hazy in her mind, she sat up in bed, glancing over at the mattress next to her.

It was empty.

"...She already left?" she moaned, her other half nowhere to be seen. Reaching her arms upward, she let out a long "Hnnggaaaaah..." as she stretched the sleep from her body.

"We're tight'nin' our search," Loki proclaimed first thing once the group had gathered around the breakfast table that morning. "I wanna concentrate our efforts on three things: *Njörðr Familia*, the Guild, and the old Murdock estate. Now, we don't want any of these folks to know we suspect anything, so we're just gonna act like it's a continuation of yesterday. Make it seem like we've still got nothin' and secretly sniff around for anything suspicious."

Hearing this, the residents of the hotel's first-floor dining hall quickly descended into chaos.

Loki, however, simply continued.

"Having said that, ol' Njörðr'll know somethin's up the moment we start pokin' around, so I'll handle that one myself. But y'all have to take care of the other two."

"And what of *Kali Familia*?" Riveria inquired.

"Ignore 'em for now. But if they do try and stick their noses in where they aren't wanted again, stay together. No heroics, ya hear?" Loki instructed, throwing a glance in Tiona and Tione's direction. "Tiona, Tione, you'll stick with Aiz and Riveria. Those two sisters of theirs are somethin' fierce, but so long as you're in pairs, you should be fine…even if they do pick a fight. By the way, I'm officially vetoing any right to object at this point," she added before Tione could open her mouth to protest. "And unless y'all wanna get shipped back to Orario, I'd suggest you behave like good little girls, yeah?"

Tione scowled, sitting back in her chair with a huff.

Aiz and Riveria simply nodded, accepting their duty to watch over the twin Amazonian sisters with their deep connection to *Kali Familia*.

"All right, then! Any questions? No? Then y'all are dismissed!"

"I wonder if Tione'll be all right…" Tiona murmured as she let her eyes turn skyward, taking in the ever-blue swath of sky spread out above the port.

She and Aiz were currently walking along a small alleyway away from the hustle and bustle of the main street, while the residents carted baskets of laundry and shopping bags nearby and children ran back and forth around them.

"I wouldn't worry. Riveria is with her…" Aiz pointed out as she walked along beside her.

"I would if I could! But…eh, I do understand what Loki was thinking. The two of us together would be a perfect target," Tiona mused slowly.

Try as she might to act normal, in her heart, she wished she was with Tione right now. Her mind was already coming up with all sorts of unlikely scenarios that could be playing out at that very moment. Still, she couldn't help but notice that Aiz's mind, too, seemed to be fixated on something.

"You're worried about Old Man Murdock, aren't you?" she asked, changing the topic of conversation.

"A little, yes..." Aiz nodded.

The two of them were on their way to the manor of the man in question, the Murdock estate, with plans to infiltrate the grounds. They needed to think of a way the two of them could get inside unnoticed in order to continue the investigation Lefiya and the others had started the previous day. Maybe, just maybe, they could find some clue.

Still ruminating on the matter, they found their walk brought to a sudden halt by a young animal girl stumbling across their path.

"Ah—!"

"Whoa there! You all right?"

The book she'd been carrying tumbled to the ground together with a handful of gold coins. Perhaps she was on her way home from shopping?

Aiz was quick to help the young girl to her feet. Tiona lent a hand, too, by gathering up her scattered possessions—that is, she was about to, until she saw the book's title and immediately stopped in her tracks.

...Argonaut.

Her eyes were glued to the book's cover—an image of a hero battling a mighty bull. It was a volume of the epic she was familiar with.

"U-um...Miss, could you...?"

"Oh! Sorry, sorry!" Tiona replied sheepishly as she handed the book and coins over to the teary-eyed girl.

The girl responded by hugging the book protectively to her chest.

"You just buy that?" Tiona inquired, bending down so she was at the girl's level.

"Yeah, the—the man at the store, he...told me they got lots of new books from the ship..."

"...You like that old legend?"

"—Yeah!" The girl's face lit up like a sunflower.

With a quick thank-you, she waved her hand before running off down the alley.

"Tiona...?" Aiz asked as Tiona continued to stare silently in the direction the girl had gone.

She stood there another moment, a soft smile playing on her lips.

"I liked them, too...back in Telskyura..." she murmured. The sight of that girl running away so happily, a great big grin on her face, joined the images from her dream that very morning—of the little girl who'd smiled the same exact way.

Bache had been training her that day, same as always, in the arena's training room.

Her face covered in blood, Tiona rummaged for the paper she'd hidden in a corner of the room and held it out to the older Amazon with both hands. "Will you...read it to me?"

It was the same scrap she'd found in one of the arena's aisles shortly before practice.

Though presumably dropped by one of her peers, it wasn't of Telskyuran origin—she had never seen these Koine letters. Considering she didn't even know how to read and write in the Amazonian language, the words on the paper were positively indecipherable, no matter how much interest she had in them.

Tiona would never forget the look Bache gave her.

The ever-taciturn Amazon was clearly taken by surprise.

Rather than respond with her typical emotionless apathy, she seemed deeply flustered, and after standing there for a good couple of moments, body swaying, she took the scrap of paper and left the room with nothing more than a "...G-give me some...time."

It wasn't until a few days later that Bache returned, and once their training for the day was over, she read the contents aloud.

She shouldn't have given a second thought to the whims of an inquisitive child, and yet, somehow her pride wouldn't let her move on. To think she and a girl ten years her junior would be on the same level, unable to read the same characters! It had been enough of a blow to her dignity that she'd gone to Kali herself, red-faced as she'd asked the goddess to teach her the meaning behind the words.

"I want to know...what it says..."

Though Kali had guffawed quite heartily at the request, she'd diligently translated the Koine words for her.

"Not realizing he was being deceived, the young man said to the king, 'Understood, my liege. I will, without fail, save the princess being held captive deep within the labyrinth.'"

"What happens next? What happens next?"

Tiona urged Bache on beneath the torchlight, sometimes kneeling, sometimes sitting cross-legged on the cold stone floor and not even bothering to tend to her wounds. Bache herself seemed bewildered, this being her first time in this sort of position, but slowly she worked her way through the entire text, relaying the story bit by bit after each training session.

But like every story, this one eventually came to an end. Especially considering this was only a scrap torn from a larger book, the ending came all too quickly. Though this meant concluding their secret post-training story time, the "damage" had been done, and Tiona no longer saw Bache as the terrifying authoritarian she'd once been.

"Lead your enemy's attacks. Draw them in until you can feel the wind against your skin, then parry."

"Parry how?"

"...Just parry."

The rigorous training sessions became more than mere pain and suffering. In fact they became almost...fun.

At the same time, the young Amazon who'd been taught to know nothing besides combat found herself dreaming of other, bigger things.

—She wanted to know how the story ended.

With every day that passed, her desire became stronger.

Then, one day.

Upon completing another rite, Kali happened to ask her if there was anything she wanted.

Tiona responded immediately.

"I want to know the end to this story."

Her wish was granted, and a complete, undamaged book was sent for.

Tiona may have been an idiot at times, but she wasn't stupid. And the pliable mind of a child was a powerful thing. Her interest sparked a flame inside her head, and soon, with Kali's help, she was reading Koine with ease. She could still remember the looks Bache gave her—dejected, almost. In the cheerless world of the arena, she had discovered another type of excitement, one different from fighting, and Tiona found herself instantly enamored.

From then on, every time Tiona won a fight, she would ask for another book to add to her collection as a reward. It became a sort of bait, but also drew favor from Kali. And so, Tiona devoured more and more and more stories. She carted them back to her stone room, lost in their pages, rolling around in her bed as she pored over them late into the night by candlelight. With every day that passed, her collection grew larger, until Tione finally kicked the giant mountain over in a huff. This, of course, led to one of their habitual fights, and Tiona retaliated with her fists as tears welled up in her eyes.

The pieces of the story—the fragments of the epic—were changing her.

First and foremost, they acted as a catalyst for her idiocy and carefree optimism.

She began to laugh more.

Her laughter was childlike, imbued with bottomless joy.

She couldn't even imagine how she must have looked in her sister's eyes. It was probably just one more reason for Tione to be mad at her. After all, while Tione was slowly descending into her own personal hell, Tiona's eyes were sparkling before the pages of books as she laughed and smiled like the village idiot.

Though raised under the same harsh conditions, the two sisters had diverged into light and dark—and all because of some story written on a little scrap of paper.

It was an abnormal thing for a happy-go-lucky soul to last long in this world of fighting and bloodshed. "Crazed warrior" indeed—before anyone had even realized it, the young girl was already taking full advantage of her title of "Berserker." So much so that the other Amazons came to wonder if this emotionally stunted girl wasn't touched in the head, far as that was from the truth.

Anytime anyone spoke to her, she laughed. In fact, she was always laughing.

She'd been saved by the power of the epic.

"..."

Aiz stared at the silent Amazon.

Tiona was completely motionless, watching the young girl disappear down the alley with her copy of the epic. Finally, she opened her mouth.

"You know, Aiz..."

"...Hmm?"

"You don't think I'm...weird, do you? Laughing all the time?" she asked, bringing her hands up to lightly touch the sides of her cheeks.

Aiz was quiet for a moment.

Then she shook her head.

"It's thanks to you that...I'm able to have as much fun as I do now."

The words may have been few.

But they were enough to convey her message.

Tiona turned around with a smile, her cheeks flushed.

"Thanks, Aiz."

And yet, despite her gratitude, something about her seemed off.

Rather than leap upon Aiz with her arms outstretched, she simply took off, continuing down the alley as though nothing had happened.

"..."

Aiz watched her friend walk away before finally falling into step behind her.

Around the same time that Aiz and Tiona were heading toward the Murdock estate, Lefiya and her small team were conducting a diligent investigation of their own.

If the Guild really is involved in this whole affair with the violas... we could be in for a mountain of trouble! Well, the same would be true for Njörðr Familia, *I suppose...*

The Guild here may have just been a branch, but it was still an administrative authority. If it was colluding with the remnants of the Evils, it'd be more than a problem—it'd be a catastrophe! Lefiya hadn't been able to shake the feeling of dread in her stomach since Loki had announced them as one of their three targets that morning.

Despite her inner turmoil, she did her best to keep a straight face—Riveria and her beloved Aiz would do their best to get to the root of things—focusing, instead, on her current task of information gathering.

"...Hey, Miss?"

"?"

Lefiya turned around, only to find herself face-to-face with a young girl with light cocoa skin. Her immediate reaction was to brace herself—*Kali Familia*?!—but almost instantly, she relaxed her guard.

Having received the gods' blessing herself, she knew not to let herself be lured into a sense of safety no matter how young or how small her enemy was, but the girl in front of her now didn't have the aura of a familia member. She didn't carry herself like someone with a Status on her back. There was no way she could have had anything to do with the adventurer or warrior professions.

Also there was the fact that the girl in front of her was decidedly human—not Amazonian. Height-wise, she came up to only about Lefiya's abdomen, and from the lightweight clothes on her back, one could immediately recognize her as a resident of Meren.

Her shoulder-length black hair gave a tiny tremble as her dark tea-colored eyes gazed up in Lefiya's direction.

"Are you an adventurer?...From Orario?"

"I am, yes. Is something the matter?"

No doubt, *Loki Familia*'s presence in the port town the last few days had made them a topic of conversation among the populace. As Lefiya bent over, the girl seemed to gather up her courage before leaning forward to whisper in Lefiya's ear.

"I—I keep hearing this scary scream. In the place I like to play."

"Scary scream…?"

"Yeah! It…it sounds just like those looooooong monsters that came outta the lake…"

"!"

Lefiya's senses snapped into focus. "Long monsters" could only mean—the violas.

"I'm not supposed to tell any grown-ups. But…but I'm scared…"

"Where is it you heard the scary scream?"

"From…from over there…" she responded, finger pointing down the alley behind her.

"Rakuta! Elfie!" Lefiya called out, head snapping upward. The rest of her group, currently scattered about the area conducting their investigations, quickly gathered around her.

"You really think she…heard a monster?"

"It doesn't seem to me like she's lying…"

"It's not like we have anything else to go on. Let's see what we can find out."

Lefiya listened to the Level-3 hume bunny and her human mage roommate back in Twilight Manor, then came to a decision. She glanced down the little back alleyway, quite a ways away from the main road, before returning her attention to the young girl.

"Do you think you could show us the way?"

The girl nodded.

"My name is Lefiya. What's yours?"

"Chandie."

And thus, the girl named Chandie began leading the group down the alley.

The tangled mix of throughways and byways behind the city proper was quite different from the main road, and Lefiya could imagine it would be all too easy to get lost if one wasn't familiar with its twists and turns. Nevertheless, their young guide seemed well at home as she led the group along, navigating the narrow streets with ease.

"...?"

As Lefiya followed immediately behind the girl, her long, slender ears suddenly twitched, almost as if they'd picked up on a slight, faint tremor.

Someone's...watching us?

No one else seemed to have noticed. And, in fact, had Lefiya not participated in various adventures with Aiz and the other first-tiers, Lefiya wouldn't have, either.

Uncertain as to whether she should say something, Lefiya found that the girl responded first—almost as if picking up on her hesitation.

"Those Amazons are here...aren't they?" she asked without even turning around.

What?

She asked, or at least she'd been about to ask, when.

From directly overhead, the mysterious presence landed behind her without a sound.

"———"

She didn't even have a chance to turn around.

With terrifying speed, the figure came at her with a dagger, slicing into the back of her neck with pinpoint accuracy.

"Lefiya?!"

The world around her shook, and a dizzying sense of vertigo overtook her. Knees crumpling, she slumped to the ground.

Rakuta's and Elfie's dissonant screams swirled around her as the sudden intense sounds of fighting pounded in her ears. The cobblestones in front of her spun and warped as she fought the urge to vomit, what was happening, what was happening—

Chandie's voice cut through the confusion above her.

"—There are those among the gods capable of suppressing their divine will."

Though the voice itself was still childlike, her manner of speaking was dignified, like someone much older.

Lefiya's azure eyes widened with a surprised start, even as her vision clouded.

"Zeus and Odin and the other great kings of the gods are not the only ones. They disguise themselves as children, blending in among the populace unnoticed…reveling in their own versions of merriment in the lower world."

With what little strength she had left, Lefiya raised her head, just in time to see the young girl remove her wig. From beneath her black hair cascaded a waterfall of crimson locks. And from within her clothes, she retrieved a demon-like mask adorned with two long fangs.

Lefiya gazed up into the two open holes of the mask, where the goddess's eyes, the same bloodred color as her hair, stared back down at her.

"You learn something new every day, child of Loki."

All too quickly, the tables had turned.

The girl had become the goddess, radiating an almighty authority, while Lefiya had become the child, unenlightened and ignorant.

Even as her consciousness began to fail her, she felt shame wash over her, and she cursed her ineptitude.

"I hope you don't mind if I borrow that body of yours for a while. I won't do anything…too uncouth with it."

The sounds of fighting behind her had stopped. A sandy-haired warrior, Bache, stepped forward to stand beside Kali, completely unharmed. That was the last thing Lefiya remembered before she completely blacked out.

"Argana…!" Tione screamed.

The woman in question simply smiled, her lips curled upward in snakelike amusement.

They'd been on their way to the Guild Branch Office when the Amazonian warrior had appeared in front of them, and she clearly had no intention of letting them pass.

"Didn't you have enough already…?!" Tione growled, fists clenched and liable to jump forward at a moment's notice.

"Tione, fall back! Calm yourself!"

Riveria shouted the warning, stopping the enraged Amazon in her tracks. Her weapon was being worked on like Aiz's and Tiona's, so the magic user's only equipment for offense was a substitute staff. Still, she stepped forward, unafraid to face the Amazon in the road, even as the rest of her group shrank back in fear.

"If there is something you want, then speak. Otherwise, you will step aside."

"…"

Argana simply stared at the unflappable high elf.

Eyes narrowing, she tore her gaze somewhat reluctantly from the dauntless high elf to lock eyes with the Amazon behind her, still staring daggers in her direction.

"Rhada fa arhlo. Nahaak jhi deena, noy phæ garaahdo sol die Hyrute."

"——"

The words brought time to a screeching halt.

Riveria's brows furrowed as the rest of the group looked around in confusion, none of them able to understand the words, but Tione snapped.

"And just what is that supposed to mean, huh?! Tell me!!" she shouted, unable to keep herself under control any longer.

Argana just kept smiling.

At any second, it seemed Tione would lose her cool completely, when suddenly…

"Lady Riveria!"

The shout came from the opposite direction.

Everyone turned around to see an out-of-breath elf running toward them.

"What is it?" Riveria inquired, a sense of foreboding washing over her.

"R-Rakuta and the others…Lefiya…They're…!" the elf tried to explain, looking very much as though she'd just seen a ghost.

The color drained from their faces. Startled, Tione whirled back around, only to find that in that tenth of an instant, the sandy-haired Amazon in front of them had disappeared.

"...!!"

Tione's eyes dropped immediately to the ground, where a certain something had been left in Argana's place.

Snatching it up, she hurried after Riveria and the others, her body still shaking.

"...Whoa, what?"

Loki deadpanned at the sight in front of her—her followers, covered in cuts and bruises with blood staining their clothes.

"Sorry, Loki...They were too much for us." Rakuta apologized, her voice hoarse.

Loki had practically sprinted from *Njörðr Familia*'s home the second she'd heard the news, arriving at the port's entrance only to find her followers looking very much worse for wear.

None of them had escaped serious injuries. And the wounds were clearly from combat—almost as if fists hard as steel had bludgeoned them a hundred times over. They'd used bits of cloth to staunch the bleeding, but those were already stained a dark red.

Rakuta was the only one who was still conscious.

"Rod! Could you lend me a hand? Quickly!"

"Roger that! C'mon, you good-for-nothings! Get your asses in gear!"

Njörðr called his captain, who was quick to respond. Rod shouted to his men, spurring the temporarily stunned fishermen of *Njörðr Familia* into a flurry of action.

"Who did this?" Loki asked, her voice low.

"...*Kali Familia*...They just...suddenly attacked..."

No doubt they'd thought this group would be easy prey given its lack of first- and even second-tier adventurers. And from Rakuta's tearful account of the events, it seemed Bache alone had been responsible for taking them down.

"They...they took Lefiya...!"

It was humiliating.

They had made a completely unexpected attack in broad daylight, rubbing dirt in their faces and making a complete fool of the normally peerless *Loki Familia*.

But it was the damage they'd done to her precious followers that really made Loki's blood boil.

"That damn midget…Pickin' a fight with me, is she?!"

Loki's normal indifference had all but disappeared, and a fiery hot flush of unadulterated rage had taken its place. As the rest of the familia began gathering around the scene after hearing the news, even those who'd been with Loki the longest—Aki and Alicia, to name a few—found themselves fearfully hesitant in the face of this new side to their goddess.

"Hey, hey, let's not start a war right in the middle of the city, shall we…?" Njörðr grimaced wearily. He knew all too well how dangerous Loki could be when she got this look on her face.

But his words fell on deaf ears. Despite the fury boiling within her, her eyes were as cold as ice. As she watched her followers being attended to, something caught her gaze, and her scarlet eyes narrowed.

The familia emblem had been torn off one of her followers' clothes.

Tearing off the emblem…Is she declaring war here? But no, when they ran off with Lefiya, they would have…Ah. So that's what's goin' on.

Loki scowled upon realizing just what it was her opponent was thinking—the atrocious, detestable plan Kali was currently concocting.

She raised her gaze toward her followers gathered around her.

"Get Tiona and Tione back here. We can't let them out of our sight," she ordered, though in the back of her mind, she feared she might already be too late.

"Is somethin' happening?"

Around the time Loki was giving her order to find Tiona and Tione…

Tiona and Aiz were already on their way back from their

infiltration mission at the Murdock estate. As soon as they heard that members of *Loki Familia* had been attacked, they took off, practically running full tilt the rest of the way to the pier.

"!!"

First Aiz, then Tiona shot past the trade pier, about to continue on to the fishing quarter, when...

"—Tiona. Over here."

"Huh? Tione?!"

Tione appeared from out of nowhere, grabbing Tiona's wrist and yanking her away.

She didn't stop until the two of them were separated from Aiz and in a dark alleyway a short distance away, where Tiona finally shook off her sister's grip.

"What the hell are you doin', Tione?! Didn't you hear? Somethin' happened! We need to be out there seein' if we can—!"

But Tione didn't let her finish.

"Rhada fa arhlo. Nahaak jhi deena, noy phæ garaahdo sol die Hyrute."

We've taken a hostage. If you want her back, you and your sister will come to the shipyard tonight—alone.

"!"

"That's what Argana said to me earlier. Rakuta and the others were attacked and...Lefiya was taken hostage," she explained.

Tiona's eyes widened.

"Those...those bastards! Using the rest of our familia to lure us in...!" Tione hissed. She was having trouble holding back the tumult of emotions, both a relentless rage to rival her goddess's and a sense of responsibility for involving her companions.

Tiona, however, kept her cool.

"...What are you gonna do?"

"You even have to ask?!"

Tione's sharpened gaze met her sister's honest one.

From far off, practically in a distant world, they could hear the commotion taking place on the pier.

"We're going to settle this. Once and for all."

To take responsibility for what they'd done and ensure this never happened again.

As Tione's words swelled with unwavering conviction, Tiona remained silent. Finally, she looked away.

"Tione..."

"What is it?"

"Can't we...ask for help? From Aiz and the others?"

"You—?! Just how thick can you possibly be?! It's our fault that Lefiya and the others—"

"But we're a familia, aren't we?" Tiona raised her gaze, interrupting Tione's tirade. "We're different from how we used to be...aren't we?"

Now it was Tione's turn to squirm.

Brows furrowed, she bit down on her lip, masking her lack of response by chucking the item Argana had left behind at her sister.

"What's this...?"

Tiona glanced down at the strip of cloth in her hand—the *Loki Familia* emblem.

The smiling face of their mascot, the Trickster, had four large gashes across it.

"It's a warning. We're to come alone. If we go to Aiz and the others... those guys will never leave us...and them...alone."

"..."

One of the gashes was vertical while the rest were horizontal, laid out across it. It was a symbol of the rites they'd suffered day in and day out back in Telskyura, used to represent the monsters they'd faced over and over in battle during those competitions in the arena.

If they were to go to Aiz and the others for help and use their combined power to save Lefiya, *Kali Familia* would continue their attacks in that same way. They wouldn't stop until they were once again able to reenact those rites—and have their showdown with Tione and her sister.

Tione understood all too well the warning they'd received.

"If we don't go there and reenact the rite, they're gonna keep on doing things like this. As many times as it takes. They won't let anything get in the way of their little game."

"..."

"We're the only ones who can finish this. We can't go to Aiz and the others...or the captain."

Silence settled over the two sisters.

Tione knew she was being stubborn. Her aversion to involving the rest of the familia could very well be taken as a lack of faith in them.

But she wasn't going to fold on this one.

This was something they had to do themselves, to sever their ties with Telskyura once and for all.

"...Okay."

Had she gotten through to her?

Another moment, and then, ever so slowly, Tiona nodded.

"I don't like hiding things from everyone, but...it really seems like we don't have any other choice," she agreed.

Tione turned her eyes downward at the sadness visible on Tiona's face.

At length, the two of them began to walk, backs to the main street, away from the sounds of civilization.

Saying nothing to Loki, to Aiz and their companions, they simply vanished into the dark alley.

"It feels like before somehow..." Tiona murmured, staring upward at the shape of the sky formed between the rooftops above their heads. "Just the two of us."

The words felt like a punch in her back.

Tione said nothing.

The sun had begun its descent toward the western horizon, disappearing from the sky overhead.

"Aiz, were you able to find them?"

"No...I looked everywhere..." Aiz replied, having just arrived back at the inn after a furtive search throughout the city. It was already growing late. She walked over toward Loki and Riveria and past the rest of her flustered companions restlessly pacing the first floor of the establishment. "I'm sorry. It's all my fault…I was with Tiona…"

"Nonsense. If that was the case, I would be most at fault. I got so caught up in wanting to help Rakuta and the others that I forgot to keep my eyes on Tione…and, no doubt, she is the one who absconded with your Tiona, as well." Riveria shook her head, eyes closed. She'd already accepted the blame for the entire situation, shame evident in the crooked arc of her brows. "However, pointing fingers will get us nowhere."

Aiz agreed, imitating the high elf's shift in focus and swallowing the rest of her apology.

"What about Rakuta and the others?"

"Leene and the other healers are looking after them. Certainly they won't be up and moving again for a while, but it shouldn't be long before their strength has returned."

Aiz let out a sigh of relief before continuing. "And what about *Kali Familia*? Have there been any signs of them?"

Just as Tiona and Tione had disappeared right out from under them, the rest of *Kali Familia*, too, seemed to have vanished into thin air. Apparently not a single soul had caught sight of them after the attack on Lefiya, not even the residents of Meren.

"Aki and the other gals split up to go look for 'em…Speakin' of, they should be comin' back right about now." Loki spoke up from her cross-legged spot atop the table, and, indeed, no sooner had the words left her mouth than the door opened to reveal Aki and Alicia back from their search.

"No good. The inn they were supposedly staying at until today was completely deserted. We snuck in but couldn't find anything."

"And even though the galleon they sailed in on is still there, it's completely empty, as well…"

The two second-tier adventurers explained despondently. Loki hummed softly as she scratched at her chin.

"Considerin' this is their first time here, you wouldn't think they'd be able to hide themselves so well…They've gotta have someone helpin' 'em."

The goddess's words triggered a jolt of fear in her followers.

Alicia clenched her fist. "But what is it they're after…?"

"Well…I'm about ninety-nine point nine percent certain they're gonna make Tione and Tiona reenact those rites they used to carry out in Telskyura. That bastard of a midget they call a goddess is nothin' but a natural-born battle junkie. And I wouldn't put it past Tione and her sister to be tempted, too," Loki posed.

"Attacking Rakuta and the others, kidnapping Lefiya—it was all a ploy to spur them into action," Riveria continued.

"Lefiya…" The name stung Aiz's heart. As worried as she was about Tiona and Tione, she couldn't help her concern for the spirited-away mage, too.

"Anyway, we continue our search…and if we find 'em, we blow 'em away. Aiz should be able to handle 'em by herself, but Riveria, feel free to blast 'em as much as ya want, too."

"In the middle of the city. What a wonderful idea…" Riveria brought a hand to her temple.

"And what about Lefiya…?" Aki retorted, eyes narrowed in disbelief.

But Loki just discarded their concerns with a dismissive wave of her hand.

From what Aiz could tell, Loki's anger hadn't subsided even slightly. As much as her usual tomfoolery colored her words, her eyes themselves weren't laughing at all.

"Look, I'm just gonna come out and say it—Lefiya's nothin' more than bait to lure in Tione and her sister. No one's gonna be threatenin' her life or anything. Then again, who knows what might happen if worse comes to worst."

"Then what you're saying is that our enemy desires nothing but combat in and of itself?" Riveria asked, though she already knew the answer.

Loki smiled. "Thaaaat's it. A hostage is just a blip on the radar for someone who wants a full-on fight to the death. Most likely she's just there to dissuade us from interferin'. That way, they can have their death match without worryin' about us gettin' in the way."

Aiz could tell from the goddess's smile—she knew Kali had no plans to kill Lefiya.

"So, Aizuu. You're the only one who's gone up against 'em. Aside from the sisters with the boobs, how tough d'ya think they are?"

"...Of the ones I fought, Level Threes or Level Fours," Aiz guessed, thinking back to yesterday's skirmish in the main street.

Their fighting style, however, would prove difficult, much like Tiona and Tione's. They fought with a complete disregard for their lives, at an insanely close range, and with no hesitation at taking someone else's life. They would always have the upper hand against someone lacking that same motivation to kill. Or at least that's what Aiz thought.

Aki and Alicia found themselves grimacing as they listened to the Sword Princess's prognosis.

"So even their mid-level warriors will prove a handful," Riveria mused.

"Unfortunately, yes..."

"The fact that Aiz and I are both using temporary weapons doesn't help matters any, either."

Loki let out a sigh as she turned her gaze toward the ceiling.

All of a sudden, Aiz raised her head with an "Ah!"

In all the commotion, there'd been something she'd forgotten to add.

"Loki."

"Hmm? What's up, Aizuu?"

Aiz undid the small bag from beneath her loin guard, handing it over to the goddess. It was something she and Tiona had found during their earlier search of the Murdock estate.

As Aiz leaned forward to explain its contents, a smile began to form on Loki's face.

"Good work, Aiz!" she exclaimed before sliding down from off the table. Grabbing a quill pen and parchment from one of the hotel staff, she quickly took to writing.

"Aki! Would ya mind playin' messenger for me?"

"Well, no, but...you mean now?"

"Faster than now. This is an emergency! Everything you need to know should be written right here," Loki asserted, handing her a small slip of paper.

Aki glanced down at it with a nod, then grabbed the two pieces of parchment and took off out of the inn at the speed of a cat.

Loki watched her with the rest of the group, then turned her eyes toward the window and the crimson sky painting the horizon.

"Now, then! All that's left is Tione and her sister..."

Why did she have to remember now, of all times?

After she'd killed the person who'd meant the most to her, after a wild light had begun to appear in her eyes, a certain Amazon had arrived to hurl her life into an even deeper level of hell.

Argana Kalif. The top contender for the rank of Telskyura's next captain.

And the warrior whose mentality was closest to Kali's. Her training was nothing short of gruesome.

The day they'd met, Argana had broken her. For no specific reason, other than that the combat-obsessed warrior Argana did not distinguish the training in their dark stone room from the battles to the death in the arena.

As Tione was reduced to blood-soaked skin and bones, she came to hold the same fear toward Argana that Tiona held toward Bache—along with an even more powerful anger.

Through the scalding pain and her hazy consciousness, she came to see Argana as a symbol of Telskyura itself. The very custom that had forced her to kill Seldas.

"...You're good."

Argana immediately took a liking to the young girl who couldn't be broken, who refused to relinquish her will to fight or her unbridled rage. She licked her lips hungrily, her long tongue twitching like a snake's at the sight of all that blood and Tione's murderous eyes as she lay battered and bruised on the ground below.

Argana's fighting style and brutality were feared even throughout Telskyura. She would drink her opponents' blood, digging her razor-sharp teeth into their skin and sucking their very life force from their body even as they wailed and cried in pain and despair. It intoxicated her; it was the highest grade of alcohol there was as she feasted on the flesh of the strong.

—Those who survived the rites were simply known as "True Warriors," and the inhabitants of Telskyura weren't given aliases as the adventurers of Orario were, save for Argana. She was referred to as Kalima, a cruel, villainous warrior recognized even by Kali herself.

She was a monster who'd go so far as to drink her own blood. And for Tione, there wasn't a day where she didn't loathe Argana with every fiber of her being. There wasn't a single moment when she wasn't overcome with rage at that Amazon and her tyrannical laugh. And ironically enough, it was during this very training that her second skill, one grounded in all that untapped fury, manifested itself.

It was when Argana rose to Level 5 that her antipathy toward the Amazon took its complete hold. Argana had been on her way out of the arena after one of her battles when Tione had finally asked the question.

"...You don't feel anything...do you?"

She murdered her peers—those she'd shared the same room with, eaten out of the same pot with, just as Seldas and Tione had. She had drunk their blood, ignoring their moans as she mercilessly dug into their flesh.

Argana had stood there, her body suffering heavy injuries and dripping blood that could either have been hers or her opponent's, with the strangest expression on her face.

"I consume them to become strong. That is all. What else am I supposed to feel?"

Telskyura had created that answer in her. The secret to power was so simple it was...disappointing.

In order to create Level-4 warriors, you had to kill Level-3s.

In order to create Level-5s, you had to kill Level-4s.

It was a sacrifice that had to be made.

It was like putting rats in a barrel to kill and cannibalize one another until only the strongest remained. That was just the type of country Telskyura was.

And yet even within that country of monsters, the one before her now was the deadliest, most despicable monster of all. That much, Tione was sure of.

"When are you going to let her go? There's no point mourning someone who's nothing more than an offering."

That had made Tione see red, and she'd launched herself at Argana when the other woman was already wounded from battle.

For too long had she been forced to suffer and seethe in Argana's training sessions, for too long had she been made to kill her sisters in those detestable rites—her eyes and heart were being worn down at an accelerating speed. Though she had sometimes longed for death, she knew that dying would be nothing more than giving in to those she abhorred the most, which was something her anger-fueled instincts would never allow.

And yet, somehow, almost in direct opposition to Tione, her sister, Tiona, had grown all the more cheerful.

She knew why. It was that epic.

The many volumes of that story had nurtured her idiot sister's sense of idealism. But even as Tione turned its pages, her empty eyes scanning the hollow words, and even as Tiona tried to teach her their meaning, she just couldn't understand where the enjoyment came from.

When Tiona looked at her with those eyes, so different from that of her peers, it made Tione's stomach roil.

She didn't like it.

Maybe even hated it.

"How can you act like that when I'm living in a never-ending hell—?"

The words had crossed her lips so many times at this point, she'd lost count.

There was no question that Tione and Tiona were two entirely different breeds of Amazon. Though they were born of the same generation and raised in the same kingdom of violence, for better or for worse, Tione had raged while Tiona had laughed.

Tione was antagonistic to a fault, even going so far as to curse her own goddess. Kali herself couldn't get enough of the girl's abuse, taking everything her beloved child could deal as her eyes twinkled in amusement.

Tiona, on the other hand, was as innocent as they came. Not only was she full of laughter, but she elicited laughs from her goddess, as well. In fact, it became commonplace for Kali to invite the girl to her chambers.

The two sisters were the only ones able to talk back to Kali, making them objects of jealousy among the other Amazons. And, of course, this led to widespread hope that one day, the two of them would be placed in front of each other in the arena.

It happened two years after they'd leveled up to Level 2. It was the day before their seventh birthday and the perfect opportunity for them to reach Level 3, given how their Statuses had grown by leaps and bounds thanks to Argana's and Bache's merciless training. Tione could practically feel it on her skin—all too soon she would have to fight her sister.

And no matter how much Tione fought back, no matter how much she rebelled—a single sentence from her sister was all it took to reduce her efforts to nothing.

"Kali, I don't wanna fight Tione."

Kali had invited the victors of the day's rites to her hall to laud their efforts.

There had been no forewarning; her stupid sister had simply blurted it out.

"We wanna leave."

Even Bache and Argana hadn't been able to believe their ears, every eye in the room turning directly toward Tiona. Kali, however, had simply narrowed her eyes beneath her mask.

Tione couldn't remember what she had thought as she stood among the other Amazons. And yet, the very wish she'd put on hold all this time...was about to come true only a few days later.

Was it a whim of their goddess, perhaps? Either way, Kali released them from that arena of stone, and soon they were sailing far, far away from the vast peninsula.

—Why?

Tiona clearly had Kali's favor; she had given her those volumes of the epic and spoiled her like a child.

But then what had those days spent trapped there even meant? What had the suffering been for, if her dolt of a sister just had to laugh to break them free of this prison? Was this even what she truly wanted?

As Tiona had run about excitedly beside her, taking in the unfamiliar sights of the cerulean sea, the steep precipices of the mountains, the clean air, and the mesmerizingly gorgeous world outside, Tione had cried. And even at the tender age of seven, she'd known enough to understand the tears weren't from the scenery before her eyes.

Sister versus sister, dusk versus dawn, darkness versus light, rage versus innocence.

How had they turned out so different, though the same blood ran through their veins?

Tione couldn't stop the feelings from welling up inside her. If she didn't let them out, scream them out, she might very well have wrung her sister's neck.

And what she found down there, deep down among the amalgam of emotions flooding through her, was jealousy—of what her sister possessed that she did not.

That was the first time Tione realized she wanted to kill herself.

"..."

Tione grit her teeth as the memories of her past faded from her mind.

She bent forward, the side of her face burning under the crimson light of the setting sun.

"Whoa! Who woulda thought all this'd be here, huh?"

Her thoughts were interrupted as the cheerful voice of her sister, much older than the girl of her memories now, reverberated off the walls of the wide room.

They were in an old, abandoned factory a ways away from the city. Piles of rusted iron and steel lay strewn among battered ship parts, and weeds grew up in patches all across the floor. The darkening light of the sky overhead peered in from the tattered shutters and many holes littering the ceiling.

"We wait here till nightfall then, huh, Tione?"

They'd come here in their search for a place devoid of people, away from Aiz and the rest of their familia.

As twilight's hue colored the world outside, Tione narrowed her eyes, shooting her happy-go-lucky sister a sharp glare.

"Tiona."

"What?"

"Let's practice."

Tiona looked back in confusion, blinking at her sister's sudden suggestion. "...You don't mean now, do you?"

"I do."

Under normal circumstances, the two would use every chance they could get to spar in Twilight Manor's courtyard, but these were hardly normal circumstances.

Ignoring her sister's look of skepticism, Tione placed one foot behind her, falling into position.

"I'm serious. We're going all out here. There's no point if we don't."

Realizing it was no use arguing, Tiona slowly fell into position, as well.

Thus the duel began in the middle of that old, abandoned factory.

"——"

Tione made the first move.

Stepping forward, she hurled her fist toward her sister.

She held nothing back, letting her anger carry her forward.

It caught Tiona off guard. Though the younger Amazon was able to block it, the sheer power behind the strike made her take a step backward.

"Yeeeoowch! That hurts, Tione!" Tiona cried out.

"I said we're going all out here!" Tione responded just as loudly, in the same tone she'd used so many times back in Telskyura.

The change was enough for even Tiona to discern, and knowing there was no other way, she began fighting, too.

Their strikes echoed off the walls, the scraps of iron and steel, and the perforated ceiling. The punches and kicks they couldn't dodge or block tore deep gashes in each other's skin. Blood dribbled from Tiona's lip where one of her sister's strikes had grazed her, and a deep purple bruise was already forming on Tione's arm where she'd blocked one of her sister's roundhouse kicks. Their original intention in seeking out the factory—to escape from any watchful eyes—had all but left their heads completely.

"Gngh…!"

At some point during their exchange of fists, Tione's vision went white with rage.

And with that white heat came all the feelings, all the words she'd been keeping locked away in her heart these many years.

For so long, she'd been using her emotions as strength; now, she finally voiced them.

"You know, I used to hate you."

Tiona laughed. "As if you need to tell me!"

"I still hate you!"

"Oh really?"

Her lips were curled upward in a familiar smile from her memories.

Even in the middle of their deadly fistfight, she still had that same damn smile.

This only fueled Tione's anger further.

"Laugh, laugh, laugh! That's all you ever do! You haven't changed one bit!" she snapped, unable to control herself and directing a high kick toward her sister's head.

"You have, though!" Tiona shot back instantly.

"———"

Tione's eyes widened with a start.

"Ever since we met Loki and the others and you started liking Finn…you've changed so much!"

The punches and kicks kept coming with no signs of slowing.

But even as Tione's strikes carried with them all those tumultuous emotions that'd been weighing her down, Tiona countered every one with a smile.

"That made me so happy!"

"Oh it did, did it?!"

Tione felt the fury rising up inside her, her eyes trembling as she put everything she had into her next strike.

"You make me so angry!!"

"What? I can't heeeeaaaaaaar you!"

"Damn you!!"

"Grah!!" Even as she let out an incensed roar, Tiona seemed unruffled. Laughing innocently, fighting as though she didn't have a care in the world, returning her strikes in the midst of her happy, childlike dance.

—She would never change. She would always be the same stupid idiot.

—And whenever Tione looked at that infuriating grin, it would always make her think the same stupid thoughts.

As her rage built and built, the exchange of blows gradually slid into a harmonious dance, and somehow, that stupid, stupid smile found its way onto Tione's face, as well.

Before she even realized it, both of them were laughing.

She couldn't even remember why they were there, what they were supposed to be doing—she just enjoyed their fight.

Until.

""Guwaaah?!""

Practically in sync, their fists found each other's cheeks.

For a single instant, they stood there frozen, like statues, then, finally, their legs gave out beneath them and they crumpled to the ground. The tufts of weeds growing out from the warehouse floor cushioned their descent.

"Another draw…" Tiona sighed.

"Yeah…"

"I'm still in the lead, then, hee-hee-hee."

"As if! You've lost way more times than I have. I'm clearly in the lead."

"Nuh-uh."

"Uh-huh!"

"Nuh-uh!"

"Uh-huh!"

The girls spread their arms and legs on the ground like two twin starfishes, their bickering morphing into laughter. They were like kids, their voices echoing off the walls of that long-forgotten building.

"Why were we even doing that again?"

"Who cares? It doesn't matter now."

Tione could tell without even looking that her sister was still chuckling. She could practically see the gentle smile that had no doubt formed on her face.

The sky above them was brilliant. Its blazing crimson shone through the holes in the ceiling, lighting their faces on fire.

As Tione narrowed her eyes at all that beauty past the warehouse walls, her mind traveled back to another time, another place, where they'd had another conversation just like this.

Yes, it had been back in Telskyura, when her anger toward Tiona had risen to a breaking point just as it had now.

Tiona's favor with Kali had caught the attention of many of the other Amazons. Theirs had been a world where it didn't pay to stick out from the crowd, and some of their peers had devised a surprise attack out of jealousy, or perhaps anger. And somehow or another, it had come down to Tione to put an end to it.

Tiona and her raucous laughter had been an eyesore to Tione back then, constantly grating on her nerves. There were times even she'd bad-mouthed the other girl and her ability to chat with Kali like it was nothing. How dare she act all buddy-buddy with the good-for-nothing goddess who'd kept them trapped in this horrible place! It was only natural that someone like Tiona would drive Tione mad.

And yet, still, the other girl was family. She was the only bond

Tione had in the cold, unfeeling world of the arena. The one person she could always turn to. And so, she'd protected her without even having to think about it.

She'd ambushed the group of Amazons who'd been planning their attack in the hallway late one night, and she took out the whole lot of them. Some of the women were ranked even higher than her, which led to a vitriolic exchange of verbal abuse followed by a life-and-death game of tag.

By the time she'd returned to her stone room, run completely ragged, Tiona was fast asleep, snoring among her piles of books. This had only irritated Tione all the more, and she'd kicked her right in the middle of her sleeping face. The resulting fight had lasted till morning.

"*Why were we even fighting...?*"

"*...I forget.*"

They'd muttered to each other, spent of their energy and splayed out like starfish. The morning sun had shone in on them from through the latticework of their small window.

It was at that moment, as Tiona had laughed amid that soft light, that Tione had realized just how irreplaceable the other girl was in her life. Not that she'd ever say it to her face.

A deluge of emotions swept through her mind as the scenes played out in her head.

Though fury and bloodthirst had been her two best friends in the harsh world of the arena, she had had emotion, too.

There was something nostalgic about those memories, and she felt her cares and reserves slowly begin to slip away.

"Hey, Tione."

The sound of her own name brought her out of her reverie.

Sitting up, she looked over to see Tiona do the same.

"What are we going to do if...if Kali makes us fight each other?" her sister asked as their gazes met.

It was what they'd escaped all those years ago—a fight to the death between sisters and a resurrection of the rites.

"Fight," Tione responded casually. "And I'd kill you. Or at least I'd try. If not, you'd kill me." She didn't even flinch, relaying the words as if they were simply a matter of fact.

Tiona's face grew solemn. "I don't think it'll come to that, though. No way."

"Huh? Why?"

"Because of Argana and Bache. Argana's too attached to you, like Bache is to me. If the two of us are gonna be killed, then…I'm positive they'd wanna be the ones to do it."

And it was true—they'd taken a risk going up against *Loki Familia*, attacking Lefiya and the others, and even taking a hostage. It sounded just like something the coldhearted, murderous Argana of her memories would do.

After a moment, Tione pulled the high potions she'd already prepared from the pouch around her waist, tossing one toward Tiona. As the other girl caught it handily, she downed one herself.

"You doin' okay?"

"Huh? Whaddaya mean?" Tiona started, already having guzzled down her high potion and cocking her head to the side curiously. It took a moment, but then she seemed to infer what Tione meant. She glanced down at her hands, tightening and loosening her fists. Finally, she looked back up at Tione with a nod.

"What do we do now?"

"Nothing until nightfall. Rest, I guess, or do whatever." Tione shrugged as she made to get to her feet but found herself stuck quite firmly in her cross-legged position thanks to Tiona's grip on her arm.

She immediately glowered at the other girl, who merely responded with her typical laugh.

"It's been so long—maybe we could take a nap together? Like we used to?"

"…What?!"

"So we can save our energy for tonight!"

You're one to talk about energy, Tione wanted to respond, but she lost her chance as Tiona kept talking.

"We used to do it all the time!"

"…Yeah, but only while traveling. You don't have much of a choice when you need to sleep outside, and you're like a human space heater!"

"But…!" Tiona frowned.

Tione's eyebrows rose as she remembered her frustration. "You're the worst sleeping partner, you know that? I can't even begin to count the number of times you've smacked me in the face."

"You've hit me, too, you know!"

"Yeah, in retaliation!!"

But even as the bickering began anew, it wasn't long before Tione decided to appease her sister and rest beside her until night fell. Wearily, she watched as Tiona found a dust-covered piece of cloth off in a corner of the warehouse and happily wrapped the two of them up inside it.

"Nighty-night."

"You better wake up later…"

Tione could barely hold in her sigh, her back against one of the piles of old scrap metal as she wondered how in the world things had come to this. The sigh of grief changed to a sigh of acceptance, though, as Tiona snuggled in beside her, resting her head on the older girl's shoulder. Soon, she was snoring softly—another source of irritation, but Tione simply put up with it.

It felt just like before, after they'd left Telskyura and had traveled around from country to country, city to city.

They'd had no choice but to sleep out under the cold sky, no roof over their heads save the occasional rocky outcropping or forest overhang. And even back then, Tiona had always fallen asleep first.

Tione let her eyelids fall.

——Somehow, she knew the two of them would be dreaming the same dream.

Nothing but the magnificent expanse of nature awaited the two sisters after their departure from Telskyura.

Oceans, mountains, forests, valleys, hills, endless fields of flowers and grasses–they'd never laid eyes upon any of it in that stone prison of the arena. It was a brand-new world to them.

It took their breath away, and they trembled with the rush of emotion.

They could never have imagined that the world would be so vast.

They had never dreamed the sky could be so beautiful.

Back then, it had only been as wide the arena, and they had loathed its very existence.

For Tione, who was still at a loss as to how she was supposed to feel being separated from Telskyura, it did much to restore the life and color to her raging heart and strained eyes, almost like water poured onto a desiccated wildflower. Together with her ever-enthusiastic sister, she found herself finally, ever so slightly, able to smile.

And every time Tiona saw this, she'd break out in a wide grin.

Beyond simply allowing the two of them to leave the country, Kali had also taken pity on them. Not only had she released them from their contract, she'd also left their Statuses untouched. This meant they were able to forge new contracts with any other god, combining their old Status with the new. This was also the only reason the two young girls were able to get by for so long on their travels, as they still had the enhanced power of their Statuses to rely upon. Kali had explained this by way of a "parting gift for her two adorable daughters," but to Tione it was too little, too late compared to how she'd treated them these many years.

Though the two girls had learned how to overcome just about everything through that miserable hell of an arena, their knowledge was limited to pure combat, and there was still much they didn't know. Money was difficult, of course, but even something as simple as human interaction was an ordeal. Tione had lost track of the amount of times Tiona had gotten swindled by some passing peddler. Not that they didn't always retaliate and get the money back, but still. From a survival perspective, the two excelled, to the point where "feral children" could have been an adequate phrase to describe them. As it happened, Tiona did teach her sister some Koine, at least enough that she could get by, shameful as it was.

The first time they came across another "tribe" similar to their own was in a small fishing village along the sea—much like Meren, actually. Accepting requests to hunt down monsters was about the only way they could make enough money to get by, and so, despite continuous objection from Tione, the two decided to temporarily join the local familia. This was what allowed them to update their Statuses and what had helped them level up to Level 3 during their stay in the village.

Be that as it may, Tione was never quite able to open up to the more erratic, pleasure-loving gods and goddesses, nor the members who made up their familias. And so, they made each other a promise that after a year of various bodyguard and labor duties (for there was a one-year rule when it came to converting to a new familia), they would revoke their contracts and leave the familia.

This was a tradition they continued, no matter what countries or what cities they visited. Though the gods and familia members might beg to keep Tione's and her sister's strength for themselves, Tione never listened. In fact, her impertinence often had her butting heads with her other familia members, and more than once they ended up leaving their familias on not-so-great terms.

The only person Tione would permit to stay at her side was Tiona.

She wouldn't acknowledge those who weren't strong, and even those who somehow earned her acceptance weren't allowed close, aside from her sister. Perhaps it was her residual trauma from Telskyura—this refusal to form connections with anyone save the sister who'd survived with her. She was scared.

As the two of them earned glimpses into these many new worlds, they made all kinds of discoveries. And yet, never did they have anyone besides each other.

It was no different from their time in Telskyura. They refused to open up their hearts to anyone besides their other halves. No matter how far they traveled across the vastness of the lower realm, their world never expanded beyond that of their dual existence.

Tione wasn't sure what her warmhearted sister felt on this matter, but whatever she may have thought, Tiona stuck by her side. It was almost as if she understood innately that Tione was the only one she could turn to.

Tiona would never let go of her sister's hand, no matter what happened.

"We'll be leaving again soon, right, Tione?"

"We will, yeah. Why? You don't want to?"

"Well, no, but…it's just that the god here is so nice, and…and so is everybody else, so…"

And then she'd laughed. The same laugh always followed her.

"But being with you is all I need, so…it's fine!"

The relief Tione had felt then, along with the feeling of being pushed out of her world, couldn't have been just her imagination.

Tiona was the sun.

There was nothing more dazzlingly radiant, nor more frustratingly ingratiating than her. Though the idiotic grin she always wore grated on Tione's nerves, the longer she looked at her, the looser her tightly clenched fist became.

Just accept it already. She saved you.

Sure, they'd fight over the stupidest, most trivial things, then eat their meals together as though nothing had happened, but as Tione sat next to that brilliant shining smile, sometimes she'd even find a smile forming on her face. This was fine. So long as she had her idiot of a sister, she'd be fine. As someone who'd known nothing of forming connections with others, Tione was able to adjust to this two-person world thanks to the sister at her side.

And so their aimless journey continued.

It was a paradox—two girls who cared not about being alone traveled in search of a place to call home. They joined one familia after another, training and developing the two vessels that were their bodies, leaving behind those they met along the way, all the while being careful not to let themselves get too comfortable in one place. This went on for quite some time as they continued their strange, aimless quest for something they themselves didn't even seek.

It was five years into this journey.

That the two sisters decided to stow away on a ship and travel to the "Center of the World"—the Labyrinth City, Orario.

"C'moooooon…it's just a way to kill time, is all!"

"…"

The cherub goddess's face twisted into a frown at Lefiya's refusal to open her mouth.

She'd only just awoken a short time ago after Kali and Bache whisked her away, and she was currently in some sort of cave-like recess no larger than a typical pub. As Lefiya looked around at the black stone, she had no clue as to where she could be.

It's humid…Near the lake, then? No, the ocean, perhaps?

She licked her lips, trying to sort out her surroundings without being noticed. Though she couldn't be sure of the time, from the stiffness in her muscles, she could hazard a guess that she'd been out at least five hours. In fact, it felt very similar to taking rest in the rooms of the Dungeon. Night was surely drawing near.

There were five others in the room besides herself—Kali, who was sitting cross-legged in front of her, and four guards. From what she could tell, everyone was at least her level or higher, and chains had been carelessly wound around her wrists.

They're not strong, either…They're normal chains, not mythril or some other type of ingot. I could probably break them if I wanted…

Her movements weren't even restricted. If it were just these restraints holding her back, then she'd surely be able to escape.

"Don't even think about it, missy. I'm sure you've noticed already, but one move outta you, and these girls'll be all over ya."

"…"

"I don't recommend tryin' to whisper out a spell or whatever else you may be plannin', either," the goddess warned with a smile, almost as though reading her mind.

Lefiya didn't respond.

"They're some of the best warriors in Telskyura, too, you know.

They could pick up on a mouse tiptoeing a kirlo away, and they're highly skilled in crushing chants. You wouldn't wanna have that pretty throat of yours pulverized, would you? I doubt you wanna see what it's like to be barely able to breathe as you drown in your own blood, yeah?"

"...Guh?!"

A chill ran up Lefiya's spine.

The battle-hardened Amazons had spent enough days in the arena to understand how to stifle a mage's spell. Mercilessly, without hesitation.

Lefiya's face paled at the thought. Kali continued with a sage nod.

"But if you just sit tight like a good little girl, you'll come out right as rain, yeah? As soon as this is all over, you'll be free to go."

"I'm...bait, aren't I? For Miss Aiz and the others...Misses Tiona and Tione?"

"Maybe you are...maybe you aren't," Kali teased, slippery as an eel.

This was what she got for thinking she was ready to level up to Level 4—kidnapped by her enemies and completely powerless to do anything. Her heart dropping in despair, she said a silent word of apology to her familia companions, all the while glaring at the goddess in front of her.

"But so long as you're askin' about Tiona and Tione, maybe you can tell me a bit about 'em."

"...Like I would tell you anything!"

"Hey, I'm not huntin' for weak points or anything like that! I just wanna learn a bit about 'em, you know? After they left Telskyura and all," Kali explained, giving Lefiya's cheek a few smacks with her tiny hand.

Lefiya winced, pulling away with a whimper as Kali continued to smile.

"What're they like now that they've settled down, huh? A mother wants to know!"

Lefiya found herself at a loss, not knowing how to proceed before the childlike goddess's affection-filled eyes.

Finally, after much thought, she opened her mouth, unable to take Kali's penetrating gaze any longer.

"I'm afraid I…can't talk about more than trivial matters, but…"

"S'fine! It's the trivial stuff I wanna hear about!" the goddess urged, keeping Lefiya talking.

And talk she did…It was a rambling, somewhat incoherent string of stories, everything from her jealousy at Tiona and Aiz's bond to Tione's incessant courting of their captain, Finn.

"Bwa-ha-ha-ha-ha-ha-ha-ha-ha!! You…you can't be serious! Tione? In love?! What a crock! Bwa-ha-ha-ha-ha-ha-ha!!"

"It…it's not quite that funny…" Lefiya remarked as she watched the tiny goddess, her hands on the ground and clapping her feet together in a simulation of applause, her undergarments bared to the world. Considering the lovelorn version of Tione was the only Tione she'd ever known, Lefiya found the tears of mirth in Kali's eyes to be a bit much.

Once the spasms of laughter finally subsided, Kali removed her hands from her belly and righted herself.

"So that little runaway of mine has fallen in love…Huh! She really has changed. Here I thought she'd be a barren witch the rest of her life. *Ha!* I guess she's a different breed than us after all."

There was an emotion behind her words, similar to the affection Lefiya had felt from her earlier. Perhaps there was some way to persuade her against all this, appeal to the goddess's emotions, and keep this senseless fight from coming to pass. She did truly seem to care for her followers.

"Erm…" she began, these thoughts running through her head. "Do you…really need to do this? I highly doubt Misses Tiona and Tione want to fight. If you could possibly show them some mercy…"

Kali's face was calm beneath her demonic mask, and the slightest of smiles played across her face.

"No can do," she replied curtly, eliciting a jolt of surprise from Lefiya. "I descended to this world seeking war and bloodshed. Don't get me wrong—I love my children. But even they can't come between me and my life's one true pleasure. So I'm gonna hafta decline."

"...!"

The terribly honest words sparked a flame in Lefiya's belly. They made her forget where she was, and a shout built up inside her throat before bursting past her lips.

"Then you're the reason why Telskyura is nothing but a land of death! That's why so many people have died!"

"Whoa, whoa, simmer down, would ya? Telskyura was like that even before I came along. We gods highly condemn distortin' a country's history and culture for our selfish whims...That'd be a crime against the mortal world! Not to mention your kids would resent you for it, yeah?" the goddess explained.

Lefiya felt her anger start to subside. "Oh..."

"The only thing I did when I got there was bequeath 'em my blessing."

No longer able to look Kali in the eye, she turned her gaze to the Amazons around her, who offered not a word of opposition. Their silence acted as a show of approval—the loyalty they'd pledged to the goddess before her.

"Child of Loki, do you know why I let Tiona and her sister go?"

"...?"

"Because they were the first ones. No one had ever requested to leave Telskyura."

"!"

"Reject none who come, chase none who leave...If you wanna skedaddle, I have no business keepin' you. Of course, you'd have to give up all the benefits from my blessing as collateral, but that's how things go, you know?"

No one else had ever requested to leave, neither before them nor after. Every other Amazon had remained in Telskyura, where their days of ceaseless combat had continued. After all, what was the point in putting time and effort into a bunch of spineless wimps who'd give up before they'd even started?

Everything was the will of her children. As much as possible, Kali had tried to make Telskyura the holy land of Amazons they wanted it to be, or at least that's how she put it.

"Did you confuse me for an affectionate goddess, Child of Loki?"

"..."

"I'm no different from every other god and goddess out there, not even some everlasting child-saving goddess of the hearth or what have you. All of us came down to this world seeking the excitement of our own. We're nothing but hedonists."

An impish smile formed on Kali's face as she rose to her feet. Then, entrusting Lefiya to the watchful gaze of her Amazonian guards, she made to leave.

"W-wait! What is...what is it you're trying to do?" Lefiya called out reflexively, realizing that her attempt to persuade the goddess had failed.

"Trying to do...? Hmm, a lot of things, I suppose, but if I had to name one..." Kali came to a stop, red hair swishing as she turned around. "Create a future of war. I want to see it with my eyes...The perfect warrior born from the very limits of ceaseless bloodshed."

As Lefiya's eyes widened in horror, Kali's face broke into a smile.

The sky was tinged with bluish shadow.

Night had settled over the port town of Meren. Passing clouds hid the twinkle of stars and the outline of the moon as they drifted ceaselessly along. Every so often, a gap would appear, and the moon's golden light would drift through the haze to illuminate the city below.

"It's time...We should get ready."

"Right."

Their nap finished, Tione and Tiona gazed out across the city and darkened night sky from the vantage point of their abandoned factory.

The meeting time Argana had given them was fast approaching, and they began to prepare themselves for their confrontation with Kali—their chance to sever the ties to their past once and for all.

"Hey, Tione."

"What is it?"

"What were you and Loki talkin' about yesterday?"

The question came as such a surprise that Tione found herself unable to move for a moment.

"...You're asking me now?"

"Well, I got curious!"

Curious, indeed, Tione thought as she let out a sigh. She was no better than a cat! She fended off her sister's question with a flippant wave of her hand.

"It's nothing, seriously. Don't even ask."

"Oh really?"

"Yep. I'm gonna go check out the road into town." She changed the subject before unconcernedly making her way out of the factory.

However, rather than checking out the road like she'd said, she came to a stop in a small alley, leaning back against the wall and turning her gaze toward the sky.

—"Have a drink with me, won'tcha, Tione?"

It had been last night, after her crushing defeat in the fight against Argana.

Tione had been out on the balcony by herself, unable to be by Aiz and Tiona any longer, when Loki had approached her on her way back from the pub.

"...Sorry. Afraid I'm not much in the mood."

"'Zat so. You know, Tione, if there's somethin' on your mind, you can always—"

"Come to you? Don't bother. You don't act like a patron deity any other time, so stop trying now." Her words were harsh, even more so than usual, a reflection of the damage her earlier defeat against Argana had done to her heart. She simply couldn't bear it.

Loki didn't seem bothered. "It's all the same to me. But maybe you'd be better off thinkin' of Finn."

Tione felt a chill run down her spine at the mention of the captain's name.

"The way you're actin'...reminds me of when I first met you. You're even more on edge than you were then."

"..."

"So try to think about when you first met Finn," Loki continued with a little laugh at the way Tione struggled to keep a straight face. "I like ya much better all mellowed out and cute-like, y'know?"

—I'm glad I can entertain you so much!

Tione started to snap back, but she couldn't seem to get the words out of her mouth. Instead, she simply walked away, dragging her feet along behind her.

"...Captain..." Remembering the scene, Tione murmured softly.

An intense feeling of dread had settled over her, as though the ground beneath her was shaking. No, she couldn't look back now. She'd come too far already, or at least that's what she desperately told herself.

"..."

But her despondent sigh didn't go unheeded.

Her sister had crept away unnoticed and returned to the abandoned factory, mimicking Tione by turning her eyes skyward.

It felt so long ago—the day the two of them first arrived in Orario. The day their two-person world came to an end.

She could still remember how that soaring white tower and those lofty city walls had loomed over her head.

It had taken them more than a few days to finally make it inside the city; Tione had gotten so irritated they'd almost given up entirely. It seemed they were really cracking down on those with blessings from outside the city in an attempt to weed out potential spies, and not even travelers like them, with no affiliation to any familia, were free from scrutiny. And certainly the sudden arrival of twin Level 3s—second-tier adventurers—with no patron deity or familia to their name, was a little hard to swallow.

The Guild had only allowed them entrance to the city on one condition: that they join one of the city's familias. The condition was born from an ulterior motive—a dog collar, so to speak, to ensure the two Level 3s didn't slip away.

Getting in will be easy but getting out will be a nightmare. That was how it had been explained to Tiona, which meant her first impression of Orario was nothing more than a bothersome cage. No doubt, it had been the same for Tione, and yet, Orario turned out to be anything but boring.

Barely a day had passed after they set foot in the city, and already they'd been swarmed. News about their arrival had spread like wildfire, with every god and goddess of a Dungeon-type familia flocking to snatch up the two beautiful Level-3 Amazons for themselves.

It was the Dungeon, after all, that had drawn Tiona and her sister to Orario in the first place. Though they'd left Telskyura, Amazonian blood still flowed through their veins, and they were anxious to test their skills against its many floors. In order for them to enter the Dungeon, however—or perhaps more accurately, in order to register as adventurers and obtain the full support and money-exchanging privileges of the Guild—they'd need to join a familia.

They'd never been entirely particular as to the familias they'd temporarily joined in the past. All changed, however, thanks to the sheer number of familias that came to scout them now. Crowds would form outside their cheap hotel. It grew so intense at times that fights began to break out, as no one was willing to give up their chance at claiming the two Amazons.

As Tione grew more and more incensed at the riotous clamoring of the scouts, Tiona stepped out in front of the crowd of adventurers, shouting as loud as she could—

"You want us? You gotta beat us!"

—and promptly instigating a free-for-all, with everyone giving it their all to best and bag the twins.

Of course, everyone there ended up losing miserably, even those who'd attempted to cheat the system and wait until the two Amazons had grown tired from previous battles. They were just too good, too used to the lifestyle of combat back in Telskyura, and not even the first-tier adventurers of Orario stood a chance.

This continued for some time, with adventurers knocking on their door for days to come, though mostly it was their defeated opponents coming back for more. To this day five years later, their deeds were still spoken of, mostly with the pure fear they had created in the citizens' hearts—"Oh, shit! An Amazon!!"

It seemed that no familia would be strong enough to best the two Amazonian twins.

In fact, it was just when Tiona and Tione were beginning to lament the ineptitude of the supposedly great "adventurers of Orario" that *Loki Familia* showed up.

Tione had hated them immediately.

From their goddess, already panting in lustful excitement at their revealing clothes, to the feeble-looking prum with that stupid smirk on his face, to the stunningly beautiful elf staring at them with one eye closed, to the dwarf observing them in amusement as he stroked his beard—she couldn't stand the way they looked at her and her sister, visibly sizing them up.

"Heard there was a pair of lively Amazons over here."

"We've killed so many of our brethren, and you still want us to join you?"

That's what she'd asked them as a test, trying to scare them.

"A mistake that came to pass only because we weren't there to watch over you. Though you don't seem all too concerned about it," the prum captain—Finn—answered, almost sympathetically.

—This bastard!

Everything about him had rubbed her the wrong way. In fact, it probably wouldn't have been possible to make a worse first impression.

The prum called to his dwarf friend, confirming the conditions of battle and that they'd have to defeat the two to induct them into the familia. To this, Tione was quick to reply.

"You're the boss, aren't you? Then stop letting others do your dirty work for you! Fight me! Or are you too scared, you cowardly prum?!"

Finn looked taken aback for a moment before that same smile from earlier returned.

"Saucy little lass, ain't she? And here I thought Bete was bad! Are all the young folk this hotheaded nowadays?"

"I can't say you were much different when we first met, Gareth."

As the dwarf and elf murmured behind him, Finn took center, consenting to a one-on-one battle with Tione. Next to her and as spirited as ever, Tiona awaited her own fight with Gareth.

Tione had thought nothing of the weak, feeble prum she saw back then. There was no way, after all, she could lose to someone so tiny. And besides, while she might have fought plenty of opponents tougher than her out on the road, none of them came close to the monsters Argana and Bache had been. This had not only made her careless but had greatly narrowed her point of view, as well.

The renown of the so-called top-tier adventurers of Orario meant nothing to her.

And she didn't know this prum's name, either.

"________________"

The battle was over in an instant. Grabbing her arm, the tiny prum sent her flying through the air.

Even as she ran at him again for a second attempt, fury coursing through her, the results were the same. She was completely, thoroughly trounced. And Tiona didn't fare much better against that Gareth character, either, having been promptly flung to the ground.

As Tione sat there on the stone cobbles, entirely dumbfounded, the prum warrior approached.

"That's it, then. You're to join our familia."

She looked up to see those calm, composed eyes gazing down at her, and for the first time in her life, she felt something grow inside her. Something she'd never felt before as her heart thudded loudly in her chest.

Tione began to change after that.

Meeting Finn had birthed a change inside her.

By beating her so thoroughly, that detestable prum had punched a hole into her heart. And in that hole, love formed.

It wasn't an uncommon thing for Amazons to get their hearts stolen by powerful men who could best even them. They all talked of one day hoping to give birth to such a man, and Tione had been no different.

If Tione had had to come up with one thing about Finn she didn't like, it was that he was too intellectual, not wild or rugged enough—but even those thoughts would betray her, as with just one spell, Finn could turn himself instantly into a crazed warrior. Hidden deep inside him was the most ruthless soldier of all.

Shit, he's the one—!!

As he fulfilled more and more of her requirements, she came to realize that he was truly her ideal man, a heroic warrior.

And the more she learned about him, the longer she stood by his side, the more of her heart he stole. He was so kind, so brilliant, so strong. It had to be fate! It simply had to be!

Thus, the young Amazonian girl who'd never known anything but fighting fell in love for the first time.

And with that, she revealed the blushing young maiden she'd long kept hidden within her.

"Captain!... What...what kind of girl do you like?"

"Hmm...I suppose someone who's upfront and honest would be enough for me. Though if I had to say more, perhaps someone graceful?"

Her new life as part of *Loki Familia* changed her. It wasn't just consciously, either, but subconsciously, too—the same way her sister influenced her. And though it may have made others laugh at her, she did everything in her power to be exactly what Finn wanted. Even going so far as to clean up her dirty mouth and unrefined mannerisms. She even let her hair grow long, all the way down to her waist, in hopes it would make her appear more scholarly, much like the high elf constantly by Finn's side, Riveria.

An all-new Amazon, with love burning even brighter than that of the greatest of lovers, burst onto the scene. But this newfound love wasn't the only thing about her that changed. She started to look forward to the opportunities each new day brought with it. She began to smile and laugh enough to annoy even her own sister.

As far as battles went, the Dungeon was enough to get her blood boiling. The very first expedition they participated in was enough of an adventure to propel both Tione and her sister to Level 4. It was within that underground labyrinth that she learned the value of teamwork—a world where not even she and her sister, let alone her by herself, could have survived—and her first bonds with other people began to form.

And then there was the mysterious girl.

Aiz Wallenstein. The "Sword Princess." A beautiful girl with golden hair and golden eyes, whose features rivaled even those of the gods. Tione hadn't been able to believe her ears when she was told this girl held the fastest record for leveling up. Aiz had reached Level 2 even before Tione and Tiona, which was saying something considering the two of them had been killing things since the day they were born. In a single year, the young blond swordswoman had reached Level 2, something Tione and her sister had taken five years to achieve. Finn and the others were already proof enough of the strangeness of Orarian adventurers—this Aiz girl was practically a heretic.

Even so, Aiz rarely interacted with the rest of the familia. If they did see her, it was usually out in the manor's courtyard, training with her sword, or disappearing into the Dungeon unnoticed despite there being no expedition to join. The only ones who'd said more than a few words to her were Loki, Riveria, and the other elites.

In the beginning, Tione didn't have any particular desire to approach the young, otherworldly girl. Tiona, however, was quite different.

"That girl Aiz. She reminds me a lot of you way back when."

"What?!"

But Tiona had only laughed, like always, at the skepticism on Tione's face.

"No way I can let that slide! I'm gonna be friends with her!"

Which was how, little by little, the three of them had formed a small group. Though Aiz had been hesitant to accept Tiona's (aggressive) advances at first, it didn't take long for the smiles to start. And soon, they'd even taken on another member—Lefiya and her undying affection for Aiz.

Tione had found someone to love.

She'd found companions.

She'd found a place to call home.

The despair, the strife, and the annoyances of her past had all been leading to this day.

It was by telling herself this that she'd been able to make a clean break from her past, or so she thought. It had seemed, for the most part, like she had.

Until now—

"It seems like before somehow...just the two of us."

The words Tiona had muttered earlier that day echoed in the back of her mind.

"..."

Tione turned her head forward, breaking free of her memories of Orario.

Not allowing herself to get lost any further in her thoughts, she made her way back to the abandoned factory.

"Let's go, Tiona."

"Got it."

Thus, the two sisters set forth, to cut their ties with fate and to free themselves from their past.

"Miss Aiz! One of the fishermen saw some Amazons down by the pier!"

Back in Meren proper, Aiz was out searching for any traces of Tione, Tiona, or *Kali Familia* when Narfi came bounding toward her.

"...Keep a lookout, then, by the pier. If you see anything, shoot something into the sky—a light bullet or magic or something."

"Roger that!"

"You're not to engage them yourself. If you see anything, wait for Riveria or me before taking any action," she instructed, somehow giving a rare complete set of commands.

Narfi and the other girls nodded in confirmation before quickly running off to relay the news to Riveria and the rest of the familia.

"I hope they're...okay..."

Aiz turned her gaze skyward for a moment, thinking of her friends, before dashing off herself down the bustling street.

"According to the guards stationed along the city walls, there's been no sign of anyone resembling Tione or her sister...nor any members of *Kali Familia*," Riveria reported.

"Which means they're still hidin' in the city...or maybe...the lake?" Loki mumbled. The two of them were in their hotel "base camp," out on the balcony with its panoramic view of the entire city.

"Additionally, it seems Aiz and the others have gotten wind of a possible lead down near the pier."

"That does it, then! I'll head to the fishing pier myself." Loki nodded as she turned away from the balcony's railing.

Riveria took a few steps toward her, backlit by the light of the hotel room.

"We'd best abandon our original mission. We've far too many matters to attend to even without our search for the violas."

"Huh? Oh yeah. Thanks to Aizuu, that's all covered. The strings're all comin' together," Loki remarked flippantly.

Riveria sharply turned her head. "What?"

But all she got from Loki was a wave of her hand and a nonchalant "Tell ya later!" as the goddess went back to staring out across the city. "Though we still don't know just who's pulling those strings..." Loki muttered, eyes narrowing against the dark expanse.

"It's quite nice watching the ants scurry about from on high, hmm?" Ishtar mused from atop her decadent chair on the highest floor of the city's most extravagant hotel. "Taking out even one of Loki's top men would bring with it significant advantages. As much as it might incur their resentment, she has no choice but to turn her attention toward those hillbilly hicks...And if that lot becomes useless, so be it—I'll simply find someone else, even if it does delay my plans."

The goddess curled her lips deliciously around the end of her kiseru pipe, gazing down upon the players of her game. Outside the window and past the haze of purple smoke rising up from between her teeth, the lake and port town lay dormant in the moonlight.

"Lady Ishtar..."

"Back already, Aisha? Is there a problem?"

"I was on my way to do as you'd instructed, but...this? What is this?"

A long-legged Amazon appeared by her side. Back from her report, she gave a tense, dubious look.

"Ah, this is your first time seeing one of these, is it?...Truthfully, I don't know much about them, either. Only that they have some kind of connection to those constantly sneaking around."

"..."

"You have something to say, Aisha?" Ishtar's amethyst eyes narrowed with a bewitching edge, and Aisha sucked in her breath. Quite suddenly, her right hand gave a twitch, almost as if she was remembering something, then she yanked her gaze away.

"...I shall return to my duties."

"See that you do."

Ishtar watched the Amazon leave the room, a hint of a smile playing on her lips as she placed the kiseru back on her tongue.

"Lenaaaaa! Did you bring my armorrrr?"

—The voice came from a large room a short ways away from Ishtar's top-floor suite.

The enormous Phryne was meeting with another Amazon who'd just returned from Orario.

"Your...your axes, too..."

"It took you so longggggg. Are you really ssssso incompetent? You evennnn left yesterday! You should have had plenty of timmmmme."

"It...it took time to get out of the city! I had to use that...that company who's getting us in and out...I'm sorry!" her younger colleague responded fearfully.

Phryne grabbed the bag of equipment out of the girl's grip with one hand. The heavy vermilion armor glinted in the light as she eased open the bag's tie.

"Hee-hee-hee...Thissssss time...this time I will crush you, Sword Princessssss," she hissed. The smile on her face was a mixture of exhilaration and unbridled rage. She threw a glance toward the side of the room. "Prepare yourselfffff, Haruhime!"

"...Yes, ma'am."

The girl responded faintly from beneath her white veil.

Arms across her chest and eyes glued to the floor, she followed solemnly behind the giant woman.

"Come on out, my little Tione..."

Argana's voice cut through the darkness. Her eyes glittered with a kind of reptilian ferocity, bound hair swaying to and fro.

Behind her, the rest of her fellow Amazons stood biding their time in the lake's breeze.

"Meditating, Bache? That's rare for you," Kali called out from her place on the floor.

"..."

Away from where Argana stood impatiently, Kali and Bache were in a large stone cavern, larger than the cave in which Lefiya was currently being held captive.

"You can't wait to fight her, can you?"

"..."

"Heh, I can see it on your face."

Bache opened her eyes wordlessly, her mouth still hidden by her ever-present neckerchief. In those eyes burned a desire for battle, the same as the one in her sister's.

"I look forward to it, too...Let the feast begin." Kali's lips parted in demented laughter. Her voice echoed off the cave walls before melting into the shadows.

Unknowing of the matters at hand, the lake waters trembled silently, cresting against the cliff face.

The long night was about to begin.

CHAPTER 5
A Duo of Sun and Moon

Гэта казка іншага сям'і.

Duet ў месяцы і сонца

Meren's port lay flush with the elliptical curve around the brackish expanse of Lolog Lake. To the east of the port rose its trade and fishing piers, easily its busiest quarters, and to the west, its massive wharf and shipyard, where the giant galleons sailed in and laid anchor.

On the occasions when the wharf wasn't full, it opened its docks to overflow passenger ships from the trade pier. Even now, enough ships to form a fleet were tethered to its moors. In the shipyard, which jutted into dry land, a number of ships in either mid-repair or mid-construction lay in wait.

Now that high-seas monster attacks were all too common, it had become common these days for shipwrights to coat ships, especially the bottom, in various types of sturdy ingots, though the most expensive (and most effective) ingots like mythril were reserved for boats of the wealthy and other large-scale vessels.

Minerals and ores from the Dungeon like the resilient noh steel sold especially well here. And because the exchange and sale of Dungeon drop items were handled by commercial familias and merchants as well, this made for some rather aggressive negotiations when it came to the minerals they bought up from adventurers.

Currently, the shipyard was devoid of shipwrights of any kind under the veil of night. The magic-stone lanterns had all been snuffed, and the warped outlines of wooden ships floated against the night sky. An eerie quiet, unsuitable for the "gateway to Orario" that Meren was, had settled over the perimeter.

It was in this shipyard that they found Argana.

"I've been waiting for you," she greeted them in the tongue of their country. Behind her, a great many other Amazons awaited.

"What happened to all the people here, huh?" Tione responded in kind. Argana's smile never faltered. "I thought they typically worked late into the night."

"They...decided to turn in early."

Tione scowled.

"Where's Lefiya?" Tiona asked next to her.

"She's with Kali and Bache. Not here."

Compared to her crude Koine, Argana's Amazonian language was smooth and fluent, with not a single stutter. She raised her arm, pointing off in a direction away from the city proper.

"You're to continue on, Tiona. The way will become clear. Bache is waiting for you."

The two sisters glanced at each other.

Then, a nod.

They had no choice but to obey their opponent's demand and split up, effectively negating any chance they might have had to work together.

"Don't lose, Tiona," Tione whispered behind her just as the moon peeked out from a gap in the clouds, bathing her in its light. Her eyes never left Argana.

"...I won't. You don't, either," Tiona replied briefly before running out ahead. Parting from her sister, she took off in the direction Argana had indicated.

"You'll follow me, Tione."

"..."

Remaining vigilant, Tione made her way toward the other Amazon.

They boarded a large galleon currently docked at the wharf, bodies melding into the darkness.

"We're going to fight here? Don't you think this is a little conspicuous?" Tione remarked, brows furrowed, but Argana simply laughed. The rest of the Amazons quickly disappeared inside the ship.

"Seeing us won't do them any good if they can't follow us."

Almost as if on cue, the ship began to move.

As Tione gave a jump, large oars plunged out of the ship's hold, landing in the water below, and soon they were sailing, farther and farther away from the wharf.

"It's a bit of an impromptu battlefield, so I'm afraid it won't give us quite as much space as back home."

The ship sliced through the surface of the lake as the oars of the powerful Amazons belowdeck propelled it forward.

"They've put some thought into this, huh…?" Tione murmured under her breath as the ship shuddered beneath her feet. *No way anyone's getting between us this far out at sea…It won't be over till one of us kicks the bucket.*

Considering the ship's "engine" was an entire host of Telskyuran warriors (each of whom was as powerful as a top-tier adventurer), even if another oar-driven ship set off from the coast now, they'd never be able to match their speed.

It was an unreachable arena, a ring atop the sea.

The perfect location to conduct the rite Argana so desired.

And it had Kali's name written all over it.

"—Found them."

At the same time as Tione was boarding the ship, Aiz was focusing on a certain glint of light far off in the distance. She rose to her feet from her hiding place atop a building near the pier, alerting the girl behind her.

"Narfi, go get the others," Aiz ordered.

"Roger!" Narfi responded, but Aiz was already gone. Darting out ahead of the group, she raced her way toward the shipyard.

Tione…!

She could already surmise *Kali Familia*'s plan the moment she saw Tione board the ship together with the group of Amazons. She had to catch up with them before that ship crossed over the ravine in the lake and disappeared into the open sea.

Her legs moved even faster, turning her into a golden bullet as she sped forward.

Only then—

—Guuuuuwwwwoooooooooooooooooaaaaaaaaaaaaaaaggghhhh!!

"?!"

A thunderous roar shook the very air around her.

"Violas?!"

"At a time like this?!"

Her peers shouted out in surprise from atop the roof behind her.

There were seven of them, emerging with an explosive boom from the cargo area where multiple ships had unloaded their freight. Vibrantly colored petals parted to reveal spine-chilling jaws, sending tremors all throughout the peaceful port town.

"Wh-whhhhuuuuaaaaaaaaaaagh?!"

They'd appeared in the middle of the port, close to the trade pier, and upon seeing the monstrously large flowers reaching for the sky, the few sailors who remained in the vicinity let out screams of terror and ran for their lives.

Why now? It couldn't possibly *be a coincidence, could it—?*

But Aiz didn't have time to process the multitude of questions currently racing through her head. She had to act. And she had to act now.

Ahead of her, she could see Tione's ship putting more and more distance between them.

Behind her, the violas were already going to town on the passenger ships currently moored at the dock, tentacles flying.

Screams were now rippling all throughout the trade pier, and though it pained her, Aiz shouted instructions behind her.

"Gngh—take care of them first!!" she screamed, sliding to a halt before spinning around.

Though Tione's ship was now disappearing behind her, she had a duty to protect the lives of the town's civilians.

"Violas?!"

Tione looked out from her rapidly accelerating ship to see Aiz and the rest of her companions facing off against the swarm of man-eating flowers. As she stood there, slack-jawed, Argana's voice rose to meet her.

"Those are nothing but a diversion. Nothing more, nothing less. Pay them no heed."

"...Then...then you're involved with those monsters after all?!"

"I'm afraid I have no idea what you're talking about. We here knew nothing of the method of diversion prior to now," the other Amazon responded noncombatively, her gaze fierce.

Tione felt her rage begin to grow as the ship passed over the lake ravine and out into the open sea. Meren got smaller and smaller on the horizon, together with its accompanying cliffs.

"But enough about that. Let's begin." Argana smiled with a sort of pure, unadulterated joy now that the time had come.

Tione turned around, her mouth still closed as she faced off against her opponent for the rite.

"..."

The golden-haired, golden-eyed swordswoman struck out against the giant man-eating flowers. A ship was wrenched in two by those flying tentacles and flipped over on its side; the sailors fled for their lives; the fishermen pointed at the spectacle in frozen fear; shrill screams began to echo from every corner of the city.

He watched all of this as he walked against the flow of the fleeing crowd of demi-humans and away from the scene.

"——Riveria."

Loki took note of the man in question.

The fishing pier was enveloped in a catastrophic cacophony as crowds of people came racing one after another out of the trade pier, joining the fishermen as they raced toward the safety of the city up on its higher ground.

Riveria and her small group were standing by on the fishing pier, ensuring Aiz and the others could keep the monsters firmly contained within the net of the pier. She'd just started to make her way over to help them fight when Loki stopped her.

"Now of all times! What is it, Loki?" Riveria and her comrades turned toward the goddess with a start.

"I'm peacin' out. Gotta go chase down a culprit...the one who set those violas loose in the lake, that is. Detective Loki has arrived!" Though her words were jocular, her eyes held a very real sense of sincerity.

"Then we're to come, too? But what of those monsters?"

"Aizuu and the rest of 'em can handle those critters. 'Sides, all of us groupin' together is exactly what the enemy wants," Loki explained.

The timing was simply too perfect for them to be anything other than a diversion, and Loki knew it. "You noticed it, too, yeah?" she continued, throwing a glance at the silent Riveria. "Not even our opponent knows what's goin' on anymore…Maybe they'll turn tail and run."

"Then you're saying now's our chance?"

"That I am. It's time to present them with some evidence they can't talk their way out of." Loki's eyes turned toward where the man she'd been watching previously had vanished.

Though most of the group had no idea what Loki was talking about, Riveria remembered their conversation from earlier and the "threads" Loki had been hoping to follow.

"…You're right that Aiz and the others should have no trouble taking care of the situation on their own. But what of Tione and Tiona?" she asked after a moment of silence. The entire reason why Riveria had chosen to take out the violas immediately rather than wait—even despite the obvious trap—was so that either Aiz or she could continue to chase after Tione and her sister.

Loki could see the high elf was concerned, perhaps thinking that Loki was simply hanging the two sisters out to dry. She replied optimistically all the same.

"I've got faith in my kids! Everything'll be fiiiiiiine."

Riveria didn't have a response to that.

Instead, she simply sighed.

"'Sides! S'not like you can just go burning things up with your magic in the middle of town, right? Even you said so earlier! Leave the city destruction to Aiz and the others."

"…I suppose there's nothing for it, then. Understood."

"Great. Then I'm leavin' you in charge of that."

"Leave it to me. Alicia!"

"Y-yes, m'lady?…What is it?"

Riveria quickly leaned forward to whisper in the young elf's long, slender ear.

Alicia's eyes widened in surprise, and then she nodded.

As the two mages ran off ahead, Loki turned toward the rest of the group. "Rakuta! Elfie! Come with me, if you would? I know you just recovered, but yer gonna be my good luck charms. Leene, you and the other healers'll stay here to look after anyone who gets hurt."

"U-understood!"

Then Loki sped off into the night, followed by a very flustered hume bunny and elf.

"We're into the endgame now, girls!"

Tiona continued straight along the path Argana had indicated.

She walked out through the back of the shipyard, up and over a pile of ship parts in the far corner, then into an outcropping of wild trees near the lake's cliffs.

The way will become clear. That's what Argana had told her. Just as she was beginning to wonder what on earth the other Amazon had been talking about, a sudden certain odor made her nostrils twitch.

"This smell…"

She knew this smell.

Sniff, sniff. Her nose twitched like a dog's as she made her way among the trees, when all of a sudden it came to her.

Iron. It was iron. Iron mixed with rust.

It was a smell she was all too familiar with, her daily bouquet back in her stone room in Telskyura.

It was the smell of home.

She understood what Argana had meant now. No doubt, they'd left her a trail of blood from wounds cut with rusted blades. Following the unforgettable smell through the woods, she began to run.

"Here…?"

She burst out of the trees, coming face-to-face with a small inlet, remarkably similar to the one she and the rest of the familia had played in upon their arrival in Meren.

It was a little smaller, making it even less noticeable than their previous oasis, and deeper, too, more like a miniature ravine. The biggest difference, though, was its lack of a beach. Rather than facing the lake, this inlet took on the brunt of the sea, and the salty waters cut away at its walls of rock.

"A sea cave…?"

She spotted a small opening in the rock, carved away by the waves and large enough for a gathering of people to pass through. Descending down the cliff, she made her way over to it and found that it didn't stop there, instead traveling deep into the earth. The black rock formed a cavernous tunnel of sorts, and after standing there studying it for a moment, Tiona made her way inside.

The salty water barely came up to her knees, perhaps a result of its proximity to the lake, and after walking a short while, she found it disappeared completely, as the higher ground held the water back. Soon, the tunnel itself began to split off into all directions, almost like an ant colony, and her bare feet slapped against the darkened rock as she continued along.

"Geez, it's like the Dungeon down here."

There was no way anyone was going to be able to find them. Even if one were to stumble across the cave, sniffing out anyone hidden within its passageways would be near impossible. It was no wonder Kali and the others had chosen this cave to conceal themselves, and now Lefiya was down here, too.

Most of it formed naturally, but…human hands certainly helped it along, she thought as she eyed the magic-stone lanterns hanging from the ceiling. The light was mixing with the faint moonlight peeking in through tiny cracks up above. The smell of blood she'd been following continued down one of the tunnels, and Tiona hastened her step, occasionally descending farther into the long, vast cavern.

Finally.

"So you made it."

"!"

She found herself in a large open grotto.

High above her head, the ceiling formed a wide cylindrical shape. The jet-black stone of the rest of the tunnel continued into the expanse, making the cave feel almost like the inside of a giant stone coffin.

Atop the piles of rock to her either side stood her former colleagues, the warriors of Telskyura, and sitting cross-legged on the highest of the peaks was the source of the welcoming call—Kali herself.

In front of her, though, was the one who mattered the most.

The sandy-haired Amazon, her face half-hidden by her black neckerchief, stood there in silence, waiting for her.

"Bache..."

"..."

Bache didn't respond, instead merely directing her gaze toward Tiona. Her eyes glinted beneath the strands of her sandy bangs.

"...Where's Lefiya, Kali?"

"We've got her somewhere else. Don't worry, though. We'll let her go...once the rite's been finished," she explained, her bloodred eyes narrowing in a look not dissimilar to a child who'd just recovered her long-lost treasure. "I must admit, I never thought this day would come. The opportunity to watch pupil challenge teacher, to see just how far they've each developed." Her words crackled with an earnest zeal.

She glanced toward Tiona's chest, eyes narrowing in disappointment.

"Though some parts haven't developed as much as I would've liked..."

"Can we cut it with the comments on my figure already?!" Tiona shouted back with an angry wave of her hands.

As an aside, while Argana's and Tione's bust sizes were approximately the same, Bache's surpassed both of them. Between the two younger sisters, Bache had beaten Tiona by a landslide.

"—Prepare yourself, Tiona," Bache spoke up, uttering her first words since the now red-faced Tiona had entered the room. Her voice was cheerless, a signal that the pleasantries were finished. "This is a fight to the death," she continued matter-of-factly as she flung out her right arm to settle into a battle-ready position.

"...We really have to?"

"A little too late for that now, isn't it, Tiona?" Kali said from above.

"Yeah, but...I don't wanna kill Bache..." Tiona responded without looking, her eyes focused directly on the woman in front of her. It was much the same as when she'd expressed her unwillingness to kill Tione all those years ago.

"I should never have read those books to you..." Bache stated, her tone callous. She didn't even move.

Tiona scowled, but even as she did, she couldn't help but notice something. Bache was cold, much more so than she'd been ten years prior. In fact, it almost seemed like she was now so sharp that the icy aura of antipathy around her was tangible.

She was now more powerful and heartless than Tiona could have ever imagined.

So close to becoming a "true warrior" of Telskyura.

"You...killed Elnea, didn't you?"

"I did. Just as Argana killed Belnas...It's what allowed us to reach Level Six."

Elnea and Belnas were the other two candidates in the running for familia captain. The last time Tiona had seen them, they'd been Level 5s, powerful enough to make Tiona shudder in fear and awe. Killing Elnea had been Bache's final test—the rite that had propelled her to Level 6.

Just like Argana.

Both of them had become monsters manufactured by Telskyura, the sole survivors in the barrelful of rats, cannibalizing the others to make their way to the top.

"I'll give you no choice but to fight."

If Argana was the snake...

...then right now, the warrior with bloodlust permeating her eyes was...

"*—Die Asura.*"

The ultra-short chant from Bache's lips cut off her thoughts.

It was similar to Aiz's spell. Bache's only magic.

"*Velgas.*"

Bache thrust out her right hand, a blackish purple film of light surrounding it.

Then it solidified, growing rich and viscous enough to completely hide the initial radiant image summoned by the chant; it wriggled and squirmed to form a raging spiral.

This was Velgas. An enchantment Bache cast upon her right hand.

Element: poison.

An undefendable, venomous fang she'd already used to incapacitate so many of her brethren in the rites.

Yes, if Argana was the snake, then Bache was the venomous insect.

Even her magic itself had been appropriately dubbed the "Poison Queen."

"——————————————!!"

As though waiting for just this moment, the crowd of Amazons surrounding them stamped their feet down in unison. Amid the tremors and shouts, the excitement and roars, a volatile sense of passion and fervor erupted throughout the stone coffin, bringing the rites of Telskyura to life before their eyes.

"...!!"

The poison in Bache's magic guaranteed a swift kill.

If Tiona didn't fight back, she'd be dead before dessert. She had no choice but to ready her own fists as her former teacher—and another younger sister—aimed for her life.

Standing there in the middle of their grotto battlefield—no, arena—their gazes met.

"Heh. Perfect. Let's begin."

Kali smiled as she looked down at them—then the two Amazons struck.

"Nowwww, Haruhime."

Heavy clouds shielded the moon up above. Down below, the woman in question responded with a resigned "Yes, ma'am."

"—*Grow.*"

She began the spell, chanting softly.

"That power and that vessel. Breadth of wealth and breadth of wishes."

Though her voice was delicate as it wove the ephemeral tune, the magic it summoned was strong.

"Until the bell tolls, bring forth glory and illusion."

As the sky shook with a thunderous roar, the shouts of adventurers shrill in the air, not a single soul noticed the hum of her chant.

"—Grow."

The heavenly, commanding sound of her voice drew forth a golden light. It formed a mist, a golden cloud of luminous particles, rising from the ground.

The veil hiding her face fluttered.

"Confine divine offerings within this body. This golden light bestowed from above."

She hated this chant.

Even if it ended up hurting someone, she had no way to save them.

"Into the hammer and into the ground, may it bestow good fortune upon you."

No, she couldn't save anyone, this puerile girl who refused to stand up against the laws that bound her. And to hold such a hope was nothing short of shameful.

But perhaps, this light by itself would one day become a blessing.

Though someone as stupid as she couldn't be saved, perhaps it could be the sliver of hope that could save someone else.

If that moment ever came, she would bestow everything upon that person, her body, her heart, and this light.

Her jade-green eyes now uncovered, she looked away, then released her light.

"—Grow."

The light became strength.

"Guuuuuuuuuuwwwwwooooooooooooooaaaaaaaarrrrrggghhh!!"

The deafening roar ended in a cry of agony as it pierced the very heavens.

With one arcing swing of her sword, Aiz severed the head of the final viola.

"That's all of them!"

"Are there any casualties?"

"At the moment, no...The citizens have all been evacuated!"

The voices of her fellow familia members filled the air of the loading dock, Narfi at their center.

Though for many this had been their first encounter with the giant man-eating flowers, they'd come out of the battle relatively unscathed thanks to the intel Aiz and the others had already gathered on the beasts. They were, after all, members of the famed *Loki Familia*, which meant the whole lot of them were prodigies, even at Levels 2 and 3.

The entire affair was over barely five minutes after the monsters had first appeared.

The lights have all gone out...Could it be because of the battle?

Aiz thought, having taken out four of the seven flowers herself. A sense of unease passed through her as she eyed the mostly snuffed magic-stone lanterns decorating the trade pier. It was almost as if someone, or perhaps the violas themselves, had purposefully smashed them in the midst of all the chaos.

"...!"

She didn't have time to think about it long, though.

Tiona's and Tione's faces sprang to her mind, and she immediately dashed off and into the night.

—I'm afraidddddd I can't let you do that.

All of a sudden, she could have sworn she heard the croaking laughter of a frog.

Then.

"That was a wonderful show you all put on!"

"?!"

As the frigid voice gave a hiss, an entire swarm of shadows came flying out of the sky.

"What—?!"

"*Kali Familia*?!"

The rest of *Loki Familia* was just as surprised, letting out shouts as the ambuscade of mysterious foes surrounded them, brandishing their weapons. The girls flung back a barrage of weapons of their own, from atop the storehouse and among the shadows of strewn cargo, sending them screaming toward their assailants the second they hit the ground, but every one of them missed.

There were more than twenty enemies against only ten of them, Aiz included.

And they had them completely surrounded.

"What do we do?!"

The faces of their enemies were hidden beneath turbans, but the exposed skin visible from their necks down was noticeably tanned and their armor was minimal, nothing but the bare essentials in order to maximize their movement. They were Amazons, no doubt about it.

Though Aiz had escaped the initial attack, she turned back to them now, fully prepared to aid Narfi and the other second-tier-and-under adventurers in their fight against the twenty-plus masked assailants, until—

"You'll be facinggggggg me."

"———"

All of a sudden, Aiz found herself veiled in an enormous shadow from behind.

"Ngah—!!"

"Gngh!!"

The vertical strike came at her with incredible force. It was only thanks to her godlike reflexes that she was able to jump out of the way.

There was a monstrous crack as the paved surface of the road underfoot exploded, sending splinters of wood, smoke, and debris flying up into the air. Aiz spun around, putting space between her and her new opponent as she turned to look at them head-on.

She readied her sword, senses keen…then saw a quivering silhouette emerge from the cloud of dust.

"…!"

"Hee-hee-hee, you are gooddddddd. You are!"

A flickering metallic glint reflected in her golden eyes, opened wide in shock.

It was a full-body suit of armor, easily more than two meders tall and a nauseating crimson color.

Its wielder currently flaunted a giant ax in both their massive hands. There wasn't even a trace of visible bare skin. Everything was completely covered by the glimmering armor, and from the fierce twinkle of the ingots within, it was as sturdy as an ox. It had to have been top-tier. And yet at the same time, there was something about it that was even more astounding, on multiple levels. The make was simply perfect, fit to its wielder's body like a glove, almost as though it had been custom-made…

An image flashed in the back of her mind, of the earthenware figurines she'd seen in that antique dealer's shop while hunting around for a sword. The suit in front of her now looked almost the same, though a bit fatter around the middle.

Almost like that monster…No, that voice…

Shaking away the somewhat rude thoughts, she instead focused on the voice. As its timbre tickled the threads of her memory, she felt a name rise naturally to her lips.

"Phryne Jamil…?"

The armed figure twisted in a strange show of corpulent torment, almost as though sighing.

"Was it thattttttttt obvious? Even through the armorrrrrrr?…It truly is a crimmmmmme to be beautiful."

Aiz's brow drew tight at the confirmation.

Phryne Jamil, otherwise known as Androctonus, the Man Slayer, was the captain of *Ishtar Familia*.

—Which meant it wasn't *Kali Familia* attacking them but…*Ishtar Familia*?

Then the other assailants, too—were they Berbera? Aiz found herself at a complete loss, filled with both disbelief and a rising sense of urgency. There was no chance she'd be able to aid Tiona and Tione with one of Orario's largest familias standing in her way.

Meanwhile, Phryne, unaware of Aiz's inner turmoil, popped open the visor on her helm with a sharp *clang*, revealing her frog-like features.

"Nnnnnno bother. If I simply kill you nowwwwww, no one will be the wiiiiiiser!"

Loki Familia's Sword Princess, Aiz Wallenstein, and *Ishtar Familia*'s Androctonus, Phryne Jamil, shared a long history. Though it was perhaps one-sided, as Aiz, for the life of her, could not figure out why the atrocious frog of a woman had it out for her.

Three times now, they'd crossed swords.

In their first duel, Aiz had been a Level-2 rookie who'd left Phryne with nothing but malicious resentment.

Their second duel had come two years later, a chance encounter deep within the halls of the Dungeon.

And their third duel had taken place right after Aiz had leveled up to Level 5.

The first time, Phryne had had Aiz right where she wanted her when Riveria and the others had intervened, leaving the actual outcome up in the air. The second time had been a draw. And the third time had been a sound victory on Aiz's part.

"What reason could you have to attack us? And now?"

"Do I need a reaaason to beat you until that mouth of yourssssss no longer works?" Phryne shot back.

It was the same basic reasoning she gave every time they fought—pure, unadulterated hatred. Even the first time, Phryne had only wanted to give the hotshot record breaker a proper "baptism." Of course, she had no way of knowing that the hotshot record breaker would go on to rise in power at an almost phenomenal rate, nor that she'd quickly surpass Phryne in terms of status, fame, and strength.

Stronger than you. More beautiful than you.

Though Phryne would never admit it, her valuation of others was different. And there were just some things that were unforgivable. With every fiber of her being, she hated this beautiful young girl who'd zoomed up the ranks to first-tier in the blink of an eye. The same way that Ishtar despised Freya, in fact.

Phryne's bloodshot eyes stared out from within the confines of her open visor.

Even though she wasn't privy to Phryne's thoughts, Aiz knew this fight was inevitable, both from the wrath and bloodlust practically radiating from the other woman, as well as from her experience with their past encounters.

—Are those...particles of light?

She thought with a start as something caught her attention.

And indeed, tiny light particles seemed to be drifting up from Phryne's face—the parts exposed to the open air, anyway.

"Today will be the day I finnnnnnnally crush you, Sword Princessssssssss!!"

Her booming voice brought her visor slamming back down, and with it, Aiz's view of the light particles was cut off.

A mere second later, Phryne was charging, giant axes held high.

"____________"

The attack was strong.

A true threat, faster and more powerful than Aiz could have possibly expected.

"Gngh?!"

The spot she'd been occupying only a moment ago went up in a catastrophic wreath of debris, just like before.

Though she was able to dodge the ax in Phryne's right hand with a hairbreadth to spare, the ax in her left hand came down on her before she had a chance to react.

She brought up her sword, and the incoming attack slammed into it with such force that it sent a rippling tremor through her body.

—She's strong!!

So strong she could barely believe her eyes.

Her power, her speed—everything was on par with Aiz's own, despite the Amazon being an entire level lower than her.

"Hee-hee-hee! What'sssss wrong, Sword Princessssssss?"

"...Ngh?!"

She moved her sword in desperation, hurtling toward the twin ax attacks coming at her from all sides.

The violent duel was enough to make the rest of Aiz's familia and the other Amazons, currently observing from off to the side, gulp in fear. Sparks flew as the three blades clashed against one another again and again, echoing all throughout the trade pier.

Could she have leveled up? Maybe she's a Level 6 now, too...?!

Her strength, speed, perception—everything was far too high to belong to a Level 5.

Perhaps they hadn't informed the Guild of her level-up? Or perhaps the official report was never updated? She could think of many possible circumstances that would have led to word of her achievement never making the news. Could she truly have reached Level 6?

But if so, what was this strange feeling Aiz couldn't quite shake?

Almost as though her opponent were doused in a heavenly sort of nectar—?

"Miss Aiz!!"

The shrill voices of her companions shook her from her reverie, returning her to the duel at hand. Even as she focused on her own fight against two Amazons at the same time, Narfi, as well as the rest of the girls, couldn't help but shout in response to Aiz's peril.

"Sssssssso irritating! Stop with the screaminggggg!" Phryne shouted before chucking one of her axes in Narfi's direction.

She seemed completely unconcerned at potentially hitting her own comrades currently surrounding the girl, putting enough force behind the ironhanded throw to smash all of them into dust.

Narfi and the Amazons both froze at the sight of the ax hurtling toward them.

"?!"

And in that second, Aiz ran, taking advantage of the space she'd put between her and Phryne and racing toward the direction of the flying ax.

She flung herself in the path of the spinning cutter, stopping it with her sword.

"Hee-hee-hee, what a fool!" Phryne laughed with scorn. She immediately dashed forward, eliminating the distance between Aiz and her. With one mighty swoop, she brought her remaining ax down on Aiz, who was still shaking from the tremendous force the flying cutter had applied to her body.

"Gnnngahh!"

Aiz's sword caught the ax just in time with a direct block to her front. The impact sent her to her knees with enough force to split the ground below.

Phryne's face broke into a smile, eyeing the swordswoman like a butterfly caught in a net. "Nowwwww, Sharay! Do it nowwwwww!!" she screamed.

The command's intended recipient was currently waiting outside the scene of the battle.

Hiding herself atop one of the nearby buildings, she directed her staff toward Aiz and the others in perfect sync with Phryne's shout, her lips forming the words of a chant.

"————————————?!"

All of a sudden, a wave of high-pitched, high-frequency sound washed over them.

It felt like it was boring into her chest. Unable to take it any longer, Aiz flung away Phryne's ax before tumbling out of range of the spell.

"What was…that…?"

Though her ears continued to ring, there was no real damage done to her body, and she didn't seem to be suffering from any sort of status effect, either.

Back at the scene of the attack, Phryne seemed to have taken the full brunt of the hit, but from what she could tell, nothing about the armor-clad woman had changed. Instead, she was now simply gazing in her direction, almost curiously.

Aiz felt a feeling of dread rush through her. Her instincts as a swordswoman were tingling.

—She couldn't have…?!

Hoping to suppress the foreboding thought before it could become reality, she parted her lips.

"*...Awaken, Tempest.*"

Only the wind enchantment that should have formed around her at those words failed to respond. Her Airiel was gone.

"...?!"

"Hee-hee-hee-hee, it worked, it woooorked!!" Phryne let out her loudest belt of laughter yet.

The frog woman's glee said everything, and Aiz realized all too well what had just happened.

"A curse...!"

"Biiiingo!"

Much like its name implied, a "curse" was a type of jinx, different from other "pure" magic spells. It debilitated a target via a variety of witchcraft-like effects that magic couldn't produce, in exchange for a penalty placed on the caster. Status effects were ineffective against it, and only by a very limited number of methods could it be fended off or lifted.

No doubt, the curse she was afflicted with now was a silencing curse—capable of rendering its target incapable of magic.

And that frog's never been able to use magic in the first place...!

Aiz realized this with a start, which was why the curse had had no effect on her. Had this been her plan all along?

Saving her Airiel for later had proved to be her own undoing.

Her trump card had been effectively nullified.

"I readddddddied these anti-statuses and curses for my fight with Ottarrrrr, but...hee-hee...you'rrrrrrre proving to be a fine guinea pigggg!" Phryne hissed as she studied Aiz carefully, sliding her tongue across her lips within her mighty helm. "Though I wassssss hoping to try it out on that Nine Hell, toooooooo. Seemssssss she was able to sniff me out!"

"...!"

"An elffffffff without magic? You might as wellllllllll replace her with a steaming pile of dog shit!"

"*You monster!!*" Aiz shouted, or at least she would have, had Phryne's ax not come tumbling down out of the sky toward her.

She quickly brought her sword up to block it, and the high-pitched screech of the resulting impact echoed all throughout the pier.

"Muchhhhhhhhh like you now, hmmmmmm? You're no match for me nooooooow!!"

"Gngh…!!"

The only way Aiz could think of to break the curse was to take out its caster, but the one in question had already flown the coop. She had no choice—she'd have to continue like this.

Waiting it out wouldn't do any good, either, considering she had to get to Tiona and Tione as quickly as possible.

Aiz's eyes flashed. She'd have to face this monster of a woman, whose strength was on par with any Level 6, with nothing but her sword.

—It's almost like the fairy tale.

The young animal woman hidden among the shadows atop the storehouse couldn't help but think to herself as she watched the Sword Princess fight gallantly.

"…"

An assortment of feelings reflected in her jade-colored eyes as she watched the swordswoman surrounded by all those Amazon envoys, the long-legged one included.

Beneath the veil disguising her features, her golden locks, the same brilliant gold as Aiz's own, trembled with abashment.

Tione and Argana's ship had already made its way well out to sea.

This far away from the coast, nothing but the gleam of the cliff-top lighthouse could reach them.

And atop that boat, a similar scene to the one deep within the bowels of Tiona's sea cave was currently taking place, Amazons whooping in virulent passion as the sounds of fist on skin reverberated throughout the deck.

"Gnnngh!"

Tione aimed a kick for Argana's head, but the other woman blocked it with her arm before jumping out of reach.

Argana cocked her head to the side curiously. "You're fighting much better than yesterday…Why is that, Tione?"

And it was true—Tione's strikes were hitting with much greater precision than they had the day prior. The increased speed and accuracy enabled her to actually fight on par with her opponent.

"You sure it's not just you gettin' soft?" Tione snapped back, though not before she cursed internally.

Tione and Tiona had leveled up only a mere day before they came to Meren. Neither one of them had been able to fully come to terms with their new boosted abilities. There was still a bit of a gap between their bodies and minds, which, though slight, could prove fatal in a match against another top-tier adventurer.

Her fight with Tiona back in the abandoned warehouse had been to rectify exactly this. Just as Aiz had gone up against that giant swarm of monsters immediately after her own level-up, Tione, too, had "adjusted" herself—the sister vs. sister practice duel let her put her new abilities into practice.

She'd been able to rein in the stampeding horse that was her own body. She wasn't going to be defeated this time. And she assumed it would be the same for Tiona, now able to hold her own against Bache.

Still…she's got the advantage when it comes to sheer power…

Argana and Bache, too, might have leveled up only a short while ago, but it was still a longer period of time than Tione and Tiona had. Ability-wise, at least, they'd always be ahead. She also hadn't been able to sense any openings in the other woman's moves, at least nothing like some of the ones she'd seen in Finn and the others.

Which meant everything was going to come down to technique and strategy. Victory would fall to the one who craved it the most.

"Hmm, yes. Perhaps that is it. I've grown soft." Argana laughed—a remarkable feat considering she was currently locked in a duel to the death. She seemed to be thoroughly enjoying herself. "Then I suppose I'll have to up my game."

"…!!"

Brimming with an almost tangible thirst for blood, Argana sprinted forward. Tione rose to meet her, kicking her leg up to block the incoming attack. Argana's fists flew at her, from the left, from the right, like deadly sickles slicing through the air.

Her nails were long, like a monster's claws, and her attacks were all the more snakelike when she didn't have her hands curled into their ironlike fists. Tione quickly crouched in order to evade the relentless blows as the close-range duel of fist on fist continued.

"Ha-ha-ha-ha-ha-ha! Finally, you're back to the old you!"

"Just shut up and fight already!"

It wouldn't do Tione any good to remain on the defensive in a fight against someone like Argana, who had killed so many of her own kin. There was no one in the world who'd be able to endure this woman's monstrous attacks for long. At some point, she herself would need to attack.

The two Amazons whaled on each other, spurred on by burgeoning waves of fury and rage. They were like crazed bulls in an arena; each strike soliciting a return barrage; one hit turned into two. It was almost as if the battles they'd waged so long ago in that stone training room were returning to life before their eyes, only fiercer, more savage.

"Huuuuuuuuuwwwwwwwwwoooooooooooaaaaaaarrrrrgggghh!!"

Their attacks were as sharp as razor blades, their techniques swift and sure enough to elicit gasps of astonishment. And as the other Amazons watched this duel of the fates unfold, they let out bellowing roars. The sheer power erupting from their lungs was enough to change the minds of any monsters thinking of approaching the ship.

The light of the magic-stone lanterns on deck trembled.

"Gnngh?!"

Argana's claws grazed Tione's cheek, drawing blood. The Amazon curled her long tongue upward to lick at the drops that had splattered on her own cheek.

"You...you snake!!" Tione exploded, all the thoughts of her youth, those memories of anger and pain rushing up through her. Not even realizing she'd activated her Berserker skill, she let her fist fly with the weight of every one of those poignant memories behind it.

"Your blood is as delicious as I always thought it would be..."

"You're sick!!"

"I've wanted to drink it for so long...so long, Tione. Down to the very...last...drop," she murmured, dodging Tione's attack as her eyes lit up with the fiery passion of a woman in love.

Tione would have backed away in disgust if she could. Argana's eyes were more reptilian than ever. Her ex-teacher's claws bit into her again, her arms this time, and she was quick to lap up the red blood.

"—Ngh."

A strange feeling of discomfort washed over her.

It started out slight but grew and grew, and to Tione's horror, she saw the wounds on her arm grow, and more and more blood flowed from the split skin to sate her opponent's snakelike tongue.

She sent an enraged fist flying in Argana's direction, but the other Amazon was already long gone.

More and more of her attacks were missing.

—Wait a minute.

Just as Tione's power was growing with the help of her Berserker skill, so, too, was her opponent's—.

"You're too slow, Tione."

"____________"

Argana nimbly sidestepped her punch, disappearing from her field of vision.

Before suddenly wrapping herself around her back, limbs sliding around her like a snake curling around its prey. There was a hiss in her ear, then Argana's incisors sank into Tione's neck.

"——Grrrrrrraaaaaaahhhhhh?!"

Her nerves burned with a fiery pain. She could actually feel her skin and flesh tearing and hear her blood being sucked out.

Then came Argana's tongue, groping inside her like some kind of parasitic centipede, triggering a violent revulsion that sent goose bumps down her whole body.

She tumbled to the floor of the deck as Argana quickly rose to her feet, on the defensive once again.

"You…you hag…!" Tione hissed as she staggered back to her feet, trying to suppress the blood pouring freely from the fresh holes in her neck.

Argana merely narrowed her eyes, tongue sliding over and savoring her bloodstained lips.

It was a sight Tione had seen far too many times back in Telskyura—the aberrant warrior mercilessly draining the blood of her opponents as they screamed in vain.

Body trembling in pain and anger, Tione reaffirmed her resolve.

"That's how you get your power, isn't it…? From the blood of your opponents…?!"

Argana sneered.

Tione was right on the money.

"You've noticed, have you?"

"Is it the same magic as Bache's…?!"

"Mine is a curse," the other Amazon responded, caressing her exposed skin. "It's known as Kalima. As you've already guessed, it allows me to strengthen my abilities through the blood of others blessed with the power of the Falna."

"…?!"

"Kali refers to it as 'Blood Drain.' Only she and Bache know about it…and considering I never used it during your training, it's no surprise you never noticed it, either."

Kalima. Blood Drain. A curse.

As each of the words passed Argana's lips, connections began forming in Tione's memories.

She'd always assumed Argana's bloodsucking attacks, and even that nickname, Kalima, had simply been a show of force used to strike fear in her opponents. But looking back now, it had a legitimate purpose. And it was why that annoying name had come to be used as her own alias to boot. Everything made sense.

The impact of this revelation was enough to throw Tione for a momentary loop. "Is there no end to how strong it can make you…? How…how is that even fair?!" she spit out, her voice husky.

"Of course not. Break the curse, and my abilities return to normal.

Also, a piddling splash of blood would do no good. It needs to be an ample amount, like the mouthful I took from you earlier."

"...Then, the sacrifice?"

"My endurance. It drops significantly."

Just tell all your deepest secrets, why don't you?! Tione couldn't help but think even as she remained in awe of the information being revealed.

A secret technique that, upon fulfilling its requirements, would grant its user a truly limitless increase in their Status in exchange for a sharp drop in endurance? Curses were rare enough as it was among magic users, but this one in particular had to be the rarest of the rare.

A skill known only to Argana. A blood sacrifice. There wasn't a more perfect skill for the powerful yet despicable warrior.

"You remember, don't you, Tione? When you asked me whether I felt anything about killing my own brethren?" Argana asked, Tione's breath ragged opposite her. "I feel elation. By feasting on their flesh, I grow stronger. They're not gone—they're inside me! They get to live forever, cheating death as they propel me to the highest of plateaus, the strongest warrior in all the world!" The Telskyuran monster was shouting now as she offered up her prayers of gratitude to the many souls she'd consumed.

"They have no reason to mourn! Their blood shall become mine, and we'll live together...forever!!" The snake laughed, childlike joy bubbling up and out from her lungs. Her eyes sparkled, her mind truly convinced that she was nothing short of a savior to the victims who'd died at her hands.

"And Kali...Kali is waiting, too. She's waiting for me to become the strongest in all the land. Which is why...I'll be feasting on your flesh soon, Tione."

"Like hell, you monster...!!" Tione shouted back, her teeth bared in anger. All around them, the other Amazons swallowed hard in fear.

"From the moment I saw you in the lake...I knew it was fate."

Meanwhile, a similarly violent duel was taking place down in the cave by the sea.

Bache's and Tiona's strikes swung at each other back and forth in the middle of their arena of stone, as Kali and the other Amazons spectated from above. Like Tione and Argana, they, too, wielded nothing but their bare fists and feet.

There was only one weapon, Bache's Velgas, which came at Tiona like a deadly storm in her flurry of attacks. With each sweep of the poisonous crystal of purplish-black light coating her right hand, the ground below let out a monstrous *phwooooooooooom* and a plume of smoke, its surface now stained the same color as her hand.

There was no way for Tiona to defend against this type of magic attack, and she found herself unable to do anything but evade the incoming strikes again and again.

"I hated Kali at first…for letting the two of you leave. You were supposed to be mine to kill…and yet you got away."

"…!"

"Argana felt the same," Bache continued, stoic. The only thing that betrayed her true emotions was the sheer ferocity behind her attacks. As she attacked, Tiona attempted to use the same combat techniques she'd instilled in her so many years ago to send her own Velgas flying back at her.

"For us to be fighting like this…now…here…it is truly our destiny."

"Geez, Bache. I didn't even know you had that many words in you!"

"Yes. I do have a tendency to talk more when I get excited," Bache responded, though none of the excitement she mentioned was revealed on her face. Tiona couldn't help but feel glad that Lefiya wasn't present.

Their conversation was a mix of Amazonian language and Koine, the differing languages enough to make her head spin. And what was worse, she felt like Bache was already gaining on her. Her opponent's strikes were simply too powerful.

My body's actually doing what I want it to do thanks to that warm-up fight with Tione, but…that magic is somethin' else!

She couldn't even get close to the other Amazon. Her head flashed with memories of the past, of her fellow brethren writhing in pain from a mere graze from Bache's Velgas. As a young girl, the sight of that coolheaded warrior woman calmly exterminating her prey had been enough to traumatize her for life.

Yikes! Thinking's not gonna do me any good here! I don't have Tione and the others to back me up! she thought—a thought very unbecoming to an adventurer who had to be ready with a plan at all times when Dungeon crawling—before effectively turning off her brain and simply darting forward.

"Me, though? I was always pleased as punch, you know? How you'd read books to me and sometimes even wipe me down after our training sessions?"

"...All of that was nothing but...ways to pass the time."

Tiona flew at her, even with the threat of Bache's venomous fist looming in front of her. There was no way she'd be able to dodge every one of the incoming punches, and in due course, one of the magic-infused strikes grazed the side of her body.

Pain flared up across her skin in an instant, a strange odor mixing with the rising smoke.

With the hit, Bache's defense rose, as well.

"Hngh!"

"————————————?!"

Bache's eyes narrowed, and she aimed a strike straight toward Tiona's chest.

Though Tiona was able to block the direct attack with her left arm, it screamed with the sting of Bache's Velgas. The rippling pain of her skin melting before her eyes was enough to make her realize she couldn't keep this up for long.

From atop her vantage point, Kali watched everything with a thin smile, reveling in the way Tiona refused to back down despite repeated hits from Bache's Velgas.

"Status resistance, hmm? No doubt something she picked up in Orario. But how long will she be able to keep it up? The venom of those Dungeon monsters doesn't hold a candle to my Bache's."

Not once during their training back in Telskyura had Bache used her magic on Tiona.

But it was not out of kindness. No, Bache used her magic only when she was sure that she was going to take down her prey. Never would she allow her opponent to take countermeasures or develop a resistance to her venom.

It had to be a sure kill.

—Swifter and deadlier than even the toxin of a poison vermis.

Colder than the venom of any monster writhing and squirming down in the Dungeon.

Tiona felt that chill pass through her now, but at the same time, something warm was forming inside her.

It was her Berserk skill, the same as her sister's. A skill that boosted her attack power the more damage she took. Feeling the power surging within her, she gave up on petty tricks and simply launched everything she had straight at the woman in front of her.

"!!"

Bache's eyes widened for the first time at the unexpected assault.

The attack sailed toward her like a river breaking through a dam, and she flung up her Velgas to ward it off, but Tiona paid it no heed. As it carved through her shoulder, it only increased her power, and she drove her head straight into her opponent's body with all the force her skill could lend her.

"Hnnguh?!"

The plump roundness of Bache's chest took the full brunt of the attack, and her legs crumpled beneath her.

Tiona took that opportunity to spin around into a powerful roundhouse kick even as her charred shoulder wailed in pain.

Tione's favorite kick——!!

"Strong enough to cut through flesh and bone."

Her entire body whirled to drive the kick straight at Bache's face.

It happened in an instant—*THWACK!!*

The dull sound of flesh on flesh, bone on bone, echoed throughout the cavern, hushing the exuberant cries of the surrounding Amazons. Silence settled over the crowd. Kali, too, said nothing as she looked down at the two warriors, her legs still crossed beneath her.

Then, just when it seemed the silence was liable to carve through their very eardrums...

Tiona's eyes dilated in shock.

It wasn't because Bache had somehow gotten her left hand up just in time to block the incoming kick.

No, it was at the purplish-black tangle of light that now *enveloped her entire body.*

"What...?" she gasped as she heard her right foot begin to thrum with an unnerving *phroooooom.*

What the...hell?

"You didn't know, did you...?"

But the voice wasn't from Bache, who was currently directing her gaze toward Tiona in cold silence, but from Kali up above them.

"When Bache reached Level Six, her Velgas leveled up, too. Not only did its power increase...but so did its range."

It was the blessing that came with every level-up. The increase that was applied to not only one's abilities but one's magic power, as well. Though Bache had only ever been able to enchant her right hand with her Velgas before, now she was able to enchant her whole body, the same as Aiz did with her Airiel.

Even now, Bache's bewitching copper skin seemed awash in an almost electrifying purplish-black light, turning her entire body into a glowing insect shell.

"Gnnngah, hot, hot, hottt———?!" Tiona screeched, forced to retreat as the stretched seconds sped forward to catch up with reality.

Her leg had turned an unsettling color, now seemingly devoid of strength. Bache, however, paid this no mind, already racing toward her in merciless pursuit.

"My magic may not be strong enough to act as armor, but it's plenty strong enough to enhance the pain and suffering of my opponents."

"Eek! Unngah?!"

"Why don't you attack? If you just stand there like a bump on a log, I'll take you out with ease."

Tiona stumbled backward as Bache advanced, her every ominously glowing limb attacking from all sides.

Even before, the Amazon's uncanny strength was enough to crush a person whole, but now with the added power of her Velgas covering her entire form, she could easily rend even a sturdy-bodied first-tier adventurer limb from limb.

Bones cracking, skin prickling with a searing pain, Tiona spat blood from between her teeth.

—What gives, huh? How'm I supposed to beat this lady?!

She couldn't let herself get hit. She couldn't do the hitting.

Which meant…she was gonna die long before she'd have any chance of taking Bache down—.

Despair began to gnaw away at her heart like little worms as the view in front of her became ever more clouded with incoming strikes.

"Have I broken your spirit, Tiona?"

"Hu—gggnnnnnnnnwwwwuuuaaaaAAAAARRRRRGGGHHH!!"

Bache's hand grabbed ahold of Tiona's face and lifted her.

She couldn't see, coughing up smoke and muck as her face sizzled beneath Bache's fingers. She screamed. Grappling desperately at the fingers digging into her skin, she attempted to pull away the other woman's grip, but the powerful vise was simply too strong.

Bache began to squeeze, slowly crushing her head like a ripe berry.

"Tiona…do you know why it is that I trained you so diligently?"

"……!!"

Bache's icy voice filled her ears, her world shrouded in light—blackish, purplish, venomous light.

"It was for this very day. The day when I could fight against you in all your glory…and feast upon your flesh."

"?!"

"I've been preparing myself since the moment we first met. Yes, you would grow strong…so strong…and through that strength, I, too, would reach a new plateau—by killing you."

She would level up. That's what she was referring to. The ritualistic act where lower-world denizens would break free of the container of their Statuses and reach new heights in their abilities.

By felling Tiona now that her strength had matured, by feasting on her, Bache would accomplish a true feat, propelling her to that coveted next level.

"Not once have I ever thought of Argana as a sister. In my eyes, she's nothing but a predator." A momentary glint of fear flashed across her steely eyes. "A predator I refuse to let consume me. I… don't want to die."

They were just like Tiona and Tione.

Since the moment she was born, Bache had been plagued by a monster—her sister.

This was the reason for Bache's reticence, for her paucity of emotion. She didn't want to die. Even letting the words pass her lips sent tendrils of irrepressible fear squirming throughout her entire body.

Bache knew. Even if she were to escape the confines of Telskyura, her other half, the other being with whom she shared her talents and abilities, would follow her to the ends of the earth. That bothersome bond of blood would always draw them together.

Back when Kali had stepped in to keep her sister from killing her, Bache had learned there was only one truth she could cling to:

"Strength. I needed to be strong. I needed a power that couldn't be stolen from me."

Combining her fear of death with her insatiable thirst for life, she'd fostered the fighting spirit inside her. And from the amalgam of survival and fighting instincts, a new warrior, in her purest form, was born.

She coveted strength, craved it as a coldhearted, inhuman warrior.

"I will kill you and your sister…I will kill Argana…and then I will become the most powerful warrior in the whole world," the Poison Queen hissed, as Kali watched over her with intrigue and love.

"!!"

Tiona willed up every ounce of strength she could muster, even as the poison continued to scald her face. Swinging her leg upward in a mighty kick, she somehow managed to make contact with Bache, who released the confining grip on her head. Around and around she spun, not even caring about the burn the contact had left on her leg, focusing only on putting distance between herself and her attacker.

"Hah…hah…?!"

Her whole face felt like it was on fire; pain and a strange sense of intoxication ravaged her being. The venom was strong. Like a fever, it washed over her body, and beads of sweat developed across her skin. Even the globules of blood she coughed up from her mouth had begun to take on a blackish hue.

Down on all fours, she supported herself with shaking arms, and the excruciating pain was enough that a tear fell from her eye and ran down the length of her cheek. Inside, she could feel a crack working its way through her heart—the callous confession of the woman she'd once regarded as her second sister hit where it hurt the most.

It hurts.

It hurts so bad!

I can't do this anymore!!

"Tio…ne…"

Tione——Tione!!

Help me, Tione!!

It hurts too much! I don't wanna fight anymore!

I don't wanna fight——.

Tiona's consciousness lost itself somewhere along the line between past and present as poison consumed her body and cracks spread across her heart.

Deep inside the dark reaches of her soul, Little Tiona was crying.

She didn't wanna fight. She didn't wanna fight.

"————————————————*!!*"

The Amazons roared, Tiona no longer able to move as her chest heaved up and down.

"*On your feet!*" they cried. "*Kill her!*" they cried.

Bache turned her cold, ruthless eyes toward the girl on the ground, and the writhing blob of light around her hand let out an audible crackle as it flashed.

And then she started toward her, slowly, as Kali watched from above.

"Gngh…ah?!"

With a loud *thud*, Tione flew backward, breaking through a nearby barrel and colliding with the side of the ship.

Her body was already a bloody mess. Blood poured like rivers from her open wounds and mouth, her skin littered with swollen bruises and sores.

The spectating Amazons let out excited whoops and hollers as Argana approached.

"Have you had enough yet, Tione?"

"...!"

Argana ran her arm across her cheek, licking at the mixture of blood—some of it Tione's, some of it her own. Her body, too, looked decidedly worse for wear, and her garments, dragon-scale belt included, were tattered and ragged.

"Though you've lost your edge as a warrior...you've lasted longer than I thought you would. I must admit that you've grown stronger. You're not that sad waste of flesh that you were so many years ago."

Her voice sounded so far away. It buzzed in her ears.

Damn you, Tione cursed the woman in her head. But she'd lost too much blood. It was hard to think. Her mind was hazy and slipping in and out of consciousness.

She let herself slide down the side of the ship, her head starting to droop.

"I'd never given much thought to you so-called adventurers...but now I've actually started to look forward to it. That boaz in particular. I'll be interested to see just how strong he is."

Argana was saying something.

Prattling on about something.

"Ah, but first things first. You'll allow me to eat you now, won't you?"

Yakking, yakking, yakking—.

"I suppose if Bache has been defeated...heh...then I'll just have to kill Tiona, too."

—In that moment, something snapped.

There came a resounding crack, the likes of which she'd never heard before, and her vision went red with flames.

Her head rolled upward, the entirety of her being exploded with a fiery heat—and then she was off.

"__________"

Argana didn't even have time to react.

Nor to evade the incoming fist.

Tione pushed herself off the side of the ship, spraying splinters of wood as she sent her fist into the side of Argana's jaw.

"Wha—?!"

The Amazon went flying.

Now it was her turn to sail through the air, breaking through barrels to slam painfully into the opposite wall.

Blood dribbled down from between her lips as she looked up in shock at the crimson snake of fury now staring her down.

"I'll kill you…!!"

Tione's fist was clenched in rage, her body stained a brilliant red, her own blood dyeing her skin.

She was furious.

A pure, unadulterated enmity churned through her veins, stronger than any she'd ever felt before, stronger than when she'd been pelted with blows, stronger than when she'd had her own blood sucked from her body and the shame had been seared into her memory.

And as all that ire flowed through her like flames licking at her skin, she roared.

"If you kill her, I'll kill you!!"

"…!!"

The sheer force of all that furor was enough to steal the breath of every Amazon on board.

Not even Tione herself knew what had caused it.

It was a livid inferno the likes of which she'd never felt before.

But she didn't have to understand it to let her mouth run away from her.

"Lay one finger on her. I dare you!! You'll rue the day you were born!!!!"

As Tione screamed, she began to realize just where her shouts were coming from.

Oh, how she hated that stupid smile.

But oh, how she needed it.

She always had. And she'd always do whatever it took. She had a duty to fulfill.

Because that stupid idiot was her other half—her one and only little sister.

"I'll never let you touch her!!"

She would protect her. She would protect her Tiona.

She had to keep her safe. Because they only had each other.

She protected her when the other Amazons targeted her in the arena. When she fell asleep first next to her.

She'd always quietly protected her—the dazzling sun that shone its light on her life.

And she wasn't about to stop now.

"You two are…really a different breed of Amazon," Argana mused. The fact that the sisters had been able to retain their bond even in the cutthroat world of Telskyura was a miracle, indeed. She smiled. "You love each other, don't you?"

"What?!"

"Since you seem to be in the dark, I guess I'll go ahead and tell you. It's been so long, after all." Argana rose to her feet, that same amused smile still playing on her lips. "Tiona has always been protecting you."

—Tione, Tione.

Again and again, Little Tiona called out her sister's name through the darkness.

She could see her back quivering as she cried and cried, only a few steps ahead.

Little Tione would never be a warrior.

She'd strayed from the warrior's path.

Tiona knew why. As thick as she could be at times, she still understood why.

It was simple. Because she was simply Tione.

On the day she saw her sister crying, reduced to tears after having killed Seldas, a feeling took root inside Tiona.

—She needed to protect her.

It wasn't because she empathized with her. But simply because it seemed natural to do so. She was her other half, after all. Just like she didn't need a reason to protect herself, she didn't need a reason to protect her sister.

And so, from that day, Tiona began *killing the other girls in their room.* Or, perhaps more concisely, she volunteered to fight them in the rites. Whenever Tione was scheduled to fight against one of their own roommates, Tiona would go to Kali and request that she be switched in for her sister. It was her way of protecting her sister's heart, haggard and broken as it was from Argana's training.

But there was still the anxiety Tione always felt as the days for her rites grew near. Tiona didn't like that, either. And so she went to Kali again. And agreed to do whatever Kali asked so long as her wish was fulfilled. She killed all of them. In a single long night of rite after rite after rite, she piled their bodies high. Tione never even noticed.

It was that one bond she had with her sister that let her simply be Tiona Hyrute rather than a warrior of Telskyura.

Perhaps if she'd never seen Tione crying in her room that one night, she, too, would have turned out just like Argana and Bache—an Amazon who filled the hole in her heart with nothing but ceaseless fighting. She would have become a true berserker, mercilessly slaughtering her opponents, awash in their blood yet radiating a pure and innocent smile all the while.

Tiona knew all this. She understood the paper-thin line she'd tread. And that her sister's presence had been the one thing someone as stupid as her could hold onto.

Tione was the moon.

She lit the way forward through the darkness when neither of them knew where to go. She was always there next to her in her moonlike tranquility when it came time to sleep. Tiona had always liked Tione the best at night. It was the one time the restless, angry girl of the day could settle down. She held her so, so close, a cradle of the moon, rocking her to sleep.

Tiona couldn't sleep unless she was next to Tione.

—Tione, Tione.

Little Tiona was crying. *I can't get up*, she said.

She liked to fight, but she didn't like to kill. She'd wept salty wet tears beneath her mask upon killing their final roommate. It hurt so badly. So badly her whole body and heart ached.

—Tione, save me.

Where was she to hit her on the head, call her stupid, and tug her hand?

She rubbed at her chest, looking down into the darkness, into the deep, deep pool of her heart to where Little Tiona continued to cry.

Closing her eyes, she reopened them to see her—Tione, standing above her.

—Don't lose, Tiona.

That's what she'd told her just a short while ago when the two had separated.

She saw her sister's back, framed in the light of the moon above.

Standing behind her younger self, she bent down to pick up the book lying at her feet.

Then handed it to the weeping girl in front of her.

—Try to hold out just a bit longer, okay?

—Tione's doing her best, too.

She laughed, her smile as bright and gleaming as the sun.

Little Tiona placed her hand on the book's cover, blinking curiously. She flipped through its pages, and after several hundred of the paper sheets had gone by, she came to a stop on the hero of the legend—and instantly brightened.

The two Tionas, the young girl and the warrior, looked at each other and smiled, then took each other's hands.

"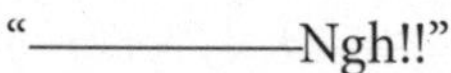Ngh!!"

Tiona's eyes shot open with a powerful snap.

Her consciousness was suddenly as sharp as a tack, and she sprang instantly to her feet.

"!"

Bache gave a start, then leaped backward. As she eyed the

rejuvenated girl suspiciously, the Amazonian spectators above let out resounding cries of adulation.

"Hoh-hoh. So you're back on your feet," Kali mused, smiling beneath her mask. "What's your plan, then, hmm? Doesn't look to me like you're doing so hot. You sure you can still fight?"

Indeed, smoke continued to rise from Tiona's body where Bache's Velgas had seared the skin.

Tiona brought an arm up to wipe at her poison-smeared face—perhaps Kali's words had reached her?—then she formed both her hands into fists before gearing up for a mighty yell.

"It doesn't hurt. Not one bit!!"

Bache's eyes grew round in surprise.

"And your words don't hurt me, either. Not one bit!!"

Now it was Kali's turn to open her mouth with surprise.

"I can still fight. I can keep doin' this forever!!"

Not a single Amazon moved, all of them as still as statues.

"You think I'd lose to the likes of you?!"

And then Tiona's smile deepened.

She squeezed her fists tighter, readying herself for combat as if her skin wasn't currently covered in poison and giving off smoke.

She'd just figured out the one tactic she could use against Bache's Velgas.

She just had to ignore it—to tough it out.

It was the plan of a girl whose head didn't quite function the way others' did and a culmination of all her thickheaded stupidity.

"Bwa-ha-ha-ha-ha-ha-HA-HA-HA-HA-HA-HA-HA-HA-HA-HA!!"

With a start, the tiny, cherubic goddess watching over them let out a great, gulping guffaw, breaking the silence like water bursting through a dam. Holding both hands to her stomach, she flapped her feet in the air, practically tumbling straight off her perch.

Down below, Bache's expression never faltered. Even as her goddess's laughter echoed throughout the cavern, she only narrowed her eyes.

"…My Velgas isn't something you can just ignore."

"'Course! It actually hurts like hell!"

"Well, then—"

But Tiona interrupted before she could finish.

"But it's not gonna keep me from smilin'!"

Bache's eyes widened for a second time.

"It doesn't matter how much it hurts, how much my heart aches, how much I wanna cry—I'll just keep on smilin'!"

True to her words, a giant smile was currently plastered across her face.

It was a smile from cheek to cheek and which was completely out of place considering her current state.

—What was it that had separated Tiona and Tione into light and dark back in Telskyura? Yes, it had been that book, the epic.

She could still remember losing herself among the pages of that story as Bache read it aloud to her. She could still remember the very first time she'd laughed so hard she couldn't stop at the ridiculous dialogue of the story's hero.

And she could still remember the burst of courage those words had given her.

"I'm not the sharpest tool in the shed…so yeah! Maybe this is the only thing I can do!"

Maybe that beautiful story had been the one place she could run when the days tried to drive her into the ground. Maybe it was only through that legendary epic that she'd been able to console herself after what she'd done.

Of all the things that story may have given her, the one that Tiona was most sure of—was her smile.

"But you can bet I'm gonna do it. I'm gonna keep on smiling!"

If she just kept on smiling, then maybe, maybe Tione would smile, too.

If someone like Tiona wasn't even able to smile, then there was no way that faded world of blood and ash they lived in was ever going to change.

So she smiled.

Because of that epic, even when it was just the two of them in that cold world, Tiona could light up the sky with her expression of joy.

And finally, she'd been able to make Tione smile, too.

"So long as I'm smiling, I don't care about all that bad stuff!"

Tiona had a favorite story among all those poems.

It was the story of Argonaut.

An ordinary boy who dreamed of becoming a hero.

A farcical story that had left her drowning in tears of mirth.

Oh, I will smile.

No matter how much I may be made the fool, no matter how many times the derisive laughter of others may scorn me, I shall curve these lips upward.

If not, how should the spirit smile? How should the goddess of fortune grin?

—Smile.

Just like the fairy-tale hero who had so encouraged her.

Just like the characters in that beautiful story.

No matter how much it hurt, no matter how much she might suffer, no matter how much she had to fake it.

She would simply smile.

Smile for that bright tomorrow she knew awaited.

She wasn't trying to play hero. She was merely doing everything she could do—and for someone like her, someone who wasn't as smart, wasn't as clever, that was fine enough!!

"I have to smile...for all those who can't!!" she declared, sporting her biggest grin yet. "And if I have to smile forever before you'll smile back, then that's what I'll do!"

"That's bullshit...!" Tione hissed with a clench of her fists, doing her best to mask the tumult of emotions in her heart. Tiona had killed even more of their sisters back in Telskyura?

But it all made sense.

When Tione's eyes and heart had grown worn and tattered, Tiona had been the one to smile for her.

—*"That girl, Aiz. She reminds me a lot of you way back when."*

And then Aiz had come along. And Tiona began to smile for her, just like she'd always done for Tione.

Tione finally realized the reason behind that smile—that idiot sister of hers was always protecting her from the shadows.

"That asshole…Thinking she can be a hero to me…?!"

Tiona might have been taken in by those stories of hero-hood, but she wasn't waiting for a hero to come save her. No, she had to be the hero. Because she had another part of her that needed protection. So her simpleminded sister had kept on smiling.

Until the day she could make Tione smile.

Tione had always thought she'd been the one supporting and protecting Tiona. But in reality, Tiona had been the one defending and upholding her.

And it had been the same for Tiona.

Backs together, the two sisters had always protected each other.

"What do you think I am? Some princess waiting for her hero to come? I'd rather eat shit and die!!"

Tiona wasn't coming. And even if she did, Tione was only going to give her an earful—with her fist.

She was the only one who could take out the opponent standing before her now.

Take her out—and protect her Tiona.

"Argana—I'm going to kill you."

"What a wonderful look that is in your eyes, Tione…Finally, you've become a warrior again," Argana mused. Tingling pinpricks worked their way up her spine at the way Tione's gaze bored into her.

Tione ignored her comment, opening her mouth as a red-stained puff of air passed her lips.

"…You haven't changed, Tiona," Bache murmured, taking in the sight of the smiling girl before her. "You always were the biggest idiot in Telskyura…the craziest animal."

No matter what kind of dilemma she'd found herself in, no matter how tight a corner she'd found herself in, that grin of hers had never vanished. She was always, always smiling.

With that brilliant, innocent, virulent smile pasted on her face, she wrested victory from her enemies. With that one smile, she'd overcome everything the world had tried to throw at her.

"What were you expectin'? Of course she hasn't changed! Even Tione may have changed over the years, but this girl'll always be the same stupid idiot!!" Kali howled giddily before bringing her laughter-induced convulsions to an abrupt stop. She slowly pulled herself back up to a sitting position, grin widening as she glanced down at the two warriors below. "—This is great! I knew I liked you better than Tione!" she exclaimed, almost as though trying to draw a sympathetic response from her immortal kin.

Tiona smirked.

Having made the self-encouraging assertion that she felt no pain, she let her lips part just slightly.

Revealing a solid red puff of air.

—This is it.

Bache's face tightened at the sight.

Tiona's breath was red. And not just metaphorically, either, but truly red—the heat inside her was great enough to stain the very air she was breathing.

It was Tiona's rare skill, Intense Heat.

Its effects activated before her Berserk ability finished, providing her a massive boost in ability if her status entered critical. It had the same activation requirements as Tione's own attack-boosting skill, Backdraft. So long as the two sisters had these skills, no matter how dire their situation, the further they were pushed, the higher their combat power would rise.

The Hyrute sisters were most dangerous when they were cornered.

From atop that boat.

From within that cave by the sea.

The two rites reached their climaxes at the exact same time.

Around both of them, Amazons stomped their feet in unison, letting out ever more deafening cries of war, one atop another atop another.

"My future of war…let's see how it plays out." Kali's voice melted into the darkness.

Then the decisive battles began.

The shadow raced through the dark night.

It hadn't stopped since seeing those monsters appear in the port.

There was something it needed to confirm. Back to the screams and chaos of the wharf in its wake, it ran all the way outside the city.

It arrived at a cave, not altogether unlike the sea cave Tiona had ventured into only a short while earlier. Cautiously, it slipped inside, not making a sound. Breath stilled, it wove its way through the ant-like tunnels of the cavern, careful not to get lost among its passageways. It didn't use a light, instead feeling the wall against its hand to lead it along, a shadow melting into the surrounding darkness as it continued forward through the gloomy tunnel.

"—!"

It was then that it saw them.

Cages, seven of them, all containing a miniature viola with flower bud closed and tentacles coiled up around it. And carved into the earth around the cages were ruts, leftover evidence from the *earlier journey the cages made from the city.*

"Someone turn on a light in here!"

"?!"

It came from behind—and suddenly the light of a magic-stone lantern illuminated the perimeter.

It was Loki, having successfully followed the shadow without being noticed thanks to the help of her familia members. Loki shone the light on her target, revealing its true form.

Everyone in the entourage she'd brought with her inhaled sharply in unison, taken by surprise at the revelation.

"Not who you were expectin', was it?"

The shadow, no, the man boasted a stocky frame of roughly two meders tall, and shining beneath his black crop of hair was a pair of obsidian eyes. Firm, tanned skin stretched over the muscles of his arms and chest, revealing a body perfectly honed for fishing.

A human man.

"Rod…wasn't it?"

"My…lady…?"

The *Njörðr Familia* captain, Rod, stood staring at Loki with his eyes as round as saucers.

His voice caught in his throat as he looked from Loki and her magic-stone lantern to the gaggle of girls behind her. It didn't take him long to realize he'd been followed.

Throwing a glance at the immature violas behind him, he finally spoke, his voice hoarse. "W-well, isn't this a surprise? How, uh…how long have you been, uh…following me? Ha-ha…Guess I was in too much of a rush to notice. Goddammit…" He let out an undeniably forced chuckle, trying what he could to smooth over the incriminating situation.

Next to Loki and her glare of incredulity, the hume bunny Rakuta spoke up, no longer able to keep her thoughts to herself.

"Y-you're the one who's been setting loose the violas in the lake?"

"—That, uh…Yes! Yes, I am! It was all me! You caught me!" he suddenly blurted out, seemingly out of desperation. Eyes flashing, he raised his voice even louder. "It was definitely me! I was the one who set loose all these monsters into the—!!"

"All right, all right. We get it already," Loki cut in before he could finish. She waved a flippant hand in the frozen man's direction, ever so slightly widening her vermilion eyes.

"You're really gonna let your kid take all the flak for this, are ya, Njörðr?"

A heavy silence settled down over the cave.

Only after Loki's voice had echoed into the depth of the cavern and a painful silence descended did a figure emerge from the shadows.

The sandal-clad foot of a finely shaped calf appeared first, followed by an auburn-tinged ponytail, hanging down loosely from the back of the man's head.

It was none other than the god Njörðr, his face taut with pensive reflection.

"S-Skip, don't…!" Rod pleaded despondently, but it was too late.

"What the…hell is going on here?!"

"Two scumbags for the price of one, that's what's goin' on here," Loki explained.

Rakuta and the rest of Loki's followers could only look back and forth between Rod and Njörðr with identical confounded looks. The person, or rather god Loki had seen escaping from the scene of the violas back at the wharf had, in fact, been Njörðr.

But Loki hadn't been the only one to notice Njörðr's hasty retreat. Rod had, as well. Unable to shake his god's questionably timed exit, Rod had followed him all the way to this cave, only to have Loki and her followers show up only moments later behind him.

"Then that 'confession' he gave us…?"

"He was just coverin' for his pop…You've got yourself a good bunch of kiddos, don't you, Njörðr?"

While discovering his own god was behind the viola attacks must have been a considerable shock for Rod, the moment Loki and the rest of her followers had shown up, he hadn't hesitated even a second to cover for Njörðr—his faith in and respect for his "Skip" were just that great.

Behind Rod, Njörðr grimaced, his features a mixture of regret and shame.

"It…it can't really be true, can it, Skip? How could you unleash these monsters into the lake…?"

"I'm afraid it is, Rod."

"Why? Why would you do something like that?!" Rod's face was twisting now, tears threatening to spill from his eyes.

"…I'm not the wonderful god you all believe me to be," Njörðr responded, avoiding Rod's gaze and looking, instead, toward Loki. "Loki, this is all my doing…"

"Yeah, cat's out of the bag already. No use hidin' things now." Loki lobbed a small bag at Njörðr's feet. The multicolored powder mixture Rod had shown Aiz and the others down at the pier the other day spilled out of the opening—the "magic dust" Rod and his men used to ward off monsters out at sea.

Njörðr's brows creased further still.

"I've been sending my kids all over. To the folks at the Guild and even to Old Man Murdock himself. Finally, I've got my evidence," Loki continued, alluding to the bag that Aiz had given her not long ago.

"...!"

Njörðr brought a hand to his head in resignation, visibly pale.

But before he could offer up a response, Rod did for him, voice laced with surprise. "Master Borg? And...the Guild? But...but what do they have to do with any of this, milady?!" he asked shakily.

"Well..." Loki started. "It goes somethin' like this—"

"—one of you isn't the culprit. All of you are the culprits!"

A similar conversation was currently taking place in an empty storehouse behind the Guild Branch Office.

The Guild Branch chief himself, Rubart, paled in the face of Riveria's accusation.

"What are you...? A-an accusation like that is an insult to the Guild—!"

"Then what does that make you, the one who carried out the actions in question?"

As chaos overwhelmed the city of Meren, the branch chief had been taking advantage of the similar commotion in the branch office to slip out of sight and cart with him a certain item to the storehouse.

What he hadn't expected, though, was the sudden appearance of a green-haired high elf, and—caught red-handed—he let one of the items in his arms drop to the floor as his face twitched. The item in question was of a decidedly magic-stone make.

"The reason Meren has not called for aid from Orario, even in a dire situation such as this...is because you control the signal!"

And, indeed, the telescope-like signal itself was right there in his hands. The series of magic-stone flashes it created was strong enough to reach the guard post along Orario's great stone walls, allowing Meren to alert the city, even from kirlos away, of any urgent distress.

"You know that if any adventurers from Guild Headquarters were to come now, they'd become instantly aware of all the dirty dealings currently occurring. For instance, our little viola situation...Am I correct?" Riveria stated, one eye closed as she stared Rubart down with the other.

"...!"

Rubart's face began losing its color at a nigh unparalleled rate.

"All that earlier chicanery about not being on good terms with the Guild was simply to keep us from discovering your involvement as a conspirator, yes?"

"*L-Loki Familia*...!"

In yet a third similar conversation, Alicia was currently accosting a certain Borg Murdock, head of Meren, at his family estate. The village chief's hands were gripping the sides of a large hemp sack containing, quite clearly, the "magic dust" in question.

Though he at first attempted to conceal the sack, he quickly realized such actions were too little, too late, instead simply slumping to the floor in resignation.

"But what could all of them have to do with those flower creatures...?"

Loki could hear her followers' bewildered voices behind her but didn't reply; instead, she looked first to the motionless violas who appeared to be sleeping in their black cages, then next to the powder scattered around Njörðr's feet.

"There're magic stones mixed in with all that stuff...ain't there?"

"...There are," Njörðr responded, defeated.

There was another collective gasp of surprise from Rod and the rest of Loki's familia. Loki, however, just moved the conversation along.

"Crushed 'em up good and small to keep anyone from noticing... then mixed 'em up with fishy parts and all other sorts of raw, stinky gook...That sound about right?"

"Indeed. I'm impressed, Loki. I put a lot of work into that to make sure even other gods wouldn't see through it..."

"I had Aizuu sniff things out. She's got a nose for this kinda stuff. Snuck into Murdock's place and found his little stash of magic stones in the basement."

Njörðr's lips curled upward in a self-deprecating grin.

Rod, still stunned between the two, cut in with his own request for clarification. "W-wait just a second here, milady! By magic stones you don't mean...mean *those*, do you? Those...stones inside monsters' chests?! How the devil would something like that keep those same monsters at bay?"

"Those flowers...Seems there's one thing they like even more than the taste of human flesh—other monsters. Or, more accurately, the magic stones of other monsters. This was news to me, too," Loki explained, and the eyes of Rakuta and the other girls behind her widened further.

This had been what Aiz and company had reported following the last expedition. The vibrantly colored monsters such as the violas and the caterpillars were merely "tentacles" for the corrupted spirit, seeking out magic stones for the spirit to feed on.

"Scatterin' this stuff with its magic stones out in the water makes the violas go crazy, drawing their attention away from the boats themselves and allowin' 'em to sail through without so much as a scratch."

When Tiona had called the magic dust "monster bait" the other day, she'd been right on the money. This was an item perfectly crafted for viola-repelling use.

"But...but...but it just doesn't make sense! Why would...But other monsters, too! They didn't attack the boats, either!" Rod insisted.

"Didn't I just say those flower beasties prefer the taste of their own kind?" Loki explained with a sigh. "They ate everything! 'Magic dust' and other monsters alike. Why else do you think the seas have been so peaceful lately?"

As Rod's eyes widened in realization, first he, then Rakuta and the others, and finally Loki, too, all threw their gazes in Njörðr's direction.

"I'm pretty sure I know the answer already, but…I just hafta ask," Loki continued. "Why'd ya do it?"

Njörðr took a few steps farther inside the cavern, walking over toward a small spring before plunging his hand in the water. When his fist emerged, it was wrapped tightly around the tail of a fish.

"…Take a look at this fish, Loki."

It was a dodobass, big and black. Though still young, it was already as long as most other fish in their prime, and its tough ovular scales were already growing in all across its body.

"Wonderful batch of scales it has, yes? All of it a result of evolution—to protect itself from the monsters in the lake."

"You don't have to tell me. Things like that have been happenin' since monsters first emerged on the surface. The whole ecosystem's careening out of control."

"Exactly, exactly…But this dodobass, you see, is actually quite lucky. It was somehow able to keep itself alive; its children were able to find food. Others, however, weren't so lucky…"

"And…that's why you set loose all those violas into the lake?"

Njörðr nodded, his face cheerless. Around him, Rod and the others couldn't help the somewhat sardonic half smiles that rose to their lips.

"The oceans of this world, they're in a…horrid state. The increase in monsters these past five hundred years has simply been too great."

"I guess that makes sense…Up on land, we're somehow able to keep 'em under control, but there aren't a lotta people who could do the same thing out on the open sea."

"Yes. Poseidon and his followers did what they could, but it was a Sisyphean task from the start. If it had gone on much longer, my men and I, well…we'd have been out of jobs. And not just us—fishing would become a fool's errand in every sea of the world. I simply couldn't let that happen."

Njörðr was, after all, a god of the rod.

The whole reason he'd descended to the human world was to reap the bounties of its waters. Next to him, Rod, his fellow fishing captain, stood stock-still, simply listening to his deity's confession.

"Meren almost reached a breaking point not long ago," Njörðr continued. "The fish dropped to dangerously low levels. The lake's monsters nabbed all of them before we fishermen could reel them in. Orario, of course, had enough money that it could simply import its fish from elsewhere, but what were my men and I supposed to do?"

"..."

"Fishing is our livelihood. We have no other way of making money. But fishing requires that we venture out to sea, and with each passing voyage...my men were dying. Rod's father...and his grandfather both met their ends this way." He smiled sadly at Loki, silent for a moment before continuing. "My blessing did them no good. They were no match for those monsters."

"Skip Njörðr..." Rod sniffled, looking as though he was about to cry.

"Alternatively, I could have gone the Poseidon route and militarized my familia...The thought had crossed my mind. But my men would, no doubt, have had none of that. It would have been as impossible a task as Poseidon's attempt to clear the ocean! Needless to say, I'd reached quite an impasse...until I learned of these monsters' existence," he concluded, throwing a glance at the violas in question.

"When was that? And how was that, huh?" Loki prodded.

"Seven years ago, perhaps? Or, no...six? One of them washed right down the sewers from Orario and landed in our lake."

While it had caused some damage, the beast had eventually been taken care of by a familia who'd just so happened to have been there on a trip. It was exactly when the viola had been about to attack another monster, actually—something Njörðr hadn't failed to miss. Following the source of the creature, he'd made his way into Orario's sewers to investigate the matter for himself. Quite opposite of the raider fish that made their way to Orario from the lake, these man-eating flowers were, in fact, making their way from Orario. Of course, this was before the mythril gate had been installed on the sewer's drainage pipe.

"It was there, prowling around as I was in the sewers without permission…that I met a human most strange."

"A human? What kinda human?"

"Deathly pale, almost as though his very skin simply refused to absorb light from the sun. And with eyes hidden beneath long bangs…"

If the strange gentleman hadn't accosted him first, Njörðr likely wouldn't have approached. But seeing as he had…

"I ask for only a few things in return. Then, you may use these monsters any way you see fit, my lord."

With those words, a secret pact had been forged between them.

And in return for releasing the violas into the lake and nearby ocean, Njörðr agreed to help the man smuggle his goods out of Meren.

"…Then that's why the Guild Branch Office and the Murdock estate had to get involved?"

"Indeed."

Loki sighed as Njörðr let his shoulders droop.

It would have been pretty difficult to smuggle anything out of Meren without the aforementioned entities' help, after all. And given that Njörðr's plan would lead to safer seas and a more sustainable crop of fish, Borg had agreed. The Guild Branch Office's cooperation, meanwhile—or more specifically, Rubart's—had come out of a monetary necessity.

"In order to make the powder, we needed magic stones…and getting our hands on those, or shall we say, stealing them, required the help of the Guild Branch Office…"

Rubart controlled the flow of magic stones from the main headquarters.

Borg processed the powder in the basement of his estate.

And Njörðr had simply feigned innocence, continuing to fish in the lake and ocean as the violas effectively culled the overwhelming monster population.

As much as possible, the three conspirators attempted to disguise their involvement.

Meanwhile, Borg made sure that every incoming and outgoing ship received a batch of the powder to ensure their safety in the waters. It was a process that had been going on for years.

"And what about those folks who don't have the powder, huh? They'd still get attacked by the violas," Loki pointed out. "Did you take them into account as part of your little plan?"

"Compared to the numbers I was losing to the myriad monsters out at sea…it seemed a small price to pay," Njörðr responded with a short laugh, to which Loki just sighed.

Fishing, the sea, and all those of the lower world involved in the two—Njörðr simply loved them too much. As charitable as he was, he'd even lent his aid readily to Loki and her followers in their own investigation.

"You really are an idiot…" Loki muttered.

Rod, too, could do nothing but silently hang his head.

"One more thing I wanna make clear," Loki started again. "In any of your dealin's, did you ever come in contact with any of those Evils remnants? Or those human-monster creature hybrids?"

"I'm not sure I know what either of those are, so…I would assume no?"

Then the true enemy they'd been tracking had nothing to do with the goings-on in the port. Loki felt a sense of futility wash over her, but she continued all the same.

"But somebody had to have hauled all these violas here, right? From Orario? Then you did the duty of tossin' 'em in the lake? Who's your delivery boy?"

"That's, erm…well…"

"Spit it out, Njörðr."

"…*Ishtar Familia*," he finally admitted sheepishly. "They acted as a sort of…contact for us. Or perhaps *intermediary* would be a better word. With our mutual friend in the sewers. At any rate, they've done a lot for us, always coming to our aid when we needed it. Apparently they use some sort of agency to get in and out of the city without being seen, and they always take care of any flowers who've grown too big for their britches…"

"Then they're also the ones who set loose those violas in the port, I assume…" Loki mused.

"…I would imagine."

Seeing the unbelievable sight of the violas at the pier had been the reason Njörðr had come down there in the first place. Hearing that *Ishtar Familia* was the one responsible got the cogs of Loki's brain turning, and she mulled the familia's name around in her mind.

Seeing as she'd about exhausted her supply of information from Njörðr, she said, "I won't tell anyone about what you've done here, all right?" and turned toward the other god. "After all, peace has returned to the city. *But*…I'm gonna have to tell the Guild about the violas. And you're not gonna be able to use 'em anymore."

"All right…"

"Also, I'm gonna work you like a damn packhorse after this for all the trouble you put me through, y'hear? I got plenty more things I'm gonna wanna ask you."

Njörðr's head fell with a dispirited slump. "…Right."

Loki took a moment to survey the perimeter. "That miserable midget—erm, Kali's probably usin' these tunnels as her own personal fort, isn't she?"

"I believe so. She and Ishtar have…some sort of agreement."

"Then that means Lefiya and Tiona are here somewhere, too." Loki nodded with a hum before turning around to face her followers. "Rakuta. Elfie. Let everyone else know that Lefiya and the others are here, would ya?"

"Everyone, Miss Loki…?"

"You, Miss Aiz, and…Lady Riveria…?"

Loki just grinned.

"I mean everyone."

A short while before Njörðr was making his confession…

Aiz and company were still continuing to defend themselves

against *Ishtar Familia*'s assault. The lights of Meren or, perhaps more accurately, the lights of Meren's pier, had all been snuffed out. With the violas repelled, the last thing the citizens of Meren had expected was to find themselves with yet another violent battle on their hands in the middle of the wharf—a two-familia duel, no less—and the chaos and confusion had reached an all-time high.

"Why the hell isn't the signal going off?! What's the Guild doing—sitting on their asses?!"

"How should I know? Everyone down at the Branch Office is in a right tizzy, too. Seems somethin's gone missing—not sure if it's the signal or the branch manager himself!"

The voices of the two men came from near the port city's token short walls. Standing atop the watchtower, they stared morosely off into the distance at the motionless gate of Orario's grand bulwark, the signal that should have been emanating from the Guild Branch Office nowhere to be found.

"Goddammit! At this rate, we're better off gettin' the hell outta this pl—"

The animal man's rant stopped short, and the telescope he was currently gazing through fixed on a spot on Orario's walls.

"Oh…"

"What is it? You see somethin'? Don't tell me it's somethin' else!!" The human man next to him grabbed the telescope out of his hands before peering through it himself.

And then. "Oh…" he replied simply, frozen to the spot the same as his partner.

The telescope was directed toward the highest point on Orario's mighty walls.

At a certain item fluttering just in front of the parapets.

"The…Trickster emblem…?" the first man murmured in wonderment.

And, indeed, the flag of Orario's strongest familia was currently whipping in the breeze atop the city's walls.

"Like hell we're gonna let the girls have all the fun…" spat a certain young werewolf, standing atop the wall bordering Orario's

© Kiyotaka Haimura

southwestern district. "Come on, you ingrates! You gonna let those girls walk all over us? Let's do this!"

"Hoo-rah!!"

As Bete glanced behind him, eyes glinting, the gaggle of men to his rear let out a simultaneous cry of fortitude. They thrust their weapons in the air with a zeal that bordered on manic. Meanwhile, next to them, Aki brought her hands up to cover the catlike ears on top of her head.

Every one of them atop that wall had their sights set on Meren's trade pier, currently devoid of light in the distance. Even from Orario, they could see the relentless flashes of light staining the darkness like firecrackers—evidence of the sword duel currently under way.

"Ha-ha-ha, Bete certainly knows how to rile up a crowd," Finn mused with a smile.

"Aye, but they're already fit to be tied, the whole lot of 'em...What's gone and crawled up their arses, 'ey, Raul?" Gareth turned his attention to the young man next to him.

"Well, that's, erm...We ran into a certain, uh...Little Rookie at the Flaming Wasp earlier..." Raul responded, clad in armor from head to toe and sporting his own weapon.

"Aki! That's the *Kali Familia* in question over there, is it not?" Finn called out to the young catgirl.

Still flustered by the testosterone pressing down around her on all sides, Aki attempted to focus. "I-it is, sir! Which means Tione and Tiona must be there, too..." She'd come rushing to Finn's and the others' sides not too long ago with the news from Loki's messenger—three pieces of news, in fact.

One, a brief summary of what *Kali Familia* had done.

Two, instructions to ready Aiz's and the others' weapons.

And three, an order to rally the troops and launch an attack on Meren.

"Is everyone here?"

"This should be everyone, yeah!"

After Aki's report, Finn had ordered their flag to be erected atop the city walls posthaste as a symbol for the rest of the familia to assemble. Now, they stood there complete, with the comical grin of the Trickster gazing down at them.

"Seems we're drawin' a bit of a crowd. Ye think it'll be a problem, Finn?" Gareth pointed out.

"*Ganesha Familia*, at least, hasn't shown any signs of movement. We should be fine. You've delivered the magic letter to the Guild as I instructed, right, Aki?"

"Sure did..." Aki replied with a tired sigh.

Indeed, the Trickster flag had garnered the attention of more than just *Loki Familia*. Even now, far down on the ground below, gods and civilians alike were beginning to gather, all of them pointing up at the *Loki Familia* assemblage as they whispered, "What's going on?"

The magic letter, on the other hand, was a memo written by Loki for Ouranos—it explained the current situation in Meren, the underhanded dealings of the Guild Branch Office, and more than a few threatening complaints regarding the entire affair. Aki had expedited the letter just as her goddess had asked, which explained her current fatigue.

"What of Aiz and the others' weapons?"

"Primed and ready. Thanks to the servicin' Tsubaki gave 'em during the expedition, it didn't take much to get 'em ready for the next fight," Gareth assured him.

"I've got Aiz's sword," Bete added.

"W-wait a second! Does this mean I have to carry Misses Tione's and Tiona's weapons all by myself?!" Raul this time. And it was true, the weapons had already been passed out, with Aiz's Desperate going to Bete, Riveria's staff going to Finn, and Tiona's giant oversized Urga falling directly into Raul's unlucky hands.

But no one paid him any mind, Finn turning around to address the rest of the group now that their preparations were complete.

"All right then, everyone! Our mission this time is to meet up with a certain pair of rambunctious sisters. While this may not seem like much...I assure you we're going to have our hands plenty full."

"You're tellin' us!"

"I just hope Miss Tione doesn't let me have it too hard!"

As Finn shrugged, the rest of the men half joked, half yelped in fear.

But even as they jested, ferocious grins of anger toward the ones threatening their companions proliferated throughout the entire group.

"These are direct orders from Loki. We're to find the two of them…and bring the hammer down."

The eyebrows of everyone present lifted in surprise.

Then Finn's smile vanished. In four words, he spurred them into action.

"Troops! Let's move out!"

The reaction was immediate as they all leaped off the side of the towering walls in one fell swoop. Bracing themselves for landing, they made sure their eyes never left their target—the city of Meren, veiled in darkness in front of them.

Loki Familia's ridiculously powerful reinforcements were on their way.

CHAPTER 6

WAR'S END

Гэта казка іншага сям'і.

канец смуты

"D-damn elven wench…!"

Moonlight trickled in through the window of the dim storehouse to reveal a certain branch manager tied quite securely to one of the pillars with a length of rope.

Riveria's handiwork, obviously.

"Someone from the Guild will be along sooner or later. You'll be able to confess to your crimes then."

—She'd left him with this before vacating the premises not long ago. Calmly accosting him in his desperate attempt to hide the mountain of transmissions and documents that evidenced his embezzlement—not only remunerations from Njörðr but evidence as to his own personal smuggling efforts, as well—she'd opted to simply leave the whole pile for whomever happened upon the unlucky man first.

For a man living in fear of a soon-to-come investigation from Guild Headquarters, things had taken an all-too-real turn for the worst.

"If I could…just…get free of these…confounded ropes…!!" he huffed, the long-faced man wriggling his body to and fro as blood pounded through his eyes. The secret knot-tying tricks of the forest high elves were not something an ordinary person could easily extricate themselves of no matter how much they struggled. And as he pulled and tugged at his bonds, face as red as a ripened tomato, he was just beginning to realize this all too fully, when suddenly.

"Rubart Ryan! So you were up to no good, you wretched man!"

"…?! Wh-who's there?!"

The voice was unfamiliar, reverberating around him in the dim space of the storehouse.

Jerking his head first left, then right, he searched nearby, but there was no one to be found.

The only company he had was that same disquieting shadow wrapped all around him.

"So ambitious and so accomplished, too. Even Ouranos had agreed that you might be able to turn things around for the Branch Office... and yet here you are. Oh, how the mighty fall."

"I—I command you to show yourself!" Rubart shouted into the darkness, his body trembling at the strangely ethereal voice that was neither male nor female.

Then.

"Though some of your actions may be pardonable considering your oh-so-laudable cause of restoring peace to the oceans—"

A cloak of blackest night cut through the darkness, revealing a shadowy figure in front of him.

"A gh-gh-gh-gh-gh-ghost?!" Rubart screamed, half-crazed by this point as he remembered all too vividly the long-running rumors of the spirit haunting the Branch Office.

"—that doesn't condone the fact that you took advantage of your position to line your own pockets. Disciplinary measures must be taken, Rubart."

No sooner had the words left the cloaked figure's mouth than a glowing green particle of light worked its way from one of its darkened sleeves. Rubart's face went white, the green light filling his mouth and lungs and rendering him unconscious almost instantly with his eyes still open in fright.

"To think I had to come all the way out here for this..." A grumble came from under the dark hood. With Rubart now sleeping soundly, the "ghost," Fels, looked down at the man with a good-natured slump of the shoulders. The Magus and right-hand man to the god of the Guild, Ouranos, let out a sigh.

"And here I thought Loki worked her men hard. But who am I to talk?" Fels added before looking up toward the window overhead—and the sudden sound of commotion coming from outside the storehouse. "Dear, dear. I should be making haste...It would seem they've already arrived."

Indeed, the cacophony of voices was already transforming into the battle song of a forward advance.

"Wh-what was that?"

Back in Meren's trade pier district…

As Aiz and the rest of *Loki Familia* squared off against Phryne and her assailants, the ears of the Amazons on guard perked up at the sounds behind them. They'd been stationed there to ensure no civilians made their way out onto the wharf, but the timbre of the earlier city commotion had taken a sudden shift. In fact, the sounds of fear and confusion as people fled had given way to…excited shouts, almost as though they were welcoming someone.

They turned their gazes to the rear, peering suspiciously through the blue shadow of nightfall—only to come face-to-face with an entire army charging straight in their direction.

"What the hell?!"

"L-Loki Familia?!"

The Trickster flag waved on high as the troops barreled their way into Meren. Making a beeline toward the pier, the men of *Loki Familia* stopped for nothing, stampeding straight through the city.

In less than an instant, the Amazonian guards were obliterated, completely overwhelmed by the galloping throng of male aggressors and their accompanying deep-bellied battle cry.

"Finn! You're here!"

"Apologies for our late arrival, Riveria. What's the current status?"

Finn and Riveria convened atop the roof of a nearby building, Meren's citizens mistaking the group for emissaries from Orario and welcoming them with buoyant cheers.

"Aiz and the others have been brought to a standstill farther down the road…As for Tione and Tiona…" Riveria began, filling Finn in on the rest of the situation.

Finn responded promptly, tossing out orders to Gareth and the rest of the troops following along on the road below. "Gareth! Take Raul and the others and head toward the western border of the city!"

"The west? The devil's goin' down over there?" Gareth asked in confusion.

"Tiona, Loki, and the others were last seen headed in that direction. Where's Bete?"

"Knowin' him, he's already tearin' things up at the pier!"

"Perfect. We'll leave that to him, then!"

"And what of us?" Riveria this time.

Finn glanced up at the question, turning his gaze toward the high elf next to him. He tossed her the long silver staff he'd been carrying—her Magna Alfs—and she responded with a nod.

"As for us, we'll—"

"Hrrggggrraaaaaaaaaghhhh!!"

"Ngh!!"

Silver sword met twin axes in a flurrying whirlwind of strikes.

With every incoming barrage, Aiz deftly knocked away the two bludgeons and retaliated with the wild flash of her blade, but no matter the angle of her sword, the fully armored giant of a woman always just barely managed to fend off her onslaught.

Phryne flinched beneath her visor. This wasn't some giant battle-ax she was up against—this was nothing but a single sword. But then why was her armor already covered in scratches? Why was the duel leaning in Aiz's favor?

Because she was the Sword Princess, that's why. And it didn't matter that their levels were now the same or that her wind magic had been sealed.

The temporary strength Phryne had gained for this duel was no match for the swordsmanship Aiz had perfected through hours upon hours of rigorous training. Aiz's technique and tactical prowess were simply too great for Phryne's own abilities to catch up.

"Youuuuuuuuu…annoying biiiiiiitch!" the giant woman wailed, putting everything she had into a single massive diagonal strike of her ax.

With blinding speed, Aiz sidestepped the incoming attack in all its overflowing, rage-induced power. Time came screeching to a halt as the Sword Princess retaliated with a spinning cut, so fast Phryne couldn't even register the movement.

"Ruuuuuuuuuaaaaaaaarrrrrrggggghhh!!"

The tempestuous horizontal strike collided with Phryne's torso, slicing across the armor with a magnificent flurry of sparks.

"Gnnnggraah…!! You…you scratched ittttt! My beautiful armor-rrrrrrrr!!"

—It…It only nicked it!

Aiz looked on in dismay at the superficial mark her attack had made on the armor's surface. She'd put everything she had into that hit, yet she'd still failed to fell the beast. And it wasn't that Phryne's reaction time had simply been too fast, either. It was for the same reason she'd already let so many other good opportunities during this fight pass her by—both literally and figuratively, her weapon just didn't cut it.

The sword she was using was not her own but a substitute, and her opponent's suit of armor was easily top grade. It put her at a distinct disadvantage, especially with their levels already so close.

Aiz glanced down at the blade of her sword, covered with nicks and chips. She had no idea how many more of Phryne's attacks the metal could take. As blood and light particles oozed their way out of the neat gash in Phryne's armor, Aiz turned to the woman with a sharp glare, the inklings of anxiety working their way up under her collar.

Then, suddenly.

"——————————————!!"

"!"

Her reinforcements arrived.

With a raging howl, the slew of *Loki Familia* men threw themselves at the surrounding circle of Amazons. Narfi and the other lower-level familia members, barely hanging on by that point, could only look on in speechless wonder as the sudden blitz stole their opponents from them.

Soon one, two, three, the Berbera fell one by one, no match against these new enemies.

"What the helllllllllll?! What'ssssss going on—?!"

But the Berbera weren't the only ones. A similar shadow quickly overtook the thunderstruck Phryne. Gray curls dancing, the werewolf leaped toward her like a starved animal, thirsty for blood.

"Gyyyyyyaaah———?!"

There was a brilliant flash as the kick connected with her armor.

Phryne barely managed to defend herself, bringing an ax down just in time, but the sheer force of the kick still sent her careening backward and forming deep grooves in the dirt with her heels.

"Yo, Aiz."

"Mister Bete…!"

Bete turned his gaze toward Aiz with an incredulous look, and Aiz herself was taken aback.

"I thought you were supposed to be goin' up against that *Kali Familia* whatsit! But this is just that nasty frog from *Ishtar Familia*."

It didn't take long for Aiz to realize that Loki must have been the one to call in the cavalry. A bit shamefaced, she quickly filled in Bete on the current situation.

"I don't understand…a single bit of what you just told me, aside from the fact that these cows are keepin' us from Tiona and Tione," Bete started, face darkening as he spoke. He could tell that the normally emotionless girl was desperately trying to string together her words in a way that made sense. "Aiz, you go on ahead."

"What?"

"Y'gotta save those numbskull Amazons, don'tcha? They'll do a lot better with your help than mine anyway," Bete continued almost languidly, ignoring the way Aiz's brows rose in surprise. "I'll take care of things here." The red glint of Phryne's armor reflected in his amber eyes.

"B-but she's as strong as a Level Six! And…and my magic, it was sealed, so going up against her alone would be—"

"Awww, shut the hell up, would ya?" The werewolf cut her off with an irate growl, already a Level 6 himself. "Only a little longer now..." he hissed, looking up. "Only a little longer, and I'll become stronger than even you...at least without that wind of yours."

"!"

Confused, Aiz, too, turned her gaze upward to the night sky. To the clouds drifting among all that inky blue and the moonlight just starting to peek through the veil.

Taking her Desperate from him, she nodded.

She ran out of there as fast as she could.

"Stop right there, Sword Princesssssss!"

"You're not going anywhere!"

"?!"

Enraged, Phryne made to follow the swordswoman, only to find her path cut short by a werewolf. She brought her axes up to fend off the incoming kick, revealing her monstrous tongue. "Donnnnnnnn't mess with me, Vanargand! I know youuuuuuuu can't get enough of me, but I doooooooon't have time for this!!" Her face was already the same color as her crimson armor.

"You smokin' somethin', froggy?" Bete spat out, not even trying to disguise his disgust.

Whether or not she knew of the rage surging through the werewolf's entire body, Phryne let out a grand peal of laughter.

"Hee-hee-hee!! I'll warn you! I'mmmmmm a great deal stronger now, after chasing that sssssssorry girl! You think I care that you leveled up? You're nothing but a dog with itsssssss tail between its legs!"

The air around Bete froze with a *crack*.

"Yer gonna regret those words..."

A dangerous glint appeared in his eyes.

Almost as if in response to his call, the clouds parted to reveal the light of the moon.

"Hee-hee...hee...?" Phryne's echoing laugh came to an abrupt halt.

The scene outside her visor was...changing.

Golden light flooded the once-dark pier, sending faint tremors up and down Bete's body, and the werewolf's shadow trembled ever so slightly against the ground.

And then the pupils of his amber eyes suddenly turned to slits that split the irises right down the middle, almost like some kind of feral beast's.

"N-no way..."

He stood with the moon at his back, his canines enlarged and sharpened, and his gray hair practically standing on end.

Phryne could only stare in horror as the shadow on the ground warped into a terrifying, crazed wolf.

"Nhag loy! Korru jhi roojeh!"

"Negrub fuu Kali?!"

Wh-what are they saying...?

Lefiya thought back in one of the caverns in the winding sea cave. The Amazons left to guard her had burst into a flurry of anxious activity, and though she had no idea what they were saying, she could hazard a guess in response to their reactions.

Someone's here? Maybe they came into the cave...At least that's what it seems like. Why else would they be scuttling about so?

And certainly invaders could mean only one thing—Aiz and the others were on their way.

Lefiya swallowed hard.

I can't very well sit here and do nothing, then, can I? At the very least, I need to inform them of my location...!

But the question was how, especially with these brutish guards keeping watch.

Even in the current commotion, the four of them had yet to avert their eyes from Lefiya. And Lefiya, well, she had nothing but magic in her arsenal, and if Kali's words were to be believed, if she even tried to whisper a quick chant, they'd crush her little neck faster than the words could pass her lips...

The mental reminder was enough to make her shake her head in furious refusal.

"...?"

Until, all of a sudden, she realized something.

There was a crack running through the rock face overhead, just high enough that it entered her vision when she tilted her head up. While not wide enough to let a mouse or rat pass, it was just wide enough to let a sliver of moonlight filter through.

—Light? Then...it connects to the world outside—.

With that revelation came an idea, and quite suddenly she knew exactly what she needed to do.

It was a reckless plan. In fact, she might as well have been gambling on the impossible, and it was going to require ample courage. But if she couldn't even do something as simple as this, certainly she would never amount to anything more than excess baggage for Aiz and the others to carry around—!

With her hands still bound by their chains, her body gave a shiver. She was ready.

I'm a ridiculous magic powerhouse, I'm a ridiculous magic powerhouse, I'm a ridiculous magic powerhouse...

The words Loki had spoken to her back when she'd updated her Status reverberated in her heart like a mantra of courage. Then, gathering every tiny ounce of pure determination she had, she sucked in her breath in one mighty *whoosh*.

"...?"

The action was enough to draw suspicious glances from every Amazon in the cave. But it was too late.

"*—Unleashed pillar of light, limbs of the holy tree!!*"

"?!"

Her chant had already begun.

She bellowed it from the top of her lungs, not even bothering to hide it, not resorting to any tricks and simply singing with everything she had.

For a single instant, the Amazonian guards could do nothing but stand there in shock, and during that time, an enormous magic circle formed around Lefiya's kneeling form. Just as the guards were about to spring into action, the golden light seared into their eyes with a brilliant flash.

—A smoke screen?!

Or at least that was the Amazons' first thought, but in fact, Lefiya's intentions were quite different.

No, her goal was to fill up the cave with so much light that it escaped that crack in the rock and lit up the sky—.

"*You are the master—*"

"Rhu moona!"

"Guh?!"

One of the Amazons leaped toward her, cutting her chant short. Down came the knife, directly toward her throat, but with a yank of her chains, Lefiya somehow managed to block the incoming attack.

Her magic circle was still intact. There was no snuffing it out now. And as Lefiya's light shone through that crack in the wall, she willed her friends to see it.

Miss Aiz, Miss Aiz, Miss Aiiiiiiiiiiiiz————!!

Her heart cried out desperately for the one she loved, and just as the other Amazons drew near, reaching for her—there was a ground-shaking explosion.

"?!"

The ceiling above them gave way, rocks and shrapnel flying as a lone adventurer came bounding down into the cave. Her call had been answered, and the one who'd shattered rock and stone to save her was none other than—

—Miss Aiz!

She turned her trembling eyes in the direction of her savior and took in the sight of that gorgeous, slender swordswo—Since when did Aiz have muscles like that? And a-a beard?!

"Ye all right, lass?"

It wasn't Aiz at all but, in fact, Gareth.

Her magic circle went out with a *hiss.*

"...Not as easy on the eyes as the one ye're expectin', am I?"

"That's—?! N-n-n-no, Mister Gareth! I'm not—, I wasn't—,

s-s-surely you're just imagining things!!" Lefiya desperately tried to explain, sweat breaking out across her temples.

But Gareth saw right through her all the same. "Sorry, lass. I know I can never be Aiz," he muttered with a sigh before reshouldering his Grand Ax.

"Gha-gha reem?!"

The flabbergasted Amazons stood rooted to their spots at this new development, then quickly readied their weapons and began to move. The tense cry had clearly been some kind of command, because one of them shot forward, straight at Gareth.

In response, Gareth readied his own arm, balling his free hand into a fist to promptly bash the incoming body out of the way.

"———"

BAM!! The Amazon went flying, and the cave shook with noise as she collided with the far rock wall. She wasn't getting up after that.

Once again, time seemed to slow to a crawl, neither Lefiya nor the Amazons saying a word.

"Reminds me of the first time I met those two ragamuffins." Gareth laughed before tossing aside his ax. The day played out in his head like it was yesterday—when he'd sent Tiona flying just like this not more than five years ago—and the giant dwarf warrior turned to face his remaining opponents. "Ye seem pretty confident in yer skills, don't ye, lassies?" he said, cracking his knuckles with a popping sound that echoed off the walls. "But yer still green."

Then he laughed an uproarious, fearless laugh.

"————————?!"

Something stirred inside the Amazons. They might not have had any idea what the dwarf was saying, but they did know one thing—he was making fun of them, and almost in sync, the whole lot of them came charging at Gareth at once.

What happened next was enough to drain the color from Lefiya's face—Gareth's fist sent each of the incoming Amazons flying into the wall one after another.

The moon glimmered in the blue sky overhead.

The clouds had all but disappeared, and its golden light poured down on the ground below.

And beneath that watching gaze, in the middle of Meren's trade pier, clash after clash of a raging battle echoed throughout the docks. Again and again the clamorous percussion of metal on metal punctuated the air.

"Grrrrraaaaaaagggggghhh…!!" Phryne belted out, her voice hoarse and her face exposed to the night breeze. Her fat arms, short legs, and even her round torso engulfed in shimmering particles of light had been laid bare. At her feet, the crimson pieces of her armor lay like bloody shrapnel, still glinting in the moonlight. Nearly all the reinforced plating had been torn off. The full-body suit of armor she'd been so proud of was nothing short of decimated.

Thanks to a certain werewolf.

"This is…this is innnnnnsane! How can you…be even more powerful than…than the Sword Princesssssss…?!" She ground her teeth, and her ghastly, froggy face had become all the more ghastly once it was stained with blood and vehemence.

Across from her, the werewolf stood in stark contrast, backlit by the light of the moon as a heavy globule of drool leaked down from between his lips. The pieces of her strewn armor crackled under his feet like mere crushed pebbles.

Phryne's bulbous eyes dilated before the glare of his silvery metal boots.

"Hr-hrrrrrrruuuuuuuuuaaaaaaAAAAAAARRRRGHHHHHH!!"

With a roar that split the air, she charged forward, ax flying.

She put everything she had behind that strike, barreling toward the wolf and still surrounded by light particles, and he responded in kind, moving at a near impossible speed to meet her with an accelerating kick of his own. They collided.

"____________"

Her ax met the same fate as her armor.

As the broken fragments scattered in slow motion, the particles around her fizzled into nothing.

"M-my time rannnnnnnn out—?!"

But before she could so much as lament her life's choices, Bete's metal boots were streaking toward her face. Her expression froze in horror, the word *"Wait!"* stuck between her lips, but even if she'd been able to get it out, it wouldn't have stopped the charging wolf, and with a kick that made the very air groan, the heels of those silvery boots hit her head-on.

"GUUUUWWOOOOOOOOOOOOUGH!!"

It was a direct hit that sent her rotund body sailing through the air, obliterating every object it encountered along the way. She flew all the way past the docks, plunging into the waters of Lolog Lake beyond.

There was a tremendous splash, and the Berbera still fighting on the pier nearby looked up in shocked dismay. Even the Amazons still hiding in the shadows on the roof of the storehouse could only look on in horror.

"A-Aisha…?!"

"…!" The long-legged warrior, Aisha, grimaced beneath her turban. "He's transformed!"

Werewolves had long been considered the least-suited race for Dungeon crawling all across Orario because deep within the bowels of the Dungeon, they had no access to the moon—the source of their true power. These sorts of "transformations" had been confirmed only in a limited number of animal-person species. It was an ability that unleashed not only their untapped power but their innate animalistic nature as well, "trading rationality for strength," as the saying went. And for werewolves, the key to their transformation was none other than the light of the moon.

While this werewolf skill was well-known across the globe, none of the Amazons had ever seen it in person, nor anything like the sheer overwhelming boost of power it gave to his abilities now.

"Vanargand…!"

With blazing speed and honed strikes, he could decimate his opponent in an instant, turning the battlefield into a bloody brawl. Even the werewolf's alias on her lips was enough to make her shudder.

"Gngh…?!"

She could feel the fear radiating off her veiled companion behind her.

The werewolf's gray fur was standing on end, giving off the illusion that it had grown in length. His amber eyes, still split down the middle, emanated a kind of savage lunacy.

Looking at him now, the veiled girl felt her tail, similar to his own, begin to tremble in subconscious terror.

"—There you are."

Snorting, Bete turned in their direction, eyes staring straight through the darkness to where they shielded themselves in shadow.

None of them so much as breathed—and then he charged.

"Shit!" Aisha hissed, the first to spring to her feet, and though the other Amazons leaped to defend them, it was too late.

Pudao swords and other weapons came at him, but they couldn't so much as graze his fur. His single flying kick connected with the group of hidden warriors, hurling them away.

"You damn animal!"

"Don't try it, Rena!!"

But the girl wouldn't listen, flourishing her scimitar and sending it toward one of Bete's gauntlets. It glanced off with barely more than a haphazard bounce.

Bete turned to her, now frozen in the air, and punched her straight in the gut.

"Nnguuuuuh!"

Her scream followed behind her as she was sent flying. Bete, however, turned toward the lone animal girl, now helpless without her Amazonian guards.

"—!!"

"You're the one controlling that light, aren't you?!"

Just like Aiz, Bete, too, had noticed the Level-6 Status Phryne currently boasted. But as soon as the particles of light flitting about her had disappeared, she'd turned into nothing more than a hapless civilian. Not about to leave the source of all that power—this conspicuously out-of-place girl who looked more like a shrine maiden than anything else—at large, he stood ready to bring his full strength down right on her head.

"Ah—"

Until.

He caught a glance of her through the pale-white shroud of her veil, and the trembling green eyes staring back at him brought his hand to an abrupt halt.

"Hngh!!"

Aisha saw her opening and took it, jumping forward in the nick of time to pull the girl to safety.

"M-Miss Aisha—!"

"There's no time to talk. All of you, run!!" Aisha commanded, her voice ringing out across the battlefield even as she struggled to push her injured body forward. Her fellow Berbera were quick to follow her order, all of them retreating into the darkness.

Soon, none but *Loki Familia* remained.

"..."

The battle on the pier was over. Finally, silence had returned to the dark city.

All that was left was the quiet lull of the tide from the direction of the lake. With a slump, Bete let his left arm, still held aloft, drop to his side.

Whether his froggy opponent had sunk to the bottom of the lake or floated her way to safety, he didn't know, and he didn't care, either. He wasn't in the mood to go running after her.

He couldn't seem to shake those jade eyes from his memory. Lips curling in disgust (and his tattoo with them), he shot a wad of spit toward the ground.

"If yer not willin' to fall in the fire, don't jump in the pan..."

Back in the sea cave.

The rite continued down within the arena nature had built. It should have been over already, but instead, the two women continued to go at each other with undiminished strength, coming closer and closer to the grand finale of their battle.

"Hiiiii-YAH!"

"Ngh!" Bache quickly dodged Tiona's incoming attack. The other Amazon no longer feared the armor of Velgas surrounding her body, nor each strike aiming to kill. And as she swung her leg with enough force to break bone, attempting to throw Bache off her feet, Bache took to the air and brought her own heel up for a downward swipe at the top of Tiona's head.

Tiona was too fast, her catlike reflexes moving her nimbly out of harm's way, and Bache's ax kick went flying into the ground. Her heel connected with the stone and cracked it in two. For a moment, the rock burned, smoke rising from the effects of Bache's Velgas.

"Hey, you guys! If I win, do I get some sorta prize, just like before?" Tiona shouted as she chucked a rock she'd picked up during her evasive maneuvers in Bache's direction.

Bache didn't reply, Velgas-coated fist rising to meet the rock and shattering it into pieces as she charged. Kali, on the other hand, furrowed her brows in curious doubt as she watched the goings-on down below.

"You're really somethin' else, you know that?…But what the hell. What were you thinkin'?"

"If I win…I want you to make it so Bache and Argana don't have to fight anymore!"

This was enough to widen not only Kali's eyes but Bache's, as well.

"I'm not sayin' you have to stop the rites entirely, 'specially for those who like 'em! But Bache doesn't wanna fight anymore, yeah? She doesn't wanna die! Just like Tione and me! So I want her to be able to do whatever she wants!!"

A chance for Bache to escape from Kali's command, from the brunt of Argana's bloodlust. Even now, in the midst of their close-quarter duel, Bache's movements dulled ever so slightly.

"…Don't listen to her, Bache. You think I'd be stupid enough to release you for losing? Don't make me laugh! Victory is the only path to survival."

"...I understand, Kali," Bache replied, devoid of emotion, and soon her attacks packed the same punch as before.

"But why?!" Tiona shouted.

"You think your words mean shit? *Ha!* As if I'd grant you any old stupid request."

"You're just a greedy old hag!" Tiona was whining now, bickering like a small child even as she was pummeled with attacks.

"And that's good enough for me!" Kali shot back, sticking out her tongue in an equally childish riposte. "...It's a good thing I'm here to watch over your fight," she continued, going stoic beneath her mask. "At least with Argana and Tione, I know they'll complete the rite. They'll continue fighting until the bitter end, offering up their opponent's dead carcass in triumphant victory."

"...!"

"Because Argana and Tione...are made from the same mold."

Tiona twisted her head upward. "That's not true!"

"Yes it is!" Kali simply laughed. "Argana may have her relentless fighting spirit, but Tione has her anger, and they're both the same, ever-enduring and ever-abiding. When that girl gets really, truly angry...she wouldn't hesitate a moment to end her opponent's life."

Almost as if in response to Kali's murmured allegations, a similar battle to the death intensified, far away atop its ship out at sea.

"————————————————HrrrruuuaaaaAAAGH!!"

Tione roared, all her rage and all her fury sending her fist into Argana's abdomen. The force sent a waterfall of blood down Argana's chin.

"Guh-guaagh...ha-ha, ha-ha-ha-ha-ha-ha-ha!! You're still...growing stronger...are you, Tione?!"

"I thought I told you to shut up!!" The sight of all that blood, the sound of Argana's vicious laughter—it only served to spur Tione on further. It didn't matter how much of her own life Argana's strikes had already carved away. It didn't matter how much blood came bubbling out between Argana's lips. Tione couldn't stop; her fists, her feet—all stained red—just kept flying.

Relentlessly, mercilessly, she threw blow after blow, the aura of vibrant red air around her darkening as her every strike sought to rend the other Amazon limb from limb.

Argana had her curse. But Tione had her skill.

And Argana was forced to admit that these two weren't exactly the most compatible of abilities. As her own defenses took a sharp decline, Tione's attack power only climbed and climbed.

One strike. One strike was all it would take. Tione was becoming the sword that would behead the snake.

While there were any number of ways Tione could have overpowered the other Amazon using her technique and skills, she forgot all of them—simply railing on her again and again, her entire mind, her entire being focused on wringing the very life from Argana's body. And with every punch, more and more blood came spurting from Argana's mouth.

Argana took all of it, making no move to cancel her curse.

Perhaps it was a sign of respect, perhaps a way of not turning her back on the battle at hand. So as not to dirty the sacred rites of her country.

And Argana, who refused to put nothing but her best foot forward, was dying.

"Are you going to kill me, Tione? Good!" She laughed, even now trembling with excitement, with a scorching pain. "My blood will become yours, and I shall live forever! Together with those I've already consumed! We shall arrive, all of us, at war's end!!" She was howling now, her state of mind practically no different from Kali's own.

"We shall become…the strongest warrior!!"

—Shut up, shut up, SHUT UP.

Argana's words were like white noise to Tione's ears.

—I'll defeat her. I'll kill her. With my own hands. I'll steal the life from her eyes.

This monster of Telskyura, who represented everything she and Tiona had been made to suffer—she was going to kill her. And she was going to protect her sister.

There was one key difference between her and Tiona—and that was how much they condemned Telskyura. Tione, who'd never been able to smile the way Tiona had, retained nothing but a quietly amassed resentment, like a shadow hanging over her. Without even realizing it, Tione was becoming every bit the warrior she'd so tried to escape.

Kali had been right on the money.

While there might have been a temporary slump in Tiona and Bache's rite, Tione and Argana's never faltered. On and on they fought, showing no signs of hesitation or misgiving. Tione's rage was propelling her toward the future of war Kali desired.

Kali had all of them in the palm of her hand. It had been she who'd ordered Argana and Tione's fight to take place out at sea, where no one could interfere, and she who'd decided to remain in the cave and watch over Bache and Tiona.

Everything was going exactly as she'd planned.

"I'll kill you, Tione! Come here and let me drink the life from your veins!!"

"RuuuuuaaaaaaaaaaaaaaaAAAAAAGGGGGHHH!!"

As Argana coaxed her, voice dripping with joy and rage, the Amazonian warriors beside them raised their own voices in vociferous climax.

The final curtain call so lusted after by their goddess was growing steadily nearer.

Tione...!

Back in the cave, Tiona scowled. The constant drumming in her ears was louder now, sending rippling waves of heat all the way to the tips of her fingers.

"Ngh!"

Not missing the opening, Bache threw a knife-hand strike toward her face, and Tiona had less than a second to dodge the incoming Velgas. She leaped backward, narrowly avoiding the attack as it went into the wall, sending shards of smoking, toxic rock flying.

Tiona's cheek and hair, too, sizzled where Bache's hand had grazed her, and moving back, she reestablished the distance between them.

I can't be worrying about Tione now. I have to focus on winning this battle first...

If not, she was in for a world of hurt from her sister. She turned her gaze toward Bache and the icy-cold stare the other Amazon was directing her way. Feeling the sweat running off her in droves, she let out another breath of crimson air.

"My big hits keep missing..." she mumbled beneath her breath, and it was true—three times now she'd tried to lay the finishing blow on Bache only to miss her target. While she knew pecking away at the other Amazon with short, quick strikes would do nothing but get her own body further scorched by Bache's Velgas, Bache herself wasn't so negligent as to leave herself open for any type of critical hit. "What should I doooooooo?"

She didn't have much time. That much she knew.

She could keep smiling all she wanted, but pain was still pain, and heartache was still heartache.

In fact, if she had any choice in the matter at all, she'd much rather have curled up right there on the floor and taken a good long nap.

Kinda reminds me of those caterpillar critters down in the Dungeon. If only I had some sorta weapon...then I could figure somethin' out.

Not that it was an acceptable scenario, considering she'd probably kill Bache right out.

But if I had my Urga...then what would I do? she mused, looking down at her fist as her mind went to her beloved weapon still under maintenance.

This poison was different from that of those caterpillars. Though her skin may change its color, lose its feeling, and squirm with an agonizing pain, it didn't melt or lose its shape.

Her breath grew darker, saturated with more and more red.

"..."

Then slowly, she began to stretch.

Bending her knees, she let out a deep puff of air.

"Bache."

"..."

She looked the other woman straight in the eye. Bache's face was expressionless, and her lips were closed tight beneath the black of her neckerchief.

"—I'm coming for you."

And with that, their final duel began.

Tiona's inaugural strike was a flying punch, straight from the front.

"?!"

Both of them attacked, counterattacked, blocked. They went at each other like dogs, and the swirling mass of toxic light circling Bache's body seared Tiona's skin every time they touched. As she danced out of harm's way, her feet as bare as the elves', Tiona was foregoing all manner of evasion and simply throwing herself at the other Amazon with everything she had.

What is she thinking?

Bache's eyes hardened as she watched Tiona come at her. It was ridiculous, really, coming straight from the front like that. Her Velgas was not only a method of attack but one of defense, as well. And every time Tiona's fist came at her, no matter if it hit, no matter if it was blocked, no matter if it was fended off, the toxins ate away at her bit by bit. It didn't matter how high of a status resistance she might have—if she didn't heal herself soon, she had only about five minutes of fight left in her.

And as for the finishing blow she'd been trying to lay on Bache for some time now, she had only about one.

Had the other girl really let herself go this time? Abandoned all reason in her desperation? The thought had only just crossed Bache's mind when—

"____________"

—her attacks began hitting nothing but air.

And the attacks landing on her came faster and faster, the accuracy of Tiona's punches and kicks seeming especially on point.

Bache threw punch after rock-crushing punch. But none of them hit. Tiona was gone. Then suddenly she'd be right next to her, landing a kick to her shoulder. She could hear the sound of Tiona's skin sizzling against her Velgas. Again and again and again.

—She's...

Their timing no longer matched.

Tiona's speed was rising.

Alarmingly so.

And not only that, the power behind her punches was rising, too.

Bache's eyes shook in their sockets. And all of a sudden, that painfully smiling face came directly into view.

Sh-she can't be—!

Tiona's skill, Intense Heat.

Similar to her Berserk skill, every time she took damage, it increased the course-correcting effects of her abilities. The more cornered she was, the closer she came to death, the more her survival and battle instincts turned into pure, concentrated power, flaring up inside her.

—Which meant Bache couldn't let her land an attack. But Bache couldn't attack her, either. Or to put it another way, whether she turned the other cheek or simply let it all fly, Tiona's Status would simply keep on rising.

The damage from her Velgas was going to keep on strengthening the other Amazon no matter what she did.

"Gngh!!"

Tiona's two boosts had stacked themselves.

Bache, on the other hand, couldn't land a single hit. She couldn't dodge a single blow. And she couldn't guard against a single incoming strike.

Bone-crunching punches slammed into her face. Flailing toes met her chin in earsplitting kicks. Throws sent her hurtling through the air to slam hard against the ground.

Higher, higher, higher.

Speed, endurance, power—all of it rose, seemingly without limit.

Up, up, up, up, up, up—it never ceased.

"Nothing can stop me noooooOOOOO*OOOOOOWWWWWW*!!"

The wave of attacks beat against Bache's body with the force of a raging river.

Wounds opened up all over her faster than she could even register them, shaking her so much she couldn't even maintain her Velgas.

Blood was leaking from her every pore now, coloring every inch of her copper skin.

Tiona, you—

Tiona was on fire. Burning brightly, ablaze with life.

Despite the pain and despite the heartache, she'd stood tall, utilizing the most relentless method she could to bring Bache down. Her eyes were hazy, evidence of the struggle her own body was enduring to keep her alive.

And yet through all of it—her smile never once faltered.

Instead, she was creeping toward her, looking more and more like the snake Bache had come to fear—her sister, the embodiment of death.

"Gngh…gnnnnrrrraaaAAAAAGHH!!" Bache screamed, the first time she'd even raised her voice during the duel, trying to dismiss that horrible building fear of death shaking her to the core. Her mask of insouciance gone, her eyes glinting, she gathered together all the power deep down inside her and wrung out every last drop of the murderously toxic venom exuding from her pores.

Who would fall first? Tiona or Bache?

Faster and faster their fists flew, and the great abyss of death transformed into their final arena.

"——*RRRRUUUUUUUUUAAAAAAAARRRRRGGGGGHHH!!*"

They were boiling now.

Battering punches. Flying kicks. The fire burning within them both set their fight ablaze.

Even their voices met in a battle of roars, shaking the very walls of the cavern.

"HA-HA-HA-HA-HA-HA-HA! This is it! This is truly a rite of the arena, a life-and-death duel! This is the fight I've been waiting for!!" Kali laughed gleefully, her eyes wide and glimmering as the rest of the Amazons found themselves taken aback at the sheer power behind the echoing voices.

"Tiona!!"

Bache's voice screamed as her fist came in contact with Tiona's abdomen.

The air rushed out of the other girl with an audible *guhhh.*

"Are you smiling now?!"

The poison ripped through her, all along her skin, burning her nerves, and the pain and shock practically sent her to her knees.

But even through all of it, even though the hellish torture ravaging her entire body, Tiona still smiled.

"—You bet I am!!"

And then she punched back.

Her fist sank into Bache's abdomen with the same force the other Amazon had just inflicted on her. Bache's body curved into an unnatural C shape at the force, blood shooting from her mouth.

"Hurt me all you want! Bleed me all you want! I'll never stop laughing!!"

A spinning kick.

Bache dodged this one, both of them jumping back to put distance between them.

"I'll smile…for those who can't!!"

The treasure she'd received in that story of legend, that unwavering promise, two sisters smiling and laughing together.

She'd smile for tomorrow. She'd smile because she believed in the happiness that awaited.

The gazes of the two Amazons met. Then they drew their arms back, preparing themselves for the final strike.

Tiona clenched her fist.

Bache focused the light of her Velgas.

Then they charged, smile meeting bloodlust in a mad dash toward the center.

"Gnnnngh!!"

They collided.

Red-hot air hit purplish black light particles at point-blank range.

It happened in an instant, Bache one step ahead, her fist flying and, with it, her Velgas.

"TIONAAAAAAAAAAAAAAAAAAAAAA!!"

She hurtled straight at her face, straight at that smile—but Tiona ignored it.

Instead, she was focused on Bache's arm, on a spot of skin where the light of her Velgas seemed to have disappeared, and reaching her own arm around it, she pushed down.

The strike barreling toward her face suddenly wasn't anymore.

"————————"

Bache's eyes dilated in surprise.

"Bache—"

Her attack was gone. All that was left was that smile—and then Tiona roared.

"Here I...GOOOOOOOOOOOOOOOOOOOOOO————!!"

The explosion was instantaneous.

"Gungh?!"

Tiona's right fist came straight into Bache's chest.

So much power. Bache's body was launched away, crashing into the far rock wall with a horrific crunch.

Urga. The Amazon word for "great destruction."

Letting herself get within a hairbreadth of death, she'd built up the effects of her skill to its very limits, releasing a truly "final" finishing blow.

It was the strongest attack she had in her arsenal.

"—Gn—gh..."

Peeling away, Bache took first one step, then two steps, then, wobbling, she fell to her knees. She collapsed to the ground, right then and there, robbed of her voice aside from the stuttered grunt making its way past her lips.

Tiona had won.

"—Se wehga! Se wehga! Se wehga!"

Thou art the true warrior! Thou art the true warrior! Thou art the true warrior!

All around her, her fellow Amazons raised their voices in

thunderous praise, extolling her, the victor. It was enough to shake the walls of stone and rock surrounding them—Tiona with her breath ragged and Bache facedown on the ground.

"Well done! Well done!"

Two tiny hands came together in excited applause. Kali smiled beneath her mask, more than satisfied, as she lauded Tiona from above.

"That was just wonderful! Guess that settles it, then. Letting you go truly was my one big mistake, Tiona. I was too soft. Too soft!"

"..."

"You've proven victorious in the rite...However, your opponent lives," Kali continued, her eyes flitting from Tiona, exhausted and covered in wounds, to Bache, still lying on the ground.

Indeed, the chest of the sandy-haired Amazon continued to rise and fall. The blessing Kali had bestowed unto her long, long ago yet endured.

"Go ahead and kill her." The smile was audible in her command. "Only then can the rite be complete."

Tiona's response, however, was all too direct.

"Don't wanna."

It was no different from that day, so long ago, when Tiona had looked her goddess in the eye and insisted that she didn't want to fight her sister.

"I'm not a warrior anymore."

"..."

"...and Tione isn't, either. We're adventurers now."

Kali found herself at a loss for words.

"I'm not gonna kill anyone else...not anymore, Kali!"

Now even the ovation of her sisters quieted.

Tiona glanced up, meeting that of her goddess's gaze in the middle of that silent stone arena.

"...You really have changed."

Kali finally muttered slowly, almost mournfully.

But it didn't last, her earlier smile returning to her face.

"...But one thing certainly hasn't changed, and that's your connection with your sister."

The goddess raised her arm, and all of a sudden, the other Amazons who'd been watching over the match charged into the arena, descending upon Tiona.

They surrounded her in an instant.

"Tione is with Argana right now…far, far out at sea. There's no one to save you."

"…"

"You're coming with us…back to Telskyura!"

Even Tiona knew it would be pointless to put up a fight at this point. Even now, she walked the line between life and death—it was the only way she'd been able to release her inner Urga, after all—and standing there was taking everything she had. She couldn't even think of raising a finger, let alone a fist. And then there was the poison from Bache's Velgas to contend with, still coursing through her. It would be so easy for them to simply carry her back to their ship.

"Which of them will come, I wonder. Argana? Tione?…Whichever one lives will be your next opponent. An offering to the strongest warrior!"

The goddess of war and bloodshed couldn't be swayed. As Tiona looked up at her through blurred eyes, she couldn't think of a single way out of this mess, and around her, the circle of Amazons grew smaller and smaller.

When all of a sudden—ever so lightly.

A breeze brushed past her cheek, playing with the strands of her hair.

Wind. Faint yet very definitely there, reaching out all the way to her deep within that cave.

"…You're wrong, Kali," Tiona said with a smile, her eyes closing. It was a different kind of smile this time, quiet and peaceful.

Kali raised an eyebrow dubiously.

Then Tiona opened her eyes. "Because Tione and I aren't alone anymore."

It was then that it happened.

The trickle of air turned into a rushing blast into the cave.

"We have friends now!"

One brilliant, gleaming slash, then another, hundreds of them, raced around the group as Kali and her followers' eyes opened in shock. Before her lightning-fast onslaught, the circle of Amazons around her was blown away.

"The Sword Princess…?"

The golden-haired, golden-eyed swordswoman appeared before them, barring their path to Tiona and flourishing her silver sword with an audible slice as it cut through the air.

"—Are you all right, Tiona?"

Even as bedraggled as she was, Tiona burst into a smile, at her companion who had raced to save her, faster than anyone else.

At her beloved friend.

"I am now!"

Almost as if on cue, the rest of *Loki Familia* came barreling into the cave with a mighty war cry. They flung themselves on the remaining Amazons with weapons flying.

Kali shot to her feet, her seemingly impenetrable calm demeanor gone in an instant.

"That damn Ishtar…Were they defeated already?!"

The battle below her was practically over before it started, Aiz and the rest of her peers quickly suppressing Kali's warriors. At *Ishtar Familia*'s retreat, the curse restricting Aiz's Airiel had been undone, and she released it now in waves across the battlefield. The other adventurers, too, not wanting to be outdone, raised their voices in murderous, frenzied cries as they set themselves on the Amazonian warriors. Their power was overwhelming, a result of their knowledge that a companion, one of their own, was in danger.

Kali's gaze narrowed as she grit her teeth in scarcely contained rage.

"—Looks like you picked the wrong people to mess with, you damned little gremlin."

The voice came from out of nowhere.

From above even her as she stood over the battlefield.

She looked skyward with a jolt, only to find a certain ginger-haired goddess seated on a rock ledge jutting out not far from the ceiling.

It was Loki.

"How ya feelin' right about now, huh? All your glorious plans crashing down around you with your precious children lyin' face-down in the dirt?"

She'd just appeared from the hole behind her that led into the rest of the cave. The smaller goddess's unsightly development was all too amusing.

"Don't patronize me!" Kali snarled, pointed canines snapping.

Loki's vermilion eyes opened ever so slightly as her smile widened. "I'm just sayin', is all, you pint-size ignoramus. You really…really picked the wrong people to mess with." The smile accompanying her sentiment this time could easily have rivaled that of the most nefariously wicked god, all her anger at the smaller goddess coming back a thousandfold. It was the ultimate depraved sneer, enough to make even the faces of Njörðr and Rod, who'd accompanied her into the cave, twitch in fear.

Kali's face burned with shame and humiliation beneath her mask, the screams of her warriors echoing around her.

"…And yet, Tione has never strayed from my will. She's gone already. She's far away where you miserable scum can't reach her, continuing her own fight," she hissed between her clenched teeth with a vengeful smile.

"Oh pish. You think I'm worried about her?"

"…What do you mean?"

Loki flapped her hand dismissively before looking up and behind her toward the hole from whence she'd come. The two figures that appeared from the darkness were none other than Gareth and the very much no longer captured Lefiya.

The dwarf nodded at his patron deity's glance.

"I've got my strongest knight on the job."

Back on the Amazonian ship still far out in the ocean southwest of Meren.

The rite currently taking place was reaching its finish.

The spectators knew this, all of them Telskyuran warriors who'd seen more than their fair share of battles. The end wasn't far off. And facing the two combatants now, Tione and Argana, still at each other's throats in violent repartee, they clamored for victory, for glory, and, most importantly, for death.

Tione and Argana were giving everything they had to take down their blood-covered opponents. They no longer saw anyone else; Argana reflected in Tione's eyes the same way Tione was reflected in Argana's.

—I'll kill her. I'LL KILL HER!!

Tione's vision had gone red. Argana, however, only smiled deeper the more Tione's true warrior's nature shone through. Each one of them was looking for an opening, a shot at landing the finishing blow and bringing down their opponent once and for all.

Nothing but pure, concentrated rage controlled Tione now. Her every move was dictated by a need to kill. No one could stop her. Not her goddess. Not even her friends.

But if there was someone.

If there was someone who could stop her…it would have been her other half. Her younger sister—

"That's far enough."

—But the voice was not that of her sister. It was someone who'd bested her, who'd stolen her heart.

"?!"

No sooner had Tione and Argana been about to lay into each other for the last time than a spear thrust its way between them, lodging itself in the wooden floor. It was long and boasting a tip of pure golden alloy. The two Amazons found themselves frozen where they stood, and all of a sudden, a tiny figure came flying down—a single prum landing on the deck of the ship and reclaiming the spear for himself.

Brilliant green eyes, like the all-knowing surface of a vast lake, stared out beneath his sweeping bangs of gold.

Finn Deimne had inserted himself right smack in the middle of the rite.

"Cap…tain…?"

All it took was one look at that pint-size frame and heroic profile for the anger to dissipate from Tione's eyes. In fact, all too quickly, her rage was replaced with the thump, thump, thumping of her giddy heart.

As Tione found herself at a loss, Argana, too, could do nothing but stare in shock.

"A prum…?!"

Murmurs of bewilderment passed through the audience of Amazons beside them. They were on a ship out in the middle of the ocean. An arena on the open sea, where not a soul should have been able to reach them. Nothing but the fading light of the far-off lighthouse was even visible off Meren's coastline.

"You…you…How did you even get here…?!" Argana could only mutter in awe.

Her eyes went first to the surrounding waters.

But there was nothing, no other ships, nothing that would have delivered this prum to where they stood. And swimming was out of the question—a thought that she quickly eliminated, considering the prum's clothes didn't have a drop of water on them.

"How—?"

Her confusion seemed just about to get the better of her—when her eyes narrowed in on a sight that truly took her breath away.

"A…bridge of ice…?!"

"I do apologize. I'll return it momentarily."

Flowing locks of shimmering jade-colored hair fluttered in the salty breeze.

Below her, waves lapped against the coast, while above, the soaring outline of the lighthouse stood tall.

Silvery staff in hand, Riveria responded calmly to the dumbfounded gazes of the lighthouse attendants currently looking down at her from the building's windows. In front of her, traveling for kirlos and kirlos out into the sea, ran a winding bridge of ice along the water's surface. Boasting a breadth of five meders or so, it cut a direct line from the coast to the ship just visible in the lighthouse's line of sight.

It was a bridge of magic, formed of her glacial spell, Wynn Fimbulvetr.

Using the high-output spell, she'd frozen the very sea itself. By focusing an immense amount of Mind, she'd been able to narrow the scope of her magic's effects while also lengthening its path to an unimaginable degree. To put it mildly, it was a feat none other than the strongest mage in all of Orario would be able to pull off.

What followed her stunt was, no doubt, obvious. Running across this new bridge, Finn made his way to the ship, took a flying leap, then landed artfully atop the ship's deck, spear in hand.

"Bring Tione back soon, Finn..."

The high elf mage murmured from back on land, no traces of doubt in her voice as it made its way across the waves.

"Honestly, I've no idea if my words will get through to you, but I figure there's no harm in trying. I was hoping we could reach some sort of agreement, warriors of Telskyura," Finn began calmly, his back to Tione and shielding her from any further blows.

The reaction to the Koine-spouting, spear-wielding prum was immediate.

"*—KILL HIIIIIIIIM!!*"

Finn had interrupted their sacred rite, and the Amazonian warriors were incensed.

They leaped at him from all sides, weapons flying as they prepared to make this new intruder pay for the heinous crime of defying their goddess's divine will.

"That could have gone better," Finn muttered. "Then you leave me no choice."

All at once, the prum captain began to move. Like a spinning top, he twisted, never once leaving his spot as his Fortia Spear sliced through the air in every direction, golden tip gleaming. His speed was incredible, repelling the female warriors, weapons and all, as they launched themselves at him; he sent them flying over the side of the ship as they screamed in shock and disappointment.

"You lot have been giving certain members of our familia considerable trouble, haven't you?"

All around the ship, giant pillars of water soared upward as the Amazons plunged beneath the waves. Soon, the only ones who remained on deck were Finn, Tione, and Argana.

"...Ngh!!"

Finn's strength was in a league all its own, and Argana couldn't even try to hide her astonishment. Behind Finn, however, Tione was experiencing her own crisis.

"St-stop it! Please stop, Captain! Don't...don't get in the way!!"

"Get in the...way?"

But even as she screamed, the damage had already been done, her inner fragility revealed. Looking at his back now, she saw in her mind the bond they shared growing weaker and weaker.

"I...I have to bring Argana down myself! If I don't—...If I don't, then Tiona, Aiz, and everyone else, they'll...they'll be hunted down!!"

She shouted what was in her heart, disorganized and inarticulate though it was.

Yet even as she stood there stammering, the tiny prum didn't move from his spot; no, he didn't even flinch.

"Tione. Since when did we become so weak and frail as to need your protection?"

"...!"

"That you would go to such lengths...Is it out of pride? Or perhaps some sort of personal resentment? If it is out of enmity, I'd say you certainly got your revenge."

The words cut into Tione's heart like a knife.

It was cold, almost, this direct attack on her past actions and rationale.

—She was being scorned. By the person she loved the most.

The mask of boldness she'd so desperately attempted to hide

behind began to peel away. She felt a heat spread through her battered body, a heat that had nothing to do with her earlier anger, and in her eyes, all that she'd been keeping suppressed fought for release.

"However..."

Just when despair had begun to overtake her features, Finn turned back, looking straight toward her.

"...Somehow, despite all the time you've spent pushing, you've finally learned to pull."

"Huh...?"

"When did you learn such tactics, hmm?"

Tione raised her gaze, meeting Finn's own, and the prum gave her a wry smile as he balanced the handle of his spear on his shoulder.

"You really should try not to make us worry so much, Tione."

Now Tione's eyes began to tremble.

"I'm just glad you're all right."

Strange though it may seem, a part of her, the smallest, most infinitesimal part, had always wanted to play the heroine waiting for her knight in shining armor. Just like in those stories Tiona had read to her.

It was the smallest, tiniest part buried deep down within her.

The part of her that had found someone to love so, so much.

"You're going to get an earful from me after this, you know that, right?" Finn said with a soft smile.

"Y-yes..." she responded, tears clinging to her eyes.

And then she sat, spent of her energy and sinking to the floor. She'd already been on the verge of collapse, having suffered almost more than she could take, and this new attack melting her heart had severed the final thread holding her together.

It wasn't rage scraping at her heart this time; it was something else, burrowing its way into its deepest recesses.

"—You can't be serious! What the hell is all this?!" Argana suddenly barked, no longer able to watch in silence. Rage made itself plain on her face as she glared daggers at Tione on the ground. "To your feet, Tione!! We will continue the rite! You really think you can just end it with this lunacy?!"

She couldn't bear seeing the cowardly image of Tione on her knees before her.

This wasn't the face of a warrior, of an avenger ablaze with fury.

This was nothing but an ordinary, run-of-the-mill, unremarkable girl.

As someone who yearned for a future of war and combat, this was something she could not permit.

"You understand Koine, I see." Finn turned his attention now to the enraged Amazon in front of him. "Then our conversation will be short. I was wondering if you would be willing…to let me take the place of Tione in the rite."

He thrust his spear into the boards of the floor below. Watching Argana, still shocked, out of the corner of his eye, he stooped down into position, fully prepared to fight sans weapon. "If I win, you're to leave Tione and her sister alone. Make one move toward them again, and we'll completely decimate the country you call home."

"A man…and a prum, no less?! Don't make me laugh…!" But even as the mere thought made her body quiver in shame, she readied herself all the same. Long tongue reaching out to lick the red liquid off her cheeks, her eyes turned bloodshot. Her body coursed with bloodlust, absolutely prepared to slaughter the tiny fool of a man in front of her so she could continue her fight with Tione.

"Die!!"

Tione knew how the fight would end before it even started.

"I've heard tell that those of Telskyura consider it an insult to be shown sympathy in a fight."

Argana's wounds were too deep and too many from their own fight.

Her body had just about reached its limit.

"So I shall give it my all, as well."

And even more than that.

The Argana in front of her now was no different from the Tione who'd gone up against Finn those five years ago.

She knew nothing. Not of the strength of adventurers, nor of the world.

Nor that the tiny figure standing before her was not only a prum hero…

"*—Spear of magic, I offer my blood! Bore within this brow.*"

…but a berserker, too. One as strong and crazed as even her.

"*Hell Finegas!*"

His green eyes, as calm as the lake's surface, suddenly flashed a brilliant red.

"?!"

Argana's fist came at him, but he caught it in his own, in his fist no larger than a human child's. And as Argana gulped in surprise, he unleashed everything he had. His abilities were now enhanced to an unimaginable degree and his mind gone wild with a thirst for blood.

Fingers digging into her fist, he yanked her forward in the blink of an eye.

Argana could barely believe what she was seeing, and time ground to a screeching halt as she saw the tiny prum ready his other fist.

He roared, lungs bursting with all the intensity of a bloodthirsty warrior.

"HUUURRRRRRAAAAAAAAAAAUUGGGGGHHHHHHH!!"

His fist collided with Argana's face.

"GUGNNNNH———"

She tried to scream, but the vicious crack of her bones snapping interrupted the sound.

Then she was flying. She crashed through the railing, sending up splinters of wood as she plunged into the water far, far away from the side of the boat. The deluge of water that rose up from the impact might as well have been caused by a magic explosion for all its magnitude.

"——————————!"

The recoil was enough to send the ship rocking back and forth, its boards creaking noisily, and Tione waited for the motion to subside before moving. When finally silence had returned to the deck, she raised her head, finding Finn standing in front of her with his eyes still red.

"Ah…" She instinctively closed her eyes, unable to face his red ones head-on as they stared at her huddled form on the ship's floor.

A few seconds passed.

When nothing happened, she slowly, ever so slowly cracked open her eyes, only to feel something come down on her shoulders. Taken aback, she quickly turned her head to find that Finn had wrapped his waistcloth around her.

"Captain…" she murmured, lips trembling.

Finn just smiled, his irises having returned to their beautiful green shade.

"Let's go home, Tione."

Then he walked past her, giving her head a soft pat.

That was the final straw for Tione, already spent in more ways than she could imagine, and her eyes welled up with salty tears. Completely abandoning all modesty, she turned on her heel before promptly tackling her beloved's back.

"Captaaaaaaaaaaaaaain————!!"

Her arms wrapped around him in the tightest squeeze she could muster.

Finn, on the other hand, was sent straight to the floor by the emotional Amazon's giant bear hug, his nose cracking against the hard wood of the deck with his arms spread-eagled above him.

"Captain, oh, Captaaaaaaaain! Thank you soooooo muchhhhhh… Ahhhh, I'm so sorry…!!"

"…There, there," Finn could only reply with a knowing smile as Tione sobbed his name again and again into his shirt, her arms still wrapped around his waist.

He'd wait there, the prum captain of *Loki Familia*, with his cheek pressed into the floor, until she was done crying, simply smiling at the night sky up above.

The two rites, one within the cave and one atop the ship, had come to an end.

The fate the two girls shared had been broken at the hands of their companions.

By the time Tione and Finn made their way back across the ice bridge to the shore (Riveria had re-created it to allow them passage), traces of light were already starting to color the sky. It took a while after that, mostly due to Tione's wailing, for Riveria to apply the proper healing and care for her battered body. But once finished, the three of them continued to the wharf, Tione sandwiched between the two elites with Finn's waistcloth still wrapped around her shoulders. They found the rest of *Loki Familia* gathered in front of the fishing pier and causing a horrible racket.

"I...I brought Misses Tiona's and Tione's weapons for nothing...?! But her Urga almost broke my back...!" Raul lamented.

"Don't sweat it, Raul! It's the thought that counts, yeah? We're just happy you had us in mind! Thanks!" Tiona replied, as boisterous as ever.

"How does Miss Tiona still have that much...energy...?" Leene asked.

"Indeed," Lefiya agreed. "Only a few hours ago she was knocking on death's door and plagued by poison, no less...Just healing her took considerable time."

"All thanks to you, Leene! And I've gotta apologize to you, Lefiya. Gettin' you all mixed up in our problems!"

"No one's gonna forgive ya when yer runnin' around like a damn crackpot! You even realize what all these guys did for ya?" Bete growled.

"Well, *sor-ry* for wantin' to apologize when I've done something wrong!...Not that...you know...an apology's probably enough...I'm really sorry for puttin' you guys through all that."

"*Somebody hold me!* Tiona? Bein' all meek 'n' submissive? A new world's bein' born in my soul!"

"Let her be, Loki," Aiz said.

"All right, all right! You win, Aizuu! You and your damn perfection—Nnnnggaaah!"

"Bete, *do* something! Look how sad Tiona looks now!"

"H-how the hell should I know what to do?! You think I can do anything to fix that crazy woman?"

"You could start by *apologizing*, you big ol' asshat!!" Tiona finally squawked.

"Oh, why don't you just shove it, you shit-for-brains Amazon!!"

As Tione looked out across the clamorous group with her sister at its center, she felt the muscles in her face relax, her earlier anxiety washing away. Next to her, Finn could only shrug as Riveria sported her usual one-eyed smile.

"Huh? Oh, Tione!" Tiona suddenly spouted, noticing her sister immediately.

"Lady Riveria!" "Captain!" the rest of the group shouted as the younger Amazon came sprinting toward them.

"You all right, Tione?! The rite! What happened with the rite? Where's Argana?!"

"...The captain sent her on a one-way trip."

Tiona was silent for a moment, her face blank in puzzlement.

Then she laughed, great guffaws that forced her hands to her stomach.

The sight of it was enough to make the corners of Tione's mouth twitch upward ever so slightly.

"I beat Bache! And you know what? No one had to do any dyin' or killin'! How about that, huh?"

That smile. That smile. Always that smile.

What was behind that smile? What did it hold? What had it saved?

To the east, the sun broke across the horizon, coloring the surface of the lake a brilliant, fiery gold.

Tione's face softened, her lips curling upward, all the way upward—in a true smile.

"Thanks, Tiona. For saving me. I can't thank you enough."

Tiona glanced up at her sister, now smiling as brightly as the rising sun, and for a moment, something in her heart caught. The more she looked, the more her own face flushed and the more her own smile grew.

"You bet!" she finally answered, the two sisters now sharing the same smile as Finn and Riveria watched like protective parents.

Almost instantly, though, Tione's smile fell, and a look of despondence washed over her. "I…need to apologize to everyone. You're too much of a dunce for people to stay mad at, but me…? I guess we'll see."

"It'll be fine! It'll be fine! You'll see! Everyone'll forgive ya! Just shoot 'em that same smile and everything'll be right as rain!"

"Smile?! During an apology? That's just asking for a punch in the face!"

"Naaaaaaah! C'mooooon! Just do it!"

"Ugh, you're so annoying! Go over there somewhere!! You really are the worst!"

"But Tioneeeeeeeeeeee!!"

And so the two sisters walked toward the group.

They walked to that place of light where their friends awaited them with smiles.

Their days of loneliness were behind them.

EPILOGUE

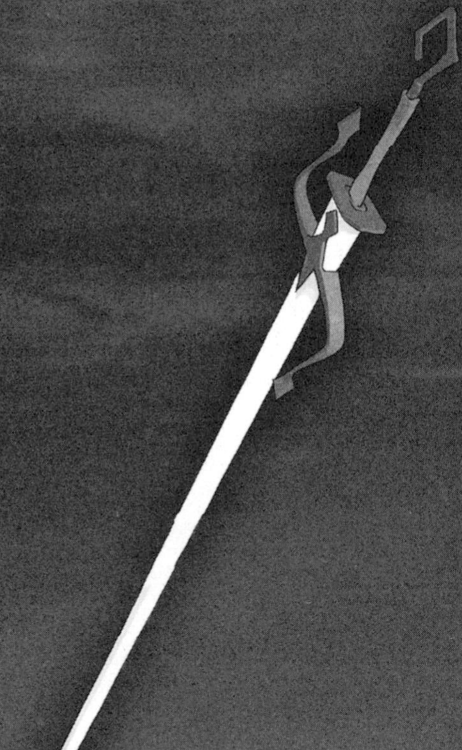

Disturbing Elements

Гэта казка іншага сям'і.

трывожныя элементы

All in all, the "Meren incident" was just about cleaned up that night.

The Guild decided to blame *Kali Familia* for *Loki Familia*'s fight in the middle of the wharf. "An unfortunate accident brought about by savage Amazons from a remote land," was how they described it. As for the violas, well, those were just monsters who happened upon land at a most inopportune time.

The Guild's top brass didn't have much choice on the matter given how Loki had dragged them into the investigation. From the violas' release into the sea, to the involvement of wonder boy Njörðr, of all people, to the conspiracy of the Murdock estate, and perhaps most egregious of all—that a high-ranking Guild member would be involved in embezzlement—they knew that going public with everything would shake Meren to its very roots. The Guild, being the Guild, could already picture the kinds of criticism they'd receive (and the many ways other familias would be able to take advantage of them and invite them to ruin).

If details of this incident got out, plots to reveal their weaknesses would come out of the woodwork. It was almost as if they'd received a warning already, from the "thread" connecting the separate points of the scandal: "If I'm going down, you're going down with me."

Truthfully, the Guild had long been getting information from *Loki Familia* on the secret maneuvers of Orario's organizations, but they'd never acted upon any of the tips, perhaps already afraid of the retaliation (and mutual destruction) it would bring.

"See, the reason they released the violas then...and also the reason why they only had 'em do so much damage...was to make it seem like they were never even there."

"I see. It was more than a diversion...It was insurance."

—was the explanation Loki and Riveria came up with.

Then that "thread," that queen of beauty, could make her way back to Orario, smiling as though none the wiser.

While nothing would happen to Njörðr or Borg, what with the strong influence they had on Meren's administration, there was no question as to the deal that was made behind the scenes promising their allegiance to the Guild.

Thus, it came to pass that Guild Branch Chief Rubart would be the only one taking the fall.

"The hell. So that guy Rubart was the only one to go down, huh? He really drew the short straw on this one."

It was the day after everyone had returned to the port city proper, making it the second day after the events had transpired at Meren's wharf. After dealing with the constant belligerence that was the Guild, Loki had made her way quickly—escaping, perhaps—to Njörðr and company to wrest out the full details of the proceedings.

"It would seem so. Quite awful, what happened to him. Losing his job and everything."

"Well, isn't that just a cryin' shame. Imagine, one of yer own kids gettin' caught up in my all-powerful plan and endin' up on unemployment the rest of their life."

"I know. Which is exactly why I forcibly carved my blessing in his back and welcomed him into my ranks of fishermen."

"Yer really the devil himself."

The two joked back and forth, faces deadpan. They were in Njörðr's chambers in Nóatún, *Njörðr Familia*'s home.

"Like throwin' a farmer onto a battlefield, you are."

"Still…it's about the only thing I can do to atone for what I've done…"

It seemed Rubart hadn't taken too well to the change, already resentful enough over what had happened and now surrounded on all sides by slightly too affectionate fishermen. "Don't worry! We'll take good care of ya!" The entire thing had gotten a bit out of hand, no doubt making the gesture of goodwill feel more and more like punishment…

"And what about you, huh? Fixed things up between you and your kid?"

"You mean Rod?...I'm not sure things will ever be the same between us..." he answered somewhat vaguely, with a weak smile that contained dozens of emotions. "What was it he told me? Ah, yes...'we'll keep doing our best so long as you try not to get involved in anything else strange.'"

"...You really do have some good kids."

"Indeed." Njörðr smiled at Loki's sincere reply. "Though I still haven't solved the whole monsters-in-the-sea issue, I'll try to think of a way to do so without the violas going forward. To do so would, no doubt, put me back in your sights and in line for another scolding, as well."

"That it would."

"We'll keep on slogging away here...Rod, Borg, and everyone else."

With their plans for the future laid out, both of them turned around to face the same direction, where a certain young goddess currently sat tied up on a chair.

"Now it's your turn, you demonic urchin. Ready to spit it all out?"

"...Hmph," she replied with a jerk of her head. Loki just cackled evilly from her spot a short distance away.

Once the fight in the sea cavern had come to an end, she and her followers had taken pity on Bache and the other injured Amazons, healing their wounds and sending them back on their ship to Telskyura. Not so their patron deity, however, who'd been forcibly brought back with them. Seeing the tiny brat hopping mad at her current arrangements only made Loki all the more gratified.

"First off, ya better goddamn well promise not to lay a finger on my Tione and Tiona, ya hear? And make sure those battle junkies of yours know it, too..."

"...If you're talking about Argana, she's no use to me now anyway."

"Huh?" Loki asked dubiously.

"And not just Argana, either...but all of them. Everyone except Bache has done the dishonor of losing to a man..." Kali continued, with a deep frown. Her eyes turned dark and glassy as she mumbled invectives: "If only they could have been Amazons," "And don't even get me started on Tione," "Damn girl. Fall in love, will she?" "With Argana down for the count, Bache doesn't even have a reason to fight anymore..." "The future is dark indeed..."

"This may very well be the end for Telskyura..." she finally said out loud. "My poor beloved kingdom..."

"I have no idea what you were just mumblin' up a storm about... but let me get one thing straight. And this is for the sake of my cute little Tiona and Tione," Loki started. "You're gonna put an end to all this killin', you hear? Or at the very least, release those who don't like these 'rites' of yours."

"Oh, right, because if I say, 'If you don't wanna die, just say so, and you can leave,' everyone won't raise their hands. What are you, an imbecile?!"

"You wanna die, you asinine punk?!"

"All right, all right. I got it, I got it! Love will save the world and all that. Love and peace, love and peace. All hail Lady Aphrodite."

"You little shit—"

"This approach seems to be getting us nowhere. Perhaps you wouldn't mind lowering your fist, Loki?"

Loki's clenched fist was trembling at the masked goddess's infuriating expression and cheeky comments, but when Njörðr interrupted with a well-placed jab of his elbow, she somehow released the breath she'd been holding.

"...Fine. First off, why did you all come to Meren?"

"Not sayin'."

"I thought I just asked if you wanted to die, punk!"

"And that alone is what I can't tell you. Not after coming this far."

Kali harrumphed, once again turning her head to the side as big blue veins rose atop Loki's forehead.

"Come on now, you two..." Njörðr attempted to mediate for Loki—a skill he'd developed far too well thanks to the long friendship they shared from back in the upper world.

"If anyone, Ishtar certainly seems to have done a lot for him and his familia. You don't suppose she has something to do with it?"

"All right, out with it, midget!"

"—♪"

Kali responded with a brash whistle.

Though she examined things from underneath her half-lidded eyes, Loki had somehow narrowed down the candidates in her mind after hearing about Ishtar's involvement. The first face that popped into her head belonged to the abominable goddess of beauty she couldn't seem to get rid of...But considering she had no duty to warn Kali of the kinds of trouble she could get her into, Loki chose to keep her mouth shut.

"...Next. What do you know about those man-eating viola flowers?"

"Nothing, actually. I'm being honest."

Loki stared down at Kali but spotted no sign of dishonesty in her crimson eyes.

"Though come to think of it, Ishtar certainly seemed to know a great deal about those flowers, no?" Kali mused.

"Not Ishtar again!...Njörðr, you said yourself Ishtar and her gang were the ones who supplied your violas, right?"

"That's true. However, they were simply a trading partner...introduced to me as the perfect entity to help in transporting the violas to Meren."

Once the deal had been struck, they'd both used the sea cave near Meren to their own advantage. In exchange for their delivering the violas, Njörðr had agreed to finance their activities in the city. It had never been anything more than that, and certainly there was no sort of trusting relationship between the two.

"She really chewed you up and spit you out, you know that, right?" Loki commented, holding nothing back.

"Tell me something I don't know..." Njörðr replied with a sigh.

"Hmm...Then our two leads are Ishtar and that mysterious human skulking about in the sewers..." Loki mused as the two finally turned toward the table where *Ishtar Familia*'s emblem—one of the insignias on the Guild's official list—had been placed alongside a refined portrait of the mysterious figure Njörðr had drawn up. The illustration depicted an unhealthy-looking person with bags under their eyes, or, at least, under the one eye not hidden by a set of long bangs.

*A shadier-lookin' guy than Soma even…*Loki couldn't help but think as she eyed it.

"…Come to think, what kinda stuff did this fella want you to smuggle anyway?"

"I'm afraid I never looked inside the boxes themselves, but likely valuable goods, occasionally alcohol…One time there was even a box that made a horrible ruckus. Something alive, no doubt. According to that human, he desperately needed money."

"Money, huh…?"

Certainly, if the remnants of the Evils and those creatures had any hopes of fulfilling their dreams of destroying Orario, they'd need sufficient capital to support their activities. Then had everything been a wasted effort? At any rate, she'd at least gotten her hands on another clue, which was enough for the time being.

"Yo, short stuff. Ishtar mention anything else? Doesn't even have to be anything important."

"Hmmm…I'm afraid we didn't talk long. Both of us had things to do, you see…So I can't remember much else," Kali began, her expression somewhat pensive beneath the gazes of the other two gods. "But…" she added. "What I can say is…that woman is terrifying."

"…? What's that supposed to mean? Your familia is kirlos ahead of hers when it comes to sheer power…" Loki said, confused.

"I mean she's as crafty as they come. And she has an ace up her sleeve to boot. Surely you've heard something from your children concerning this matter, hmm?"

And certainly, Loki had.

Thinking back now, Loki remembered Aiz and Bete telling her that Ishtar's Level-5 captain, Phryne Jamil, had been wielding the combat power of a Level 6. And what's more, according to Bete, she'd had some kind of magic user in her arsenal, too…If that goddess really had gotten ahold of some kind of magic or curse that effectively leveled up her followers, she'd be a force to be reckoned with. For instance, if those same effects had been used on either Argana or Bache, the situation they'd just dealt with would likely have gone much differently. Sure, she'd been able to play it cool knowing she had reinforcements in the form of Finn and the rest of the men, but had her calculations been incorrect, she'd have been in for a world of hurt. The mere thought of it was enough to send a drop of cold sweat down her temple.

At the same time, though, another thought crossed her mind.

This was exactly what the lower world was about—the most thrilling board game, brimming with possibilities even she and her other gods couldn't predict.

And it was for this reason that she couldn't get enough of it—a thought that had her indiscreetly licking her chops.

"And one more thing..." Kali spoke up again. "This is just a hunch, but...the reason she didn't bat an eye at leaving my girls and me out to dry even after going all the way to invite us here? She's got something else. Another one of her hidden aces."

"Another ace in the hole..." Loki ruminated on the words as Njörðr threw a gaze in her direction.

Outside, night had already blanketed the building in shadow. Inside, Loki heard the sound of two unexpected divine wills interlocking.

"That incompetent fool...falling to *Loki Familia*. It's just as I predicted..."

A bewitching figure made its way along the stone passage.

Woven hair swaying with each step, Ishtar cursed the tiny goddess under her breath. Her human manservant remained silent alongside her.

But her grumblings were not to last long, and her frown turned into a smile as she let out a puff of noxious purple air from her kiseru pipe. She'd reached the end of the dimly lit passage.

"If I can't rely on them, I'll have to rely on myself...even if it means using *it*."

The room in front of her opened up.

In a grand hall of stone, robed figures were walking to and fro across its floor. She looked down at them from atop the balcony-like plateau jutting out into the room, and to that which was tied up at the room's center.

It was a monster, a giant beast bound by countless chains.

"The Bull of Heaven...milady?" the young human behind her murmured, his voice low as his body gave a shudder. The goddess of beauty simply narrowed her amethyst eyes.

Two colossal horns protruded from its head, warped and twisted in gallant depravity.

And from its forehead, a female figure, feasting itself on magic stones, rolled its hideous eyes upward.

Status Lv.6

STRENGTH:	G 243	ENDURANCE:	G 277
DEXTERITY:	C 651	AGILITY:	C 609
MAGIC:	S 989	MAGE:	E
HEALING:	G	IMMUNITY:	G
SPIRIT HEALING:	H	MAGIC RESISTANCE:	H

MAGIC:	Vas Windheim	• Attack Magic. • Concurrent Casting. • Level 1: Wynn Fimbulvetr • Level 2: Rea Laevateinn • Level 3: Vas Windheim
	Via Shilheim	• Defense Magic. • Concurrent Casting. • Level 1: Liv Ilusio • Level 2: Veil Breath • Level 3: Via Shilheim
	Van Alheim	• Healing Magic. • Concurrent Casting. • Level 1: Fil Eldis • Level 2: Luna Aldis • Level 3: Van Alheim
SKILLS:	Fairy Anthem	• Increases magic effects. • Increases magic range. • Greatly increases magic power according to the length of the chant.
	Alf Regina	• Strengthens magic abilities. • Increases magic effects for all elves within own magic circle. • Converts magic energy of all elves within own magic circle into Mind and absorbs it.

EQUIPMENT: Magna Alfs

- Weapon for magic-users only.
- Was actually commissioned by Loki rather than Riveria for an exorbitant sum of money in Altena, the kingdom of magic. The highest grade of staff and considered even in Orario to be one of the mortal realm's most powerful five staves, the "Supreme Five" or "Magia Venti."
- A nonstandard-build staff inlaid with nine of the highest-grade magic stones. Increases magic power to its utmost limits. Lenoa of the Witch's Secret House handles magic-stone replacement.
- Boasts a strong handle made of mythril and holycite; also capable as a long-handled weapon.
- Worth 340,000,000 valis but even more when taking into account the magic stones.

EQUIPMENT: Fairy King's Holy Robe

- Sewn from the fibers of the Sacred Royal Tree towering above the high elf forest, giving it exceptional magic-resistive properties.
- Fashioned from the dress Riveria was wearing when she fled home. Though she pushed it onto her pupil, Aina, it passed through many hands before finally being made into first-tier adventurer armor.

RIVERIA LJOS ALF
Riveria • Ljos • Alf
BELONGS TO: Loki Familia
RACE: High Elf
JOB: adventurer
DUNGEON RANGE: fifty-ninth floor
WEAPONS: staff, bow and arrow
CURRENT WORTH: 147,000,000 valis

Afterword

I took a trip recently where I got to take a leisurely stroll along the coast.

While the sea was certainly beautiful, great blue sky spread out up above, it was the sound of the waves that left the deepest impression on me. As each new wave lapped up silently toward my feet, my mind unknowingly constructed a scene: a man and woman having a conversation. I've never been much of one for romantic comedies, but I can remember quite clearly wanting to take to my keyboard with a fervor at that point. Once I finally finished the manuscript, however, it had somehow turned into a brutal slugfest between Amazons. My life!

At any rate, this is the sixth volume of my little side series. Time-wise, it takes place before the sixth volume of the main series, ending just about when that book begins.

My original plot for this book (at least my outline of it) somewhat muddied the sisterly bond of the two Amazonian sisters, as well as their enemies. Try as I might to depict it, I almost always found myself at a loss, and I'd end up simply slapping some bare-bones characterization together as best I could. Tione is a bit like this; Tiona has a very one-track mind. It came to the point where even I, as the author, wondered if they had a bond at all! (That and the fact that it felt a bit awkward for me to describe sisterly love...).

However, as the setting began to come alive across the page, and as I dove into depictions of the girls' past, I finally managed to banish my misgivings and take to writing about their bond with gusto. Likewise, I was also able to fully flesh out the villains. While this may be all too obvious, I very much believe characters have life in them, countless stories just waiting to be told. And this book was the first time I truly felt these two became "sisters."

Aside from that, I also tried to do a bit of world building in this book and really expand the setting as much as I could. It makes me think how lovely it would be to create an entirely new world someday. I also tried to insert characters from the main series wherever I could, which should hopefully make it all the more fun when you pick up volume seven.

And on that note, let me segue into my thank-yous for this volume.

To my editors, Otaki and Takahashi; to my illustrator, Kiyotaka Haimura; and to everyone else who made this book possible, I sincerely apologize for falling behind in the delivery of my manuscript. At the same time, I thank you from the bottom of my heart for lending me your strength. I'd also like to thank all of you, my readers, who now hold this book in your hands. I hope we'll be able to meet like this again and again for books to come.

According to my current schedule, the next item on my plate is the backstory for volume six of the main story, meaning that volume seven will most likely be at least a full main series book's worth of time down the road. Though when I say "mostly likely," I mainly mean "certainly"...At any rate, I shall endeavor to do the best I can.

Thank you for reading my little ramblings.

All the best.
Fujino Omori

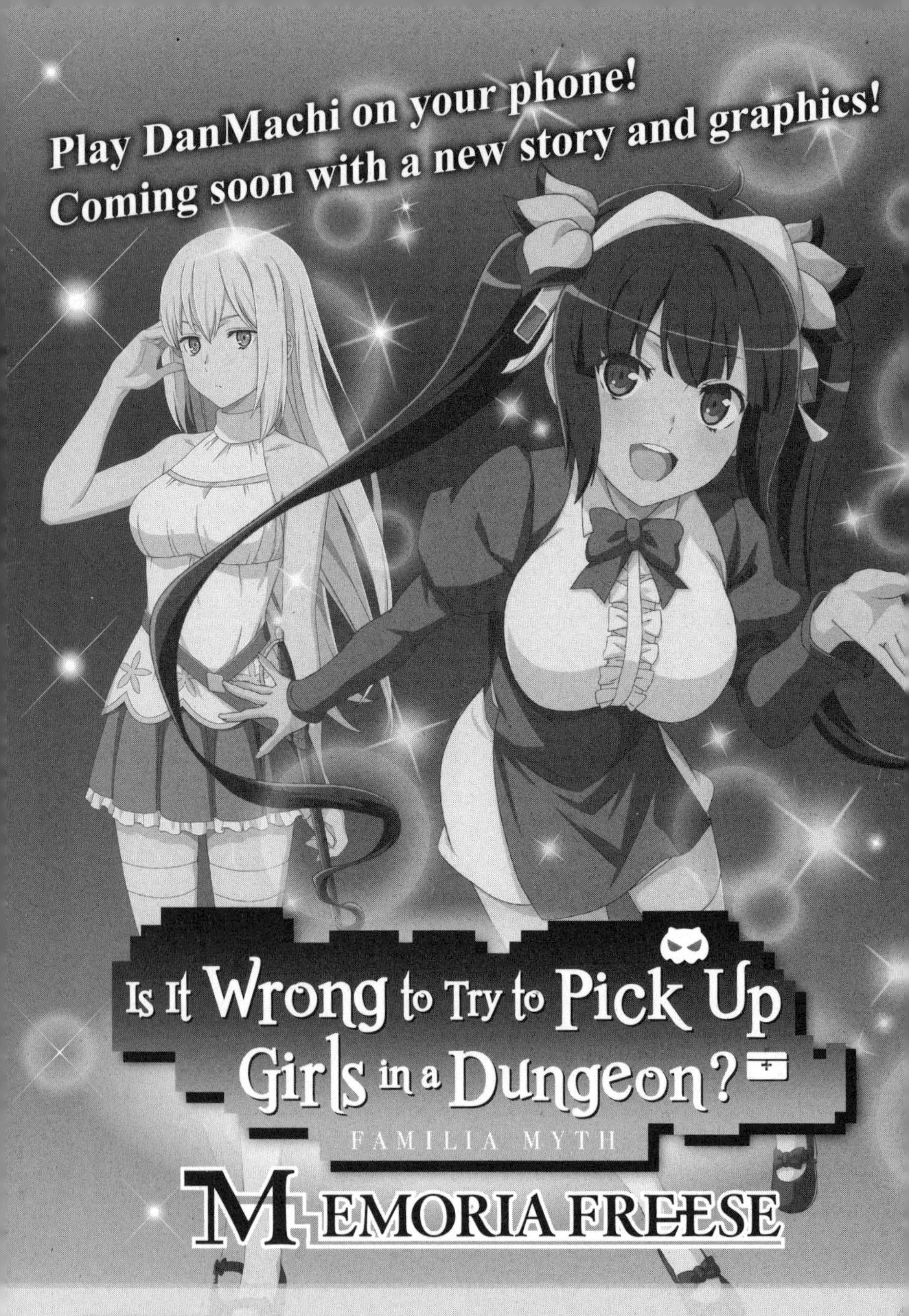
Play DanMachi on your phone!
Coming soon with a new story and graphics!
Is It Wrong to Try to Pick Up Girls in a Dungeon?
FAMILIA MYTH
MEMORIA FREESE